SCREAMER

*Never, ever
steal from a banshee*

By Frank J. Vizard
An Irish-American Novel

ISBN: 978-0-692-18494-3

Dedication

For Deborah and Nuala

"A solitary
A lone one
Small woman
Dressed in white
To kill?
Ugly-beautiful
Youthfully old
Small and tall
In a dark bright dress…

…Don't touch my comb,
My one and only,
Lay no hand on it.
Steal it,
Pick it up,
I'll come get it,
Burn, burn all I
Touch."

--Seoirse Bodley
"The Banshee"

Chapter One

They say the eyes are windows into the soul but he knew from long experience no one wanted to look into his. He couldn't blame them one bit. But it was becoming too dark to see properly so he removed his black tinted sunglasses. That's when the people nearest him began to slip away. Their slow recoil was one of his small pleasures. He watched them as they looked at him and then tried not to. At first they didn't quite know why they were doing it. The realization typically came in stages, beginning with the most perceptive and then floating like a wisp of dread from one person to the next. In the old days, people would have just run. The brave and the foolish might have drawn a weapon.

It was his eyes that made them uneasy—they were all black with no whites in them at all. He knew what they were thinking. Some kind of eye problem, they rationalized. Maybe that's why he had been wearing sunglasses indoors, although that was hardly unusual at a ski resort. The hipper crowd guessed the whites of his eyes had been tattooed with black ink. But the eyes made them uncomfortable. Those eyes looked like they belonged to something from the dark part of the forest, beyond the safety of the nicely groomed ski runs outside.

And the man with black eyes wasn't dressed for skiing either. No fancy waterproof fabrics made of bright colors for him. He

1

wore a black pinstripe suit that bordered on formal wear, a black shirt fastened at the top with not just one button but three arranged in a tight vertical line, a shirt perhaps from another country, they thought. That observation seemed supported by the black fez-like hat, minus the tassel, that crowned a lean, angular face that was in marked contrast to the well-fed visages of those around him. His face, framed by straight jet-black hair that fell to a hard jawline, was paler than most as well and set him apart from the tanned or sun-kissed skin of those who had spent the day outdoors. Some mentally surmised that he was here to pick someone up, maybe a friend or family members who had been left there for the day. But he approached no one and no one approached him. He lingered. And that had made a few uneasy. And now with sunglasses removed, that uneasiness increased and a few heads began turning his way. Those casting him sideways glances guessed he must have sensed the feelings of those around him or maybe he spotted the woman angling her smartphone to take a picture of him because he produced another pair of smaller framed sunglasses from an inside pocket and put them on with one hand while placing the original pair into the same inside pocket. These new glasses had a light yellow tint that made those sneaking looks at him now guess that he was some kind of musician, maybe someone famous although no one could put a name to his face. But the yellow-tinted glasses made them feel better and they were soon re-focusing their attention on their respective companions. The woman with the smartphone took a picture of her friends instead, one framed so that the bar's name could be seen in the background. It was called *Cloudsplitter*. Still, he could hear her whispering that he was an ex-con just released or even escaped from the maximum security prison in nearby Dannemora.

Disturbing. The Heer of Dunderberg knew that's the word they were looking for to describe him. It was a word people, even the Dutch who knew him the longest, used when they told others about him. Not for the first time did he consider that he would have to develop some way of lowering his profile. He should stay out of sight of the larger populace. He didn't want to attract attraction. But he had to admit being seen--maybe even possibly anticipated-- was a rush because there was a small element of risk. He allowed himself a tiny smile. It wasn't like he was a regular at the bar. It would be years before he would set foot in this place again, so many perhaps that by then everyone here today would be dead.

"Just two more weeks of skiing left," he heard the bartender saying to a customer. "The slopes shut down after the second weekend in April."

Through the window, the Heer of Dunderberg watched as the light began to fade over Whiteface Mountain, the brightness of the snow-covered ski trails slowly being covered by the shadows of pine trees that lined the slope and funneled skiers downhill. The snow was man-made, he knew, making the whole tableaux false in his estimation. It was late in the season and the surrounding area was only patchy with snow. He detected the same falseness in the tall, bearded man at the corner of the bar who was feigning interest in what the pretty young woman next to him was saying. He recognized the bearded man for the predator he was. He hoped the bearded man wouldn't become a problem. That fancy green and gold ski suit would be ruined if he did.

The Heer of Dunderberg was far from his usual haunts in the lower Hudson River Valley. He had avoided this area in years past when it had a booming iron works trade. The smell of burning iron in the air had been enough to keep him away. But enterprises like the AuSable Horse Nail Company were long gone and now he ventured northwards closer to the source of the river. The Hudson began as a thin stream emanating from a lake called the Tear of the Clouds atop Mt. Marcy, the tallest peak in the Adirondacks Mountains, the stream growing ever larger as it caromed hundreds of miles the length of New York State before emptying into the Atlantic Ocean amidst the skyscrapers of Manhattan. There was never any need to venture too far from the river's banks. He'd always go where the river went. He was bonded to it. Tear of the Clouds was only as short distance away.

Once more, the Heer of Dunderberg quickly glanced at the woman talking to the bearded man before shifting his gaze elsewhere. He knew that sometimes people could sense his interest in them if he looked at them for more than a few seconds. He didn't want her to notice him at this point but she was the one. It was just a matter of deciding when to take her. He looked over at the liquor bottles behind the bar as if contemplating his next drink. He already knew a lot about her. She was a recent arrival in this country, visiting Lake Placid and its Olympic winter sports facilities in the hope of taking a few good marketing and environmental tips back to her native Slovenia. She was attractive but didn't dress in a way that would turn heads. The brown hair was held in check by a black knit hat covered with a snowflake design. The unzippered black ski jacket, also peppered with the same snowflake design, was probably a size too big and did little to accentuate her figure although the tight green sweater underneath made up for it. She had no friends here and only one or two acquaintances might notice her absence. And they would probably think she had returned to Slovenia.

But the woman's lonely existence didn't make her foolish. Something about the bearded man gave her pause and she excused herself. The Heer of Dunderberg watched as she headed for the ladies room and then turned abruptly toward the exit door.

The Heer of Dunderberg looked back. There was anger in the bearded man's eyes and those eyes told the Heer of Dunderberg what he was thinking. He had seen her leave. She had told him she was coming back. She was never coming back. That was a mistake. She should never have lied to him. Now the bearded man would feel his subsequent actions were justified. Of course, he was lying to himself. His intentions were always malicious. Yes, the bearded man was now a problem. There was no way around it. He would have to act sooner than desired. Inconvenient but there would a degree of pleasure to be had nonetheless. He didn't like men like him.

"Lying bitch!" The bearded man tossed down his drink in a gulp and slammed the glass hard on the bar but no one other than the Heer of Dunderberg paid him any heed. The Heer of Dunderberg shook his head slightly. The bearded man couldn't even curse well. And there was ice in his drink, the sign of a man who didn't respect the whiskey he was imbibing. The water should always be on the side. The bearded man left by another door that led directly outside onto the slope. The woman would leave by the front entrance to the ski lodge, exiting past the ski rental shop and the booths where lift tickets were sold. The Heer of Dunderberg recognized the tactic. Circle around and cut off your prey. Attack with the element of surprise on your side and thus avoid a long pursuit that might attract unwanted attention. He followed the bearded man out the same door. The bearded man would be focused on his prey and not on anyone in pursuit of him.

New York State Trooper Urgill Douglas sat in a duly marked blue sports utility vehicle on the other side of a small bridge that connected the parking lot of the ski lodge to Route 86, the main road that led back to the town of Lake Placid and its warm hotels. The exposed rock that gave Whiteface its name wasn't visible from his vantage point. Those white, gabbroic anorthosite rocks were on the north and east sides of the mountain and offered a dramatic vista from Lake Placid. For the last few hours, Douglas had been studying the fir waves: alternating bands of live and dead balsam fir that flanked the mountain's ski trails. The phenomenon had attracted the attention of scientists, one of whom had recently given a lecture on the topic in Lake Placid. The winter winds, said the scientist, were laden with ice crystals that gradually kill the first tree needles and branches they hit. Trees to the leeward farther up slope were protected from the wind. The result was alternating bands of life and death.

A blue shuttle bus roared passed Trooper Douglas, temporarily blocking his view of the slopes. Out of habit, he glanced in the rear view mirror and caught a glimpse of himself: black hair cut short, hazel eyes, and a jaw that reminded people of Jay Leno, the famous comedian. The bus, he knew, would return in an hour to take the last of the day's skiers back to town like so many school kids going home. Some, of course, would be driving their own cars and that was his principal concern. Route 86 was a narrow, winding road that hugged the ledges overlooking the AuSable River as it headed into the town of Lake Placid. A tired, perhaps slightly drunk skier behind the wheel of a car was a danger to himself and others on the road. The trout didn't much like it either, Trooper Douglas added with a grim chuckle, when cars fell into the AuSable.

He liked to think about the trout in the AuSable, a river that ran north instead of south like most rivers in the United States and which emptied into Lake Champlain, the massive body of water that divided New York from Vermont. In his mind, he was walking the river for the thousandth time and trying to think like a fish. He thought about logjams, big rocks, deadfall and whether trout would like lurking there. He thought about where they might like to eat and what kind of flies he would use. Black Ghost, AuSable Wulf, wooly buggers, zonkers or even simple bunny leech flies to imitate leeches. He thought about the proper depth to drop bait. Every spot on the river is different. He could feel the cool water flowing around his waders. And then that moment when the fish takes the line and it leaps out of the river. Then there is that surge of adrenaline mixed with a bit of panic that he won't be able to land the three-pounder, even a feisty five-pounder sometimes. But he'd reel it in, take a quick selfie and, if fish wasn't on the dinner menu, release the fish back into the river. Then he would cast again. He'd grown to favor a cast motion halfway between a sidearm and a full overhead motion. It gave him more distance and theline seemed to drop more gently into the water—less chance of scaring a fish. He sighed. Thinking like a fish wasn't easy.

Trooper Douglas shifted in his seat, half-wishing that he was among those enjoying the après-ski scene. He was a local boy, named for the father who had lived his whole life inside the blue line that defined the Adirondack Mountain Park on the map, a vast, sparsely populated area of 9,375 square miles that included most of the land in the northern part of New York State, making it the largest park in the United States. Trooper Douglas knew Whiteface Mountain well, having taken a turn as a lift operator back in the days before the first enclosed gondola was installed. He shivered with the memory. Whiteface, with its 22 miles of trails was a cold mountain, prone to icy runs that attracted skiers who were fast on their feet. Trooper Douglas had seen the pictures from when Whiteface and Lake Placid had hosted its first Olympics in 1932 and a second in 1980. Everyone looked cold then too. On the other side of the main lodge, the old scoreboard still stood from the 1980 Olympics. Whiteface isn't fashionable Vail or Aspen by any stretch even if the vertical drop of 3,430 feet beats them both. People didn't change their ski outfits every year. They were worn until they were worn out. But that was part of the appeal of Whiteface. There was a more authentic feeling here, even if that feeling came with a distinct chill. The only real change of late had been the installation of the *Cloudsplitter* gondola, the nickname shamelessly borrowed from nearby Mount Marcy, the tallest mountain in the Adirondacks and sometimes referred to as Tahawus, a supposedly Indian name translated as Cloudsplitter. Most locals insisted the Indians had no name for Mt. Marcy at all. Trooper Douglas fell into that camp. One of his ancestors had been an Adirondack guide back in the 19th century and family lore supported that contention. Others in his family said Whiteface did have an Indian name, Wahopartenie, meaning "it is white" in the Algonquin tongue. Their enemies, the Iroquois, didn't think much of Algonquins, dissing their hunting skills by calling them "bark eaters" or Adirondacks.

There was little doubt in anybody's mind, however, that the enclosed gondola was a long overdue amenity for skiers who had endured the bone-chilling ride to the summit on open chairs. The state owned Whiteface and most people thought the state probably wouldn't put much money into it until another Olympics came their way, if ever. The gondola had come as a nice surprise. Some had wondered if the gondola was a prelude for a sale into private hands. *But Whiteface is still state property and that's why I'm here, rather than a local cop.* Douglas chuckled to himself. *I am a local cop.*

Douglas knew that wasn't entirely true. He was proud to be a New York State Trooper, a police force that answered only to the governor of the state much the way the Pretorian Guard of the old Roman Empire had answered only to the Emperor. They had worn a purple stripe on their togas. New York State Troopers found inspiration in that sense of duty and wore a purple tie with their grey uniforms. The hat band of his round, tan Stetson on the seat next to him was also purple for the same reason.

He glanced at the hat. Nearly everything about his uniform was steeped in tradition and meaning. The Stetson was tan to mark the Troopers' origin as a mounted force in 1917.The uniform was grey to signify their impartiality. The New York State patch on his sleeve depicted the goddesses Liberty and Justice flanking a shield with a depiction of the Hudson Highlands and sailing ships on the Hudson River. Unlike other police forces, however, Troopers didn't wear a badge on the uniform; they carried their eight-sided badge in their pocket. The only tradition that sometimes gave Douglas pause was the black stripe down each trouser leg in remembrance of fallen comrades.

And then there was the lore of his own Troop B, founded in 1921 as the Black Horse Brigade by 56 battle-tested veterans of World War I who soon found themselves engaged in shoot-outs with bootleggers smuggling Canadian booze during the Prohibition years when alcohol was illegal. These days, Troop B covered a five county area divided into three zones, with Whiteface smack in the middle of Zone 3. The threat from Canada now was terrorists trying to sneak over the border.

Douglas sighed. The terrorism threat seemed far removed on most days although an incident at the Seattle border crossing a few years back had underscored the possibility. The people who came to Whiteface Mountain and Lake Placid, and they were from many countries, wanted to breathe the Olympic spirit. They came to use ski jumps, bobsled runs, and ice skating rinks that were world class and which hosted many international competitions. They also came to rub elbows, when possible, with the athletes training for the next Winter Olympics. *Just like this woman, I bet.* Trooper Douglas saw her as soon as she came out the door. She walked a few steps and then stopped. A rider, he guessed, and one who had just realized she had missed the bus and would have to wait for the next one. He watched as the woman looked back toward the door, then turning away as if thinking better of it. Trooper Douglas registered details without consciously willing it: black knit hat and coat with some kind of matching design, hint of a green sweater at the neck, light brown pants tucked into darker brown boots.

The woman took a few short steps, tentatively it seemed. Then her stride became more purposeful. A walker, thought Trooper Douglas. She's going to take a walk to pass the time before the next bus arrives. Trooper Douglas watched as she came toward the bridge but she didn't come across. Instead, she followed another dirt road that rose slightly and led to the children's ski school. There's no one up there at this time of day and everything's closed, he knew. *She'll be back quick enough.*

Trooper Douglas looked up the road where the woman walked. From where he sat, Trooper Douglas could see farther along it than she could. The road rose steadily and then abruptly turned in on itself and disappeared behind a small hill. At the other end of the turn, just beyond his line of sight, was the children's ski school. As Trooper Douglas looked, he saw a flash of movement at the farthest limit of his vision, just where the road turned.

That's odd. There's someone up there.

Trooper Douglas looked back toward the ski lodge. All quiet at the moment. He looked back up the road. The walking woman was now closer to the bend in the road. In another minute or two, she would be out of sight.

The more he thought about it, the more that unknown movement bothered him. And he couldn't say exactly why. *Probably just someone working late. Or someone who had taken a wrong turn on one of the new runs. Or probably someone walking down to the ski lodge who forgotten something and turned back.*

"Probably, probably," Trooper Douglas said to the wind as he got out of the car and donned his trooper's hat and grey Gore-Tex jacket. "Probably" was not one of his favorite words. His legs felt a little stiff from sitting in the car. *I can use the exercise.*

Trooper Douglas was approaching the bend in the dirt road when he heard the woman's voice raised in alarm. He broke into a run and turned round the bend into the parking area. To the left was the complex of small buildings and yurt-style tents that housed the children's ski school. To the right stood a large, green metal structure, crowned by an operator's shed, which anchored the single ski lift on this side of the mountain. In between, a small wooden ramp led up to the school from a drop-off area and it was there that he saw the woman, struggling against the embrace of a bearded man clad in a stylish green and gold ski suit.

In almost the same moment, Trooper Douglas saw what looked like a dark shadow leap down from the top of the ski lift. Whoever it was had been lying in wait, pressed up against the wall of the shed atop the lift. The bearded man must have heard something because he suddenly let the woman go and spun around to face the shadow as it landed in the snow. The bearded man swung his fist in the direction of the shadow and hit nothing. The shadow developed arms and legs that struck the bearded man in a series of quick, powerful movements. In another moment, the bearded man lay sprawled six feet from where he had stood.

Damn, he's good. Trooper Douglas, still running, realized that he had just seen some form of martial arts display but of a type he had never witnessed, inside or outside of a police academy.

That's when the shadow noticed him. Trooper Douglas strained to see some identifying feature but couldn't—other than he seemed to be dressed in a suit. The woman, however, was now recoiling from her rescuer. *Who fears their savior?*

But the woman must have seen something Trooper Douglas didn't for a second later, a shadowy arm flicked out toward her head and her knees buckled. The shadow caught her as she fell and deftly threw her over his shoulder.

"Hold it!" yelled Trooper Douglas, drawing his gun. But even as the pistol cleared its holster, the shadow and his victim had already turned and were racing across the snow. On the other side of the children's ski school, Trooper Douglas knew, was a ski trail that followed a line of telephone poles back to the main lodge. What Trooper Douglas couldn't understand was how a man could move so fast while carrying another person. It looked like his feet were barely touching the snow-covered ground.

"Shit!" cursed Trooper Douglas as he turned and raced back the way he had come. With luck, he could cut them off at the main lodge. But even as he ran down the hill, he saw the shadow and his bundle emerge from the trees and sprint towards a black sedan.

"A fucking black car, of course," panted Trooper Douglas as he ran. *The bad guy's color of choice.* The man put the limp woman in the back seat of the car and was already speeding across the small bridge toward Route 86 as Trooper Douglas reached the bottom of the hill. Trooper Douglas ran across the bridge, the sound of water pounding in his ears. *German?* he thought as he looked after the departing car. *Maybe it's one of those high-end Japanese luxury cars.* He could never tell one from the other.

Probably stolen, he thought as he started the SUV's engine. *There's that word again.* Trooper Douglas floored the accelerator and flipped on the siren and dash-mounted red emergency light. *Talk about probable cause.*

The black sedan reached Route 86 and turned left, not toward Lake Placid, but in the opposite direction toward Wilmington. A good choice, conceded Trooper Douglas. The road to Wilmington was the one less traveled. Once through Wilmington, he could turn right toward AuSable Forks and then on north to the Canadian border.

Trooper Douglas followed the black sedan, making the same turn toward Wilmington. Then he reached for the radio.

"Three Bravo one zero nine in pursuit of a black sedan on Route 86 heading toward Wilmington. Code 11. Suspect is dangerous and is holding a hostage. Possible kidnapping in progress. Requesting assistance."

Trooper Douglas paused to catch his breath. "Victim is female Caucasian. Approximately 23 years of age. Brown hair. Wearing a black ski jacket and a black ski hat. Green sweater. Brown pants and boots."

Trooper Douglas listened for a response. *God knows where the nearest back-up is.* State troopers were stretched thin inside the blue line. Trooper Douglas thought about another imaginary line as well, one that defined patrol areas. He was approaching that line. On the other side of Route 86, patrols were run out of Plattsburgh, a 40-minute drive north. He also knew that patrols were heaviest on the Northway, the highway that offered quick passage from the Canadian border to Albany, the state capitol. Officers of Troop T, dedicated to thruway patrol, chased a regular bounty of speeders while keeping an eye out for radical Muslim terrorists that might be using the highway for quick passage into the country from Montreal. He couldn't be sure that anyone had heard him. Troop B's headquarters, a re-purposed athlete's dorm from the 1980 Winter Olympics, was in Ray Brook, a small hamlet just west of Lake Placid. The surrounding mountains often interfered with radio reception, he knew, and now Whiteface loomed between him and HQ. Mobile phone coverage was spotty to non-existent.

Terrorists. Hell, maybe that's what I've got here. Well, one maybe. Trooper Douglas drove as fast as he could past the rocky notch in the AuSable River where he'd gone swimming as a boy. He drove past a few faux-Swiss style inns and into Wilmington, a small village of relics from the 1950s that included a small, winter-themed amusement park filled with pudgy reindeer, a place Santa would have closed if he knew about it. Trooper Douglas thought about the martial arts display he had witnessed. *Somebody trained this guy.*

Trooper Douglas spotted the black sedan ahead of him. The car was approaching a three-way intersection. AuSable Forks and Canada were a right turn. To his surprise, the black sedan turned left onto state road 431. *There's nothing that way but another small village called Franklin Falls.* He made the left and sped past a long driveway that was the entrance to the Atmospheric Research and Analysis Station operated by some university eggheads from down state.

There was another alternative but it was so unlikely that Trooper Douglas didn't even consider it until the black sedan veered left off of 431 onto a road with a long steep incline.

"I got you now!" yelled Trooper Douglas, pounding the steering wheel and reaching for the radio. "Three Bravo one zero nine. Suspect is driving a black sedan on Whiteface Mountain Memorial Highway. Code 11. In pursuit. Requesting assistance."

Douglas thought for a second, wondering if he should repeat the transmission. Code 11 meant an assault had occurred. That should get everyone's attention by itself. *Can't hurt.*

"Three Bravo one zero nine. I repeat. Code 11. Whiteface Mountain Memorial Highway. In pursuit. Requesting backup."

Douglas realized his voice had a little more urgency in it this time around. He didn't relish the idea of facing some martial arts expert on his own. He could handle himself but one-on-one situations meant there was always a chance the bad guy could get lucky. *Shit. Stay calm. Think.*

Whiteface Mountain Memorial Highway is a five-mile dead end. It leads nowhere but up. The two-lane road was a Depression-era make-work project begun by then New York governor and future President Franklin D. Roosevelt. Now it was a road for summer tourists seeking a mountain top view without having to hike for it. Just below the summit was a medieval-looking castle built with the granite from the road's excavation. At the very summit—elevation 4,867 feet--was a round structure housing an automated weather station. The road was closed this time of year. No one would be at the top of Whiteface.

Of course, the barricade blocking the road at the tollbooth up ahead won't be much of a deterrent, thought Trooper Douglas. The tollbooth and its adjacent stone and wood buildings were such exact copies of their European counterparts that Trooper Douglas would have believed it if someone told him they had been air-lifted from the Alps before World War II. Sure enough, the wooden barrier, a single bar across the road, was smashed. Past the barricade, the road extended straight uphill at a slight incline. After two miles, the road then switched back and forth as it climbed more steeply up the mountain. Trooper Douglas drove as fast as he dared, trusting the four-wheel drive to take him across icy patches of road as he gained altitude. The roadway was in need of repair—there were cracks in the pavement as well as the occasional sinkhole.

The stone guardrails had settled and there was the odd loose rock that had fallen onto the road. There hadn't been a big maintenance project here since the 1980s. Most of the toll money collected from tourists was funneled back into the ski center and the bobsled/luge track by the Olympic Regional Development Association.

Trooper Douglas had plenty of time to paint a mental image of the physical layout that awaited him at the top of the mountain. The summit area was hundreds of feet higher than the highest point where skiers were allowed to go so there was no chance of seeing them there. *At this time of day, skiers will have cleared the mountain anyway.* He'd be driving into the parking area by the castle which would qualify as a fortress in anybody's mind. There were two ways, then, to get to the actual summit which was another 276 feet or 27 stories higher. One was to traverse a 424-foot long tunnel to an elevator that made the trip up through the core of the mountain and that had been installed at the behest of a polio-stricken FDR who wished the summit be accessible to the disabled. *That should be locked.* The other way was to take the Stairway Ridge Trail, a narrow path of cement and stone steps that left one perilously exposed to the elements and strong winds for about 130 long yards.

The last time I walked up that trail it felt like the top of my head was going to scrape the sky. And I covered some of it on all fours. Now it will be all ice. I don't want to do that this time of year. Hopefully, neither will this guy.

Trooper Douglas slowed the SUV as he neared the castle, half expecting trouble to come leaping at him before he came to a full stop. The sun was setting, its last rays reflecting off Mirror Lake in the distance, even as the lights of the town--Lake Placid-- along its shores began to flicker on. Ahead was the black sedan, stopped lengthwise across the road, with its doors open and its occupants gone.

Trooper Douglas stopped his SUV and got out, drawing his Glock 37 pistol. The gun fired .45 GAP bullets with plenty of stopping power from a 10-round magazine and that was reassuring. To his left was an access door that opened into the long tunnel that led to the elevator that went up to the summit and the weather station. Trooper Douglas checked the door and found it was locked. That left only one place to go. Trooper Douglas walked forward toward the mountain's edge and the castle itself.

The castle looked like it had grown out of the solid rock of the mountain, extending itself to a precipice with a wonderful view of the surrounding area. On a clear day, you could see Canada to the north and Lake Champlain to the east. The castle itself was basically a long rectangle with a round stone tower, marked by a small door, at its center that led to a cafeteria and indoor observation area. On either side of the tower were two passageways large enough for a single car to pass through. A car could enter the right passageway and then loop around through the rear courtyard for an exit through the left.

Trooper Douglas ran to the small, metal door that opened into the tower, noting the slits above it shaped like an inverted cross and hoping his quarry wouldn't appear there with a gun. The welcoming sign above the door noted the elevation: 4,602 feet. He tried the door and it was locked. His quarry was likely in the courtyard beyond.

Trooper Douglas knew from past visits to the castle that the right passageway afforded more cover. While the left passageway was sheer wall all the way through, the right passageway also included a narrow walkway interrupted by stone and brick pillars that supported an arched, partially enclosed viewing gallery. Trooper Douglas peeked into the passageway and saw no one. Silently, he dashed from one pillar to the next until he could see into the rear courtyard.

The courtyard was more like a large balcony in the shape of a semi-circle with another stunning view over the mountains. The road looped around a blue picnic table covered with ice patches that looked like dirty dishes at the end of a meal. A stone wall crept around the edge of the courtyard, accompanied by a stone pathway until it met a stone staircase that rose in a steep arc upwards. That marked the beginning of the Stairway Ridge Trail. The dark man was standing atop the wall near the foot of the stairs, the woman unconscious in his arms. *Don't go up there.* The other side of the wall was a sheer drop of a few hundred feet and there was a steep slope after that. The dark man's attention seemed to be focused on the other side of the wall. *He's thinking about murder and suicide in one jump.*

"Okay. Let's not do anything hasty," said Trooper Douglas. His voice didn't sound right at all. *I must have been daydreaming when they talked about this situation at the academy.* His pistol was pointed at the two figures but he knew he didn't have a shot.

"Let's talk about this a little," said Trooper Douglas. With the setting sun behind them, the two figures were just one misshapen shadow. Suddenly, he began to hear what he guessed at first to be a rising wind but then identified as harp music. *Where's that coming from?*

As if on cue, the dark man wheeled and hurled the unconscious woman over the wall. For a moment, she hung in space, arms spread as if she could fly. Then she vanished.

"No!" screamed Trooper Douglas even as he realized the situation had taken an even stranger turn. The woman had not fallen. She had disappeared. But even as this thought formed in his brain, the dark man launched himself off the wall with a leap. For a second, he was there in mid-air and then he disappeared as well.

"Fucking shit!" cursed Trooper Douglas as he raced to the wall and looked down. Directly below him, amidst some fog, was a tight circle of colored bands that seem to hang in the air just above ground. The innermost band was blue, while a middle band was yellow and the outermost band was red. In the middle was a triangular shadow that looked like a mountain. *The Spectre of the Brocken?* He recognized it from a description his father had given him after seeing it once on Whiteface Mountain in 1973. It was a seldom seen atmospheric disturbance mostly associated with a high peak in Germany's Harz Mountains but recorded elsewhere as well. His father had researched the phenomenon and learned that the shape of a man was often seen in its center. His old man had always hoped to see it again. *No figure this time. Or was there?* For a second, he thought he glimpsed a silhouette. There also was something else. His father has said the borders of the bands were clearly defined. *These bands are well-defined but are rippling intermittently as well.*

He couldn't see much beyond or around the Spectre of the Brocken. More disturbingly, he had not heard the sounds he expected. No thudding bodies. No snapping tree branches. No falling rocks. Nothing. *Right now, I'd welcome an avalanche.*

In his mind, Trooper Douglas replayed the leap of the dark man. From his body position, it was clear that when the dark man jumped, he fully expected to land somewhere. Trooper Douglas looked at the spot where he had last seen the dark man. It was a point in mid-air about five feet in front of him on the other side of the wall. There was no one there now. An impulse gripped Trooper Douglas and he fired his pistol six times at that spot in space, three bullets in a vertical line and three in a horizontal line.

"Here's your cross, you bastard, because if I find you alive, I'm going to crucify you."

Trooper Douglas lowered his pistol, already regretting what was probably a rash act. Still, he'd been shooting at nothing, out of frustration. But now he had a nagging feeling that he hit something. He could tell by the sound. It was the fifth bullet, he thought. It didn't sound like the rest. It was like it had stopped in mid-flight.

"Fuck! How stupid is this? I've got two missing bodies and I'm shooting at the sky. And I'm talking to myself!"

As if in reply, the wind picked up and Trooper Douglas again heard what sounded like a few strands of harp music. He stepped away from the wall and closed his eyes, trying to focus on the direction of the sound. *I can't pinpoint it!* He opened his eyes again. He heard seven notes but it was not a tune he recognized. He suddenly felt something hard hit him in the chest and knock the air out of him while his brain tried to register why he hadn't seen that coming. But he started to panic when he felt his mouth being pried open by something that felt like hooks, followed by a slimy something slithering down his throat, splicing into a thinner thread that penetrated into his chest that tightened into a grip. On his heart, he realized. Coming undone and pulled upward. Suddenly, there was a void in his chest, an absence that sent adrenalin shooting through his body. His eyes opened in fear. It had been so quick.

"A Bose-Epstein being," said a figure that now stood before him. The man in the suit. With darkness where the whites of his eyes should be. "That's the technical name your scientists have for what just attacked you. We have another name, one that's older. It's very rare. Prefers cold weather as you might have guessed. I sent it home."

Trooper Douglas heard himself gurgle.

"You shot her," whispered the figure in voice that seemed to be fading away with each word.

Oh, God! No! Did I kill her?

"She'll live."

Trooper Douglas wanted to move but he felt too weak to do so. The pistol dropped from his hand, its weight too much to bear. There was something in the dark man's hand. Something the dark man wanted him to see. It was a frozen heart. As Trooper Douglas fell to the ground, he knew the heart was his. The last thing he saw was the black stripe on his pant leg. His last thought was that he would now be among the remembered.

The Heer of Dunderberg reached down and placed the heart inside Trooper Douglas' left hand, wrapping the now dead man's fingers around it. He straightened and looked into the distance. A line of flashing lights streamed through the valley below like a long fiery dragon headed in his direction. For a moment, the Heer of Dunderberg regarded the display. This delivery had not gone as smoothly as he would have liked. It was getting harder to remain unnoticed, to remain the stuff of legend. The lights were a reminder of that. But more were needed. He turned and walked into the shadows. A few moments later, the wind died, taking with it the sound of a harp.

When the orange banner with the words "Orange Plus" in black letters began blinking on his computer screen, a shot of adrenaline coursed through the researcher's veins for all the wrong reasons. He was new to this posting at the Whiteface Mountain Atmospheric Analysis and Research Station and he didn't want to attract undo attention until he was sure he knew the ropes. So when the orange banner began flashing, his first reaction was one of fear, that somehow he had caused a computer malfunction and that he would be responsible for the loss of precious data being automatically collected at the observatory atop Whiteface Mountain. At that moment, he was glad he worked inside his own cubicle so that no one could see how jumpy the blinking orange banner made him. Like the three other researchers who worked at the station, his primary job was the collection of data regarding air pollution— mostly from smoke stacks in Ohio-- and ozone layer depletion high in the atmosphere. But the station was funded by 20 different agencies and institutions both inside and outside of government, a standard ploy, he knew, that devolved anyone of real responsibility. In sum, he wasn't really sure for whom he was working for at any given moment. When, after a few tense seconds, nothing untoward had occurred on his screen, the researcher more calmly assessed the situation. He pressed F7 on his computer keyboard and a series of HELP prompts appeared, including one that read "Orange Plus." He clicked on the words with his computer mouse and another screen appeared. Some type of sensor in the observatory on Whiteface had been triggered, he realized, but it was one with which he was unfamiliar.

The computer prompted him to check for a false positive reading and he confirmed that, if nothing else, there wasn't a computer or sensor malfunction. Following further prompts, he created an encrypted file and saved the sensor data to it. The computer then automatically installed what the researcher recognized as stenographic software, programs that had been residing on his hard drive until needed. Then unbidded, a picture of a buxom brunette wearing a see-through top made of black mesh appeared on his screen. With a grin, the researcher followed the prompts instructing him on how to imbed the encrypted file into the picture using the stenographic software. The researcher, again following prompts, accessed the Internet and posted the picture with the instructed file name on much-frequented soft-porn bulletin board. The picture, the researcher knew, could be viewed and downloaded anonymously by anyone but only someone with the correct stenographic software would know that another file lay hidden in the picture. And if someone did hack the stenography program, they would still have to unravel the encryption used on the original data file. The beauty of this methodology was that it employed two layers of excellent security and the intended recipient would never be known. The researcher clicked on a gray box marked "finished" when it appeared. The computer then automatically deleted all the stenography and encryption programs he had just used. New programs would be downloaded from the Internet without his being aware of it, hidden until needed.

"So what's Orange Plus?" said the researcher to a colleague sitting unseen inside another cubicle.

"No idea, dude."

The first state troopers on the scene didn't touch a thing, particularly when they saw what Trooper Douglas was holding in his hand. In short order, New York State crime scene investigators combed the castle's grounds. They were soon followed by the captain of Douglas's troop.

"What have you got?" asked the troop captain, a beefy man who had grown round around the right connections in Albany.

"Trooper Urgill Douglas," replied the lead investigator, a balding man with the crumpled look of a state bureaucrat. "Dead about two hours ago. He fired his weapon six times at something but there are no blood spatters anywhere nearby, other than what's on his left hand."

"Any trace of a woman? His radio call said a woman was being kidnapped."

"No trace of her."

"You said there is blood on his left hand?"

"He's holding a heart in his left hand."

"A heart?"

"Yeah. It's frozen. But the victim has some strange marks around his mouth. I know this sounds crazy. I think the heart is his."

Chapter Two

Those that thought of her at all considered her to be a lonely figure. But that's not how she thought of herself. She sat comfortably up to her waist in the cool waters of Lough Nasool. The lower half of the white dress she wore was wet but she didn't care. Well, she cared a little bit as it was her favorite. The thin white stripes sown into the material bespoke superior craftsmanship. But the feel of the water was so exquisite. She closed her eyes and she brushed her black hair with a practiced rhythm. The comb glinted in the sunlight as the tiny jewels embedded in it caught the sun's rays, flickering with each movement of the woman's arm.

She should be lonely, she knew, but she wasn't. She enjoyed her time alone. Those that knew of her whispered and called her a woman of the hills. Mostly, they knew of her near the end of their days when she'd come visiting, a keen on her lips that would make them tremble. They knew what a visit from her meant. In the old days, she had visited only a few families when the time came but intermarriage meant many had a drop of the old blood in them. Lately, all she often had time for was a single note that perhaps went unheard or ignored. The world was a noisy place these days and many no longer knew how to listen in the old, hard way, preferring sounds of their own choosing, their ears closed off to all else. No matter. She fulfilled her long obligations whether they heard her or not.

No one sought her out and if they did, this would be the last place they'd come. Indeed, this part of Sligo, one of Ireland's more remote counties in the northwest of the country, remained virtually unchanged and unvisited even as tourists flocked across the rest of the land. This was especially true of Lough Nasool, a small bowl of water beneath the treeless plateau of Moytirra. The ghosts of the ancient battlefield kept them all away, she told herself. Just as well. It was an empty place only the wind loved and it suited her.

Yes, it had been a fierce battle atop the plateau. The good people of the Tuatha De Danaan, led by Lugh, fought the deformed six-fingered sea-faring Formorian wretches, led by the Balor of the Evil Eye. The fighting raged on relentlessly for days, with the Formorians eating the dead of friend and foe alike until Lugh fired a stone that plucked the one eye from Balor's head, leaving the Fomorians confused and leaderless in their retreat. The eye, so the legend said, had fallen on this very spot with such an impact as to form a depression that became Lough Nasool or the Lake of the Evil Eye.

The woman was still lost in her thoughts when Balor blinked. At first, the woman didn't notice anything amiss. It wasn't until the suddenly swirling water grabbed her by the legs and swept them from under her that her eyes flared in alarm. The comb flew out her hands and landed on the grass above the shore. She tried to steady herself by gripping the lake shore with her hands, digging her fingers into the dirt, but the current was too strong. In a moment, she was on the other side of the lake, caught in the grip of a whirlpool.

The water is disappearing! She caught glimpses of muddy ground where there had been water only minutes before. The woman cried out but her voice was muffled by the sound of swirling water and a great sucking sound coming from somewhere beneath her. Like some giant creature that hadn't been fed in a long time.

Is this my end? With no voice raised in mourning? She fought to swim and her arms flailed twice before her head disappeared under thewater.

Ryan Connor sank his long, lanky frame into a wicker chair in the front yard of his cousin's house and stared back at the twin cows in the field opposite eyeing him while they chewed on some grass. He shielded his eyes from the sun's glare and brought a cup of strong tea to his lips. A car whizzed by on its way to Sligo town some three miles distance. It was a fast road but one not heavily traveled. The road was sometimes closed for rally racing but on normal days, a fast ride could become a slow journey thanks to the inevitable tractor that slowed cars to a crawl until they could find a safe place to pass. The two-lane road ran parallel to Keelogyboy Mountain, a flattened 1,400 foot high mound that looked like a sleeping giant. His cousin's house was nestled just below the giant's neck

Connor came to Ireland often. The country beckoned like a siren's call and the longest he'd been able to stay away was three years. He'd been born in New York but had been brought to Ireland as a toddler, then abruptly whisked back to America just when he was beginning to settle into Ireland, enrolled in a local school that was a small building with a massive tree in the front yard surrounded by a white wall head-high in those days. His earliest memories were of leaving Ireland, arriving in New York City and wondering what was wrong with the grass because it was such a pale green. Every trip to Ireland now seemed like a chance to gather bits of himself that had been left behind as a child. He had no regrets. In all likelihood, he'd have not had the opportunities and experiences that made him the man he was today if he had remained in Ireland.

But when Connor was in Sligo, he sometimes caught a shadow of himself walking around the country, living another life, one that had more sheep and horses in it than trains and buses, likely knowing everyone within sight of his eyes for miles versus knowing everyone in your building. Connor loved living in New York but he also loved coming back to Sligo. The landscape, with its mountains and it coasts, could still grab him by the wrist and it was a grasp he welcomed. But he had the ability to pry himself loose when he needed to go. In America, hard work could make something happen that would change your life. In Ireland, hard work often only made the obstacles in front of you more formidable. That was breaking down a bit. The country had transformed itself from an agricultural economy into one that now offered more jobs in information technology and pharmaceuticals, mostly around Dublin and Cork, the biggest cities and a long drive from Sligo. But there were still plenty of people leaving Ireland--especially those from places in the far west like Sligo-- for a better life elsewhere. Just like they had done for centuries. Some returned. Many didn't.

Smudge, a white cat with a black mark about his right eye, purred around his chair leg. Connor hoped the tea would clear the fog in his head. His cousin Rosaleen had capped an evening at Vincent's Pub with a few hot toddies and he blamed that for the heaviness of his head. Vincent's Pub had the advantage of being within staggering distance of his cousin's house and Connor liked the place for its rural charm and its centuries-old ambience. It reminded Connor of one of those taverns in the movie *The Three Musketeers* where the heroes would have stopped for refreshment and the watering of their horses. The pub was a long stone building that seemed to sink further into the ground the closer you came to it. Vincent lived next door in a newer house but Vincent could be found most nights behind the stick, dispensing pints and opinions with equal ease. There was a small fireplace and a few tables that were used mostly for card games by the local farmers. All in all, the place probably hadn't changed since the middle of 19th century. Vincent had stroked his gray hair in astonishment when he learned that people in New York City had paid top dollar to see a Broadway play that took place in a pub much like his own. Vincent, who only opened the pub in the evenings after his day job as a security guard was done, looked at the old place with new eyes while the regulars feared the revelation would surely lead to an increase in the price of a pint of Guinness. Vincent suddenly now viewed himself as the caretaker of a piece of living Irish history even as he refused to acknowledge his own graying hair.

Rosaleen, Connor recalled, had tried to sell Connor's attributes to a couple of local girls.

"Sure now, look at all six feet plus of him. Fit he is. Aye, the dark hair goes wavy when it's long but it's been short now for years. Now, his father—bless his soul—his hair didn't go gray until he was 60 so our man here will keep his looks for quite a while yet," said Rosaleen. "The face is handsome enough, I'd say. But have you noticed the eyes on him? They're blue now when he has a bit of drink in him and he's all nice and content like. But if you see him in the road tomorrow, you'll see his eyes are green. My advice to any woman interested in him is to let him have a glass or two of the black. But then I'm partial to blue eyes myself."

Connor chuckled at the memory and shook his head when he recalled two of the regulars, two brothers with heads the same size as those of the cows they tended. They hadn't said much, thank God. Connor suspected their native tongue might be something bovine. But the evening had been good craic, as the Irish called a good time, all the same. Vincent had been in rare form and had brought out his guitar for a few songs.

Rosaleen's house was probably as old as Vincent's Pub, guessed Connor, and was a welcome contrast to the new housing developments creeping out from Sligo town. The second story had gone up in the 1920's but no one knew when the original house had been built. Like most of the traditional houses in this part of Ireland, it was rectangular in shape. The downstairs rooms were the width of the house, with each one leading to the next without the benefit of a hallway. A steep staircase with steps so narrow they had to be traversed sideways led up to a short hallway with three bedrooms with low doors off it. Rosaleen had modernized things a bit, converting the old cow shed attached to the house into a large dining and living space complete with new stove and appliances. She hadn't included a hot press, though, a cupboard next to a boiler where towels and sheets were kept warm against damp days that was a fixture of many Irish homes. But many of the old touches remained. The front door opened onto a mud room and a second door opened into the house where an old but massive coal-burning range dominated what had once been the kitchen. It now supplemented an oil burner for home heating. It wasn't that long ago when the range was the main source of warmth. Small plastic tubes had extended from the range into other rooms to provide an illusion of central heating that shattered in the cool, wet dawns when the range fire went out. Those tubes were gone now. He had never gotten the knack of firing up the range to rid the house of the morning damp. Pry open the top lid. Open the flume with the knob on the far left. Add kindling. Light with match. Then add four lumps of coal. Ruefully, he inspected his lower arms and hands for black marks of coal dust. Every time Connor tried to light the range he came away looking like a West Virginia coal miner.

Other antique touches remained in full working order, however. The wood-encased clock on the wall, given to Rosaleen's grandmother on her wedding day, marked the time. A massive wood-cased radio with a shortwave band spoke of a time when places were further away and more exotic. Each downstairs room had a little wrought-iron fireplace in it. Rosaleen burned bits of coal in those fireplaces from time to time and while Connor had never asked her about it, he was sure the practice was more habitual than practical. It was something her parents did while they were alive. It was like lighting a candle in church in memory of the departed.

Each of the three bedrooms upstairs had its own tiny fireplace but the fanciest, bordered in green marble, was in the front parlor, the entry way marked by a low wood doorway that forced Connor to stoop. Rosaleen had added a "mad red" couch as a touch of modernity or, Connor suspected, of rebellion.

"I've left the house to you in my will," Rosaleen had said, "providing I don't get married."

Connor had laughed. "Yes. And the first thing I'm going to do is install a mirror on the wall in the bathroom so I can shave. How do expect a man to marry you if he can't shave properly in the morning?"

"He can do like my father did. He shaved in the light of the kitchen window using a small mirror."

"Which is what I'm doing now and I'm lucky I haven't scarred myself for life."

That was how she'd come by the house, inheriting it from her parents. And it was like her to promise him something he'd never get. At 27, Rosaleen was three years younger than Connor. She had a long life ahead of her. Furthermore, she was a good-looking brunette who'd soon attract a husband. Or so he hoped. Sligo town was loaded with young bachelors whisking off to Dublin or Brussels on one assignment or another and then returning.

Connor sipped at his tea, determined to enjoy his last days in Ireland before going back to New York City. Smudge moved off in search of a field mouse or a feline paramour. While Dublin could match New York's fast pace, time slowed to a crawl in Loughanelton. The rooster up the road didn't crow until 10 AM and Connor would have his tea finished before the old bird rousted himself. The truth was that he hadn't planned to stay in Ireland this long. He'd come for the funeral of an uncle and godfather whispered to have been active in the Irish Republican Army in its Armalite rifle heyday. The whispers, Connor knew, were true as his uncle Michael, back when he'd lived in New York, had sometimes used his parent's home as a safe house for a litany of men in transit named "Smith" or "Jones." The old man understood why the twin towers of New York City's World Trade Center were targeted on September 11th, 2001. "They've severed the horns of the Great Satan," he had told Connor over the phone. With years of Catholic versus Protestant strife behind him, his uncle knew how to cast the attack in a religious context that Connor rightly suspected reflected the frame of mind of the Islamic radicals behind the plot.

There had been a wake at the uncle's house and he had looked dignified in a suit and green tie. There had been sandwiches, whiskey and tea served in the good china. There were only two framed photos on the walls. One was of the man himself, looking like a elder white-haired statesman in a white shirt and a patterned red tie under an expensive-looking coat, holding the 1916 Proclamation of Irish Independence in his hands. In the background were a group of Celtic crosses of varying height.

"He did well that day," said Rosaleen at his elbow. "The photo was taken down below in Limerick. It was at the gravesite of one of the men executed by the British in 1916. His remains were removed from Mountjoy Prison and he was re-interred in some wee place called Ballylanders. The man had always wished to be buried at home. Your uncle read the 1916 Proclamation over his grave that day. He was a fierce Republican. I was very proud of him."

The second photo was an old black and white image of young men with warrior faces dressed in dark suits, tightly knotted ties and white shirts starched with stiff collars carrying a coffin draped with the Irish flag out of a church as a well-dressed crowd watched. Atop the coffin was a wreath. One of the lead pallbearers had a large bulge in his right suit pocket and Connor wondered if he was armed. They were led by man, also in a suit, with a high forehead and swept-back black hair, holding a hat—a fedora Connor guessed--and looking off to his right. There also were two men in an uniform Connor didn't recognize accompanying the coffin. In the background, was another man in a light suit, noticeable because while the rest of the crowd stared at the coffin, he was looking sharply to his right, in the same direction as the man with the hat. The left pocket of his suit was bulging as well. Something unseen by the many had grabbed their attention.

"Do you know who that is?" asked Rosaleen. "'Leave your jewels and gold wands in the bank and buy a revolver.'"

"You're quoting The Rebel Countess," said Connor. He was a great fan of the famous Irish poet William Butler Yeats, who had grown up in Sligo and which was the setting for many of his most famous poems, *The Lake Isle of Innisfree* being foremost among them. Yeats had been a frequent visitor to nearby Lissadell House, the home of Countess Markiewicz, a wealthy Irish woman who had married a Polish count and then fought for Irish freedom from British rule in the Easter Rising of 1916 as a sniper. Her death sentence had been commuted because of her sex.

"She died in 1927," said Rosaleen. "Most of the photos of her are in uniform with pistol in hand. I have never seen this photo of her funeral anywhere else. It was given to your uncle by the son of the man holding the hat, a friend of the Countess who helped organize her funeral in Dublin. Thousands came even though the government wouldn't give her a state funeral. She was anti-Treaty."

Connor nodded. The man with the hat looked like he was scanning the crowd for enemies. The bulge in the man's pocket was probably a revolver and Connor wondered if it perhaps belonged to the Countess herself.

"It was a bad year. The treaty that created the North was only a few years old. The Irish Free State government that backed the treaty was waging a secret war against the militant anti-Treaty supporters. There were assassinations of political figures. Men were whisked away in the middle of the night and their bodies found in the road the next day. Those men in suits in the background were IFS secret agents. Even taking this photograph would have been risky."

Rosaleen took a breath. "The photo is fascinating in its detail. The two men in uniform are former members of a youth brigade the Countess trained prior to the Rising. She taught them all how to shoot. You can see they have outgrown the uniforms but are wearing them for the occasion."

"So why did my uncle like this photograph so much?"

"I asked him about that. It took me weeks to get up the nerve. But he was very gracious. He believed the death of the Countess was the moment when the nation knew the ideal of a united Ireland wouldn't occur in any of their lifetimes. It was why so many thousands came to see her off. They buried a dream. It wouldn't stay buried, of course. But here we are all these years later and we're still divided."

Rosaleen paused. "And there was the man in the hat. I think the death of the Countess unraveled him. In the 1930s, he became a leading fascist and even advocated the Nazis invading Ireland. He lost the plot completely. Your uncle took it as a warning. Be very careful if someone tries to pass you the hat, especially if you decide to take it. Which is perhaps what the son intended."

"Who was the man in the hat?"

"It doesn't matter. He died forgotten. And I'll not curse his descendants by whispering his name. You can find that out his name on your own if you're determined enough. But you should have the photographs."

"Thank you," said Connor. "I'll make some copies and get them to you."

"It was Ken over in America, wasn't it?

"Yes. That was actually his real first name." Certain types of men in Ireland went by their middle name. Anyone asking for the man using his first name was certainly the authorities. Republican activity for a united Ireland that included the six counties in the north still owned—occupied they would say—by England was illegal.

The names of the callers were all blur but their sorrow seemed genuine and the uncle was known well locally. The funeral mass had been a sad and ritualistic affair with no mention of politics but the actual burial had been accompanied by a bagpiper playing old rebel songs and three men wearing balaclavas that covered their face but couldn't disguise their age as they fired off a salute with Armalites still retained for "ceremonial occasions," as Rosaleen had put it to him. Connor hadn't asked for any names but he'd heard one of them referred to as "Slab." Rosaleen had taken him under her wing and had insisted that he stay with her rather than at some overpriced hotel once she heard he wasn't keen on staying in his uncle's house.

"Sure, why would you stay there on your own? The place is haunted now by dead rebel ghosts," she said in a tone that made Connor think she believed there were live rebel ghosts around as well, men still operating in the shadows despite the appearance of peace. Connor didn't doubt it.

Rosaleen laughed. His mind must have been on his face. "No worries, pet. They are all above in Leitrim." That was the next county over and one well known for its rebel tendencies.

The bed in Rosaleen's house was nice as was the room on the second floor facing the front. There was a small coal-driven fireplace and lacy curtains that kept flies out—Ireland, like most of Europe, had not discovered window screens for some reason. Connor was sure the breakfast—one could only eat so much Flahavans porridge-- was more varied elsewhere.

Connor made himself a cup of tea and found a bit of milk in the fridge to put into it. Most Americans took their tea without milk but in England and Ireland a dash of milk was the norm. The English preferred to add their milk after the tea was poured but the Irish liked to put the milk in the cup first. There were great arguments about which method yielded the better drink. Connor added the milk in after the pour, letting the white liquid filter downward of its own accord only because then he didn't have to look for a spoon to stir it. No sugar either. That also required a spoon.

Connor's reverie was interrupted by the sound of the mail van pulling up to the front gate.

"Top of the morning, Connor!"

Connor chuckled. The mailman, of course, knew Connor was visiting from New York and was deliberately putting on the stage "Oirish" voice for his benefit.

Connor rose from his seat and strode over to the gate. The mailman leaned out of the van and thrust two letters at him.

"Not much today. How's Rosaleen?"

"Grand," said Connor, accepting the letters, bills by the look of them. "Off working. What's new in the world?"

"Ah, big news," said the mailman. "Lough Nasool disappeared again."

"Again?" It was remarkable enough for a lake to disappear once, thought Connor. But more than once?

"Aye," said the mailman. "The story goes that the lake disappears once every 100 years but I'd say it's been knocked off schedule."

"How's that?"

"It last vanished in 1989. Before that, it disappeared in 1964 and 1933. I remember my grandfather telling the tale."

"A whole lake?"

"Ah, sure, it's only a wee lake," said the mailman, somewhat dismissively. "Do you not know it?"

"Never heard of it."

"Where have you been all your life?" said the mailman with a wink. "Lough Nasool. The Lake of the Evil Eye. They say the giant Balor lost his eye there fighting the Tuatha De Danaan and the lough is his eye yet. When he blinks, the water disappears. Spooky shite, eh?"

"Where does the water go?"

"Ach, who knows?" said the mailman. "But it fills up again right quick, that I can tell you. The whole country over there is queer, full of deep caves and God-knows-what."

"Where is it exactly?" asked Connor. "Sounds like it would be worth a look."

The mailman studied Connor for a moment. "Go out on the Boyle road until you see a massive lake."

"OK."

"That won't be it. That would be Lough Arrow. There's another lake with a castle in the middle of it. That's not it either. That would be Lough Key. Lough Nasool is on the other side of that. If you go into Boyle, you've gone too far."

"That's a lot of lakes."

"Aye. There's more than them I just named. They can barely keep track of them over there. Be careful you don't fall into one." With a wave, the mailman drove off.

Connor smiled. In Ireland, directions like that were as good as it got. Modern tech like GPS maps wasn't so reliable around here. Connor had hiked to the top of Keelogyboy and the people wandering about that he at first thought were sheep herders were actually people trying to get a mobile signal the same as him. People would get one but it would be gone with a change in the wind.

Connor was not surprised to soon find himself in the town of Boyle. The lure of visiting a disappearing lake was impossible to resist. The day was what counted for a good one in the West of Ireland. Bolts of sunshine blasting through dark clouds moving along at a fast clip. He wore waterproof boots bought in Scotland and a waterproof jacket bought locally. He had once kitted himself out in waterproof gear made in the USA. Assaulted by Irish rain, he might as well have been wearing paper. Irish rain is a class of heavy water that goes through most American raingear.

A church steeple caught his eye. The town's most famous son, the writer and chronicler of Irish rural life John McGahern, had observed that while the ordinary people hereabouts had strictly conformed to the observances required by the Catholic Church, they had paid little attention to the institution once beyond its doors. The people, wrote McGahern, went about their sensible pagan lives as they had done for centuries, seeing the Church as just one more fiction they had been forced to endure, like all the others since the time of the Druids. McGahern had been writing about the 20th century. In the 21st century, it seemed all Ireland publicly treated the Church like a fiction and paid little heed to its observances, a trend accelerated by a series of scandals involving priestly pedophiles that made the phrase "a bunch of buggers" synonymous with the wearers of Roman collars.

"All pagan, all the time," Connor muttered, altering but mimicking the slogan of a 24-hour news radio station.

If there was a road that led to the other side of Lough Arrow, Connor missed it. Only mildly frustrated, Connor had enjoyed the drive along the shores of Lough Arrow. Some Americans were intimidated by driving on the other side of the road with the steering wheel on the right side of the car but it had never bothered Connor. Admittedly, there was a small adjustment period of about an hour when he was likely to turn on the windshield wipers when he meant to signal for a turn. There were no double yellow lines on the road, just white slashes for two-way traffic with solid white lines for no passing sections. There were a few big highways in Ireland but they were concentrated around the major cities of Dublin and Cork. In the West, two lanes were the rule and they were often narrow, Connor kept the left side mirror angled downward so he could better gauge how close he was to a wall or a ditch. Many cars had camera systems that let the driver see around the vehicle but Connor trusted his own spatial sense more than he did technology.

Lough Arrow was certainly one of the most beautiful lakes he'd ever seen. Boyle, by contrast, offered the lake little competition, being quite unremarkable, perhaps out of deference to the lake. In town, he made a series of left turns that he hoped would get him out of Boyle as soon as possible and on the road to the far side of Lough Arrow. If all went well, Lough Arrow should appear on his left. Instead, Connor spotted a lake on his right with an island in the middle of it. And in the middle of the island was a massive castle.

For a moment, Connor thought he had lost his bearings completely. That would be Lough Key, according to the mailman. But then the castle struck a chord in his memory. Lough Key. Connor remembered his Yeats. The great Irish poet William Butler Yeats loved Sligo and had planned to found a mystical order with Castle Rock in Lough Key as its centerpiece. Lough Key had also figured prominently in *The Secret Rose*, Yeats' story of star-crossed lovers.

More confident now, Connor drove on in his rented red Land Rover and soon found Lough Arrow on his left. Connor followed the shoreline until the road veered away from Lough Arrow. After another mile, Connor came to a fork in the road. Connor slowed the car to a crawl as there was no traffic to worry about. The left fork rose up a hill and near the top, Connor could see what looked like a grocery store. Connor sighed. He needed directions and someone in the grocery store might provide them. The Land Rover was equipped with a GPS navigation system but the software was hopeless. The road he was on didn't even show up on the map. Never mind the lake. Although that didn't surprise him. Navigation systems focused on the man-made, ignoring that created by Nature.

"Good day!" said Connor to the teen-aged clerk behind the counter, trying not to sound like an Australian. The store was more modern and larger than Connor would have guessed given its isolation and was brightly lit with fluorescent lights. "Can you tell me the way the Lough Nasool?"

"I couldn't," said the clerk. "It's a hard place to find, right enough, and I'm not from around here. But do you see that old fellow down by the milk?"

Connor turned and saw the man. He was tall, angular and looked to be in his seventies. The old man was staring into the dairy section as if there was more to be seen there than just milk, cheese, and yogurt.

"He's from around those parts," continued the clerk. "He'll set you straight."

Connor nodded his thanks and approached the old man.

"Sorry to trouble you but I'm told you can tell me the way to Lough Nasool."

The old man turned to face Connor, seemingly relieved that he no longer had to ponder the ins and outs of dairy products.

"Aye," said the old man, pausing then as if preparing for a recital. Connor had once heard a recording of Yeats reciting *The Lake Isle of Innisfree*. As the old man began to speak, Connor felt like he was listening to the sonorous tones of Yeats all over again. The old man's voice changed pitch as he described the twists and turns ahead. His voice continued to rise and fall as the road went up a hill and then down again. Finally, said the old man, you'll come to a fork in the road.

"Then you'll make a turn to the right," finished the old man. "Lough Nasool will be within sight."

"Thank you very much," said Connor, mustering a formality that seemed to fit the occasion. Connor felt like he had just been to poetry reading.

Connor nodded his thanks again and headed for the door.

"I will arise and go now," Connor muttered to himself, remembering the poem's first line.

The old man's tonal inflections matched the terrain perfectly and within a half hour, Connor was parked beside what had been the waters of Lough Nasool. At the moment, the lake was mostly mud.

It's a wonder there is no else around. But then it was a weekday so many people might be at work. And the narrow roads and remoteness of Lough Nasool discouraged the casual visitor or tourist. *Still if a lake disappeared in the United States, the area would have been roped off for TV crews and be under study by a team of scientists.* The Irish merely shrugged, confident the lake would return to normal of its own accord. In short, the doings of the lake were none of their business.

Like the mailman said, Lough Nasool was not a very big lake. Connor had seen bigger ponds but he knew that a lake got its designation because of its depth, not its width. Drained as it was, Connor still couldn't estimate the depth of Lough Nasool but it looked too deep and slippery to climb down into. A small pool of water was already forming at the bottom. Connor wondered if the lake could fill as fast as it drained. And that thought kept him near the lake edge.

Connor slowly walked along the muddy shore as he absorbed the scene. Lough Nasool might be about 24 acres in size, he estimated, as it seemed to be about the same size as a farm an uncle on his mother's side had once owned long ago. At one end, there was a house but it appeared to be unoccupied. Not uncommon, Connor knew, as many had emigrated, gone to Dublin or moved into town.

Connor continued his walk. The shoreline followed the road and soon the plateau of Moytirra loomed above him. Connor recognized it from pictures he'd seen. The plateau threw its shadow ahead of him. Without thinking, Connor followed the line between darkness and light until he saw something gleaming in the grass. Curious, Connor stepped toward it gingerly and then retrieved it. A large comb, he saw at once. The handle was at least six inches long and the comb's teeth were very long. Embedded into the comb were numerous tiny flecks of light that might be jewels. Connor brushed some mud from the comb and discovered a pattern of three interlocking spirals etched into what he guessed was a bone handle. A woman's comb, he thought, and very old. Perhaps a lady traveling by coach dropped it here a century or two ago.

This will be a nice souvenir. He slipped the comb into his inside jacket pocket. Better than a rock. There would be a good story attached to this. *The story of Lough Nasool, the disappearing lake. Yes, that would be a good one.*

Connor backtracked the way he had come, unsure of any other way to go, until he came to Boyle. Once there, Connor decided to play the tourist and detoured through the Curlew Mountains, only stopping when he came to Keshcorran, a small but steep mountain crowned by a ring of caves said to extend underground for miles. On a whim, Connor climbed over a gate and crossed a field with a bull at the other end. The hike to the top of Keshcorran took an hour with the last few hundred yards the steepest. More than once, Connor had to dig into the soil with his fingers to steady himself. Finally, Connor reached the ring of caves and plopped down onto a rock that guarded the entrance to the largest of the caves. The view was magnificent and his perch offered a sense of height that was greater that the 1,182-foot elevation marked on maps. Cormac

MacArt, an ancient king of Ireland, had been born at the foot of Keshcorran. A wolf had carried the baby prince into one of 13 caves behind him. The boy had been found a year later when he was old enough to toddle out of the caves on his own. Connor stole a glance behind him. That must have been some hike for a toddler, he thought. And then there was the story of how the giant Finn McCool, the great Irish hero, and his band of Fenians had been enticed into these enchanted caves by the three daughters of an evil sorcerer who magically held them captive until one of the Fenians overcame them.

Suddenly, Connor heard a noise to his right. He wheeled around, half expecting to see three old witches or the young prince himself. A lamb edged its way toward him and then stopped a few paces short of him as if startled to find any other creature other than sheep up here.

"Surprise!" said Connor.

The lamb bolted.

"All right. I'll be going. Sorry for the intrusion."

Connor laughed as he scrambled down the mountainside. The smile faded from his lips when he came to the field below. This time, the bull was waiting for him. Connor hopped over the wall and the bull began to charge. Connor took off at a run, heading for the opposite wall and the safety of the car.

It was an unequal race in the end. Connor had been on the basketball team in high school and could still sprint better than most. Connor ran across the field and cleared the gate with plenty of room between him and the bull. Nevertheless, judging from the snorts and foot stamping, the bull claimed victory for forcing him from the field.

"Thanks for the workout," shouted Connor as he climbed into his car. With a wave at the bull, Connor drove off. Within minutes, he was navigating through the small town of Ballymote.

He then opted for a small road that led past Templerock. Connor slowed as he drove by—he had always wanted to stay the night at Templerock. The Knights Templar had built a small castle here on the banks of the Owenmore River in 1200. The castle was in ruins, Connor saw, but a large two-story mansion next to it was still occupied by the St. Jacques, descendants of the O'Hara family who had built the castle. Templerock was now an inn but it didn't seem to actively attract many guests. There were more sheep in the front yard than parked cars.

Connor drove on until he reached the N17, the main road to Sligo. This was a road he knew well. Behind him was the small town of Tubbercurry, marked by a town square that was actually a triangle. It was on a nearby farm in a place called Bunnacranagh that he had spent a year of his childhood, working side-by-side with another uncle and his children—mostly milking cows and shoveling tons of cowshit out of the barn. Tubbercurry had been burned to the ground in a reprisal raid by the Black & Tans in 1920, the streets running with petrol, porter, whiskey, melted soap and candle grease. Or so his uncle said. That had been back during Ireland's fight for independence from England. There had been a firefight on the next farm belonging to the Murphy's. Bullet holes still pocked the walls of one of the sheds, he recalled.

And here he was in a British Land Rover, he thought. *If his uncle could see him now*. Connor smiled. And Tubbercurry was doing well last time he looked.

He soon drove passed Knocknashee, a mountain reputed to be the home of the fairies, also called Mullinabreena or the Hill of the Fairy Palace. Connor had climbed to the top once years ago and examined the remains of a fort said to have been built in the Bronze Age. He recalled walking along the summit on a long, wide road-like indentation in the soil that could have once been the approach to the fort.

Those thoughts were soon pushed out of his mind by a dark wall of rain sliding up the road toward him, all light ahead of it and darkness behind. The rain came down hard like some water god had stepped on the island to relieve himself. Pissing rain the Irish said of it. Within seconds, the road all but disappeared as the rain swamped over him. Connor could see the dim shapes of the cars in front of him, red lights ablaze as they followed other vehicles to the shoulder and for a moment he considered doing the same. *But then isn't this what big red Land Rovers were for, particularly rented ones?*

Connor activated the flashing hazard lights and eased cautiously forward. The road ahead descended into a valley and there was a good chance that a car could hydroplane down the hill out of control. Halfway down the hill he glanced in the rear view mirror. A procession of cars followed his lead, the red color and the flashing lights of the Land Rover serving as a marker for the route. He kept his speed slow. The visibility was low and his biggest fear was smashing into a car stopped ahead of him. He glanced once more in the rear view mirror and judging from the headlights he could see, there was now a long line behind him.

Connor maintained his speed and climbed the road ahead, which was a little steeper than the section he had descended. By the time he hit the crest, the rain had abated to a light shower and visibility had returned. Just another "soft day" in Ireland, as the local would say.

The weather continued to improve as he navigated the last roundabouts before entering the town. In the distance now, he could see Ben Bulben, a massive flattop that overlooked the coastline and stretched out of sight to the north like some huge aircraft carrier. He was always slightly bothered when he saw Ben Bulben these days. As a child, he remembered seeing a large white square in the limestone on the southern side hundreds of feet above the plain below, that was reputed to be the door to another world, one that sometimes swings open, according to legend. No mortal hand had ever touched it, he recalled being told. But to Connor's eye now, the white square was no longer there. Still, Ben Bulben was easily Sligo's most identifiable landmark and was a staple of every postcard. Beneath Ben Bulben's towering cliffs, in the cemetery of Drumcliffe, lay the grave of W. B. Yeats.

"Cast a cold eye, on life, on death. Horseman pass by!" Connor recited from memory the inscription on Yeats' tombstone, written by the poet himself before his death. Yeat's himself wasn't there. The poet had died in France just prior to World War II. After the war, Ireland had pressured France to return Yeats to his homeland. But the war had made a mess of French graveyards and no one knew where the remains of Yeats actually were. In 1947, France sent a coffin of bones to Ireland, claiming it was Yeats when it fact they were the bones of numerous people gathered from a mass grave in France. That bit of French skullduggery had only recently come to light. Locals were still digesting the truth. "Cast a cold eye," Connor said aloud. "Because I'm not here."

Connor entered Sligo Town via the Inner Relief Road and wondered once again if it was named for the feeling the locals felt upon arriving safely home after a trip away. He gripped the wheel with his right hand in the 12 o'clock position, ready to raise a finger in greeting if he passed a car he recognized. Sligo was remote but didn't feel that way. The town was a cozy place of low buildings that gave off an extraordinary air of self-sufficiency and it was easy to believe that no world outside of it existed. The best streets in Sligo were not its main, undistinguished thoroughfares but the narrow side lanes that invariably led to bridges that spanned the Garavogue River, a shallow waterway that slow-poured itself into the nearby bay. The river was at its best at night when the lights of pubs, clubs, and eateries along its banks daggered it, giving the flowing water the texture and colors of an old oil painting. Connor turned right onto Wine Street but skipped his first parking opportunity, a lot favored by supermarket shoppers and always crowded. He carried on past the old red-bricked Yeats Building on his right and the much newer and aptly named Glass House Hotel on his left. It had replaced the old Silver Swan Hotel of his youth and Connor still had trouble placing the Glass House, with its trapezoid shaped entrance and orange interior glowing like a lava lamp, in his mind as a landmark. Still, it might be a better point of reference than the town hall, built in a badly interpreted French Renaissance style with a tower that looked more like a tumor.

Connor accelerated over the Hyde Bridge which allowed vehicles to traverse the Garavogue, turned left onto Markievicz Road, named for the revolutionary countess and a heroine of the war against England, then turned quickly again up the hill toward Sligo General Hospital. But just below the hospital was a parking lot, the entrance framed by yellow bars designed to keep out caravans, Connor parked and got out of the car. This was the view he savored.

Knocknarea stood in the distance. The mountain rose above Sligo, both the town and the bay, standing opposite Ben Bulben like a separated lover. At its summit was an enormous, ancient cairn, visible for miles, and said to be the final resting place of Queen Maeve, a legendary queen of Connaught, a kingdom that included Sligo and Galway to the south. The ancient dolmens, sacred wells and stone circles that littered the fields around the town hinted at some superhuman greatness in former times and the cairn atop Knocknarea subdued all disbelief. It was customary for hikers to bring a stone to hurl atop her tomb and unquestionably bad luck to bring one down. Connor had added three to the pile over the years. Sligo had a lot of great views and they were all to be enjoyed. His eyes satiated, Connor began walking down a side street toward the Garavogue. He had a little business to attend to in town and Rosaleen would be joining him for a drink as well.

The woman broke the surface of the water with an abruptness that startled four geese into flight. For a few moments, she savored the sweet air, keeping her head above water. Gradually, she took in the surrounding shoreline and then the island with the castle. Lough Key, she realized. The underground river had not swept her as far as she feared. A branch of the subterranean river, she knew, went at least as far as Cong, many miles to the south, sometimes bubbling up at spots with names like the Round Hill of Oozing Water and the Footstep of the Hag. Knowing this, there were moments when she thought she'd be trapped below the earth forever. After falling through the whirlpool and the initial surge of water, the current had eased. She had been able to swim from one underground cavern to the next. None had offered an exit to the world above. And she was without her comb. She shivered at the thought. *I must retrieve it at once.*

That thought alone was enough to spur her into action. With renewed vigor, she swam to shore, emerging dripping wet with her white dress clinging to her body. She stood there allowing the sun to warm her. Fortunately, the dress material dried quickly.

A noise startled her. The road was much nearer than she realized. An old man walking his dog was staring at her. The dog barked and backed up a few steps. She pursed her lips and aimed the sound that came from her lips directly at the man. It was a sound that he wouldn't hear, being at a frequency just below the range of human hearing. The sound wouldn't manifest itself until it struck the man and then it would envelope him. The sound, she knew from long experience, made the human eyeball resonate. The man would now be looking at a figure that would seem to flicker like a ghostly apparition.

"Mother of God!" said the old man as he tugged at the dog's leash and hurried away.

The woman laughed to herself. She must be quite a sight but she was definitely not divine. The old man will have a good ghost story to tell tonight down at the pub, if he waits that long. If only she had her cloak—her gwynn. He'd never have noticed her if she was wearing it. *I left it on the grass by Lough Nasool.*

The comb was another matter. She had this sickening feeling that something had happened to it. The woman moved quickly to the road and started walking. Her pace was one few could match.

She reached Lough Nasool in a fit of anxiety. The water had returned and the lake looked as placid as any ever seen. Her gwynn was where she had left it, unseen and untouched, its hue only visible to her discerning eye. The comb, however, was nowhere to be found. She scoured the shore even as she became more certain of its disappearance.

It was no use. *It is gone!*

She closed her eyes and focused on the comb. A jumble of images leapt into her mind. A man had found it. She sniffed at the air and smelled his residue. *I have his scent now.*

More images came to her, choppy and imprecise. There was someone with the man now. Another woman, connected somehow to the man. She concentrated on the woman. Women were easier for her when the distance was great. Still, she shouldn't be having this much trouble focusing.

Pity her if she uses my comb.

She shifted her head slightly. Another image curved away from the first. A house. *Her house was nearby.* She could find that house.

She picked up her gwynn.

Chapter Three

Not for the first time, Connor wondered how many people carried money around that wasn't worth anything. Connor checked his wallet before entering Hargadon's pub to be sure he had enough Euros to stand a few rounds. His fingers lingered on the old Irish florin, a silver coin from the days when decimals didn't rule the world, tucked into the corner. The florin had been among the loose change found in a drawer in his parent's home. On one side of the coin was an image of harp. On the other was the image of a salmon, linked in Irish mythology to both wisdom and the warrior hero Fionn Mac Cumhaill or Finn McCool as he was known to the English-speaking world. The coin and others like it had been developed in 1928 by a commission headed by the poet W.B. Yeats, then an Irish Senator. The coin had a face value of two shillings. One shilling equaled 12 pence or cents in the American sense. The last florins had been made in 1968. For Connor, its value was the physical link to his favorite poet and his upbringing.

Connor's favorite place for a drink in Sligo town was Hargadon's on the narrow main avenue of O'Connell Street. The pub first opened its doors to a thirsty public in 1864. Properly called Hargadon Bros. from when it also operated as a grocer, the pub had a painted green and varnished wood exterior that framed a pair of large windows split by a gauzy, semi-transparent curtain that masked the identity of its patrons from judgmental eyes. Yeats himself had often drank there, arriving on "the last bus from Cavan," meaning he arrived late at night and perhaps slightly wobbly from stops at other local watering holes but still standing tall at over six feet, black hair slanting over his forehead above keen eyes. Connor wondered if the bar had been the inspiration for Yeats' six-line poem "A Drinking Song" that had been grossly over analyzed by sober literary critics. "Wine comes in at the mouth and loves come in the eye," wrote the poet. Simple enough for anyone who had ever eyed the opposite sex with a glass in hand. Connor paused at the door and inhaled the smell of old wood. There was wood everywhere. The walls were made of it and, of course, the floors, planked with wide timbers. Stools, chairs, tables—all wood with a variety of dark stains made by design and frequent use. A major centerpiece was a carving of the toucan bird nursing a pint. The toucan had been used in Guinness ads for decades, Connor knew. The only metal in the place was from the old tin Guinness ads mounted at various spots. There was a front bar immediately on his left that looked over a room of tables. Farther on, was a long hallway with tabled nooks for those who needing privacy. Connor often wondered what plots might have been hatched in those seats back during the war for independence from England.

At the back was another room with tables, shelves lined with antique clay whiskey jugs and a space where local musicians set up for a session and which was now crammed with drinkers, one a very loud fellow who could only be from the North, likely taking a breather from the sectarian atmosphere back home. The front bar was manned by a barman in a white shirt and black tie catering to a mix of tourists and locals. In amongst them was a blonde mother/ daughter package that had fallen from the same freckled tree and who were maybe not so local and very likely on the hunt. Connor spotted Rosaleen leaning out from one of the nooks and beckoning him towards him. Connor walked across the stone floor and slid in beside her, thinking himself lucky to be sitting next to Rosaleen as the woman opposite took up much of the other side of the table.

Rosaleen passed him a pint of Guinness. "Fiona Campbell," said Rosaleen by way of introduction. "I took the liberty of ordering so you wouldn't have to wait for the seven-minute pour."

The seven-minute wait was the only downside to drinking Guinness, especially if you were thirsty. The pint glass was held at a 45-degree angle and filled as far as the etched harp. Then it was placed aside until the liquid had changed from a frothy brown to a solid black with a white creamy head. Finally, it was slowly topped off with the more talented bartenders creating the outline of a shamrock in the head. It was drink that was available around the world but the black brew tasted best in Ireland. Once Ireland's national drink crossed the water, it lost something of its essence. It would make you believe in magic. Connor preferred Guinness over regular beer—all those bubbles stayed trapped in your body and just expanded your waistline. Both women were drinking Guinness as well, despite the lust for red wine that had gripped the country in the last few years.

"Thanks," said Connor. "Pleased to meet you, Fiona."

Fiona smiled and Connor studied her more closely as he sipped from the glass. She had lively eyes set above oversized cheeks. He didn't care much for the frosted mix of black, blonde and red hair that fell to her shoulders. She was dressed in a loose fitting, lightweight black sort of wrap with a touch of a blue blouse peeking from underneath. She offered him a ready smile in welcome and seemed in good spirits, remarkable considering that for most Dubliners taking the train across Ireland to Sligo was like a resident of Moscow taking the Trans-Siberian Railroad to Vladivostok. A radio in the background took a break from its music programming to announce the day's wakes for the newly departed. There were only three, all seemingly elderly, with at least two, judging from the uptick in conversation at the bar, known to the regulars.

Connor savored the Guinness. He'd been thinking of it since he'd parked the car in a lot off Connaughton Road and walked down to the Garavogue River past the monument to O'Higgins who left Sligo to liberate Chile from the Spanish Crown. He had then crossed the river via a footbridge that led to a pedestrian causeway called the Rockwood Parade. The rash of new restaurants and pubs in the area drew people from all over and not for the first time did it occur to him that Sligo town was becoming a miniature version of Amsterdam's canal district--minus the obvious prostitutes, of course.

"Fiona has become quite the mother hen to all of Dublin's young filmmakers," said Rosaleen.

Fiona chuckled and a lot of her jiggled while her hair made itself ready to fly away. She was ample in every sense of the word.

"How many films have you produced?" asked Connor

"Six," replied Fiona. "All shorts. That is why my old friend Rosaleen thought you and I should become acquainted. Tell me more about this film festival of yours. Is it for short films only?"

"Yes," said Connor, pausing while he sipped his Guinness. "It's called the Empire Short Film Festival. New York is known as the Empire State. Hence the name."

"Or Empire Shorts for short," quipped Rosaleen. "Puts strange ideas into a woman's head, that does."

"Like the Empire State Building," said Fiona. "Very phallic."

"It's an annual event," continued Connor. "Twelve semi-finalists are picked from among all the entries. These twelve films are shown during the festival that is screened in small theaters around the world for a one week in September. The audience at each screening casts ballots that determine Best Film and Best Actor. The winners are announced the last night of the festival in New York. The winner gets a free lighting and post-production package as well as the recognition."

"Nice prize," commented Fiona.

"Thanks," said Connor. "When I started this festival, the prize was enough film to shoot a feature. Now, everyone shoots digital so it's the post stuff that's really needed by new directors. The entire New York film industry is solidly behind this festival. As you know, today's short filmmakers are tomorrow's feature film directors. And the New York film community wants their business when that time comes."

Fiona nodded. "You'll have to get down to the Cong Film Fleadh down below in Ashford Castle. There's a lot of new blood that'll be there."

"I'll make a point of it," said Connor. "The international aspect of the festival is critical to its success. I don't want this to be an American-dominated festival. Most of what comes out of the American film schools is Hollywood-slick, over-produced, and predictable with a camera cut every five seconds."

"That's true enough," said Fiona. "It's like the camera cuts are used in place of any narrative forward direction."

"Independent theater owners are feeling that way about every film coming out of Hollywood. They're very keen to have original, alternate programming that will get people into their theaters and out from in front of the TV. We want people to put away their phones for two hours. Empire Shorts is a night out across the U.S., Europe and beyond."

Connor knew that he was putting a positive spin on things. He was very aware that he might be servicing a dying business. Attendance at movie theaters was steadily declining, thanks to cable TV, streaming services using the Internet, and big screen home theaters setups that sometimes rivaled that of a local cinema. He was offering cinema owners original programming but he worried that if the owners didn't make money from it right away, they would drop the festival before it had time to build an audience via word-of-mouth and social media. Ireland also was a potentially important source of English language films. Connor knew he couldn't ask an American audience to sit through two hours of reading subtitles. That would be deadly. Chatting up directors and producers was the fun part of the job. Less entertaining was pitching one theater owner after another on the art house circuit—the big movie chains that used multi-state bookers to schedule film releases wouldn't even answer his calls—and convincing them to become committed.

Connor was worried about the phone in his pocket as well. Shorts might be a perfect fit for the small screen of mobile phones. People were already watching feature films on their phones even if the small screen made everyone look the size of leprechauns. It was like films were being turned into elevator music.

"And from what I see on your web site, you've got posters and programs to support each venue."

"That's right. So tell me about what's happening in Dublin," said Connor.

"Things are improving dramatically," said Fiona with a smile. "Thanks to a growing economy and financial support from the Irish film board, there's fabulous new talent getting into business."

"Bollix! What year are you living in?" said Rosaleen. "The economy is shite and there isn't a euro to be found anywhere. You're in total denial. Even when things were good, they weren't that great around here. The Celtic Tiger wouldn't get his balls wet crossing the River Shannon."

The Shannon, Connor recalled, separated the west of Ireland from the rest of the country.

"Nevertheless, I'm optimistic," said Fiona. "I'm producing two short films at the moment."

"Tell me more," said Connor.

"One's a doc," said Fiona. "Are they eligible?"

"A documentary," said Connor, for Rosaleen's benefit. "Sure."

"I know what a doc is," said Rosaleen, "Sure, aren't we all mad about fillums?"

Connor smiled. Like a lot of people in Ireland, she turned "films" into a two-syllable word.

"That we are," agreed Fiona. "We were on about nothing else back in school, weren't we?"

"Grand days," said Rosaleen.

"So what's the doc about," said Connor hastily, before the two women took off on a tangent down memory lane.

"Underground horse racing," said Fiona. "The Irish love horses as much as they do films. So, listen close. There is the whole movement that can't be stopped. Sulky racing run by the Travelers. Horse owners find an isolated bit of road in the countryside and shut down a section of it for a quick race. They're trotters, you know, with the wee carts behind the horses. It's all over in minutes and everyone disappears before the Guards get there."

A childhood memory of a painted wagon at the edge of the village galloped into Connor's mind. The Travelers, he knew, had recently been granted ethnic minority status by the Irish government even though they'd been in Ireland for centuries. The prejudice against them ran deep amongst many. Most Irish claimed to be able to identify Travelers on sight but Connor was blind to whatever was the characteristic identifier. They'd been known as tinkers and gypsies in Connor's youth—but those terms were considered pejorative now-- and their dress had been very distinctive, like that belonging to another people. They had their own language. The Travelers wandered Ireland in RVs rather than wagons these days although there was at least one family that had been camped in a Sligo carpark for over a decade. Connor remembered staring at the wagon as a little boy. There had been a woman inside dressed in a long colorful skirt and blouse with a vest. He remembered being scared and curious at the same time.

He had heard stories of children being "taken by the tinkers" but he wasn't sure if they had gone willingly or not. He might go with them if he was asked, he had realized. He walked away before the question could be asked of him.

"There's a lot of money in it," continued Fiona. "You can imagine the wagering that goes on."

"Sounds like American drag racing but without the engines," said Connor. "Real horsepower."

"The language is a bit coarse," said Fiona. "Would you mind? There's a lot of 'fookin this' and fookin that' and "half the horses are cunts."

"Just the ones that lose," said a male voice.

Connor looked up from his seat to see a tall, blonde man of about 25 standing beside their table. He was dressed casually in a sweater and jeans and wore a loose smile about his lips. He was well-muscled in a way that spoke of the outdoors rather than a gym. "Sorry. I couldn't help overhear. When anyone talks about horses my hearing improves by leaps and bounds. Can I buy you ladies a drink?"

Connor sighed and gave the man another look. The man's eyes were politely moving back and forth between Fiona and Rosaleen but he lingered on Rosaleen. Connor wasn't in the mood for small talk with a man on the make.

"We're in the middle of a business discussion," said Connor, sharply.

"Are ye now?" said the man.

"And we're not talking about horses."

"I see," the man replied. The man glanced at the women's faces and finding no encouragement there, he nodded and walked off.

The man's departure was followed by an awkward silence.

"When Connor was small, he didn't always play well with the other boys," said Rosaleen finally.

Connor said nothing. This was a good time for a sip of Guinness.

"Do you know who that was?" continued Rosaleen.

"No," said Connor.

"Sean St, Jacques himself," said Rosaleen.

"As in the St. Jacques of Templerock?" asked Fiona.

"The same," said Rosaleen. "I'm afraid Connor has made a civil introduction impossible."

"Never mind," said Connor. "Fiona, what's the other film you're producing?

"And this is the same man who once told me he'd love to spend a night at Templerock," continued Fiona. "It's quite the manor house. Slim chance of that now."

Connor gave Fiona a look that said 'rescue me.'

"You'll love this," said Fiona. "The other film I'm working on has no speaking parts. It's all about looks. A destitute man comes into a petrol station and pours petrol all over himself. He takes out a lighter to torch himself but the lighter doesn't work."

"Peachy," said Rosaleen.

"So he goes into the cashier's to get a book of matches but the cashier won't give him the matches until he pays for the matches and the petrol. Of course, the poor man is short a few pennies so his life is saved."

"Black comedy," said Connor. "I'd loved to see both films entered in the festival."

"Consider it done," said Fiona, raising her glass.

Connor raised his glass and they both took a long gulp as three musicians mounted the stage at the far end of the club.

"Who's the band tonight?" he asked.

"Three harmonica players," said Rosaleen. "They call themselves Triple Harp Bypass. No Crows will be playing later."

"Cute," said Connor. "That reminds me. I think I met Yeats or his ghost today. Connor quickly recounted his trip to Lough Nasool. "I even picked up a souvenir, a jeweled, silver comb with a triple spiral design engraved on the handle."

"Now you're looting the country," said Rosaleen. "Let's see it."

Ryan reached into his jacket pocket and passed the comb to Rosaleen.

"Very beautiful," said Rosaleen, as she examined it.

"Valuable maybe," said Fiona.

"It's just a comb," said Connor.

"Somebody's family heirloom, perhaps," said Fiona.

"Stealing our heritage, you are," laughed Rosaleen as she passed the comb back to Ryan.

"I doubt it's that valuable," said Connor. "It's just a souvenir."

"They say its good luck to bring a stone up to Queen's Maeve's tomb above on Knocknarea," said Rosaleen, "but that its bad luck to take one away. I hope the same isn't true of your comb."

"Quite the international crowd, you have here," remarked Fiona, nodding toward a group of Japanese men and women entering the bar.

"They're probably here to study Yeats," said Connor. "The Japanese love Yeats. They come to a school here that's teaches nothing but Yeats. Half the students are from abroad."

"Yes," said Fiona. "I've heard of it. Sligo is turning into a Yeats theme park. I saw a statue of him in the square and I passed a jewelry shop called 'The Cat and the Moon." That's the title of one of his poems, isn't it?"

"Yes," said Connor.   *"Black Minnaloushe stared at the moon*
For, wander and wail as he would,
The pure cold light in the sky troubled
his animal blood."

"Who's Minnaloushe?" asked Fiona.

"The cat," said Connor

"He thinks quoting Yeats will help him meet women," said Rosaleen. "It might work yet. Poems are like spells. If you say them aloud, they can be like an incantation or an enchantment."

"Funny name for a cat," said Fiona. "I'm not sure I'd fancy a cat as a pet. They have minds of their own. I require unquestioned love and devotion," she finished with a chuckle.

"Speaking of pets and poems, did I tell you about the new side business I'm developing?" said Rosaleen. "I'm teaming up with this artist woman down the road from me—Heidi, a lovely Welsh woman—who will draw a portrait of your deceased pet while I supply a poem about the poor animal. A nice package tastefully presented. We are getting the local vets to stock a brochure. Heidi is working on a website. Great skills she has."

"You're joking," said Fiona as Connor nearly choked on his pint.

"Your beautiful coat of fur, and long bushy tale
Fox-like in your way
Your sojourn a short stay,
And as you gaze from your portrait of fame
You look down as if to say
Roald Dahl was right,
All cats are not the same!"

Rosaleen smiled. "A short bit of a longer epic. That was the first sale."

"What spell have you cast with that poem?" asked Connor.

"One that eases the pain of the living."

"The idea sounds crazy but fair play to you," said Connor.

"Not as daft as Yeats himself, pining away after that woman Maud Gonne all his life. A big help his poetry was to him on that score," said Rosaleen, sarcastically. "Poems need to earn a living."

"Just try not to get paid by the word," said Connor.

"Yourself and Yeats are well-suited for each other," chided Rosaleen.

Connor sighed. "Okay, I know how this plays out. You'll be sniping at me all night. Would you mind if I bought St. Jacques a drink and asked him to join us?"

"He is a dote," said Rosaleen with a smile. "And he's not wearing Wellingtons." The waterproof boot was standard footwear for all farmers.

"And that's a good thing?" asked Connor, knowing full well that in the sometimes untranslatable English of the Irish to be called a "dote" was to have a halo of affection placed above your head that God himself couldn't remove. Or at least that was Rosaleen's definition. Connor rose from his seat. "Well, find an extra chair and I'll bring him over."

"He likes horses," said Fiona. "How bad could he be? Just remember I'm the one going spare."

"I'm not putting on a holy show, am I?" asked Rosaleen as Connor got up. He knew she was asking Fiona if she looked garish.

"You're aces," said Connor, smiling. He knew she hadn't a clue about cards.

Rosaleen stood in her kitchen, hands on her hips, the queen of her domain. Connor was great company and she enjoyed his visits but like most men, he never put things back where they were supposed to be.

She had driven Connor to the small airport at Knock for his connecting flight to Shannon International. The parting had been tearful but happy as they were sure they'd see each other again soon. Fiona, meanwhile, had taken the first train back to Dublin. Tomorrow would spent with interviewing more asylum seekers and with helping a local man, who fancied himself the King of the Gypsies, navigate the bureaucracy of Tusla, until recently called the North Western Health Board, but renamed to sound more Irish even if Tusla wasn't a proper Irish word at all. But the new name promised a new friendlier beginning after a few lapses in care that had damaged public perception of the government agency.

"The poorest-looking king I ever saw," she had remarked to a co-worker after a previous visit by the man and now in retrospect, she hoped her comment had not been seen as insensitive because she hadn't meant it that way. *It was so hard to say anything these days.*

But at the moment, she had just enough energy left to strip the beds and to put her kitchen back in order. Satisfied by her efforts, Rosaleen put up the kettle on the range. She had an electric model like most people but she often preferred to use the kettle on the range just for the high, piercing whistle it made when the water came to a boil. From a cabinet, she took down a red box of loose tea and spooned three heaps into a blue teapot, one with flecks of red and wavy lines along the base that reminded her of the nearby sea, made by a local artisan named Kennedy, and put out a matching blue mug made by the same potter. It was later than she thought, she realized, as the kettle began to whistle. It was pitch black out with no moon in the sky.

Rosaleen picked up her mug of tea and moved into what her mother, God rest her soul, had called the parlor. Much of her mother's furniture still filled the room. Bella had died three years ago but the room still retained her touch. There was one exception, a deep red sofa that raised Rosaleen's spirits each time she sat on it. The only problem was that her cat, Smudge, liked it too. Keeping the sofa clean of cat hair was a major chore.

Connor's departure got her thinking about the men in her life. There was her brother up the road, married to a woman content to be on a farm. Talking to no one but the animals the whole day long, she thought with a shake of her head. Then there was Enda, who was studying to be a vet, an on-and-off-again romance that was currently off. And now maybe the Sean St. Jacques was a possibility. They had hit it off nicely the night before. If Sean is interested, she thought, he will make it his business to bump into her or to come by Tusla on some innocent inquiry.

Rosaleen's thoughts were interrupted by the loud bang of the front gate being thrown open with enough strength to startle her.

"Who can that be at this time of night?" she said to her cat. "If that's a man with too much drink on him, I'll have him arrested for his boldness!" Smudge was already heading up the stairs as fast as his four legs would take him.

"Coward!" she yelled after him.

Then she heard what sounded like an army of crickets working themselves up into a high-pitch whine that seemed to undulate in intensity. Suddenly, the noise stopped but the reprieve was only seconds long for it started again at a louder volume although she thought the pitch had changed slightly. There was something wet beneath her nose and she dabbed at it with her finger, surprised to see that her finger was covered in blood. She felt like she was losing her balance and she reached out to grab the doorknob to steady herself.

Rosaleen had just touched the doorknob when a force like a giant sledgehammer hit the house, rattling it to its foundations. Rosaleen screamed as she was knocked to her knees. Looking up, she could see that a crack had appeared above the door. The door itself had been loosened from its frame but had somehow held. But even as she looked, the metal hinges that held the door began to twist. Someone was forcing the door inward. Rosaleen screamed again, jumped up and jammed her body against the door. For a moment, the force on the door stopped and she dared to hope the attacker was gone.

When the second attack on the door came, it was swift and powerful, splintering the wood beside her head. There was a hole in the door and through it came a low, loud sound that just got lower and lower until she could no longer hear it. Instead, she felt it. The sound pulsed like a strobe light through her body and it felt like her insides were turning to jelly. Breathing became difficult as pressure gradually increased on her chest. She felt a rising wave of nausea, even as the bones in her body started to vibrate, making her jerk involuntarily up and down like a puppet on a string.

Then suddenly it stopped. Rosaleen was overcome with fatigue and felt unable to move. Her eyes gravitated toward the hole in the door in time to see a hand--a woman's hand she noted with surprise--reach through the door and grab her by the shoulder.

Rosaleen had seen local cows branded and now she felt their pain. The fingers on her shoulder singed into her flesh, burning the skin and then the tissue beneath it. Rosaleen had not known such agony existed. The fingers gripped her like a vise. Already, her mind was trying to escape the pain. She was howling in pain but it was like another person was doing it. She looked at her shoulder and glimpsed a piece of charred flesh between the fingers that gripped her. *Oh, my God!*

There was worse to come. She felt her mind being probed with what felt like a hot poker, her thoughts turned over against her will like bits of coal being stirred in a fire. Her sense of detachment disappeared. She screamed, praying she would pass out but whatever was attacking her mind wouldn't let her.

That's when she wished for death. If she could die, she thought, her mind and her body would escape the pain.

It was then that the fingers released her. Rosaleen crumpled to the floor. Her once beautiful black hair was now streaked with grey locks that splayed across the floor. The wound to her shoulder was smoking. The handprint was still visible.

Chapter Four

The Cornet of Horse stood in the darkness near the media-viewing stand four miles from the missile launch pad at Cape Canaveral. This was as close as anyone not actively involved with flight operations could go. It also was a relatively discreet viewing area as only a few space-beat reporters were on hand for what they viewed as a routine event. All was quiet in the mild Florida night. Indeed, the entire Space Coast seemed devoid of activity. But the stillness was deceiving. Out of sight, technicians were waiting. The question was whether the wait would be short one or a long one induced by a poor weather forecast. The Cornet of Horse's mind was just beginning to wander when the silence was broken by the voice of mission control heard over a loudspeaker, counting down the final seconds before launch.

In the distance, engines ignited with a roar, creating a giant candle flame that grew in length and intensity as the rocket seemingly erupted from the earth itself, creating billowing clouds of white smoke visible even at night. The Cornet of Horse, like millions of others, had watched space launches on television, so the fireworks were no surprise. He was unprepared for the hot, powerful wind that made his pants legs flap like flags in gale. The heat turned his exposed skin pink. It was as if someone has opened a furnace door right next to him.

Despite the discomfort, the Cornet of Horse allowed himself a small smile as his eyes followed the rocket upwards. Regardless of the paucity of press actually present at the event, tomorrow's *New York Times* would carry a front-page story on tonight's launch. The story would hail the launch of an important new weather satellite that would monitor climatic changes at key locations around the globe. Readers might be surprised to learn that Whiteface Mountain in upstate New York, the Sumava Mountains in the Czech Republic, the Ruwenzori in Zaire, and 17 other remote locations around the globe merited surveillance. Some more media-savvy readers might also wonder why the launch of a weather satellite rated front page, upper right, above the fold placement by the paper. Those questions would remain unanswered, leaving readers little choice but to mentally shrug and chalk it up some quirk of the paper's editors. By the next day, the story would be forgotten, having failed the test of relevance and lacking in even entertainment value.

The satellite, if the story could be told, was a marvel. Most people thought a satellite looked like an oversized garbage can with a pair of solar panels stuck on with sticks. This bird was very different. It was a variant on the Gravity field Ocean Circulation Explorer (GOCE) first launched by the European Space Agency. GOCE was a sleek, five-meter-long, arrow-like satellite, often compared to a Formula 1 race car, which used a vibration-reducing ion thruster for propulsion. The GOCE mission was to measure gravitational anomalies from a low orbit of just 250 kilometers to construct a true picture of the shape of the earth down to two centimeters. The force of gravity varied from place to place, being weakest at the equator and strongest at the poles. Mountains, deep sea trenches and other features of the landscape could vary gravitational levels as well, turning the earth into a slightly bumpy, misshapen ball. These differences were captured by three pairs of extremely sensitive accelerometers mounted on three 50 centimeter arms: one pair was aligned with the satellite's trajectory, another pair was positioned perpendicular to the trajectory and the last pair was pointed toward the center of the earth.

The main benefit, from the point of view of the Cornet of Horse, was that GOCE could distinguish between faint gravitational and non-gravitational signals. With some further modification, the accelerometers were now able to detect concentrations of Kaluza-Klein particles, the faint footprint of activity that for the Cornet of Horse signaled likely enemy movement. If this new satellite, dubbed KK-1, worked as an early warning system, then the tremendous manufacturing expense would be worth it. The satellite would be a nice complement to the hand-held KK detector he'd recently accepted delivery on. The device was at the forefront of miniaturization technology thanks to the use of electronic circuits fashioned around carbon nanotubes, cylindrical molecules with a diameter of one-billionth of a meter and a length many thousands of times longer than that. The technology allowed computations to be made in the trillions of operations per second, a speed previously attainable by only the most powerful parallel computers. Unlike silicon-based computers, carbon nanotube-based devices were small in size because they ran cool so space-consuming parts like heat sinks and fans were not necessary. Better yet, data from the KK-1 satellite could be melded with local readings to produce an even more detailed accounting of KK particles in a given area.

Black gold paid for everything. In the closing months of World War II, General Yamashita Tomoyuki of the Japanese Imperial Army had buried tons of gold, the accumulated hoard from a dozen conquered countries, in 175 treasure vaults built all over the Philippines. The gold had been found, of course, along with the bodies of the vault builders, but its discovery and the interrogation methods used to find it, were never made public. The gold was secretly removed to banks in a variety of countries all too willing to accept a gold deposit, no questions asked. The black gold was initially earmarked as a secret slush fund for the fight against Communism but as time went by, it was used to fund all kinds of covert operations. A small percentage of the interest alone funded most MEDEA operations, the Cornet of Horse knew.

A slight movement to his left caught his attention. It was a tabby cat, illuminated by the faint light from the reviewing stand behind him. The animal was headed toward the reviewing stand, looking for shelter from the heat of the rocket launch. The Cornet of Horse crouched down and picked up a stone lying at his feet. In one swift movement a baseball pitcher would envy, the Cornet of Horse side-armed the stone straight at the cat. In the millisecond before the stone's arrival on target, the cat sensed danger but it was too late. The stone cracked the cat's skull just above the eye socket and the animal crumpled to the ground. *One less feline in the world.* He kept walking. Moments later, somewhere behind him, the Cornet of Horse heard a gasp. Someone had noted the cat's demise.

A middle-age woman in a dark business suit and wearing a media badge walked quickly toward him, her face full of outrage.

"I saw what you did," she began. That was despicable..." Her voice faded as she got closer and saw the physical size of him. Her eyes grew wide as she took in his height and weight. Her eyes rose to meet his, set deep beneath a brow that could have been cut from stone. She noted the ski-slope nose and the two vertical lines on his forehead that seemed to be old scars. His mouth was set straight across, bracketed by two deep folds where the cheeks began. It was a face mounted on a square jaw that looked like bruised rock.

"Sixty."

"What?" asked the woman.

"Number of species made extinct by cats. They're stone cold killers."

The woman's jaw dropped. The idea that an animal so cute could be so deadly was a notion so foreign to her she couldn't process it. The woman thought to argue the point but realized her protestations would fall on deaf ears. She could see that in his world, she had already ceased to exist and she was suddenly quite happy about that. She didn't want to find out how he felt about cat lovers.

The Cornet of Horse turned and walked away, his attention returning skyward, tracking the fiery wash of the rocket as it grew smaller in the night sky. For the allies and enemies of the Cornet of Horse, who would be able to supply the proper context and appreciate such details as the geographic locations mentioned, the *Times* article would reassure the former and warn the latter. Despite its public exposure, the article would be a private communiqué--a secret message presented in plain sight--even though he didn't know the identities of all the recipients. Of course, he could never be sure what his enemies knew or whether they even read newspapers. But they were being given fair warning.

It was a message that the majority of people would miss. *I'm fortunate to be working in the United States.* Few Americans had developed the insight to look past the obvious to see what might be there. Americans didn't even have a proper word for such capability. The Italians, he knew from his time in Rome, had a word for it, only natural for a country that spawned an empire, gave birth to the Mafia, hosted the Vatican, spirited Nazis out of Europe, and in recent years, had sheltered leftist guerrilla groups and secret Masonic lodges capable of railway bombings and political assassinations. *Dietrologia*, they called it, the study of what lurks behind it all. *A poor translation but that's the gist of it.*

The rocket was now just a shiny point of light in the night sky. The voice of mission control, heard on an outdoor speaker, noted the satellite on board was deploying and declared the mission a success. So did the Cornet of Horse as he walked toward his car. *How far I've come. From cuculatti to MEDEA. From four legs to four wheels. Only the Old Voices stay the same.*

Today's car was a bland four-door, champagne-colored Japanese model popular with older Asian ladies. It wasn't memorable in any sense but it suited his purposes. The Cornet of Horse sighed wistfully, remembering his favorite car, safely

68

stashed in a garage in New York City. The Tatra T-87 had been created in Czechoslovakia in 1936. The T-87, designed by the brilliant Hans Ledwinka, had been years ahead of its time. Porsche had been merely looking over Ledwinka's shoulder. When the Nazis overran Czechoslovakia during World War II, Adolf Hitler threw Ledwinka into prison to make life easier for German car manufacturers. The design of the T-87 had been unparalleled in its breathtaking, aerodynamic beauty--all the way to the central fin at the rear of the car. A third, center-mounted headlight turned with the car's wheels to direct light around corners, an innovation that Detroit adopted almost 60 years later. The V-8 engine was powerful enough for a smooth ride at 90 mph thanks to air intake scoops that kept the engine cool. The Cornet of Horse remembered a hot pursuit across the Charles River in Prague in which the T-87 had performed admirably despite its age. In some ways, the Cornet of Horse missed working in the old Soviet zones. What the Communists couldn't control, they ignored or buried. And there was never any publicity. Operationally, communism offered certain advantages.

Poor Ledwinka. Thecar designer had remained in prison until 1951. *Six years after the war ended. That's how dangerous the German carmakers considered him.* The Cornet of Horse drove past the security checkpoint at the entrance to the space center. The guards only checked papers going in, not coming out, he knew. But out of habit, he mentally recited the particulars printed on the identity card in his wallet. Identity changes were just a little more complicated these days in that computer databases needed to be altered as well--inconvenient only in that it was sometimes time-consuming. In a moment of introspection some time ago, he realized he'd used so many names that they had lost all meaning for him. Only his rank anchored his identity and in his mind, it is what he called himself. *Ledwinka died in obscurity in 1967 in Austria. With luck, I'll die the same way. But not today. Or in any of the foreseeable days to come.*

69

The Cornet of Horse turned east and drove past strip malls and low hotels toward the coast road. The Old Voices, as he thought of them, were silent. Even the memory of Prague had not been a prompt. There was time to linger, stop somewhere with a view of the ocean and watch the sunrise. Then it would be time for the flight back to New York. On the plane, he would examine the first signals from the KK-1 satellite for possible anomalies. Then he would cruise the Internet on his laptop for signs of activity that were not what they seemed to be and which might spark another hunt. The Cornet of Horse sighed, knowing that like always, he'd start with reports of kidnappings and missing persons.

On any given day, 2000 people disappear. But most of them were not the responsibility of the Cornet of Horse. In truth, most of them were of no interest. Most people who disappeared fell into a few broad categories: people who willingly disappeared to escape some unpleasantness in their lives, those who were involved in some domestic dispute involving spouses or children, and those who were murdered by serial killers. He wasn't looking for any of those people. He was looking for people, particularly young women, whose disappearance couldn't be explained and whose bodies were never found. In all honesty, he admitted to himself, he wasn't really looking for those people either. What he was looking for were unsolved disappearances that were an indicator of activity by those he really sought.

The task was hard on a number of different levels. One, the sheer number of disappearances made monitoring missing person and kidnapping reports a never ending job. Second, when things started happening, they happened quickly even if overall activity was years apart. In the last 10 years, there had been two big campaigns. The 14 young women in Perth were gone inside of a week and the 8 young women in Ireland disappeared in a few days. Perth and Ireland had not been areas he was responsible for but he knew that the response had been too slow and the women had never been recovered.

The failures, of course, were haunting. Even though no official record of his successes and failures existed, the Old Voices kept an accurate account of everything, reminding him of what had worked and what had not. Still, it was one thing to hear the old stories and another to see them. That's why a few nights later the Cornet of Horse sat in a plush red seat in the balcony of New York's Metropolitan Opera House. He was no lover of opera but tonight the Kirov Opera Company from Russia was performing *The Legend of the Invisible City of Kitezh*. The opera had been written in 1907, cobbled together from myths about an event that had happened centuries before. It wasn't completely accurate— after all, all official records of the battle had been expunged. What information that survived about Kitezh had found its way into poems, plays, and operas that were all dismissed as fictions.

The Old Voices supplied their own commentary, stimulated by the pageantry in front of his eyes. Yes, Prince Yuri Vsevolodich, the ruler of both Lesser and Greater Kitezh, had planned to wed Princess Fevronia, a woman who was much more than the earthy fairie presented in the opera. Fevronia and her kind had walked the streets of Kitezh, hand in hand with the native people, for many years. *The glamour was upon them*, said the Old Voices.

On stage, a giant mechanical horse with a searchlight for eyes crashed through the walls of Lesser Kitezh. The hordes of Batu Khan had done the actual storming of the walls. Fevronia was captured alive but such was her influence that no citizen could be induced to guide them to Greater Kitezh. *There were chimera among them.*

But Prince Vsevolodich came to them at the head of a small army. They must have known there were no match for the Batu Khan and in hindsight, their goal was simply to gain time for Greater Kitezh. *The Kerzhenets River. That's where we fought.* The Cornet of Horse closed his eyes. The Old Voices were reliving the battle. Swords, arrows, horses, shields, banners—all amidst a din of cries and screams. Then the Prince fell and the Batu Khan surged forward. But the Prince was carried away by Fevronia's brother, *or so we learned later from a dying soldier.*

No matter. *We had Grishka or so we thought.* He was a drunk, true, but his fear of the Batu Khan made him reliable enough. He had guided us to Lesser Kitezh and now swore he knew the way to Greater Kitezh as well. *We'll never know.* The stupid brothers who led the Batu Khan fought amongst themselves for Fevronia. The two of them killed each other over her. In the confusion, Fevronia and Grishka escaped.

Eventually, we found Grishka but his mind was gone. All Grishka talked about was ringing bells *and for a moment, we thought we heard bells as well.* A Batu Khan patrol reported seeing the reflection of a city in the waters of a nearby lake called Svetly Yar but could find no city by the shore. That report unnerved the remaining Batu Khan. In truth, they were now virtually leaderless and the sacking of Lesser Kitezh had satisfied their hunger for loot. The Cornet of Horse understood now that the Prince had fought a delaying action while Greater Kitezh faded away, never to be found.

The Cornet of Horse wondered how the opera's writer, a man named Rimsky-Korsakov according to the program, had come by his information. The writer was long dead. But still. Had there been a leak somewhere? And did it still exist?

The whole Kitezh affair had been bungled badly, thought the Cornet of Horse, as he watched the last act. Kitzeh showed how dangerously inefficient it was to use large forces of proxies. *We did better at Vineta*, protested the Old Voices. Yes, thought the Cornet of Horse, *but we're discussing Kitzeh.* How the entire city of Greater Kitezh had vanished was still a mystery and the area around Svetly Yar was still on the watch list 800 years later, a task now done by satellite. But their adversary had never been underestimated again. And yes, Vineta had been a triumph. Their adversary had rarely taken the field in large numbers since and when they did, they used an existing war to cloak their movements. In between, it was all covert operations, he thought, as the curtain fell.

The Cornet of Horse reached into his pocket and turned on his cellphone. It rang immediately. The caller ID feature on his cellphone identified the source of the call.

"Yes," said the Cornet of Horse.

"Lt. Clemente Gomez de Suarez with ICE, Homeland Security Investigations New York office. Is this Medea?"

"Proceed."

"I have a notation on my computer screen to notify you regarding kidnappings and missing person cases of foreign nationals. We handle human trafficking investigation, among other things. Funny, I was expecting a woman's voice."

"Tell me what happened and where."

"A New York state police officer has been killed while attempting to intercept a kidnapper and his victim in the town of Wilmington. That's upstate in the Adirondack Mountains, near Lake Placid where they had the Winter Olympics a couple of times. It happened on Whiteface Mountain, at the ski resort there. The kidnapper and his victim, a Slovenian national, are missing. So it may become an immigration matter. Well, maybe disappeared is a better word. And this is strange. The trooper seems to have had his heart removed and his chest resealed, according to the medical examiner. Looks like the killer is a surgeon." There was a pause. "If you don't mind me asking, who or what is Medea exactly? You're not in my directory."

"It's an ancient Greek tragedy written by Euripedes, I believe," said the Cornet of Horse and hung up. *Whiteface Mountain. Activity perhapsbut it's not like them to be so sloppy.*

Chapter Five

C onnor stood a few feet to the right of the foul line extended. He took a small step forward and leaned into it just enough so the man opposite him shifted his weight in that direction. Connor took his foot back, bent his knees and held the ball like he was going to shoot it. *Here is the big sell!* Connor extended his arms so that the ball looked like it was definitely leaving his hands. The defender leaped into the air to block the shot. But the ball never left Connor's hands. Connor was impressed at how high the guy could jump—it was like he jumped off a trampoline. Connor looked up at him for a full beat and saw the look of despair in the man's eyes. He was beat. He knew what happened next and there was nothing he could do about it. For Connor, the look in the guy's eyes was better than what came next. Connor dribbled around the spot on the court where the defender had been and coasted to the basket for an easy layup. It was almost anti-climatic.

And a little sad. The man guarding him was thoroughly embarrassed. It wasn't the first time Connor had done that to an opponent. But the male ego was a fragile thing, particularly in sports. The odds were the guy wouldn't come back for another game.

It was also the fourth basket in a row that Connor had scored on the guy.

Their ball. The music was playing loud in his head. It was a swirling mix of guitars and drums mixed with fiddles, accordions, and bagpipes. It slipped in under the sound of squeaky sneakers, grunts, curses and the slithery sound of sweaty bodies sliding against each other as players jostled for position as defenders tried to stay with an offense intent on eluding them.

The orange ball reversed around the top of the key and came to an opposing player out on the flank. Connor was the only one between him and the basket. The player put the ball to the floor like he knew what he was doing. He was wearing some kind of dark blue school T-shirt but Connor didn't recognize the logo. Division III player, Connor guessed

The guy dribbled toward him, the ball like a yo-yo in his right hand, looking like Jerry West on the NBA logo. Connor back pedaled. He knew what was coming. The tell was when the player's left hand rose to meet the crossover dribble coming from his right. Connor stepped forward, moving low and swept his right hand into the path of the ball, knocking it away. The player couldn't stop his momentum and went by him.

"On the crossover!" Connor heard the player say like a fading curse because he had already grabbed the ball, speeding down the court on the left hand side. One man to beat. Connor dribbled forward and dipped his shoulder slightly like he was going toward the middle. The defender shifted his weight in anticipation, beginning to turn his body in that direction but Connor drove left instead. The defender recovered and raced to beat Connor to the baseline to cut off the easy basket. Connor pulled up a step inside the paint for a jump shot. He didn't need to look at the basket until he was already in the air. The lines on the court told him where he was and where the basket would be. Nothing but net.

The defender took the ball out of bounds past the baseline and waited for one of his teammates to come back for the inbound pass. Connor loped back toward his teammates clustered loosely around the paint waiting for the ball to be brought up by the opposition.

"If you want to win, give me the ball," said Connor.

No one said anything. They knew Connor wasn't a ball hog. They knew he was in the zone. He had a hot hand. It was like being in some promised land but knowing that as a mere mortal, he wouldn't be allowed to stay very long. How long no one knew. But the smart play was to get him the ball for as long as he was there.

The downside was that in all likelihood in the next game, one of his teammates would try to make his own trip to the promised land and no one would pass him the ball. Connor shrugged the thought aside. That was the way it went sometimes.

Connor loved basketball. It was a game where you could see into the future. How good a player you were depended on how far you could see into the future and anticipate where the ball was going to be and where players were going to be. Good players could see into the future two or three times down the court. Legends extended it to four or five.

Connor knew he wasn't that good, of course. Otherwise, he would be a pro and not playing in weekly pick-up game in the rented basement gymnasium of a public school on the West Side. But there were moments like on this run down on the court where he anticipated a cut a teammate made and fed him the ball for an easy layup. Football and baseball were the main American past times but they were games that took place in the present. Basketball took place in the future. On the run.

Connor posted up on the left side with his back to the basket and the ball was dumped into him. He straightened his back and he could feel the defender leaning into him. The defender knew Connor was a right-handed shooter so he overplayed Connor a little to that side. Connor could feel the man's weight shift in that direction, slightly pushing him as well, hoping to get him off balance. Connor turned his head in that direction and then spun the opposite way toward the baseline, catching the defender leaning the wrong way. Connor dribbled the ball once and put the ball up off the glass with his left hand, just to give the defender something else to think about next time down the court. Connor could shoot accurately with his left hand from 10 feet and under. The defense would have to respect it. A fake left would give him the half step going right that would open him up for his jump shot. That was seeing the future. Another three or four more times down the court and the defender wouldn't know how to guard him. Scoring would be simple. Go left, sudden stop, one step back and put up a banker. That's when they would put another guy on him, maybe creating a mismatch somewhere else that could be exploited. Or they'd switch into a zone defense and maybe try to double him up. That meant there would be an open teammate heading for the basket. Connor could see that future. The hot hand was breaking down the defense. They would have to make adjustments. Defense, conversely, was about trying to alter the future. They would try to turn his hot hand cold, block his shot, force him give up his dribble or even foul him just to convince him he had no future. Connor enjoyed the defensive part of the game as well. Shutting down a player so that he couldn't score, so in his face that he couldn't even get a shot off, or rejecting a shot by slamming the ball away from his intended target. That told a player he had no future. That's why at game's end, many looked to find a future somewhere else. Game over. The music stopped. No more squeaky sneakers for the night.

Time to call his best friend while he waited to cool down before taking a shower in the school gym. Straparola answered on the second bell.

"What are you doing?"

"Playing hoops."

"How's your game?"

"Good. There were a lot of younger guys here today. My moves are so old they're new. And I had a hot hand."

"You know for 30 years scientists said there was no such thing as a hot hand."

"What happened? Some scientist decided to actually play the game and discovered otherwise?'

"No. Turned out there was a flaw in their methodology."

"I'll say. Anyone who ever played the game could have told them that a hot hand was a real thing."

"They did but science chose to believe otherwise."

"Well, at least they finally came to their senses. Can you meet me at Martell's?"

Anthony Straparola looked like a precinct detective, nearly always dressing in a black suit and matching black tie set against a white shirt. Straparola was solidly built with a big, square head set upon broad shoulders. The only thing that kept him out of the cop parade of fashion was a pair of black-rimmed glasses that made him look like a blues musician. When you found out that he was a science journalist, it was a lesson in the dangers of first impressions. Which is why Connor liked him. Straparola was no slave to fashion and kicked preconceived notions in the butt, being both physical and intellectual at the same time without seeming to give a whit about any impression he might be creating.

Straparola, Connor noticed, as his friend entered the bar, had grown a mustache while he'd been in Ireland. Now Straparola looked like a past president of Afghanistan.

"Welcome back, Ryan," said Straparola. "How was Ireland? The old sod, right? Pints of Guinness flowing like water." Straparola settled into the vacant bar stool next to Connor. Martell's had been Connor's choice. It was an upscale bar that attracted models on the cusp of fame, minor New York celebrities, and a few film types.

"Good to be back," said Connor.

"What are you drinking?" asked Straparola.

"Irish whiskey," said Connor. "I haven't made the disconnect yet. On the rocks. A mortal sin for some, I know."

"Tanqueray and tonic, thank you," said Straparola to the approaching barmaid. "Mind if I run a tab?"

The barmaid, blonde and dressed in the little black dress every woman in New York seemed to own, was agreeable and Straparola received his drink quickly.

"Black and blonde. My favorite colors," said Straparola. "The nice thing about a credit card is that she might remember my name next time I come in here."

"If she likes you."

"We all live for small beginnings. Cheers."

"How's the magazine racket?"

"Fair working on poor," replied Straparola, a senior editor for What's Next magazine. Straparola also loved film and had volunteered to edit the festival program when they had met at an otherwise unremarkable party a few years ago. Connor was soon impressed with Straparola analytical ability and his editor's knack for finding holes in a narrative. Straparola soon joined the festival's screening committee, a group that whittled down the 1,000 or so entries every year to a manageable 24 that the festival judges would view.

"Advertising is down across the board so the page count keeps slipping," said Straparola. "So we're running more stories about cars than we want to in order to pull money out of Detroit. It's not like it was years back when a magazine could survive on beer and butts ads. If you don't have car advertising, you don't have a magazine. It sucks but there it is. Truth is magazines are dying a slow death. How was Ireland?"

"Tremendous. You've got to come there with me sometime."

"But you keep telling me you've got to get Irish girls drunk just to get a hug," said Straparola. "So why would I want to go there?"

"The scenery, the language, the poetry, the pubs, the Guinness," said Connor. "Listen, I picked up something there I want you to look at."

Connor pulled out a brown wool sock out of his pocket.

"Nice sock," dead panned Straparola, "but all I know is they come in pairs."

"Very funny," said Connor. "It's all I had to wrap it in."

"That's a clean sock, right?"

Connor ignored him and reached into the sock and took out the silver comb from Lough Nasool and placed it on the bar.

"Nice," commented Straparola. "Where did you get?"

"I found it on the shore of a lake that disappeared."

"Disappeared?"

"Yes. Maybe just a few hours before I got there."

"No wonder you like Ireland. Nothing like that happens around here."

"It's from a lake called Lough Nasool. Every few decades the water drains out of it and then it fills up again."

"Fascinating. Where does the water go?"

"No one knows. But that is where I found the comb. At first, I thought of it only as a souvenir. But on the plane coming home, I started thinking maybe it was worth something. It could have been at the bottom of Lough Nasool for ages."

Straparola eyed the comb more closely. "Solid silver. Jeweled handle. The workmanship is very impressive. The markings look old. But I can't say for sure."

Straparola pulled his mobile phone out of his pocket. "Let me set you up with someone I know. He's an archaeology professor at Columbia. I'm sending him a text about you right now."

"Thanks," said Connor.

"No problem," said Straparola, smiling. "Of course, the next round is on you."

"Naturally."

Straparola looked at the small screen on his phone and then pushed a few buttons with his thumb. "Hang on a minute. Incoming."

Connor sipped his drink and casually glanced around at the crowd while he waited for Straparola to finish with his email and nodded to an associate producer he recognized.

"The bad news is that the professor is headed out of town to a conference tomorrow," said Straparola. "Something about little people in the south Pacific. The good news is that he wants to tell me about his research tonight. As it happens, he's going to be at a reception that I'm planning to attend as well. I've added your name to the press list."

"Excellent. He must like you."

"Maybe," said Straparola. "What he really likes is a friend in the press who'll quote him as an expert the next time an expert's opinion is required. Keeps his profile high."

"Where's the reception?"

"The Met."

Connor felt like he was walking in on some ancient Egyptian ceremony being performed by a secret sect that still upheld the old ways. Connor and Straparola had passed through the Great Hall at the Fifth Avenue entrance of the Metropolitan Museum of Art at a fast clip, bearing right to enter into a long hallway lined with mummies and various Egyptian artifacts housed in glass cases lorded over by a massive black sarcophagus large enough to house a giant and whose front was covered in hieroglyphics.

"Chapter 72 of the Book of the Dead," said Straparola, pointing to the inscriptions as they walked past. "and a few spells."

Connor kept his hands at his sides and walked by as reverentially as possible.

"Here's my man," said Straparola, approaching another large stature of a shirtless man with shoulder-length hair sitting cross-legged with an open book on his lap. "Haremhab, scribe to the king from 1336 to 1323 BC and a pretty good general, by all accounts. He'd be sort of like the patron saint of journalists in ancient Egypt."

They turned left at the statue of Haremhab and entered a large room dominated by a massive platform outlined in candles and surrounded on three sides by a black pool of water acting like an indoor moat. They crossed over a small, narrow bridge devoid of handrails onto the platform to join a cocktail party already going strong. Connor's gaze, however, was drawn to the large sandstone tower gate that rose above a crush of people dressed in evening finery. Behind the tower was a small patio that led to a second, larger sandstone structure graced by two round columns that marked the entrance to what looked like a tomb or some kind of sanctuary. In front of the sanctuary, a five-piece jazz band played softly, the musicians comfortable in their surroundings despite being a living anachronism. The wall to Connor's right and the ceiling overhead were made of glass. It felt like he was still outside. He could see the outline of trees beyond the glass. Central Park. It was hard to believe that he was in a wing of the Metropolitan Museum of Art.

"Welcome to the Temple of Dendur," said Straparola, walking beside him. "This is one of my favorite places in New York. The candles are a great touch. Makes the whole place a little spooky, doesn't it? You can easily imagine yourself in Nubia thousands of years ago. What a great place for a cocktail party!

"Nubia?" asked Connor.

"Dendur was in Nubia, south of Egypt, along the Nile," said Straparola. "The temple was built by Augustus, the Roman emperor, in 15. B.C. It is basically a memorial for two royal Nubian brothers who drowned in the Nile and were later deified."

Connor said nothing as he grabbed a glass of red wine from a passing waiter. Straparola took one as well.

"My bet is the Romans knocked off the Nubian brothers and made it look like an accident," said Straparola. "Otherwise, why pay for the temple, right? You gotta love my ancestors. Twisted. Come, on. I've spotted the professor.

The professor was not what Connor expected and Connor immediately felt guilty. The professor was no academic stereotype. He was, guessed Connor, in his mid-thirties, trim and with jet-black hair. The professor was handsome enough to be at the center of attention of a small group of single and obviously enamored women.

Straparola reached a hand in and snared the professor by the elbow. "Excuse me, ladies. I need the professor to comment on a new discovery of shattering importance."

Straparola led the professor over to Connor. "Professor Junot, may I introduce my friend Ryan Connor."

Connor and Professor Junot exchanged pleasantries but were cut short by Straparola.

"I won't be able to hold these women off for long. They all think the professor is the next Indiana Jones. You know, the dashing archaeologist. Anyway, Connor, show him your sock."

Professor Junot raised his eyebrows and Connor could feel his ears turning red with embarrassment even as he reached into his pocket for the wool sock. The professor looked on with interest as Connor extracted the silver comb. The professor gazed at the comb closely but made no effort to touch it.

"Nice workmanship," commented the professor. "Looks very old but that's impossible to say without testing. Where did you get it?"

"In Ireland," said Connor.

"You bought it from someone?"

"No. I found it."

"Found it?" said the professor. "How extraordinary! Irish, you say. That's not my area of interest but you're in the right place. There is lots of expertise in this room."

The professor glanced around and focused on someone standing a little behind Connor.

"Ah, of course. Derga!"

Connor turned as the woman named Derga turned towards the professor in what Connor would later remember as a moment remarkable for its choreography. The long red hair swirling in his direction was like a deep, red flame that swept across her face in a rippling wave and enveloped her bare shoulders. She wore a red version of the ubiquitous little black dress. And she had the figure to wear it well, he noticed appreciatively. When she tossed back her red mane, Connor was surprised to see a red eye patch over left eye.

"Derga, meet Ryan Connor," said the professor. "He has something you'll find interesting."

Straparola couldn't keep the professor's female fans away any longer and the women surged forward, sweeping both the professor and Straparola away. Both men looked happy to be swimming amongst the feminine tide, something Connor noticed only out of the corner of his eye. He was afraid that if he looked away from Derga, she'd vanish. Her one eye was green, he noticed.

The two of them said nothing until Derga tilted her head and looked at him expectantly. It was clear to him she wasn't expecting much.

"Oh, sorry." Connor looked down at the sock in his left hand. Without thinking, he had put the silver comb back in the sock. He was clutching the sock like a little boy who couldn't dress himself. Derga followed his gaze.

"Nice sock," she said, attempting to deadpan the comment even as Connor noticed the beginnings of a smile forming on her lips. Connor swore to himself. *Here I am meeting a beautiful woman and the first thing I do is show her an old sock.* He was going to burn the sock as soon as he got the chance.

"Generally, you wear them on your feet unless that's a sock puppet you're holding," she continued. "Or do you have some other use for it?"

Connor felt himself grasping for a reply. There was a boldness about this woman he hadn't expected. It was obvious she knew the impact she had on people, especially men. "They said you were shy," he said finally.

Derga laughed at the obvious lie and Connor smiled as well.

"Are you sure they weren't talking about you?" she replied.

"It's possible," conceded Connor.

Derga laughed once more. He liked her laugh, he decided. Very much. He wondered about the red eye patch. Was it really covering a bad eye or was it just some kind of fashion statement? You never knew in New York.

Derga looked at him as if she could read his mind. Connor got the sense that if asked about the red eye patch it would be the last question he'd ever ask her.

"Is there something I can help you with?" she asked. It seemed to Connor she was almost daring him to ask about the eye patch. He was sure now that asking about it would the wrong move.

Connor held up his wool sock and she laughed once more.

"I'm not sure I want to help you with that," she said.

Connor reached into the sock and removed the silver comb. At once, all trace of merriment left Derga's face. She stared at the comb and then at Connor, saying nothing. Connor, afraid that he'd somehow lose her, told how he found the comb in Ireland by a lake that had disappeared.

"Is this a trick?" asked Derga, finally.

"A trick? No. What trick could there be in this?"

"Who are you?"

"Ryan Connor. I run a short film festival here in New York."

Connor could feel the wariness with which she now regarded him.

"How do you know the professor?"

"I don't really. I just met him. My friend, Anthony Straparola, introduced us. He's a senior editor with *What's Next* magazine. I showed the professor the comb and he called you over."

Derga regarded him closely. "And you have no idea what that is?"

"This?" said Connor, holding up the comb. "It's a silver comb. Old, I reckon. Is it valuable?"

Derga didn't reply but Connor knew from the look she gave him that it was somehow.

"You should take it back to where you got it," said Derga.

"Why? Finders keepers, right? You don't expect me to fly all the way back to Ireland with it, do you?"

"It's probably too late now anyway."

"Too late? What do you mean too late?"

Derga eyed him with an unblinking stare. "I don't know if you are what you say you are. But if you are, then we'll meet on my terms. Be on the corner of 43rd and Broadway at 7 pm tomorrow night. I'll tell you then what I think of your comb. In the meantime, put it away and show it to no one."

Derga paused, taking in the rest of the room. "If you or anyone else follows me, you'll never see me again."

Derga backed away from him a few steps, turned and headed for the exit. Connor didn't move until Straparola came for him at the end of the party. Even though she had left, Connor felt Derga was still keeping an eye on him somehow.

"Can you believe that bastard, Junot?" said Straparola. "He slipped out with all the girls while I was in the men's room."

Professor Junot sat in a restaurant a few blocks from the museum and smiled as the two women he had met at the Met excused themselves and headed for the ladies room. The owner was an old friend from Alexandria and the Egyptian connection always seemed to impress any woman he brought here. And the owner always appreciated how a pretty woman could dress his place up. He was always given a window seat. A pretty woman turns passing strangers into new customers. He'd probably acquiesce to whatever arrangement the two women dreamed up. With luck, he wouldn't have to choose between them and he silently chuckled at the thought. Right now, there was a more important matter to attend to. He took out his cellphone and speed-dialed a number stored in the device's memory. His mind reviewed the encounter with Ryan Connor. The man didn't strike him as a smuggler of illegal artifacts but the professor decided he couldn't take any chances. To be tainted with any such charge would mean academic ruin, particularly since the pillaging of museums that had occurred in Iraq during the second Gulf War. If Connor should be arrested and if it came out that the professor had met Connor without duly reporting his suspicions. The professor shuddered at the thought even as the call was answered.

"Lt. Gomez, ICE."

"Good evening, Lieutenant. Professor Junot here. I apologize for the lateness of the hour."

"No problem, professor. It's nice to hear from you again. What can I do for you?"

"It's probably nothing and it could all be very innocent but I met a man this evening who is in possession of an artifact that may have been obtained under questionable circumstances."

"Where's it from? Let me guess. Iraq? No. Mexico?"

"Ireland."

"That's different. Did he try to sell it to you?"

"No. But I didn't really give him the opportunity to try."

"I understand. Tell me about it."

"And my previous difficulties?"

"Strictly confidential for the time being."

"I'll tell you what I can but Ireland is not really my area of expertise. I referred him to a colleague."

"I'll need a name."

"Of course."

Chapter Six

She stood on a stone quay cursing all forms of modern transportation, especially the airplane. The man who had taken her comb had left Ireland and gone across the ocean by plane. She trembled slightly. It had been a long time since she had left Ireland and she dreaded crossing water. But what choice had she? Of course, Fin Bheara would be filled with righteous anger. She was leaving his domain without permission, running the risk of exposure. Of course, his fury would know no limits if he knew she had lost the comb. His wife, Nuala, was his softer side but with a mishap on this scale, Nuala wouldn't be much help. At least she was fortunate that the families she keened for had no one in ill health. If one of them died while she was gone and she missed the keening…she couldn't bear the thought. The shame and punishment would be unbearable.

But she had no choice. The comb must be recovered.

Where is the ship? She felt nervous and exposed standing here on the quay. It was a small one used mostly for fishing boats. At the moment, it was deserted but the road that looped above her beyond a stone wall was busy with traffic. She could be seen by passers by driving along the winding road that hugged the coast and drew a crooked line around the small village of Killala Bay. It was only a few miles south of Sligo but she had crossed the border into County Mayo. She glanced up at the road but no one stopped to examine her more closely. She knew that to most onlookers, she looked like a woman enjoying the seaside view.

But the Irish are nosy bastards. Her biggest fear was that a pedestrian would notice her and take the stone steps down to quay for "a bit of chat." For a moment, she considered donning her gwynn, her cloak of concealment, but she decided against it. The cloak, she had been told many times, concealed her from the eyes of everyone except for others of her kind and the hunters. She had never met a hunter and didn't want to. The stories said they looked like everyone else until an iron blade appeared in their hands and they were bearing down on you. They killed without mercy or regret. Better to operate in plain sight whenever possible. That was the best camouflage of all. If a hunter was about, the gwynn would attract his attention.

She saw the zodiac boat approaching the quay with a single figure piloting the craft. As the boat drew alongside the quay, she could make out more of the features of the man aboard. Manny Corribson was the name he went by these days. He was tall, fair-featured, and looked about 40. Pale gold hair that looked like sea foam peaked out from beneath a black captain's hat. He wore a black turtleneck sweater and a pair of blue jeans. Nothing that would draw attention to himself, she noted.

Manny stepped onto the quay and tied up the boat. He had spotted her, of course, but he wouldn't say the first word. Most likely, he would just pass her by with a nod, taking her for a tourist or a poetic soul taking in the scenery.

"It's a beautiful day for a voyage, Captain Corribson," she said in Gortigern, the language used before the fall of the Tower of Babel. Her use of Gortigern was identification in of itself.

"A woman of the hills, is it?" said Captain Corribson. "It's transportation you're after is my guess if you know this is a regular port of call. Have you a destination in mind?"

"I must go across the sea to New York City."

Captain Corribson eyed her more closely. "That's a tricky approach. I'm not sure Ican get you all the way there."

"Somewhere close would be much appreciated," she replied.

"From which kingdom do you hail?"

"The kingdom of Finn Bheara and his queen, Nuala."

"They are aware of your movements?"

She didn't reply.

"I see," said the Captain. "You are of the Seelie Court?"

"Yes."

"Aye. We were on our way to Kilstiffen but I reckon that can wait until our return trip." Captain Corribsen seemed to deliberate with his own mind. She wondered if he was having some fun at her expense. Kilstiffen had disappeared beneath the waves below the Cliffs of Moher centuries ago. Kilstiffen, legend said, would reappear when a lost golden key that opened its castle doors was recovered.

"There shouldn't be much harm in it, I suppose. And maybe a bit of adventure," added Captain Corribsen, smiling. "The U.S. Navy is all that exists in the way of a challenge. And call me Manny."

The black zodiac bounced over the water at a fast clip, heading out to sea as the last few fishing boats pushed toward shore. The inbound crews sometimes shot them a curious glance as they were headed in the opposite direction of everyone else. After a while, the fishing boats faded away and the shoreline was a thin line in the distance. Manny maneuvered the zodiac in a large figure eight without reducing speed and she had to grasp the seat to maintain her balance.

"That's the signal!" shouted Manny over the engine roar.

On cue, a dark rectangular box about 10 feet wide rose out of the water ahead of them and Manny gunned the engine toward it. As the zodiac approached, one side of the rectangle opened like a garage door and a small ramp slid out into the water. The zodiac flew up the ramp and into a dark chamber. The door closed behind them and they were enveloped in darkness.

"Just relax," said Manny. "This will only take a few minutes."

She could hear pumps operating to clear the chamber of water. The sound ended and another began and she could feel herself descending on what must be some type of elevator. The stop was almost imperceptible and coincided with lights coming on inside the chamber.

"Welcome aboard the *Waverunner*," said Manny. "This is your first time, I believe."

"Thank you. Yes."

A large metal door opened and a younger version of Manny appeared in the entry way, although he was dressed in a one-piece outfit of blue green that seemed to shift in the light.

"My son. He handles most boat operations. Come. We'll be out beyond the ninth wave to the place we call home shortly. I'm glad we're not going back to the Baltic Sea. Last time we were there the Swedes got wind of us somehow. Thought we were Russians," he finished with a laugh.

Waves, she remembered being told, grew larger and larger as they headed toward the shore, with the ninth wave being the largest, at which point the sequence started again. Beyond the ninth wave is where the ocean truly began, a wave separating one world from the next. Her voyage had begun.

She never got a sense of how big the submarine was. Not large, she guessed, but comfortable. Manny didn't give her a tour and she spent most of her short time on the submarine sitting in a lounge on a sofa carved from a large piece of driftwood bolted to the floor. She wondered if Manny and his son were the only crew aboard or if there were others she hadn't seen. Manny didn't seem to think that detail important. She, on the other hand, did notice a detail: a large, gold key locked inside a glass box fastened to the wall.

"For a long time, I thought I should change my name to Captain Nemo but I think there are few readers around today who would appreciate the Jules Verne reference."

She kept silent.

"So much for that little joke," continued Manny. "Verne was an interesting man. The Seelie Court didn't like anyone talking to him, naturally. But there really was no cause for concern. Verne never understood how the Waverunner worked. Supercavitation was over his head. Mind you, the U.S. Navy is starting to get its collective brain around the idea. It's only a matter of time, before they develop supercavitating torpedoes. Then we'll have a problem on our hands."

"I'm sorry but I don't understand."

"It's like this, love. We're shaped like a rocket. In fact, we get our initial thrust from on board rocket engines. As we increase our speed, a nozzle on the bow—the tip of the rocket-- emits a gas that spreads around the boat like a bubble--with us inside. The ocean water flows around the bubble, exerting almost no drag on the boat."

"Isn't this a ship?"

"No, dear. Submarines are boats. Ships are targets. Anyway, this allows us to travel at the speed of sound so don't get too comfortable. A dash of thrust vectoring here and there helps us stay on course. A delicate piloting operation, of course, but my son is a natural."

"What about the U.S. Navy?"

"Oh, there really is not too much too worry about until we get near the American coast," said Manny. "First, we stay out of the shipping lanes. Secondly, we travel at a depth below that which other submarines operate. The Russians don't send subs into the deep blue like they used to so most of the opposition's submarine sensors are looking up toward the surface for the most part and they're listening for screws. We don't have screws. To their ears, we sound like a seismic disturbance in very deep water. Still, if they develop supercavitating torpedoes, then they'll have a weapon fast enough to catch us."

"What happens near the coast?"

"We have to operate in shallower water so there is more risk of being detected," said Manny. "The destruction of the Twin Towers in New York City on 9/11 has made coming and going more difficult. Because they fear terrorists, their harbors are filled with sensors. We'll need a different landing spot."

"So what's the plan?"

"It's one that I've used often of late. We'll come in behind a freighter carrying illegal immigrants. The freighter offloads the illegals along some deserted beach in the middle of the night. It will be our screen. If anyone picks up our signature, they'll think it belongs to the freighter. And with all the waves of people heading for shore, no one will notice your arrival. We're very experienced in ferry operations, you know. Our kingdoms are like individual cocoons isolated from one another. We provide a good deal of the transportation between them."

She paused to consider the plan and decided she had little choice but to follow it.

"You never asked me my name," she said.

"Someone will come along asking about you by name. I'll truthfully be able to say I've never heard of you. To know

94

someone's name is to know that person. If pressed, all I'll be able to say is that I recently transported a woman of the hills. More than that I will be unable to say."

In the darkness just before dawn, she could just barely perceive the coastline. The sound of crashing waves in the distance was better confirmation that land was nearby. The *Waverunner* had disappeared after she exited the submarine in a small raft that had its own automatic navigation and propulsion systems. Once ashore, the raft would fade into nothingness as the chemicals that preserved the craft's integrity wore off and the ocean's salt water acted as a dissolving agent.

Off to the right, she could see the outline of a freighter. Small boats were leaving the ship, headed for shore. They were filled with people from she knew not where. They had left everything behind to start a new life ashore. But they were not wanted. She looked again at the coastline. Long Island, Manny had said. New York City was due west. She resisted the temptation to dip her head into the ocean to catch a wift of whale song. She needed to keep her focus.

The first of the boats from the ship were touching the beach when searchlights illuminated the sand. She heard the cries of alarm from those aboard the boats even as voices of authority used bullhorns to issue instructions for surrender. The roar of engines behind her caused her to look over her shoulder. Two other ships were speeding toward the freighter before it could get away. She turned back towards the beach. Flashing red and blue lights atop vehicles cordoned off the beach like a net made of lights. The boat people had no chance of escape.

Her little raft caught the top of wave and as it crested, she stood, knowing full well that she would look like an apparition appearing out of the darkness. She hoped the sight of her would cause any unseen person on the beach to flee. She stepped onto the beach and the receding wave sucked her raft out to sea and it quickly disappeared from view in the darkness.

The beach stretched for miles in both directions. Welcome to the New World, she thought to herself. The boat people were being rounded up about a half mile away, she noted as she got her bearings. She took a few steps inland, somewhat tentatively at first and then with a quickening pace. A vehicle had detached itself from the cordon around the boat people and was heading her way. The wail of a siren rose above the sound of lapping waves as the vehicle drew nearer. She kept walking. She thought about using the gwynn but decided not to, simultaneously chiding herself for being perhaps over cautious. Still, you never knew. There might be a hunter hidden among the police and the gwynn would give her away.

Chapter Seven

Theresa Benning strolled out of the towering office skyscraper on Manhattan's Fifth Avenue and 59th Street, wondering for the millionth time whether she should ever have come to New York City and whether looking for a job in the music business was the right move. She had always thought of herself as a singer, starting out in what would now be a smoke-free jazz club downtown or in one of those show tunes piano bars on the West Side that gay men loved. But that was not to be, she thought with a sigh, a career over before it began at the old age of 23.

She forced herself to face reality. Her music teachers at Oberlin College in Ohio said her voice simply wasn't strong enough and didn't have sufficient range. At first, she had ignored them. No one would get in the way of her childhood dream. But then, she hadn't been accepted for some key courses that would have been the stepping stones that launched her singing career. Instead, she had drifted into classes on music history and theory. She lost 30 pounds in the space of a semester, telling her friends and her alarmed parents that she had been diagnosed with a rare stomach parasite. She even told herself that. *Not a bad thing, really*. She'd always been a bit heavy like her mother. The weight loss now put her into a coveted size zero dress. But at an inch over five feet tall, a strong wind might topple her off her heels.

She replayed the interview with the Sony recording executive over in her mind. She thought it went well but the vice president of Sony's newest recording label had been non-committal about the entry-level job on the business side of the music industry. *This city is full of young blonde girls with lots of energy. At least her name wasn't Lisa. There seemed to be a Lisa in every reception room in town, looking to get the same job she was after, no matter what it was.* She'd have to wait and hope the phone would ring. In the meantime, she'd cruise the Internet for other music-industry related job leads and hope there was no Lisa ahead of her.

Theresa decided to walk back uptown through Central Park, taking advantage of the nice, sunny weather. She was in no hurry to get back to her aunt's apartment. Her aunt was on a month-long cruise in the Baltic Sea so no one would be waiting for her. She passed the Central Park Zoo and heard the excited honking of the seals at feeding time. As she walked north, she passed joggers, cyclists and horse-drawn carriages, one of which seemed to keep pace slightly behind her for a while before breaking off, the driver no doubt smelling the lack of money for the ride. *Yes, a job is what I need. I'll meet new people, make new friends, maybe even find a date.*

Theresa quickly found herself at the 72nd Street entrance to the park. She walked two more blocks north on Fifth Avenue and then turned east on 74th Street. On Second Avenue she passed a row of bars filled with after-work singles. Theresa sighed. She needed a girlfriend to go out with. She didn't have the courage yet to walk into such places on her own.

Her aunt's building was on the north side of the street, close to the corner of First Avenue. The building rose 17 stories into the air, with each floor ringed by balconies, one for each apartment. Theresa skipped down the three steps that led to the front door of the building, momentarily bothered by what seemed to be a shift in the light that almost made her stumble. Still, she recovered quickly enough to open the door before the doorman could get out of his chair, although this was no glorious athletic achievement considering the slowness with which the doorman moved his girth even at the best of times, which her aunt said was around Christmas when year-end tips were in the offing. She smiled at the doorman, inwardly relieved that she wouldn't be the one to have put money in an envelope for him, and he nodded in recognition. She walked through the lobby past a leather sofa toward a bank of elevators and it seemed to her that one corner of the lobby was a little darker than she remembered it. One of the elevator doors opened and Theresa boarded, pushing the button for the tenth floor. A man carrying clothes on hangar suddenly came in behind her and his sudden arrival gave her a start. But the man got off just as quickly on the third floor, She glanced over to where the delivery man had been standing and noticed a dark black line on the wall and wondered idly if some kind of stain had rubbed off on it. At ten, she got off the elevator and turned right toward her aunt's apartment, taking out the door key out as she walked. She glanced over her shoulder to be sure no one was behind her, per her aunt's safety instruction, and while there was no one there, it seemed the light in the hallway was a little dimmer, as if one of the light bulbs had given out. A quick turn of the locks and Theresa opened the apartment door and stepped into a small foyer. She turned to lock the door behind her but before she could touch the lock, something pushed hard against the door, sending Theresa sprawling onto the floor.

Stunned, Theresa looked up and initially saw nothing. Then she saw the black line that seemed to be moving toward her. It stopped before her as she rose to a sitting position. Her eyes widened when a pair of black-gloved fingers began to materialize, seemingly out of thin air, and began parting the black line to make it wider. The fingers became hands and then arms in black pinstripe. Theresa opened her mouth to scream but the hand shot forward to cover her mouth. She reached up to push the hand away from her mouth but her arms now felt sluggish. *Some drug.*

Theresa collapsed on the floor and the Heer of Dunderberg emerged like someone stepping out between two black curtains in a theater. He produced a large nylon bag with a long zipper that ran from end to end. He laid the bag down on the floor next to Theresa, rolled her into it and then zippered it shut. He then pulled the black curtains together until they formed a thin black line which he then folded until it was a small square and put it into the inside pocket of his suit jacket.

The Heer of Dunderberg opened the apartment door, lifting the bag as if it were nothing more than a set of golf clubs. There was no one in the hall or in the elevator to mark his progress to the lobby and as he passed the doorman, he shifted the bag so his face was obscured. The doorman barely glanced up from his newspaper as the Heer of Dunderberg left the building. The doorman was paid to watch who entered the building, not who left.

The Heer of Dunderberg walked to the curb and a yellow taxi appeared as if on cue. The trunk opened and the Heer of Dunderberg put his large bag into the trunk and shut it. He then climbed into the back seat of the taxi. The driver, a bald man with black eyebrows that stretched in an unbroken line across his forehead, turned toward his passenger.

"Airport?" asked the driver.

The Heer of Dunderberg glared at him.

"Just joking," said the driver as he pulled away.

Forty blocks away, Ryan Connor passed the remodeled Hippodrome Building on the corner of 44th Street and crossed Sixth Avenue along with a crowd of office workers heading for the Port Authority buses on Eighth Avenue that would take them home to New Jersey on the other side of the Hudson River. *The bridge and tunnel people.* That's what Manhattanites—the ones who stayed on the island after 5 o'clock—called everyone else who spent their days working, but not living, in Manhattan. They never quite said it but the inference was clear that the people who didn't live on Manhattan were somehow inferior. Looking around, Connor could understand where the thought came from. It was as if all these commuters were zombies. People moved along without paying each other much heed, lost in their own thoughts, rushing to pick up children or to meet spouses, or just reviewing the workday's events in their minds. Manhattanites tended to think the world spun around their island and anyone who didn't live on it wasn't a top-tier human. Rising real estate prices, however, were making some Manhattan hipsters re-consider the city's poorer boroughs. *Brooklyn, or at least the parts closest to Manhattan, is cool again. What's next? The Bronx?*

Connor checked his watch—it was a few minutes before seven—and quickened his pace. He wanted to arrive precisely on time. He didn't want to appear anxious or overeager by arriving early. Conversely, he didn't want to appear cavalier about their appointment by arriving late. Connor noticed a Belgian bar across the street. Perhaps he could convince Derga to join him for a beer, something classy like a lambic. Connor could almost taste it.

I'm a little nervous, Connor admitted to himself. The comb from Ireland was in his pocket and Derga seemed genuinely interested in it. But he was hoping Derga would be interested in him as well.

Connor reached the southeast corner of Broadway and 44th Street at seven on the dot and a moment later, he spotted Derga walking across Broadway toward him. In fact, so had a few hundred other people. Her looks snapped people out of their zombie-like reveries and they watched her walk by, mesmerized. She wore a stunning, red pants suit that was tight in all the right places with a short jacket cut low enough to reveal an ample décolletage and short enough to hint at a bare midriff.. Connor wondered how she had even gotten into it. Connor could feel his breath starting to come in short, shallow bursts. *Calm yourself and focus on her eyes.*

Derga reached his side of the street and thread her arm through his like an old lover. Connor's heart rate leaped into another gear.

"Walk," she said.

Connor happily obliged, thrilled by the implied intimacy. They walked back the way Connor had come, toward Sixth Avenue. Derga said nothing more and Connor couldn't get his lips to move. He noticed a few looks of envy from passing men. Derga's red hair bounced as she walked, obscuring his view of her face. *So much for focusing on the eyes.*

Halfway to Sixth Avenue, she leaned against him and steered him up the three steps that marked the entry to the Metropolitan Hotel. Connor nearly stumbled as they entered the dimly lit lobby. At first, he thought it was moving day at the hotel. A long line of empty tables and chairs to his left were all covered with white cloth, looking like they were ready to loaded into boxes and shipped out. Derga steered him down the hall toward the elevators. The white cloths were intentional, Connor realized, as two business-types sat down at one of the tables and signaled for a waitress. The scene was lost from view as the elevator doors closed.

"I've booked us a room," said Derga.

Connor nodded and smiled. He was afraid to open his mouth. Connor had talked his fair share of women into hotel beds but he had never gotten this far without saying a word. He was afraid any sound emanating from his mouth would break whatever spell had carried him this far. The elevator stopped at the seventh floor and Derga led the way, still holding his arm.

"This way," she said. The hallway was narrow and so dimly lit that there was practically no illumination at all. Connor looked at Derga, the first thoughts of caution entering his mind. *What if I'm being set up and there are bad guys waiting for me in there?*

Derga stopped at the door of room 77 and smiled at him. She opened the door a sliver and slid him in ahead of her. The room was empty, Connor was relieved to discover, and was small and nearly as dark as the hallway. Connor stood next to an end table by the bed as Derga paraded around the room. He couldn't take his eyes off her. She checked the bathroom with an approving murmur and then walked to another door and opened it. A closet, he guessed.

"How lovely!" she said. "Come see."

Connor couldn't imagine what might make a closet lovely but he did as he was told and walked over to the closet door. The closet had a low ceiling and was well-matched to the room in that it was also tiny and dark. Derga suddenly pushed Connor into the closet and swung the closet door in behind them. The two of them barely fit. They stood face-to- face, bodies pressed against each other.

Kinky, thought Conor, not unduly alarmed until he lowered his head slightly and felt the thin prick of a blade under his chin.

Oh, shit! She's a real weird-o. "Ah, no offense, but this isn't really my scene."

"Hands up!"

Connor hesitated but a slight upward movement of the blade under his chin made him comply. *Fuck, she's a mad lesbian killer who's going to cut off my dick.*

Derga grabbed each of his hands in turn and examined them as if looking for something and then seemed relieved when it wasn't there.

"What are looking you for?"

"A sixth finger. Or a scar where there would have been one."

"An extra finger?"

"You have the comb?"

"Am I being robbed?"

"No. Believe me, I don't want it."

"It's in my pocket, old sock and all."

Derga smiled and lowered the blade—a stiletto, he noted—and it disappeared below his waist. Connor winced in anticipation and hoped he'd have the strength to strangle her. But no cut ever came.

"A thousand pardons but I had to be sure we were alone," said Derga. "For every encounter between two people, there is always a third. And in every council…"

"…there is one for whom no chair is set," finished Connor.

"You know your Yeats," said Derga.

"Yes," said Connor. "But unlike me, you seem to feel they are words to live by."

"They are," said Derga. She reached up and began removing the red eye patch that covered her left eye. Connor didn't know what to expect—an empty socket, a glass ball, a horrible scar. He steeled himself, determined not to betray any emotion. To his surprise, however, all he saw was a second eye as beautiful as the first. Both of her eyes focused on his face.

"You're wondering why I wear the patch."

"Fashion statement?"

"No," she smiled ruefully. "If that third person we just mentioned caught me looking at him with my uncovered eye, he'd pluck it out or worse. I only take the patch off when I'm sure he's not around."

"You're talking about the guy with six fingers?"

"No. Another. I live in a complicated world."

"Let's start with the guy with six fingers."

"The Nephilum. There is more than one."

"Never heard of them. What are they? Some kind of street gang?"

"You don't know your Bible very well. They're in the Book of Genesis, Chapter 6, Verses 1 through 4."

"Fabulous. Religious wackos. What are they? Like Al-Qaeda?"

"More dangerous. At least to me. These days they go by the name Medea."

"And my guess is they want my comb?"

"No. They want the owner of the comb."

"I don't know who that is."

"They do."

"And so do you."

"Yes."

Suddenly, a third deeply sonorous voice could be heard, speaking at waist level. "I will arise and go now, and go to Innisfree."

Derga's eyes widened in surprise.

"Easy. It's only Yeats reciting *The Lake Isle of Innisfree*. I downloaded his voice into my cellphone as a ring tone. It's the only known recording of his voice. I found it on the Internet .I can't believe I'm getting a signal inside a closet."

Derga stared at him, open-mouthed.

"Too weird?" And then without waiting for an answer, he pulled the cellphone from his pants pocket.

"Hello?" For Derga, the conversation was all one-sided.

"Vincent! Good to hear from you. What's up?"

A pause. "Yeah. No. I didn't forget. I was in Ireland. Don't worry. It's all set. The Gershwin is loving it! It's just the kind of event they want to host."

Another pause. "Sure. Listen, Vincent. I'm not in the office right now and I'm in the middle of something. Let me e-mail you with the details."

Another pause but shorter this time. "Red."

Connor hung up. "Sorry. Work. I'm setting up a premiere for a new film called *Bada Bing*. It's a movie about the Mafia done by one of their own. It's the new thing of theirs, if you know what I mean."

"I think I can help you," said Derga.

"With the premiere?"

"No."

Yeats chimed in again. "I will arise and go now,"

"Sorry," said Connor, putting the cellphone to his ear. "They're very insistent kinds of people."

The voice on the other end, however, was not Vincent's. "Fiona! Where are you? Dublin?"

A pause. "You're back in Sligo?"

Connor listened and his face turned ashen. "My God! How is she?"

"What is it?" asked Derga.

"My cousin Rosaleeen," said Connor. He listened some more. "OK. Thanks."

Connor ended the call and with a little squirming that required moments of body contact with Derga, put the cellphone back in his pocket. "My cousin in Ireland. She's been horribly attacked. She's got a bad burn on her shoulder and she's in a coma."

Derga thought for a moment. "Did your cousin ever touch the comb?"

"Ah, no. Don't tell me the comb as something to do with this?"

"Did she ever touch the comb?"

Connor thought for a moment and then remembered how Rosaleen had handled the comb that night in Sligo.

"She did, didn't she?"

Connor nodded, stunned by the idea that there could be any linkage between the comb and the attack on Rosaleen.

"She will be coming for you next?"

"Who?" asked Connor, confused. "Who's coming?"

"The owner of the comb. She'll kill you to get it back."

Connor took a deep breath. "Can we come out of the closet now?"

"Not just yet." Connor felt her other hand move in between them and realized that Derga was sliding her fingers down the front of her pants. They lingered for a few moments and then she brought a finger up to his mouth and traced a line around his lips. Her finger was wet. Connor could feel himself coming to attention.

Her hand disappeared once again and when it reappeared, she inserted a wet finger into his mouth. His reaction was almost involuntary. His lips wrapped around her finger while she slowly withdrew it.

Derga slid the patch over her eye and opened the closet door.

"The room is paid for through tomorrow morning," she said. "Stay as long as you like. I'll be in touch."

Then she left.

Chapter Eight

The first person she saw in the faint light of dawn was a man a few yards away who stood at the edge of the beach just beyond the water's reach, slowly waving a cane with a round disk attached to the end over the sand, his eyes focused downward like he was looking for something lost. But his wasn't the first voice she heard.

"Welcome to Rockaway Beach. I'm a federal officer." Something shiny and round flashed in his hand and then disappeared. "Do you have any identification?"

She could hear the mirth in the man's voice even as the flashlight shone in her face. She had not disembarked on a secluded beach, she realized, even though it had seemed so at first. The false sense of isolation was due to missing light bulbs on a stretch of boardwalk. Behind the boardwalk was a row of small, tattered-looking buildings and their lights were mostly turned off at this hour of the morning.

"A little light on the luggage too, I see," said the man.

She said nothing. His words were probes, she knew. He hoped his words would elicit a response. She glanced toward the man with the cane.

"He's nothing to worry about," said the man. "He's just a guy with a metal detector hoping for a big score. Speak English? Yeah, I bet you do. Doesn't everyone these days. Well, I got news for you. You didn't exactly arrive in the la-dee-da Hamptons. They used to call this stretch of beach the Irish Riviera. But times have changed. Now this is the kind of neighborhood where 99 Cent stores go out of business. Still attracts the surfers, though. The waves are eternal."

The light moved around her in a circle.

"So the question is this. Did you come off that same ship as those poor luckless Asian bastards we just rounded up? Or did you arrive on some other boat?"

Her eyes wandered down the beach where she could see a large number of people in the half-light being herded toward some waiting buses. They walked slowly like a people in defeat, eyes wild and teeth chattering. More than a few had swollen bellies from gulping salt water.

"The *cujones* on these people. What did they think they were going to do? Land here on the beach, then walk over to 116th Street station and take the A train down to Chinatown. They must be listening to too much Duke Ellington over there in Shanghai or Rangoon or wherever it is they're coming from. It wouldn't surprise me if they had subway maps tattooed on their bodies."

The reference to Duke Ellington caught her attention and she wondered if he was the local ruler. It was confusing. The Duke seemed to welcome new arrivals while this officer did not. *Duke Ellington must live in la-dee-da place.*

"You don't like the Duke's music?"

A ruler who is also a musician?

The light suddenly stopped and there was the sudden flash of a second light that made her blink.

"Nothing to worry about. It's only a digital photo. Just in case I lose you before we figure out who you are."

Other flashlights joined the first, forming a ring of light around her.

"Come this way, please.

The ring of light moved forward and she moved with it across the beach, up a rampand onto the boardwalk. She could see the men more clearly now. Some kind of police, she realized, although she was puzzled by the big block letters on their uniform vests that spelled "ICE." *Did they work only in winter?* Clearly not. She let the question go. They were all in uniform except for the one doing the talking. He was, upon closer inspection, a very thin man, comprised mostly of bones and attitude. He wore a dark suit, a lavender shirt and a tie of deep purple. He was about average height which was a relief. The hunters were big, she'd been told. She studied his face. Black eyes, light brown skin and noble nose. A man of Spain, she guessed, not that she had seen very many. He looked like a man who would dig in his heels, she judged. *Too bad.*

"Please extend your hands together."

She did so and a pair of plastic handcuffs slipped over her wrists.

"So you do understand English."

She looked straight at the man. *Enjoy your small victories.*

"Officer, can you escort this woman to my car? Thank you. I'll be along in a minute."

She sat in the back of the black, unmarked car, a barrier of clear plexiglass separating her from the driver, another man, a younger version of the first, in a suit. A jet plane flew overhead, low and noisy, and she realized she was near an airport. A few minutes later, the front passenger door opened. The talking man climbed in.

"There used to be 10 bars on very block around here," he said to the driver. "Imagine that."

The driver shrugged and the talking man turned toward her like an old friend. The driver put the car into gear and they drove away from the crowd of detainees and police.

"So maybe if I tell you who I am, you'll tell me who you are?" said the talking man. "I'm Lt. Clemente Gomez de Suarez. You can call me Lt. Gomez. I'm an ICEman."

Lt. Gomez paused for dramatic effect. "The Iceman Cometh. And I'm not talking about some Eugene O'Neill play on Broadway. I'm talking about me."

More silence.

"Like you would know Broadway," said Lt. Gomez. "OK. Es verdad. You're from out of town so I'll fill you in. ICE stands for Immigration and Customs Enforcement. We're an agency of the Department of Homeland Security. Established in 2003. Usually, I'm tracking stolen objects that are entering the country illegally. Stolen art, ancient artifacts, that sort of thing. A lot of that stuff floating around now, especially since the Baghdad Museum got trashed by the locals. You're lucky we happened to be a little short-handed so I'm helping out my colleagues in Enforcement and Removal Operations. We've got another *Golden Dragon* out there, full of illegals and probably a few dead bodies. Normally, I work in the Homeland Security Investigations office."

His voice was like a murmur. "Truth is I hate this shit."

Few realized that ICE was a house divided. ICE had two different wings. One was Enforcement and Removal Operations (ERO), tasked with detaining and deporting illegal aliens. The other wing was Homeland Security Investigations (HSI) which went after the trade, travel and financial activities of international terrorists and criminals. Illegal cross-border narcotics, human trafficking, and trans-national fraud were at the top of their to-do list. HSI had 65 offices world-wide with teams of investigators in each.

But when the general public thought of ICE, the activities of ERO came to mind. Dawn raids and round-ups of illegal aliens, most of whom had resided in the USA for many years without incident. ERO separated families, sending mothers or fathers back to their home country while their children remained in the USA. Fathers had been arrested while taking their children to school. People who had been brought to the USA as children were detained. Churches, schools, hospitals and workplaces were targets. Thousands were apprehended. Some were military veterans who had seen combat in the defense of the United States.

While they worked with the ERO division, many HSI agents were increasingly embarrassed by the methods employed by ERO. The Special Agents in Charge of 19 HSI offices across the United States collectively and formally argued that HSI and ERO needed to be two separate agencies, maintaining that the missions of the two sub-agencies had diverged to the point that they were incompatible with each other. The truth was that ERO was seen increasingly as a political police force. HSI agents wanted no part of that and noted that their own investigations were becoming hampered by the refusal of many state and cities to work with them because of the perceived linkage to politics.

"But the law is the law."

She looked past him out the front windshield. *So many houses. So much concrete. So many people. It was dangerous to be here. If my king knew, he'd be furious.*

"Being an investigator, I ask myself a question. What's a girl like you doing on the same beach as those other illegals off that ship. You're not Asian. It doesn't add up. You have no business being on a ship carrying a load of illegal immigrants from Asia."

I'm sorry, my king, my queen.

"Then I think what if you weren't on that ship but on another smaller one that we missed. The first ship would be a good smoke screen that would get you on shore unobserved. Everyone knows our coastlines are vulnerable to penetration. Almost worked. It was just your bad luck I saw you. Of course, the night-vision goggles helped. We've all got them now. Way better than that first-generation stuff we used to use. Picks up thermal images too."

She sensed the car was going in the general direction she wanted to go. The comb was getting closer.

"So I have this hunch that there may be more to you than meets the eye. So why don't you help me out and tell me who you are?"

They were coming to a massive suspension bridge, she noticed. She felt herself tightening up. Crossing over water made her edgy. She squirmed in her seat. On her left she could see the Manhattan skyline outlined by what seemed like a million tiny dots of light. *Breathtaking. I shouldn't be here.*

"OK. Have it your way. Believe me, we'll find out who you are. Photographs, fingerprints, DNA—the works. We're taking you to a little privately run prison down on Varick Street in lower Manhattan. You're not going to like the food." Gomez chuckled. "But most prisoners say that it's better than the detention center in New Jersey. People die there. God damned concentration camp is what it is. Maybe you want to go there instead?"

He's trying to scare me. He's not taking me to see Duke Ellington. I'm sure he would be nicer. The comb is somewhere amongst all those buildings. Time to go.

Lt. Gomez turned forward in his seat as they approached the western end of the long suspension that connected the borough of Queens with the Bronx and Manhattan. A row of tollbooths stood in a line marking the entrance to the Bronx but they moved right off onto a ramp that looped under the main bridge and came out onto a smaller bridge that led to Manhattan. Here too there were tollbooths and the car slowed as it came to one in the middle lane.

The driver rolled down the window and flashed his badge at the attendant on duty.

"Hey, LT," said the driver. "You think we will ever get EZpass?"

"Too much paperwork," said the lieutenant, glancing at the driver and turning away from his prisoner to stare out the front windshield.

Now is the moment. She opened her mouth slightly to let in the air and it flowed over the two uvula shaped like tuning forks at the back of her throat, one behind the other. She flicked her tongue up and down with a speed a hummingbird would have envied, a movement that began to synchronize with her now vibrating uvula. The sound she made had 20 different frequencies within it that she could emphasize with varying effect. For the dead, she employed a trilling keen, sometimes adding some subtle variations. One replicated the cries of Irish women who lost loved ones in the Irish Famine in the 19th century. Over a million died then. She had been busy.

But the ululation could be fashioned into a sonic weapon. Opening her mouth wide sent the sound everywhere at once but if she pursed her lips, she could focus it in a single direction, the sound not becoming audible until it hit the target. She snapped apart the plastic cuffs binding her wrists and brought one hand up toward her mouth and blew the driver a long kiss.

For the driver, it was like someone had dropped an invisible bag of loud angry, whining crickets over his head. Both his hands left the wheel to clutch his ears but he still had the presence of mind to jam on the brakes, tumbling out of the car as it came to a halt. Lt. Gomez heard the sound explode around the driver and just had time to brace himself with hand on the dashboard as the car came to its sudden stop and watched as the driver ejected himself from his seat. He turned to check on his prisoner and was stunned to see both her hands were free. He saw what looked like a small packet in her hands. He blinked. Or maybe there was nothing there at all. Just a dark rectangle without any actual substance. Then a black cloud filled the car and he could see nothing. The smell was overwhelming, like something that had been rotting for a very long time. It was like someone had opened a grave. He pushed open the car door and fell to his knees on the road, gagging and gasping for air.

A biological attack. Lt. Gomez berated himself. *How did I miss that?*

She waited until both men passed out before exiting the car. The nearest tollbooth attendant was puking over the half door and the other attendants further away were covering their faces and coughing. Drivers were hastily rolling up their windows while others quickly drove away from the scene. No one noticed her as she took out her gwynn under the cover of smoke and wrapped it around herself, vanishing from sight.

"A mysterious dark cloud has left six tollbooth workers and several commuters ill on the Robert F. Kennedy Triboro Bridge. Police are searching for an unidentified woman who escaped from custody during the incident, which occurred only moments ago. The bridge, however, is closed pending a police investigation. Drivers coming into Manhattan are advised to use the Midtown Tunnel or the Manhattan Bridge. Long Island-bound commuters should use the Throgs Neck Bridge or the Brooklyn Bridge."

The Cornet of Horse sat deep underground beneath a house in the hilly little town called Dobbs Ferry just north of New York City. The town was named for a man who had once operated a long-gone ferry across the Hudson River. If need be, he could be in Manhattan within 20 minutes. The red brick Victorian house had been bought years ago during the Cold War after the previous owner had built an unauthorized fallout shelter in the basement. It was supposed to be a secret but the house with the shelter eventually came to the attention of those who moved in the same circles as the Cornet of Horse. They, in turn, kept the secret. When the occupant passed away of natural causes, the Cornet of Horse had stepped in, buying the house in the name of a dummy corporation. The Cornet of Horse had since expanded it into a larger underground complex. Above ground, a high fence hidden behind a wall of bushes kept neighbors at arm's length. The Cornet of Horse spent most of his time underground when he was in the house. To passersby, the house looked vacant.

The Triboro Bridge closed? Curious now, the Cornet of Horse turned off the radio and jiggled the mouse on his computer to kick it out of sleep mode. The bridge, he recalled, had recently been re-dedicated to the memory of the assassinated senator and brother of the slain president, John F. Kennedy. His fingers logged onto the Internet and he typed in a password that gave him access to digital security cameras placed around New York City. A camera on top of the Empire State Building gave him a bird's eye view of the city. It was already pointed toward the Triboro Bridge and he could see the cloud of smoke spiraling away from the it. He hit the F6 button on his keyboard and a software program developed by the U.S. Office of Naval of Research tracked the smoke back to its point of origin. Fortunately, the point of origin was stationary. The software's biggest vulnerability was that it couldn't track a moving target. A toxic aerosol sprayed from a moving van would be difficult to trace.

The Cornet of Horse typed in the web address of camera closer to the Triboro Bridge and then accessed its memory, going back in time to when the incident occurred. He was lucky, he realized, in that the point of origin was a stationary car. He watched the footage as smoke spewed from the car and people nearby collapsed. He then zoomed in and replayed the footage. Two men in the front seat got out of the car and collapsed on the road. About a minute later, a woman emerged from the back seat, took a few steps amidst the smoke, and then disappeared. Surprised, he replayed the footage several times to be sure. Smoke partially obscured the woman and the camera used time-lapse photography so there were gaps in the timeline. He pressed F2 on the keyboard and another software package developed by the U.S. National Security Agency proceeded to clean up the digital image and then enhance it. *You can't beat the Americans on security software. They can read a license plate number through the fog using space satellites.*

The procedure took less than a minute. The flat-panel screen went blank for a moment and then displayed a black-and-white image that might have been taken by a high-priced celebrity portrait photographer. The Cornet of Horse stared at the screen for several seconds. He didn't blink as the image in front of him saturated his brain.

She hasn't been seen before, said one of The Voices. But she's one of them. She used a gwynn to make her escape.

The Cornet of Horse smiled to himself. The hunt was on. *In New York, no less.* Unusual as the quarry tended to avoid cities ever since the battle of Vineta. The words *sorcerer Pope* whispered in his mind but he cut it off. *No time to revisit that now.* A blinking light on his computer alerted him to a FBI communiqué of potential interest. His fingers danced on the keyboard. *Something to do with the woman on the bridge, no doubt.*

There were two bulletins of interest, in fact. The first had to do with the woman on the bridge. The incident was being described internally as a terrorist biological attack but also one of limited scope. It also had been classified as top secret. Publicly, the attack was now being attributed to a faulty fuel line in the car.

The second bulletin was on a different topic. There had been another kidnapping of a young woman, this time on the city's Upper East Side. A would-be suitor looking through his peephole had witnessed what he thought was an abduction. Forensic evidence suggested signs of a struggle and a sketch of the subject had been drawn based on the description supplied by the neighbor and the doorman of the building. There also was a grainy photograph from a newly installed security camera in the lobby. The Cornet of Horse clicked on the supplied link and was soon looking at the photo. His backed straightened in recognition. *We know him*, said The Old Voices.

The Cornet of Horse leaned back in his chair. *Shit, not him again.* He shook his head in disbelief. *They were never this sloppy.* Another thought entered his mind. *Maybe they think no one can stop them anyway.* Proof positive was on a wooden shelf above the computer. He looked up at an array of volumes and picked a binder marked with the number 17 on the spine. He flipped through the loosely bound pages until he found what he was looking for, a report dated April 24th, 1781 from Col. Hugh Hughes to his commanding officer, Major General Heath, seeking permission for the construction of a military prison on Pollepel Island in the Hudson River, a request approved by General George Washington. The communique was fiction, he knew, meant to provide a back story for a more covert operation. The prison had never been built. The truth was in the after action report he had written. Two women had been kidnapped. One had been saved. A sketch of the kidnapper had been drawn based on the surviving woman's description. The Cornet of Horse looked at the sketch carefully. There was no doubt that the face drawn by an artist on Washington's staff was identical to the photo on the Cornet of Horse's computer screen. The Heer of Dunderberg had returned.

And a second one, on the bridge

"Two," murmured the Cornet of Horse. *What did it mean? Were they acting in concert or separately? When was the last time two quarries had been pursued at the same time?*

Aenothesus, said the Old Voices. *He sought two at once.*

"Charlemagne's bodyguard," said the Cornet of Horse aloud. "That was a long time ago." He was getting into the habit of talking aloud to the Old Voices ever since mobile phones became ubiquitous and talking aloud to seemingly no one no longer drew alarmed looks from passersby. Still, he should watch himself.

He didn't get both, said the Old Voices.

"True that." *It's hard not talk back once you've started. I need to be around real people more.*

The Cornet of Horse closed his eyes and remembered.

Chapter Nine

General George Washington was tall but he towered over him and the other men in the room, all of whom looked at him as if Goliath had strode forth from the pages of the Bible, clad in buckskin and carrying a long rifle, a brace of large horse pistols and a tomahawk the size of a battle-ax.

"Maushop," said Major John Mauritius Goetschius. "He's one of the sharpshooters from way back in The Endless Mountains. He doesn't speak much and when he does its mostly in German."

Maushop's English was actually excellent but speaking in German curtailed inquisitive small talk. The men in the room, all soldiers, eyed Maushop with a mix of wonder at his size and respect for the reputation that preceded him. Everyone had heard of the riflemen from the wilds of Pennsylvania and their prowess and skill had been proven in battles across the 13 colonies. Like Maushop, they used a long rifle developed by German smiths in Pennsylvania as opposed to the European muskets commonly used. While the lighter long rifle took longer to reload than a musket, it was much more accurate at longer ranges. Rumor said many were once part of a legendary group of giant bodyguards who had guarded King Frederick the Great. Maushop knew that the legend was truer than anyone could imagine. In Prussia, they had been called Infantry Regiment Number 6, a designation that deliberately obscured who or what they were really were. Frederick had scoured all of Europe to find them, sometimes even kidnapping them into his service while others were given as gifts by their birth countries. Some had been just tall men; others had been more than that. Maushop had been among them before transferring to a cavalry troop, a move that had ultimately facilitated his escape. Maushop wasn't his real name but he liked using the one the Indians had given him, a name from their own legends of a giant from the distant past. The name would also muddy the trail for anyone looking for him in the years to come. King Frederick the Great's reach could be long.

"Just as well," said Washington. "No one is to ever discuss tonight's mission." And just like that, Maushop was accepted into the fold. Acceptance wasn't something Maushop was used to. It was the tone of Washington's voice that did it, a signal that everyone responded to that said what occurred here tonight was bigger than one man's differences with another.

Washington was like that, Goetschius confided on the ride to Washington's headquarters at Newburgh on the western bank of the Hudson River, perhaps a little more than halfway between New York to the south and Albany to the north.

"The English view the Dutch as a primitive race," said Goetschius, "who only worship the god of trade. It's been like that since Peter Stuyvesant handed them the keys to New Amsterdam a century ago—a little more than that actually at this point—and renamed it New York."

Goetschius paused for a few more gallops, adjusting the old black three-pointed hat he still favored from the early days of the war. Most now wore the tri-color version since the alliance with France. "The truth is that there are plenty in Washington's army who think the same, especially among the regular officers. But Holland let us go for a few islands in the Caribbean. Since then we have lived as a community onto ourselves. We need someone new to love." Goetschius laughed. "So as long as the Old Fox leads, I will serve. As will the men in my command. God willing."

Maushop knew that Goetschius was a religious man, having studied for the ministry of the Dutch Reformed Church before the War for Independence from England began. The Dutch Reformed Church itself had been in the throes of more democratic reforms even before the war so for them, religion and politics melded nicely. His religious training had also made Goetschius more accepting of Maushop's true nature as he was a believer in the Old Testament and the story of David lay there like a prelude. It also helped that the secretive Duzine, also known as the Twelve Men, who governed the affairs of the Dutch in America, were allies. Maushop had met Goetschius when the Duzine sent him west before the war to evaluate possible land purchases.

The clergy's loss had been Washington's gain. Goetschius had emerged as a genius of irregular or guerrilla warfare, leading 100 men who fought the British by night while re-assuming their roles as farmers during the day during the occupation of New Jersey. In time and with each success, Goetschius' force grew in numbers until they were able to wrest Fort Lee from the British before American regulars even arrived for the battle. At the moment, however, Goeschius' main concern were the Cowboys, bands of Loyalists who raided across what was now being called the Neutral Ground between the British Army in New York and American forces further up the Hudson River. But on this warm spring day, they were both headed to Newburgh after receiving a summons from Washington while inspecting a blockhouse in Dobbs Ferry, a small village on the Hudson's eastern shore, manned by 20 men from Goetschius's command tasked with curtailing Cowboy raids that had increased since the departure of General Rochambeau's French army from the area in the summer of 1781. Dobbs Ferry was the southernmost guardhouse on the Hudson River for Washington's army and so was a vital post that would warn of any major movements by the British still encamped in New York City some 20 miles downriver.

"You know Dobbs Ferry was where the traitor Benedict Arnold first arranged to meet Major Andre," said Goetschius. "But the dumb redcoats forgot to tell one of their own gunboats about the meeting and they fired on Arnold' barge, driving him off. Thank God, that meeting never occurred and we were able to capture Arnold when they tried for a second rendezvous. The sad part is that Arnold was a great general."

"He is very short," said Maushop.

Goetschius laughed. "Yes, that's true. And he came up very short in the end."

They crossed the Hudson at Kings Ferry by Verplanck's Point just as Washington and Rochambeau had done in 1781 after assembling the colonial army in Dobbs Ferry to march to the decisive victory at Yorktown Heights in Virginia. But Washington was back and Goetschius was Washington's first choice when it came to special operations, especially as he was outside the normal chain of command that was prone to penetration by British spies. Goetschius had known what was on Washington's mind for many months, sending for Maushop in anticipation of an action by Washington. Washington had been in Newburgh since March, 1782. And here it was, the beginning of April, 1783. The Old Fox had taken a long time to be convinced of the threat. Now he was.

"What's the General like?" asked Maushop.

"Well, he is a better dresser than most men I know," said Goetschius. "The women think he's gorgeous in a remote kind of way. But don't let his looks fool you. He likes a fight more than most and he is cunning and single-minded in purpose."

Maushop didn't doubt it. In Europe, they were still scratching their heads about how a 22-year-old lieutenant colonel in command of 160 Virginia militia had picked a fight with the French in the Ohio Country a generation ago and turned a skirmish into an international conflict called the Seven Years' War. England, Prussia, and Hanover had fought France, Sweden, Russia, Saxony and later Spain. France and Spain lost their North American colonies. It was truly the first world war, with battles fought in Europe, India, Africa and North and South America. Washington had famously written his brother: "I heard the bullets whistle and believe me, there is something charming in the sound." Locals who called it the French and Indian War tended to think it was a land grab by Virginians and most expected Washington to re-focus his attention on obtaining Western land once the fight with the British was over. Maushop knew Indian tribes like the Iroquois and the Shawnee were already preparing for war. Washington's ability to stir the pot was not to be underestimated. Or to do what was required politically—the French were now esteemed allies. Young French officers like Lafayette admired Washington while older veterans like General Rochambeau—commander of French forces in the Americas—did what was required but remembered their history.

Washington's headquarters was a fieldstone farm house owned by a local family called Hasbrouck. The man of the house had been killed early in the war and his widow had moved elsewhere while Washington was there, unsettled by the visible reminder of her husband's passing. They had come in unseen during the night through the rear door per instructions and stood in the back kitchen. The room was large, with whitewashed walls and reed mats thrown down on a wide beam floor. A pair of doors, painted in Prussian blue, led off to the right--bedrooms Maushop guessed--while a third, also Prussian blue, in the far left corner presumably led to the rest of the house. The ceiling had a few exposed beams and was very high, which told Maushop the owner had been very wealthy as it would cost quite a bit to heat the room continuously. That heat came from a large Dutch Jambless fireplace—contrary to the smaller English style fireplaces now in vogue--to the left and Maushop noted the short blue and white curtain at the top of the fireplace meant to curtail any smoke from spreading around the room. It would have looked very domestic if not for the sword hanging from a peg on the wall. The house looked small from the outside but Maushop now realized it was much bigger once he was inside.

There was a large dining table and chairs in front of the fireplace and that's where they were seated, being introduced to Sergeant John Phillips of Washington's Life Guard, a burly, dark-haired man who looked like he could handle himself, and Uzal Knapp, a cavalryman with questioning eyes whose unit also served as Washington's bodyguard. Phillips would handle any heavy work, lethal or otherwise, while Knapp would look after the horses and the boat. Both men wore linen hunting shirts buttoned at the top and with rolled up sleeves that were common on the frontier and had become de facto uniforms of sorts among many enlisted men in an army short of proper military wear. Washington, by contrast, wore a blue wool coat with buff-colored lapels and cuffs with yellow metal buttons gleaming bright as gold. The waistcoat and breeches were a matching buff color with gilt buttons and he wore black riding boots that came to just below the knee.

"Gentlemen, I pray you like boats," said Washington. "You will be crossing the Hudson River to attack Pollepel Island."

Knapp raised his eyebrows as he looked in Phillips direction, who returned a puzzled look. To the best of their knowledge, Pollepel was just a small island in the river, closer to the eastern shore than it was to the middle. More importantly, it was deserted. But a glance around the table made them believe everyone else thought otherwise so they held their tongues.

Maushop eyed the leader of the American forces arrayed against the might of the British Empire with interest. Washington stood a little over six feet tall, he reckoned, and presented a trim figure. He had large hands and feet which Maushop figured counted in his acceptance of Maushop himself. He had a long straight nose well suited for the long face with high cheek bones and pockmarks that told of a childhood bout with smallpox. Maushop could see Washington was not wearing the customary white wig favored by gentlemen. Instead, the general powdered his hair white, tied into a short braid at the back. Blue-grey eyes looked out from beneath heavy brows

"I will speak plainly," said Washington. "The war is winding down and I expect to issue an order in a matter of weeks for the cessation of hostilities that will be a prelude to political negotiations with the enemy. The time is right. The British are losing a war in India and that suits our purpose." Washington paused. "But why are we here? Our army is camped some miles to the south around Verplanck and many have wondered why I have chosen to be headquartered here in Newburgh."

Washington chuckled and Maushop was distracted by the flash of Washington's teeth. Rumor said his dentures were made of wood but Maushop guessed the ones the General now wore were made of ivory.

"I'm told the number of places I've slept is now something of a humorous jest," said Washington. "But I have remained in Newburgh for over a year, the longest I have stayed anywhere. First to assess the possible threat posed by Pollopel Island and then to remain here while a solution presents itself. Yes, the threat is serious and I worried that it might take an army to counter it. But another solution sits in my office waiting our arrival."

Washington paused before continuing. "Prudence suggests some action must be taken. Major, would you be so kind as to continue? The Dutch are perhaps most familiar with the nature of the problem."

"Yes, sir," said Major Goetschius in a low tone. "You will recall that several years ago we attempted to build a barrier across the Hudson from Pollepel Island to the western shore to prevent the British Navy from sailing up the Hudson to attack Albany and divide the nation into two halves. That barrier was never completed but another one was subsequently constructed further south. The reason that first barrier was never completed was because it was destroyed by a whirlpool that confined itself to the destruction of the barrier before disappearing once the nefarious task was completed."

Phillips and Knapp nodded, acknowledging their memory of the event. The barrier had been an iron chain across the river at its narrowest point. Goetschius was skipping over a few details. The destruction of the barrier had occurred during a British attack. Two frigates positioned behind the barrier had burned, set alight by a fast-moving figure that walked on water. Or so the story murmured around campfires said.

"We believe that destruction was caused by a being the Dutch call the Heer of Dunderberg, named for a nearby mountain that overlooks Pollepel and World's End, the deepest part of the river," continued Goetschius. "The Heer of Dunderberg is a legend among the Dutch and is blamed for the sinking of many ships from long before the arrival of the British. Being a religious man, I think he is some class of demon. His nature is unknown but he captains a ship that appears in a mist with a crew of lesser demons and then disappears as quickly as it came. He goes for long periods without activity, punctuated by short bursts of mayhem, ship sinking, and the kidnapping of young women. Sometimes, young men as well. They are never seen again."

"Fuck me," whispered Knapp, realizing the campfire tale was truer than he realized.

"The Heer of Dunderberg, like all of his kind, has an aversion to iron," said Maushop. "He would have believed the iron chain an attempt to imprison him."

Goetschius shrugged. "We believe the destruction of the Pollepel Island barrier signals the beginning of a new cycle of attacks by the Heer of Dunderberg."

"Indeed," interjected Washington. "I have already received intelligence reports about two local disappearances that don't fit with Cowboy raids. Both young ladies, I might add. At best, we have a bestial killer on our hands. At worst, an entity that could jeopardize peace talks with the British in the event this Heer of Dunderberg does something that the British Army misconstrues as an attack on them by us."

"And we are pretty sure the Heer of Dunderberg hates the English just a little more than he hates the Dutch. He doesn't like what they have done with the place," added Goetschius.

Washington eyes took in Phillips and Knapp. "So now you understand what's at stake. Get ready the horses and supplies required for the mission. There will be an additional gentleman joining your party that you will address as the Marquis de Montferrat if necessary. He will be accompanied by his manservant, Roger Zeffort. But please refrain from conversation with them both."

Maushop knew that the Heer of Dunderberg was a procurer for the Unseelie Court but decided that a full explanation of his nature could wait for another time. If they thought the Heer of Dunderberg was a demon that would suffice for the moment. And they weren't exactly mistaken. But it was the other name that formed a tingle in his mind. *"We know that name,"* murmured one The Voices as if waking from slumber.

Washington nodded toward Maushop and Goetschius and they followed him through the rear blue door past an empty room containing numerous desks and chest. Maushop guessed this was where Washington's aides worked, copying orders and dispatches. He could see on rolled up parchment bound with a red tape lying on a side table. Maushop had heard Goetschius complain about red tape when he had difficulty obtaining supplies for his men.

The room must have jogged Washington's memory. "I have signed an order that says Pollepel Island is to be a future military prison. Another Simsbury you can say. That will put the fear into any potential traitors. You can use it to explain your presence there, if required."

"The General has learned a lot about covert affairs." Goetschius whispered beside him. "You will recall Simsbury is the gateway to Hell."

Maushop remembered Goetschius' description of the former copper mine in Connecticut after he had brought some Loyalist prisoners there. A small wooden blockhouse concealed the entrance to an underground prison. At the bottom of a flight of stairs, a grate door made from bolts and bars of iron opened onto a six-foot shaft. At the bottom was another iron grate that led to Hell. Prisoners descended a ladder through a narrow shaft that led to a damp cavern 70 feet underground. The cavern was 165 feet long and varied in width from six to 20 feet. But it was only five feet in height so prisoners were perpetually bent over in the gloomy light from the shaftway, a light just sufficient enough to for prisoners to find their way to bunks lined up against the dingy green walls. Inmates soon developed twitchy eyes from straining to see in the near-darkness and had trouble breathing from the lack of air. The smell alone would weaken a man, said Goetschius. Loyalists would be thrown into Simsbury to rot along with rapists, highwaymen, burglars, and murderers. Disease was a fellow inmate. Few survived Simsbury. Goetschius' description of the place had converted more than one British Loyalist into an American Patriot.

Revolution was a dirty business, Maushop knew. England's biggest mistake was throwing out the rule book that governed war between nations when it came to those the Crown deemed rebels. All rebels were destined for the hangman's noose, said the King. England had brutally quelled rebellions in Scotland and Ireland and Maushop had learned from German sources that the English had lined up Hessian mercenaries for the grim work of repression even before the conflict in the Americas began. The atrocities that came next only served to unite the Americans in their opposition.

Washington turned right into a large room with double windows—another sign of wealth--that was obviously his office. A large desk dominated one corner of the room to the left of the windows. Seated in a chair in front of the desk was a well-dressed man writing with both his hands on separate pieces of paper. The man immediately stopped writing and stood. He was of medium height, looked to be in his mid-forties, but presented himself as a slender, graceful figure. He wore a green wool coat over an embroidered waistcoat that was a lighter shade of green with small diamonds discreetly catching the light from a nearby candle. His brown eyes, as many had noted who had met him, were of a peculiar beauty that defied description. His hair was black as a raven and there was the beginning of a black beard that highlighted his white complexion.

The man slowly smiled, accentuating the dimple on his chin. "Fee fi fo fum. My word. If it isn't the Cornet of Horse."

Maushop was so surprised he didn't immediately notice the man standing in the far corner with a pistol in his hand. Roger Zeffert, no doubt, who offered a slight bow in his direction but otherwise remained silent.

Maushop returned his gaze to the man who addressed him. By some accounts the man in front of him was 500 years old. *"Older,"* said one of The Voices. *"One of the men of old,"* said a second Voice. *"The Count St. Germain."*

"Hearing things?" said the man, tilting his head slightly to the side. "I can see the alchemists in Italy have served you well but I hope your hearing wasn't affected."

"The Count St. Germain. I am surprised to see you here." The Count was well informed. An alchemist in Venice seeking to turn lead into gold diverged on occasion, developing potions that had allowed him to better blend into society by putting into regression some inherited traits like a second row of teeth behind the first and a sixth finger on each hand.

"I am freedom's flame," said the Count with gravity in his voice.

"You gentlemen are already acquainted?" asked Washington, surprised.

There was a long silence while their respective histories ran through each other's minds. The Cornet of Horse had never actually met the Count. Yet, it was plain that the Count St. Germain was familiar with the Cornet of Horse's background although how he had come by that knowledge was a mystery. Everything about the Count, in fact, was mysterious. The man was famous but no one knew when or where he had been born. He had been known by many names, which was not uncommon among European royalty. Some said he was the last of the Medicis of Italy. Others said he was a practitioner of dark arts like alchemy, that he was immortal and that he had been handed the staff of Moses by the prophet himself while in Babylon. The Count was extraordinary wealthy and an accomplished composer. No one had ever seen him eat or drink anything but tea. The list of friends and backers read like a roll call of European notables.

"Casanova, Catherine the Great, King Edward II, Voltaire," said The Voices. *"All friends of the Count. And the Count is connected to the Seelie Court. There is no other way to explain him. If you can bleed him, we will see what color his blood runs."*

The Cornet of Horse ignored The Voices—they tended to be more bloodthirsty than helpful--and reviewed what else he knew of the Count. There was always a bevy of royal lady admirers who never hesitated to rally to the Count's needs. These days, the King of France employed him as a diplomat and certainly as a spy. He was also a Mason and that would make him a fraternal brother of Washington, Benjamin Franklin and other American notables. But why was he here?

"He's new," said the Cornet of Horse in German, knowing that it was one of at least 11 languages the Count St. Germain spoke fluently.

131

"Please. Let's all converse in English," said the Count. "You speak it so much better than you let on." With a wave of a delicate hand from the Count, Zeffert exited the room through another door behind him.

The Cornet of Horse accepted the gesture of good faith and decided to relax a little. The Count noticed. "We are on the same side of this one."

"We most assuredly are," said Washington. "The Count is a long-time friend of the American Revolution, working for our behalf in France in particular. But he has made several trips here to America. In fact, he was instrumental in the design of our flag. And I'm told he galvanized the delegates to sign the Declaration of Independence on July 4th, 1776 just at the moment when their courage was faltering as they considered the death sentence they faced from the King of England. On four occasions, the Count was interrupted by applause."

"My dear General," said the Count. "You give me too much credit."

"Not enough, Count," said Washington. "You left the room before the signers could even learn your name. They think of you now as some visiting professor. But my intelligence agents took notice. I committed to memory one of your remarks: 'Sign!—and not only for yourselves but for all the ages. For that parchment will be the textbook of freedom, the Bible of the Rights of Man forever!' I wish I could have been there."

"You're too kind," said the Count.

The Cornet of Horse was impressed by Washington's zealous endorsement of the Count. Goetschius, meanwhile, looked overwhelmed with emotion. Clearly, he fought for something greater than himself and the Cornet of Horse could feel the same spirit rising within himself, competing with an older sense of mission that had brought him here in the first place.

"And what is the Count's role in this Pollepel Island affair?" said the Cornet of Horse.

"The Count possesses the means to destroy or at least contain the so-called Heer of Dunderberg. I have been waiting here at Newburgh for his arrival," answered Washington.

"We will need special weapons," said the Count.

The Cornet of Horse nodded. "Iron."

"I have brought the necessary weapons and ammunition at my own expense," said the Count. "Your army is short on monies."

Washington sighed. "Yes, the army hasn't been paid in months."

"Be warned," said the Count. "There is a conspiracy building amongst your officers. They mean to move on Congress. Take care of that and we will take care of this matter."

Washington nodded and removed a pair of spectacles from his jacket pocket. "I intend to look into the matter, rest assured." They left him with a small grin on his face.

It was one of those inky black nights when the shoreline vanishes and the world seems divided in two: dark and darker. They floated down the Hudson River in a pair of small bateau, flat-bottomed boats double-ended like an oversized canoe, borrowed from a company of Albany militia. While the bateau could be rigged with a small sail, they had agreed man power was the best way to approach Pollepol Island. Zeffert and Knapp manned the oars while Phillips steered from the rear. A lantern hung from the bow, providing what seemed like an inadequate glow for navigation. The plan was that the first boat would land on a slip of sand that passed for a beach on the north end of the island and secure the site for the arrival of the Count, the Cornet of Horse and Major Goetschius in the second. The men in the first boat carried muskets but their musket balls were special: an iron inner core encased in the customary lead. Their bayonets had been replaced with ones made completely of iron. Likewise, the men in the second boat carried the same special ammunition. The Cornet of Horse had left behind his long rifle but carried his brace of large horse pistols and two long knives with iron blades retrieved from his saddle bag that had been used for this kind of work before. Major Goetschius carried a standard army-issue pistol and a newly-made spear with an iron point. The Count was armed with an exquisitely decorated Queen Anne pistol and carried a satchel with a strap across his chest.

"Lead and steel will have no effect on the enemy we face tonight," explained the Count for everyone's benefit but the Cornet of Horse. "Only iron will do. Remember, the ammunition you have received has a shorter range due to its weight than the lead musket ball and bullets you are used to so don't shoot until you are close."

Major Goetschius had moved to light the lantern on their boat but the Count said it was unnecessary. "Rest assured, Major. I have excellent night vision. I will guide us in if you and your colleague will handle the oars."

Afterward, the Cornet of Horse wondered if the Count knew all along what would happen next. As the first boat drew near to the island, it started moving to the westward as if some current had seized it, pushing it away from the targeted landing. The light from the first boat shifted from being directly ahead to an increasingly dimmer beacon steadily moving away to their right.

"Something's wrong," said Major Goetschius.

"Yes," said the Count. "Something is preventing the other boat from landing. An odd current or something attracted by the light, I fear."

The Count did have extraordinary night vision for they soon felt and heard the boat scraping bottom as they landed on the island.

"You anticipated the first boat not arriving," said the Cornet of Horse. "You used it as a decoy."

"A suspicion," admitted the Count. "Major, please light the lantern and be ready for whatever its light attracts."

Light suddenly pierced the darkness like a bright hole in a dark blanket. Moments later, they heard the sound of many wings flying through air.

"Bats?" asked Major Goetschius.

"Ready your pistols and keep your eyes on the Major," whispered the Count.

Something whisked by them in flight and Major Goetschius exclaimed in pain and the light wavered. "My arm is cut!"

They could be seen now, hovering above the Major, a pair with wings slowly flapping, breathing in the smell of blood like a scented flower. Their wings were bat shaped but larger. They were mostly a black outline and Cornet of Horse could see a tapered head, a long tail like some insect's stinger and four jointed appendages—two at the lower end of the abdomen and another two like arms with a thumb and three fingers with tips like talons.

The Cornet of Horse fired both his pistols simultaneously, hitting the two targets which pulled away slightly with a stroke of their wings as if only mildly perturbed. Then they exploded.

"My night eyes are pretty good too," said the Cornet of Horse.

"I was counting on it," said the Count with amusement in his voice. "I apologize. There is a slight delay in the effectiveness of the ammunition before the iron makes itself manifest."

"What was that?" said the Major with the voice of a brave man facing an unimagined foe.

"Imps," said the Count. "There seems to be only the two. That is to be expected, I suppose, as they mate for life. They hide themselves among the bats."

"Imps?" said the Major. "I have never heard of imps before."

"Well, they are not really from around here," said The Count patiently. "Our foe sometimes uses them as guard dogs. And that may be a good sign."

"How so?" asked the Major.

"We shall see," replied the Count. "It wouldn't do to let our guard down prematurely."

Fortunately, the Major's wound wasn't life threatening but severe enough to make him a one-armed man for the near future until he healed. The Major would have to stay with boat.

"Your light shall be our homeward beacon," said the Count. The Major looked only slightly mollified.

The Count and the Cornet set out toward the interior of the small island along a dirt path.

"I hope you're not thinking of using me as a decoy," said the Cornet of Horse.

"I would never dream of it," said the Count.

"You're thinking the Heer of Dunderberg isn't here at the moment and he left the imps behind as guards."

The night sky was becoming paler now and the shapes of the mountains on each side of the river were becoming apparent. Finding their way became easier with each passing moment.

"Our timing is good," said the Count. "The twilight between night and day is most auspicious."

"What are we looking for?" asked the Cornet of Horse. "A cave?"

"Or a hole in the ground," said the Count, pointing toward one. "It looks big enough for you to squeeze through. After you."

"I just hope it doesn't belong to some bear," said the Cornet of Horse as he reloaded his pistols.

The Count smiled. "You'll let me know, won't you?"

The Cornet of Horse grunted as he dropped himself into the hole. His feet touched bottom and he was surprised to find he could stand upright. While the immediate area was dark, he could see that the passageway ahead was illuminated by glowing stones set in the wall. The path seemed to curve downwards in a spiral. He advanced and heard the Count drop in behind him.

They walked on in silence, slowly and carefully. The Cornet of Horse drew a blade and a pistol while the Count drew his own pistol.

"It looks pretty," said one of The Voices. The Cornet of Horse shook his head a little as if trying to clear cobwebs from his mind. This wasn't a good time for an interior dialogue. The Voice faded away.

"Stay with me," whispered the Count.

He felt like the Count could see inside his head. But he wasn't going to give the Count any satisfaction by acknowledging his words.

They came to a large cavern and as the entered they hear a movement off to the side. The Cornet of Horse whirled, pistol raised.

"Wait," said the Count.

The movement came from a figure lying prone on the floor. It was a young woman with her legs and arms tied up and a gag in her mouth. Her eyes were filled with fear. She had dark hair and wore a dark dress down to her ankles.

The Cornet of Horse approached her and undid her gag, cutting her bonds with his knife.

"Is he here?" asked the Count.

The woman shook her head. Her eyes spoke her mind. She wasn't sure if she was safe or was just exchanging one horror for another.

"You are rescued, my dear," said the Count, putting some tenderness into his voice.

The woman visibly relaxed. Even under these circumstances, thought the Cornet of Horse, the Count had a way with women. The woman glanced at the Cornet of Horse. Clearly, she preferred the Count.

"There is another," whispered the woman. "But he took her."

"Where?"

"I do not know but I fear he will take me there next."

"Yes," agreed the Count. "and you would never come back."

The woman tried to choke back a sob but failed.

"You are very brave," said the Count. "But your trouble is at end. My friend here will lead you back into the world."

"You want me to leave?" asked the Cornet of Horse.

"Yes. We are in a portal. I intend to seal it."

"How?"

The Count patted the satchel. "Time for a bit of alchemy."

The Cornet of Horse nodded. He would be quicker carrying the woman so he picked her up and retreated the way he came. At the entrance, he lifted himself up and then reached back to haul her up. There was more light now and he found his way easily to the boat and Major Goetschius, who was quite surprised to see the Cornet of Horse acting as an escort.

Before they could speak, though, a bright flash of purple light shot upwards into the sky in a tight beam, wavered, and then dissipated into a ghostly form before disappearing. By then, the

Count had appeared, looking a little dirtier in the growing light. The Cornet of Horse noticed that the diamonds embedded in his clothing were no longer there.

"You have sealed his walkway between worlds," asked the Cornet of Horse.

"For now."

"For how long then?"

"It's hard to say, exactly," said the Count. "A few decades, maybe a century. But long enough that the Heer of Dunderberg will not be of immediate concern or a threat."

"Care to share the formula of your success?" asked the Cornet of Horse, even as he knew the answer.

The Count smiled.

"There is a voice inside my head that wants to see the color of your blood."

The Count chortled. "More than one, I'd wager."

"What now?" interrupted Major Goetschius, who sensed a rising tension and sought to calm it.

"This island will need to be continually watched but in a way that doesn't cause alarm," said the Count. "I suggested to General Washington that the creation of a military academy nearby would be a suitable disguise as to its true purpose. I saw a spot on the river called West Point that looked perfect."

The Count looked at the young woman whom they had rescued.

"But in the meantime, I know two of us need a bath!"

The woman blushed. The Cornet of Horse shook his head. The Count would vanish with the bathwater. Washington would see to it.

Chapter Ten

A building with horns on it is a rare thing, even in New York City, and these horns looked like they had been modeled after those belonging to a devil rather than a cow or a goat. The Gershwin Hotel is a solid, 13-story red Beaux Arts building dating to 1903 on 27th Street, but its character changed with the addition of the horns in 1999. Some saw the sculptured horns as flames and other as tongues but since the hotel was bracketed by a sex museum on the corner of Fifth Avenue and a swinger's club closer to Madison Avenue, most people focused on the horny idea.

The Gershwin stood only a few blocks south of the towering art deco Empire State Building, for decades the tallest building in the world and featured in over 250 films, most memorably as the perch for a giant ape in *King Kong*. Despite its proximity to one of New York City's most elegant landmarks, the neighborhood around the hotel was probably the only one in New York that didn't have a fancy upscale moniker—none that stuck, anyway-- like Soho, the East Village, or the Upper West Side.

The Gershwin's largest horns—four of them--were at street level and marked the hotel entrance and windows, protruding like awnings over the sidewalk. Smaller horns with bulbous bases decorated the exteriors of the second and third floor with a center column moving up the middle of the hotel as far as the sixth floor.

At night, white lights lit up the horns like paper lanterns, making the hotel look like some kind of post-modern Chinese bordello, a perhaps not unintentional design by its Swiss owner who lived for many years in China. Despite its slightly Asian character, the hotel catered to a steady, youthful clientele from Europe, attracted by the relatively low prices, funky rooms that often included bunk beds, and a convenient location. Each floor was painted a different color and featured at least one work from major pop artists like Andy Warhol. Ryan Connor called it home.

Connor was the hotel's artist-in-residence, an arrangement reviewed annually that provided Connor with a small office on the third floor amidst the hotel's administrative staff and a room on the 13th floor. Connor sat at a metal desk in his office working through the catering arrangements for the Friday night *Bada Bing* premiere. While the short film festival was his main gig, Ryan had agreed to help the Gershwin become a center of film-related activities that included premieres and parties. The venue for these events would be a rooftop area atop the Gershwin accessible through a door on the 13th floor just down the hall from Ryan's room. Unlike the managers of other tall buildings, the Gershwin owner was not superstitious—the number 13 button was on the elevator's control panel. The roof top area could hold about 50 people, with room for a bar at the back and a screen at the front. A wooden water tower overlooked the roof but most people's eyes were drawn to the pyramidal top of the nearby 700-foot-tall Metropolitan Life building, itself the tallest building in the world from 1909 to 1913. The cupola of the Neo-Renaissance Met Life Building is covered in gold leaf and is lit up at night to look like a crown jewel. The Gershwin roof wasn't an elegant space but it was popular because it offered New Yorkers the rare opportunity for a close-up view of the top of the MetLife Building and the ability to see a large expanse of the night sky.

That's if it doesn't rain. A small ballroom off the lobby would serve as the back-up space. Ryan glanced up at the computer screen on his desk. He subscribed to a service that recorded the number of hits and their point of origin on the film festival's web site. *Over a hundred today.* With luck, those hits would translate into entry fees for the festival. Add two or three corporate sponsors and the festival would turn a profit this year. There was also the potential income from DVD sales. Ryan was fairly certain that Leuven would recommit as one of the sponsors. The Belgian beer maker had made its own short film and was looking for a venue to show it. A Swedish clothing store chain was interested for the same reason. With television audiences routinely skipping over commercials, companies were looking for other ways to reach an audience. And the people who went to film festivals were the right demographic. Young, hip influencers is how marketing types described them.

The short film submission deadline was months away but there was long litany of things to do in the meantime. As in years past, Connor would hold the last screening and announce the winner outdoors in Union Square Park on 14th Street. That meant an annual negotiation with the Department of Parks and the local business development council for permits. There were promotional materials to be developed and the website needed to be updated. Theaters needed to be contacted to make sure they were on board. Some venues would be dropped due to poor turnout and others would be added. Connor split the gate receipts fifty-fifty with the theater owners. Then he would have to log many hours at a video editing suite to put the program together. Still, things were well in hand. *That's good because I'm having trouble focusing today.* Connor was still trying to digest everything Derga had told him. And he still didn't know whether to believe her even though she had been very convincing. *She's not a liar. But she might be nuts.*

Actually, it had been his nuts at risk for a moment. Derga had walked out of the hotel room, leaving Connor standing in the closet. He had collected himself and was just thinking about leaving when the door opened a crack and she slipped back into the room, closing the door quickly behind her..

"I think we should call for room service," she said. "I'm feeling peckish."

"I think you have a lot of explaining to do," said Connor.

"It's complicated," said Derga.

"First of all, what does my comb have to do with the attack on my cousin?"

"That's obvious, isn't it? The original owner traced you and the comb to your cousin's house. Things went badly for her from there."

Connor suddenly felt queasy. That would mean his finding the comb had precipitated the attack on his cousin and the thought sickened him. He wasn't quite ready to accept that.

"OK, let's try a different tack," said Connor. "Let's start with the eye patch. I take it both your eyes are fine."

"One is better than fine. That's why I wear the patch."

"I don't understand."

Derga sighed. "Some years ago on the Isle of Man, I worked in the maternity ward of the local hospital. Basically, I helped deliver babies. One night on my way home, a man on horseback stopped me. Now that might sound unusual but at the time, many of the local farmers still used horses to get around. The man said his wife was in labor and asked if I could come to her aid. When I consented, he swept me up on the back of his horse and we sped off. When we arrived at the house, I was surprised by the size of it and I couldn't remember ever seeing such a large dwelling in the district. And by the looks of things, the owners were very posh. Inside one of the bedrooms lay a woman about to give birth. To make a long story short, she gave birth to a boy with my help. Things got a little odd after that."

"Had you ever seen the man or his wife before?"

"No, but I didn't think that was particularly strange. At that time, everyone was moving across the old borders in Europe in search of a better life."

"So what was strange?"

"The mother asked me to dab some ointment from a jar onto the baby's eyes. She said it was a religious custom among her people and would do no harm. But, she said, I must wash my hands in a basin immediately afterward. I agreed and did as she asked. But before I could wash my hands, my hair fell in front of my face. I instinctively brushed back my hair with my hand and the ointment rubbed into my eye. It stung and I cried out."

"What was the ointment?"

"I never learned what it was. The man who brought me to the house let a yelp of alarm. And when I looked over at him, I could see a crowd of people behind him that I hadn't noticed before. They looked angry and I began to fear for my safety. Suddenly two men stepped forward, one with a shock of red hair that would equal my own and the other with jet-black hair that partially obscured a handsome face. Both wore a style of clothes that were either hopelessly-of-date or at the cutting edge of a revival."

Derga gave a little smile but Connor didn't respond to it so she continued. "The dark-haired man said his name was Robert Kirk. The redheaded man never spoke and I never heard his name mentioned. The two whisked me off away from the mob and kept me safely hidden. I worried that I would be poisoned because they warned me not to drink or eat anything I found in the house but take from their hands only. It was days before they could smuggle me out. During that time, they taught me much. They let me see for myself many things I wouldn't have believed. I came to understand their situation and because I was in their debt, I agreed to become their agent."

"What made you trust Kirk?"

"He was a Reverend."

Connor wasn't so sure that would have been enough for him. Priests were not always what they seemed and the Reverend Kirk seemed to fit the bill. "So you are what the government calls an agent of a foreign power."

Derga laughed. "You make me sound like a spy. I'm more like a lobbyist who's looking after a client's interests."

"And who is the client exactly?"

"They keep a low profile and would like it to stay that way. They don't hand out business cards."

"I'll respect their desire to maintain a low profile."

Derga paused and Connor could see she was debating on whether to confide in him or not. "You may need to know," she said finally. "I look after the interests of the Seelie Court."

"The Seelie Court? Never heard of it."

"It's an alliance..." Derga hesitated. "...of small kingdoms."

"Kingdoms? I didn't think there were that many monarchies left around."

"Yes," said Derga. "There are fewer than there used to be."

"But there are still kingdoms in places like the Middle East. Would they be part of the Seelie Court?"

"No. Of that I'm certain."

"I want to be clear on this. I don't want any part of some radical Arab agenda."

"Understood," said Derga. "You need not worry."

"So what is the Seelie Court's agenda?"

"No agenda," said Derga. "They simply want to keep the peace and maintain the status quo."

"And who would change the status quo?"

"Collectively, they are known as the Unseelie Court, for lack of a better name. Fortunately, organization isn't one of their strong suits. They don't care about the status quo one way or the other."

"What does the Unseelie Court care about?"

"Their own special interests."

"Which are?

Derga shrugged. "It's hard to say. The Unseelie Court is divided amongst many factions. Reverend Kirk has a better understanding of it than I. Their interests rarely results in anything good."

"And you work for Kirk?"

"Yes. He is an advisor of long-standing to the Seelie Court."

"And what all this got to do with your eye patch?"

Derga sighed. "You have a brutal instinct for interrogation."

"It's something I picked up from a journalist friend of mine."

Derga studied Connor for a moment. "I will be frank with you so you will be the same with me. You understand the Seelie Court is a secret alliance?"

Connor nodded.

"This is even more secret. It could cost me my life."

"I understand," said Connor.

"The Seelie Court possesses a…" Derga stopped, searching for the right words. "You would call it a technology that can render an individual invisible. It's a cloak made from metamaterials arranged in layers so it resembles a fishnet. It's called a gwynn. It bends visible light away from an object, making the wearer invisible to observers. It's not completely effective in that sometimes people can spot what seems to be a blue light out of the corners of their eyes. But in practice, it works very well. The ointment that I accidentally rubbed into my eye allows you to see beyond the visible spectrum, thereby counteracting the effects of the gwynn. I can see whoever is wearing a gwynn."

"And I'm guessing they don't like anyone using the ointment."

"Let's say its use is very restricted."

"But you're working for them, so what's the problem?"

"The problem is that only Reverend Kirk knows of my role. If any of the others notice me noticing them, at minimum they'll take my eye out on the spot. More likely, they'll just kill me. My relationship with the Reverend Kirk is not one they would approve of. They would consider my unsupervised activities very dangerous to them. So that's why I wear the patch. It's better not to see them at all."

"Have you considered changing jobs?"

"I don't think of it as a job."

"More like a calling?"

"Yes."

"That Reverend got to you good."

"The stakes are high and the work is vital."

"You know, after listening to you, I'm not sure I'll ever feel alone in a room again," said Connor. "I'm going to become completely paranoid."

"You learn to change directions and close doors behind you very quickly," said Derga. "Remember your Yeats. He knew more than he let on."

Derga reached into her pocket, took out a small, coin-like object and tossed it to him. Connor caught what turned out to be small oval stone, grayish in color but flecked with specks of red. In the middle of the stone was a small hole.

"The hole in the stone was made by flowing water," said Derga. "I can't tell you why it works but if you look through the hole, you'll see things as they truly are. If there is anyone here that shouldn't, you'll see them."

"Then what?"

"Exactly."

Connor put the stone to his eye and whirled around in a 360-degree arc.

"See anything?" asked Derga.

"Clear," said Connor, feeling a little stupid. Not only did he sound like a cop on a TV show, but, in using it, he felt like he was buying into Derga's story. *Guys will run with any story a beautiful woman tells them if it gets them where they want to go.* Connor was trying not to be one of those guys but Derga was hard to resist.

"Good," said Derga. "I'd like to try a little experiment, if you're willing. Do you have the comb with you?"

"I don't live in your world, do I?" Connor took the sock containing the comb out of his pocket and held it out to her.

"I'd rather not touch it, thanks."

"It's really a clean sock."

Derga went over to the nightstand and took an envelope from the top drawer. "Put the comb in the envelope, please."

Connor took the comb out of the sock and stared at it for a moment, not believing all the trouble picking it up in Ireland seemed to be causing. Then again, if he hadn't found the comb, he'd never have met Derga. *Hopefully, that'll turn out to be a good thing.* He put the comb in the envelope and closed it.

"Now tell me exactly where your cousin lives."

"Loughanelton. Calry. Sligo, Ireland."

Derga took out a cellphone and accessed a database. She then wrote a series of numbers on the envelope.

"What are those numbers?" asked Ryan.

"Longtitude and latitude for your cousin's home." Derga moved across the room and maneuvered a small desk so that it came between the two of them. Derga sat on the bed and motioned for Connor to pull up a chair. She placed the envelope on the desk between them and then gripped his left hand.

"This will work best if I am in physical contact with you," said Derga. "A certain aptitude is required. Do you mind?"

"Not at all," said Connor. Her touch was like an electric charge. He was getting goosebumps.

"Focus on the envelope and then tell me if anything comes to mind," instructed Derga.

"Like what?"

"An image. A picture. A shape. Whatever it is."

Connor stared at the envelope. Minutes passed.

"Maybe I'm dense but nothing is coming to mind," Connor said finally.

"That's all right." Derga opened up the desk drawer, pulled out another envelope and put the comb inside it. Then she wrote another set of longitude and latitude numbers on the envelope.

"I don't get it," said Connor.

"It's called remote viewing. The Americans and the Soviets experimented with it during the Cold War. Let's try again. Give me both your hands this time."

Connor grasped Derga's hands and focused on the envelope. It was white, just large enough to hold the comb. Connor concentrated and discovered the envelope seemed to be growing in size. Then Connor began to see what looked like as shape. Connor strained his eyes. It was a face, he realized. A woman's face. She was very pretty with beckoning eyes. But then the face began to dissolve-- even as the eyes held his stare—so there was nothing but a skull. Those eyes…

Connor felt his head snap to the side as Derga yanked his head by the hair, forcing him to break his concentration.

"Jesus!" he yelled.

"Don't try that at home alone," said Derga. "What did you see?"

"A woman. She was young and beautiful then old and ugly until there was nothing but a skull. And those eyes…"

Derga pointed to the envelope. "These numbers are the longitude and latitude for midtown Manhattan. It's as I thought. She's here and she's looking for you."

Connor put the catering invoices into a folder and filed them away into a desk drawer. The encounter with Derga was all he could think about. He needed a sounding board.

Almost as if on cue, the phone rang. Connor glanced at the caller ID number on the phone's display screen and shook his head. It was Straparola. Connor and Straparola were probably among the last straight, single guys in Manhattan that went out together. Most straight guys now forayed in parties of three. Two guys alone were assumed to be a gay couple.

"I was just about to call you," said Connor into the phone.

"You know what time it is. It's 20 minutes past deadline. Which means its time for a cocktail. I'm downstairs in the lobby. Come meet me at the bar."

"Two minutes."

"I'll order one for you."

Connor found Straparola at the hotel bar, a thoroughly modern affair of chrome and glass. Straparola sat on a stool, a tall glass of Leuven pilsner in front of him. He was dressed in his customary attire.

"Do you have any shirts that are not white?" asked Connor in mock seriousness.

"I do but they're being bleached as we speak," said Straparola.

Connor slid into the empty stool next to Straparola.. Another pilsner was on the bar waiting for him.

"May the next bar we drink at being made of wood," said Straparola, raising his glass. "And to Leuven, the great Belgian god of beer."

"Is Leuven a god?

"Must be," said Straparola "They sponsor the film festival. We get free beer. It's like manna from heaven. Remember the cardinal rule of drinking."

"Remind me. There are so many."

"Never let the facts get in the way of a good story."

"Well, I've got a good story for you and the facts are true," said Connor.

"As far as you know," said Straparola. "But continue."

"You know, I can't believe you called when you did. I really need someone to bounce this off of."

"It's all in the ether," said Straparola. "It explains why Edison and Marconi invented the radio at the same time even though they were an ocean apart."

"It's about Derga."

"This woman have a last name?"

Connor paused. "Actually, it never came up."

"I trust other things did? She's hot."

"Very funny. Let me tell you what happened." Connor then filled in Straparola on what had transpired at the hotel. Straparola eyes widened as Connor told his tale. Occasionally, he sipped at his beer but he didn't interrupt until Connor had finished.

Straparola waited a few beats before he spoke. "Weird but interesting. Typical Manhattan chick."

"Seriously."

"OK. Some of this I can speak to," said Straparola. "The invisible cloaking tech is within the realm of possibility. We ran an article about this a few issues ago. It's called a plasmonic cover. Some guys at the University of Pennyslvania developed the notion. If you can prevent light from bouncing off the surface of an object, then the object will appear so small it all but disappears. The plasmonic cover resonates at the same frequencies as the light striking it so they cancel each other out. The metamaterials thing is a different approach out of the University of California at Berkeley. They're using silver and some other metals layered on top of one other and punched through with tiny holes to bend light around an object. Still, I thought it was all just theories. I wasn't aware that anyone had something that actually worked in visible light frequencies."

"What else?"

"She's right about remote viewing," said Straparola. "The Soviets got into it first and then the CIA and the Army started their own remote viewing program at Fort Meade in Maryland. A lot of spook stuff goes on in that place. They handpicked some volunteers with apparent aptitude and then ran the op for two decades before it was shut by Congress. It's hard to tell if anything came of it in the end except there was a story that one guy drew a picture of a Soviet submarine six months before it came out of the barn in Murmansk. I heard that guy moved on to consulting for some Japanese companies. Probably explains the Nineties."

"So it works?"

"Some years ago, a couple of the Fort Meade volunteers surfaced in New Mexico and offered to train people in remote viewing for a fee. I went down to check it out. Most of the people who showed up were hoping remote viewing would help them win the lottery or give them an edge at the tables in Las Vegas. The weird thing was that after three days, these people were doing worse than the law of averages would suggest. I guess you can't remote view numbers."

"So it doesn't work?

"Not when people are self-selected," said Straparola. "Remember, the Army and CIA selected people with a perceived aptitude. And they only found a handful—less than 10—that seemed to have some ability. I interviewed one woman who was trained by the CIA who now uses her skill in missing person cases. Of course, no police department would corroborate that."

"Is there something to it or not?"

"Maybe. The CIA woman seemed to think I had some aptitude so she put me through the drill. I was hoping maybe I'd get a good first-person angle on the story. But it didn't work out. I think there is something to it but it's unreliable. It doesn't turn on like a TV. And it's difficult to interpret because the there is no sense of context or scale. You don't know if something is a bullet or a rocket."

"I'm sorry," said Connor. "I was hoping that if remote viewing was for real, then Derga would be for real as well."

"Yeah, I understand. For all we know, Derga might be one of the people the CIA trained in remote viewing. Or maybe she was trained by one of the original CIA remote viewers," said Straparola. "Let's see what else we can check out. Who did she say she worked for again?"

"Something called the Seelie Court. But it's supposed to be secret."

"OK. But who did she say was her boss or whatever? Some priest or something?"

"That's right. Reverend Robert Kirk."

"Well, let's Google the guy." Straparola lipped open his cellphone and began tapping away with his index finger. A few minutes passed while Connor silently sipped his beer.

"All right," said Straparola. "I think I found our guy."

Straparola didn't continue.

"What?"

"This isn't good. Robert Kirk was a minister in Aberfoyle, Scotland who disappeared shortly after writing a book about fairies called *The Secret Commonwealth*." Straparola looked away for a moment. "It gets weirder."

"Go on."

"Kirk disappeared in 1697."

"Excuse me?"

"You heard right. 1697."

Connor stared at Straparola.

"I think Derga's not taking her meds," said Straparola.

Connor shook his head. "I told you she put a knife to my chin?"

"Yeah. I might think hard about that second date."

"Too late. I invited her to the *Bada Bing* premiere."

"Oh, this is going to be good," said Straparola, with glee in his voice. "I wouldn't miss this for anything. Too bad there isn't a metal detector at the front desk."

Chapter Eleven

She hadn't walked far on the streets of Manhattan before she realized that invisibility was a problem. The streets were too crowded and she was having difficulty dodging oncoming pedestrians oblivious to her presence. One walker, a man in his late forties, stopped, puzzled about brushing up against something that wasn't there. She jumped to one side as another man started to jog after looking at his watch. But she wasn't quick enough to avoid the woman who walked into her back like it was a brick wall and then fell to the pavement with a cry. Two men came to the woman's aid almost immediately. *I'm invisible but I'm attracting too much attention.*

She moved into a deserted alleyway and removed her gwynn, folding it into a tiny square that fit into a small pocket inside her dress. She then stepped out into the flow of pedestrian traffic and proceeded walking. A few young men looked in her direction but didn't stop. *I'm invisible now.*

She hated the seemingly unending concrete of the city— her kind always preferred the unchanging countryside for both practical and aesthetic reasons. The time difference between here and home made the countryside a much safer entry and exit point. The Unseelie Court, she knew, wanted to drive people from rural areas and herd them into cities so that great packets of land would revert to wilderness and remain undisturbed. The campaign was executed quietly so as not to attract attention. Their weapons were disguised natural disasters—floods, fires, avalanches, mud slides—that created deserted or severely depopulated towns and villages whose people fled after what seemed like an impossible run of bad luck. It was slow work but the corralling of people into large population centers was a plan that was paying off. It would be only a matter of time before disease culled these packed-in populations.

She noticed passersby beginning to sniff the air. A sweet, syrupy smell was drifting over the city, a byproduct, she knew, of the incident in the policeman's car. She learned long ago that people would root out and destroy bad, horrid smells. Pleasant smells would be noticed but their memory would quickly fade and there would be little interest in a sustained investigation. It was human nature.

Some instinct or sign—maybe it was just the flight of the pigeons—moved her in a westerly direction toward the only large expanse of green in the city, a space called Central Park according to he letters etched into the stone wall by the entrance. She looked up at a street sign that read "116 Street" and another at a right angle to it that said "Fifth Avenue." She sensed the park was immense, a refuge from the tall buildings that surrounded the park on every side, boxing it in. She half expected the park to be crowded as well but was pleasantly surprised to find the immediate area before her virtually deserted. A small lake spread out in front of her with a low ridge of rock on the opposite shore effectively separating this section of the park off from the rest. A small two-story brick house with an outdoor patio attracted the attention of the few people in the area--an exhibit of some kind was the draw—and she steered away from it. She needed to focus her thoughts and concentrate on the comb. Contact with earth would help and she moved off the path onto the grass and sat down. Checking to see that she was unobserved, she donned her gywnn and disappeared from view.

The sun moved across the sky and the shadows created by the trees deepened as she pointed her mind toward the comb. She was having difficulty pinpointing its location as it seemed to be moving. In general, she sensed it was not too far away, somewhere to the south. It was still in the possession of the one who took it, she knew. With a sigh, she ceased her efforts. The mental noise in this city was overwhelming and prevented her from developing a more precise reading. *The night will be better.* People will be asleep and the target would likely be asleep and stationary as well, making him that much easier to find.

It was then that she noticed the black horse and black carriage trimmed with rose coming her way. It drew alongside her and she leaned backed to enjoy the spectacle of its passing. Unbelievably, the horse stopped and looked straight at her. And then so did the driver, a curious-looking individual with a bald head and eyebrows that seemed to go from ear to ear. He wore black clothes that she recognized as those typical of a livery driver. He looked to be on the short side as well.

"You'd better get in," said the driver.

She didn't reply. There was no possibility he could be talking to her.

"Yes, I'm talking to you," said the driver. "Get in but leave your gywnn on. It will look better if the carriage looks empty. I want people to think I'm done for the day."

"Who are you?"

"The local transporter. Hop in. You need to be off the street. That gywnn isn't the safe trick it used to be. Some cop with a thermal imager will come by and pick you up on his screen and then start wondering why he can't see you. That's how I found you, after all."

The driver pulled out what looked like a long pistol with a square view viewfinder mounted on top and then quickly put it away. She walked over to the carriage and climbed in, the slight movement of the carriage telling the driver she was aboard.

"Yes, it's not as easy for you folks to move about as it used to be," said the driver. "And it's going to get worse. MEDEA has launched a satellite that might make it easier to find you. Word is that it's got something called a Kaluza-Klein sensor on board."

She shuddered at the mention of MEDEA. She had never encountered one of the dreaded hunters but she knew they were relentless once they were on the scent.

"What's a Kaluza-Klein sensor?"

"It spots what they call Kaluza-Klein or KK particles. They're the evidence of your coming and going between here and there." The driver laughed. "Think of it as a pixie dust spotter."

"Technology will be the death of us," she replied. "You don't speak the old tongue?"

"I don't. Not ever. I want anyone who overhears me to think I'm a crazy bastard who didn't take his meds. Or just someone talking on a hands-free cellphone."

"How did you know I was here?"

"I didn't. That sweet, syrupy smell is all over Manhattan and then I heard about a possible terrorist incident on the Triboro Bridge. So I guessed someone was in transit and botching the job. I figured whoever it was would hole up in Central Park eventually. Your lot always heads for a park when they need to hide and this is the biggest one."

"Good guess."

"That's the trouble. Usually I know who is coming and going because I'm the one taking them." The driver turned in his seat and looked in her direction. "I suspect your little excursion is—shall we say—unauthorized?"

She didn't reply. The truth of her situation was obvious.

"Well, that happens from time to time," said the driver. "So we'll use no names if you don't mind. Who rules where you're from?

"Finbar and Nuala."

"The West of Ireland. You're a long way from home," said the driver. "The vexing question is how long do you intend to stay? I don't do overnights, generally. Most that come through here leave as quickly as they can. They're not fans of big cities."

"I've lost something and I'll only stay until I get it back."

"Really?" said the driver. "Now what would be so precious? You've got fewer possessions than a monk sworn to poverty."

She said nothing, knowing that he would come to it.

"Oh, of course," he said after a few moments. "You've lost your comb somehow and you can't get home without it. Do you know where it is?"

"Only generally. I'm having difficulty focusing."

"A common complaint of visitors to the big city. I might be able to make a few inquiries, assuming whoever has it tries to sell it. The world of buyers and sellers for such an item is a small one."

The driver took out a cellphone and dialed a number. He talked softly for a few minutes but she couldn't make out the words.

"I've asked an acquaintance to look into it," he said after hanging up. "Now the question is what to do with you."

They rode in silence toward the south end of the park, passing other rigs whose drivers nodded in recognition.

"Done for the day, are you?" shouted one wearing a top hat.

Her driver nodded and kept going, urging the horse into a trot. A few people raised their hands, bidding him to stop for passengers but the driver shook his head, not slowing until the carriage exited the park on Central Park South and Seventh Avenue.

"Here we go, right under the noses of the nation's top news editors. We'd be in trouble if they ever left their desks."

She remained silent, not sure if his remark was meant to elicit a response. She didn't know whom he was talking about and didn't really want to know. The traffic noise was picking up and would drown out any reply, anyway.

They went three blocks south along Seventh Avenue, going with the flow of cars coming off Columbus Circle and then turned west. They passed a few bars and restaurants, each with patrons smoking cigarettes outside the door, sending small clouds of white smoke into the atmosphere. Some smiled as the horse and carriage went by but the driver paid them no heed. She leaned back in the carriage and watched the passing parade of people in what was a rare moment of leisurely observation. Tall ones, short ones, fat ones, skinny ones, poor ones, rich ones—it was an endless stream. Most of them seemed totally self-absorbed, especially the well-dressed ones. *They believe themselves to be masters of the world. They think they can see everything that goes on in their universe but they know so little about it. But no one wants to set them right.*

"Do you know Duke Ellington?" she asked.

"He's dead. But he was great," said the driver. "Jazz fan?"

She wasn't sure what jazz was so she didn't reply. But knowing Duke Ellington was dead made her sad somehow. Greatness was a thing not to be missed. After a while, she saw a wide blue band in the distance with ships docked along its near shore. One ship had flat deck with planes and helicopters parked on it while the others looked the cruise ships she had seen plying the coast of Ireland.

"The Hudson River, in case you're wondering," said the driver. "That's an old aircraft carrier, the *Intrepid*, that's been turned into a museum. It's just a tourist attraction now."

160

The weapons of war. She had keened for those who had died in battle until there was none left. A steady stream of people came off the imposing carrier and she marveled at their fascination with war. She knew it wasn't possible that any of them had experienced grief the way she had. *So much for so long.*

They were almost to last corner when the driver took out a small device and pressed the small button on it. To her left, a garage door opened. She saw that the garage door served as the entrance to a narrow two-story building she wouldn't have noticed otherwise and which was jammed between two much larger ones. The second floor featured two windows that were blacked over. A yellow taxi was parked outside. The black horse swung the carriage into the opening and the garage door closed behind them with a clang. Lights came on automatically and she saw that the lower floor was a stable.

"You can take off your gwynn," said the driver. "I'd like to see whom I'm dealing with."

"Tell me," she said as she became visible. "Are you of the Seelie Court?"

"I'm strictly a service provider so I'm apolitical," said the driver, eyeing her appreciatively. "But I may have to introduce you to someone who's not. At the moment, this is his town and you're screwing things up. After that little stunt on the bridge, people are going to be looking for you. Cops. Homeland Security. Hunters maybe. He has his own agenda and doesn't like extra attention, if you know what I mean."

"I'm not interested in meeting anyone," she said. "I'm here to find my comb and that's all."

"He might be able to help you with that. But there might be a price to pay. I know he'll fancy that gwynn of yours. The ones made by the Unseelie Court seem to be defective of late. A few are emitting blue light when they are not supposed to. Some of them are so bad, people are starting to see the outlines of their wearers even in the dark. Internet chat rooms are starting to call them the Shadow People. It's making the transportation business much more difficult. Of course, that allows me to raise my rates so it's not all bad.

"Who is he?

"The Heer of Dunderberg."

"I thought you said no names."

"So what are you? The queen of trick questions."

"You're starting to annoy me," she said, taking a step toward him. Her hands were beginning to heat up.

The driver backed up a step. "Don't get wise with me, girlie. I'm more dangerous than I look."

"That's what he tells all the girls," said a voice behind her.

Chapter Twelve

L t. Clemente Gomez de Suarez walked onto the campus of Columbia University from the Broadway side through an entrance framed by Havemeyer Hall and the Mathematics Building. Lt. Gomez chuckled to himself as he watched a number of students walk by, their heads presumably full of calculus and higher geometry. The untaught math of Manhattan was the higher the street number, the worse the neighborhood was likely to be, particularly if the street has triple digits. Lt. Gomez figured he was at about 116th Street but Columbia University was on its own Bell Curve. On the eastern side of the campus, just past Amsterdam Avenue, stood a narrow, 25-block-long park called Morningside Heights that acted as a buffer and social rampart against the poorer, black and Hispanic neighborhoods of Harlem beyond, although, granted, gentrification was making inroads into all kinds of formerly tough neighborhoods. Academic life on the Heights was still not without its problems, he knew. In this semester alone, two students had committed suicide, their deaths creating a media storm in the tabloids. *Not my case, thank God.*

Lt. Gomez, a graduate of New York Univerity and the John Jay Criminal Justice College in the west sixties, was a little surprised to be here himself. It was a school he would never even have thought to aspire to. Not that he bore Columbia University a grudge, but he always figured he would be visiting Columbia the country before he ever set foot in Columbia the university. A couple of undergrads glanced after him as he walked, making him for a cop of some sort. *Of course, Columbia the country and Columbia the university may just be different ends of the same drug pipeline.*

Lt. Gomez walked on and as he came to the middle of the campus, most of the students walking in his direction veered right toward the Low Memorial Library. Lt. Gomez turned left toward the Uris Building, an unimpressive structure that aspired to grandeur with a flight of eight stairs stretched sideways beyond any utilitarian value so that it reached from one side of the building to the other. Lt. Gomez walked up a narrow, central section marked off by handrails and through a bank-style revolving door.

The bland exterior of the Uris Building did not prepare him for the interesting interior. He walked through the receiving foyer and into a circular hall with an outer ring that had periodic gaps in the walls for wide, marble staircases that led to the upper floors. Not a bad place to wait for…what's her name?

Lt. Gomez fished into the pocket of his sports coat for his little black notebook. *Derga Learmont.* Mentally, he chastised himself for forgetting such a detail but he knew what was distracting him. Lt. Gomez had a new nickname and he didn't like it one bit. A cloud of something that tasted like some kind of sweet syrup had wafted its way over Manhattan and the woman that had escaped from his custody was the cause of it. Now his colleagues were calling him "Sweets" when they thought he was just out of earshot and it pissed him off. He could have dealt with an ethnic slur better— something like the "The Spic" or "Marichon." But "Sweets" stung him to his macho core.

Lt. Gomez forced himself to focus on the task at hand. Every cop in the city was looking for the woman from the bridge. But until she was spotted, he might as well continue his other investigations and Derga Learmont was on his list of things to do. Lt. Gomez didn't know what business Derga Learmont had in the

Uris building but the professor had been sure she would be here at this time. You'll know her by her red hair and the eyepatch, the professor had said. *That'll certainly narrow the field.*

As if on cue, a woman with red hair that fluttered like a flag in a breeze descended from the nearest marble staircase. She wore a form-fitting red pants suit and red shoes but his eye sought out the eyepatch and to his surprise, he saw that it was red as well. *El mujer de la rosa. Professional and flamboyant. An interesting combination.*

Lt. Gomez put himself on an interception course and pulled out his badge. The badge stopped the woman in her tracks and she waited for him to approach.

"Ms. Derga Learmont?"

"Yes."

A very cool lady. No reaction to the badge at all. "Lt. Clemente Gomez de Suarez, Department of Homeland Security. Immigration and Customs Enforcement."

"Hello, Iceman."

Lt. Gomes smiled. *Better than "sweets" anyway.*

"May I help you?"

"I hope so," said Lt. Gomez. "We're looking into the possibility that an ancient Irish artifact may have been brought into the country illegally."

"Has the Irish government filed a complaint?"

"No," admitted Lt. Gomez. *I wonder what happened to her eye.*

"Then how could you possibly know what you're looking for?"

"We're working from a tip, Ms. Learmont. Our understanding is that you may have met the man who has this artifact."

"Really?"

"Yes. You may have met him at a reception at the Museum of Modern Art at the Temple of Dendur?"

"My, it sounds like you were there."

"I'd love to been invited but I don't usually make museum guest lists."

"Don't tell me you're looking for the next Marion True."

"Perhaps." Marion True was an antiquities curator at the J. Paul Getty Museum in Los Angeles who had been indicted in Italy on smuggling charges. The case was complex and exposed the dubious methods and pedigrees surrounding some antiquities acquisitions. However, many museum people thought True had been unfairly victimized by headline-hungry prosecutors. The net effect, however, had been a chill in the relationship between museum staffers and authorities worldwide.

"You met someone that night who showed you an Irish artifact?" continued Lt. Gomez.

"Yes. But I couldn't vouch for its authenticity. I only saw it for a moment."

"Could you describe it for me?"

"It was a silver comb about a foot long and embossed with jewels in the handle."

"Good description."

"Thank you."

"Do you remember the name of the man who showed it to you?"

"He may have mentioned it but I don't recall. Frankly, Iceman. I thought it was a prop. You wouldn't believe the lengths some guys go to meet me."

I might. "So, you don't think the comb was of any value?"

"It would be hard to say without a close examination. For all I know, it belonged to his old Irish grandmother."

"You think the man was Irish?"

"Just a guess."

"Did he have an accent?"

"I'm not a linguist."

"Did this man say where he lived or where his place of business was?"

"No. But he's not in the museum community, if that's what you mean. I mean, he carried the comb in a sock, for crying out loud."

"A sock?"

"Yes. It was ridiculous. You can see why I didn't pay him much attention."

"Yes. Perhaps you are correct and there is nothing of value at "That would be my assessment."

"Your professional assessment?" Her hesitation was only momentary but he noticed it.

"Yes."

"Very well. Ms. Learmont. "Thank you for your cooperation."

"Good luck, Iceman."

"May I ask you one last question? I apologize in advance. You don't have to answer it. How did you lose your eye? It's a terrible thing to have had happened."

She hesitated. "A domestic accident."

Lt. Gomez watched her walk away. *She is hiding something. She remembers some details vividly and forgets others completely. She knows more about the man with the sock than she admits.*

Lt. Gomez sighed. *Every rose has its thorns*. He would put a tail on her.

The Cornet of Horse was like an electronic shadow that monitored all communications involving Lt. Gomez, who, the Cornet of Horse surmised, would be like a dog on a bone tracking down the woman from the Triboro Bridge. The Cornet of Horse still wasn't sure that this unknown woman was within MEDEA's purview of operations but his instinct told him it was. And now there was this new report on Derga Learmont. It couldn't be just a coincidence. But it was clear the name meant nothing to Lt. Gomez.

Thomas of Ercildoune. He went with the royal bitch of his own accord.

"Bitter, bitter," said the Cornet of Horse aloud.

True Thomas, some called him, but that was a corruption of another name. *Druid Thomas*. He was a seer, who delivered his prophecies in verse. *Thomas the Rhymer*.

The kingdom of Strathclyde had been his home until he left to marry the queen of another realm. That had been in the 13th century.

And now eight centuries later, his surname, Learmont, reappears in connection with an ancient Irish artifact, a comb, according to the report. But was there a connection to the woman that had bedeviled Lt. Gomez? *She's a woman of the deenee shee.* A pause. *Maybe.* The Voices were divided. *Track Learmont!* The Cornet of Horse winced.

No, go after theother two first.

They are deenee shee. There is no doubt.

Be sure. Remember the compact with the sorcerer Pope!

The Voices hurt his head when they were not in accord. But the last voice was right. The ancient compact with the sorcerer Pope must be observed.

168

The Cornet of Horse tapped a few keys on his laptop computer. Unfortunately, there was no picture available of Derga Learmont. Lt. Gomez, however, had assigned one of his men to tail her.

Who is Gomez? Is he a potential ally?

The Cornet of Horse accessed the Department of Homeland Security personnel files and reviewed the jacket on Lt. Clemente Gomez de Suarez. Originally from Cuba, he noted. Divorced. Ex-wife and two children live in Miami. His home address looked as if it was in Spanish Harlem. Arrived in the U.S. as a teenager when he defected from a Cuban art tour in New York. Once on American soil, he was granted U.S. citizenship, an anti-communist policy designed to rankle the Castro brothers who ruled Cuba.

Probably ready to invade Cuba if the opportunity presents itself. He had done some anti-drug undercover work in Latin America and then was assigned to immigration. He participated in some raids to round up illegal aliens but then transferred to a unit that dealt with the recovery of stolen art and ancient artifacts. But political pressure to get tough on immigration had put him back in the field again, at least on a part-time basis, looking for illegals to deport. *Funny, if it wasn't for the need of the U.S. government to needle Fidel and Raul Castro, Lt. Gomez would have been an illegal as well. He hit the illegal alien jackpot.*

The Cornet of Horse read through the lieutenant's report a second time. Derga Learmont. Red hair and a matching eyepatch, he noticed. For the moment, he would let the lieutenant do his work for him. *She'll be easy to find.*

Chapter Thirteen

Ryan Connor walked into the Gershwin Hotel after a glass of Pernod on the rocks and a quick meal around the corner at a Vietnamese restaurant that offered 134 entrees. Tonight, he had sampled the tom hap le ve otherwise known as jumbo shrimp sautéed with beer. Connor had never been to Vietnam but he looked upon his restaurant forays as a vacation of sorts and he viewed the each item on the menu as a traveler would view an itinerary. So, far the lettuce wraps were his favorite destination while the frog legs with curry sauce had been his least.

The glass doors of the hotel closed behind him as he stopped at the front desk to check for messages. Out of the corner of his eye, he noted a yellow taxi parked a few feet down from the front entrance although the driver didn't seem to be around. That was odd.

"And you are?" The model-thin brunette behind the desk was new and from her attitude, Connor guessed her last job was working the door at some velvet-rope nightclub or restaurant.

"Ryan Connor, artist-in-residence. I'm here everyday. And you are?" Connor stretched out the query. "Tell me it's not Buffy."

"Lisa," said a female voice behind him. Connor turned to find an attractive blonde wearing a shade of red lipstick that made you shift focus from her blue eyes to her lips, a focus that then slipped even further downward into a plunging décolletage seemingly barely contained by the low neckline of a blue blouse.

"I'm Seventina," said the blonde, extending her hand while her chest moved out of the way.

"Not Lisa," said Connor, lightly shaking the offered hand. Silky smooth and warm.

"No, she's Lisa," said Seventina, nodding toward the woman behind the front desk. "We met earlier when I checked in. I'll be staying here the next six weeks or so."

"That's nice," said Connor.

"Oh, it's wonderful," said Seventina. "This is my first time in New York. You're Ryan Connor, the artist in residence."

"Yes. But how did you know? I don't think I'm very famous."

"You're not," she replied with a small laugh. "Urs asked me to keep an eye out for you. He's so sweet. He rescued me from the clutches of this short, funny looking man with no hair. But he had these eyebrows that looked connected. Do you know that look? Not my type at all. Definitely not the One, if you know what I mean. Well, maybe you don't. It's a girl thing. Anyway, Urs spirited him away to some private poker game upstairs. That sounds like a guy thing. He told me what you look liked—it was a very accurate description—and said I should bring you up to Suite 403 when you came back from Nam. I know that's far away so I was worried that you might be awhile but Urs said you'd be along any minute and he was right. You didn't bring any luggage?"

"It's coming later," Connor deadpanned, figuring it would be easier to just play along. Urs had taken to hosting a monthly poker game and he would often shanghai hotel guests as players. Connor had been drafted as a regular, an unspoken condition of his appointment as artist in residence.

Seventina intertwined her arm into his and moved them both toward the elevator. "My father married my mother when she was seventeen and didn't care who knew. Neither did my mother. That's how I got my name. Everyone always asks so I thought I'd get it outof the way up front. That okay with you?"

"At least your parents weren't related," said Connor.

"Did I say that?" Seventina smiled. "Just kidding. It was a small town, though."

She is sharper than she lets on. "What brings you to New York."

The elevator arrived and they squeezed into its narrow confines and Seventina pressed the button for the fourth floor. "I'm an air hostess for a private airline. Small jets for people with big money. I'll be working out of New York for a while."

"Here we are," announced Seventina. They walked down the corridor to Room 403 and Seventina knocked as they entered.

"Hey, look what the pussy dragged in," said Urs with a smile. "Gentlemen, this is Seventina."

Connor rolled his eyes. Urs was getting a divorce and was trying to be one of the guys again. The poker night was part of his remedial training. That's how he explained it, anyway. Tonight, he wore a red cowboy shirt with white cuffs and a pair of jeans. Urs sometimes overdid the regular guy bit. Connor'secret fear was that Urs would start wearing Hawaiian shirts.

Connor looked around the room. Urs had removed the beds and installed a large, round table with chairs in its place. A bar was pressed into one corner next to a credenza piled with snacks. Straparola was seated to the right of Urs. Anthony Immediato, his contact for the *Bada Bing* premiere sat to Urs's left. The few strands on Immediato's head got ruffled if anyone called him "Tony" because he thought it sounded too downmarket. Next to Immediato sat one of his bulky associates, a man with black, slicked-back hair and known to Connor only as Carmine. Both men were dressed in dark suits. Connor guessed Carmine was the *bada boom*, if things ever came to that. Next to Carmine was a player Connor didn't know, the man with the connected eyebrows. This crowd would soon be asking Seventina for lap dances if she stayed.

Straparola must have read his mind because he rose to his feet. "Connor, play my cards, will ya?" Without waiting for a reply, he escorted Seventina back out into the hall and closed the door behind him.

"He's in love," said Urs.

"She looks older than 17," said Carmine.

"Connor, this is Dwerg, a guest of the Gershwin. A Dutchman a long time ago, he says, but a New Yorker for years. He's in the transportation business. Dwerg, Ryan Connor is the hotel's artist in residence."

"Goedenavond," said Dwerg.

"Likewise," said Connor, guessing Dwerg was the driver of the parked taxi outside the hotel. Most taxis were kept rolling all the time so Connor figured Dwerg must be the owner and likely owned a few if one could afford to be idle. He could see why Seventina didn't think he was the One. The man was a short dome-head bordering on dwarf with the worst case of connected eyebrows he'd ever seen. Connor guessed Dwerg was local, more or less, but must have booked a room for the night. Nothing unusual there but word of the game must be getting around.

"What's the game?"

"Draw poker," said Immediato. "Jacks or better. Progression. Buck ante. It's Carmine's deal."

Connor nodded. Something in Immediato's voice told him the game was kept simple for Carmine's benefit. Connor also knew this was just a warm-up period. The stakes would be higher later in the evening when new players appeared. That's when Connor would yield his chair. Carmine too, no doubt. Connor fished a few singles and a $20 bill out of his pocket and exchanged the money for poker chips. Connor threw a chip into the center of the table along with the others and Carmine dealt the cards.

"I hear you're just back from Ireland," said Immediato. "Do they play cards over there?"

"They do," said Connor. *"He so bewitched the cards under his thumb*
That all but the one card became
A pack of hounds and not a pack of cards,
And that he changed into a hare."

"Fucking Yeats again," said Urs, familiar with Connor's obsession.

"That would have been some poker game," said Immediato.

"It was probably a game of 25," said Connor.

"Never heard of it," said Immediato.

"I have," said Dwerg. "It's a trump game, with the five of the trump suit being highest, and then the ace."

"Followed by the queen of hearts," said Connor.

"Each trick is worth five points," continued Dwerg. "The first one to 25 wins the pot."

"Not much of a betting game," said Urs.

"The bet is the bet," said Dwerg.

"Sounds tricky," said Carmine as he finished dealing five cards to each player.

"The main problem with cards is that the card player always seems to lose the girl in the end," said Dwerg.

174

"Anyone here got a woman to lose?" asked Urs, prompting general laughter.

"See what I mean?" said Dwerg.

"We're working on it," said Immediato. "Who's got openers?"

Everyone shook their head and folded their cards. No one had a pair of jacks. They all tossed another chip on the pile as Carmine gathered the cards and shuffled.

"You bring any of that Irish whisky back with you?" said Immediato.

"No," said Connor. "I found something more interesting, maybe." Connor reached into his jacket pocket, a move that seemed to alarm Carmine and he dropped his cards. Connor slowly pulled the sock from his pocket, removed the comb, and placed it on the table in front of him.

Carmine glanced at the comb, picked up the cards and resumed dealing.

Immediato leaned over for a closer inspection. "Very nice. What do you think, Dwerg?"

"I know little of such things," said Dwerg.

"I thought you said you were in the moving business," said Immediato. He looked at Connor. "You looking to move it?"

"Maybe," said Connor "How much do you think its worth?"

"Hard to say," said Immediato. "If it's real old, you might get a few grand from a collector. Of course, the feds are all over that kind of stuff since the fuckup at the Baghdad Museum."

"I still can't believe the Iraqis looted their own museum," said Urs.

"I couldn't believe it either," said Immediato. "A lot of that stuff was on order. The inventory was no secret."

"Queens or better," said Carmine, finishing the deal.

"Connor, I'll ask around," said Immediato. "A finder's fee applies, of course."

"Of course," said Connor, putting the comb away as they all looked at their cards.

"Who's got openers?"

"I do," said Immediato and threw a five-dollar chip into the pot. Everyone followed suit and then discarded the two or three cards they deemed worthless. Carmine dealt the appropriate number of cards to each player.

"So who's got the Baghdad stuff?" asked Urs.

"I wouldn't know," said Immediato, perhaps a shade too quickly. "So Connor, we all set for tomorrow night? Some people think it's a big deal, you know what I mean? And don't forget the expresso and the anisette."

"I drink it the same way. Everything's cool," said Connor.

"There's a film premiere tomorrow night here at the Gershwin," said Urs for Dwerg's benefit. "You should come by if you're not busy."

"Thank you for the invitation," said Dwerg.

"Since when are you a Sicilian, Connor?" said Immediato, pushing another five-dollar chip into the pot. Carmine folded but no one else backed down. "My bet."

"Call," said Urs.

"Kings up jacks," said Immediato, laying his cards on the table.

"Three sixes," said Dwerg, as he put one card down at a time.

"Beats me," said Urs, putting his cards face down.

"Trip sevens," said Connor and laid the three sevens down apart from the other two cards.

"The Quiet Man wins," said Carmine to Connor's astonishment. Connor didn't think Carmine capable of a cultural reference, no matter how lame.

"Carmine! You've seen that movie?" asked Immediato. "You watching fucking mick flicks now? No offense, Connor."

"None taken."

"Hey, it's a John Wayne movie," said Carmine. "It's not my fault there's micks in it."

"Hell is an Irish bar, Carmine. Remember that," said Immediato. Obviously, a *Sopranos* fan.

"What's your favorite John Wayne film?" asked Connor.

"I like them all, especially the Westerns, except the ones where he gets killed in the end. They suck," said Carmine.

"John Wayne's real name was Marion something, wasn't it?" asked Urs.

"You looking to get hurt?" asked Carmine. "That's just a nasty rumor."

"No, of course not," said Urs. "I didn't mean anything."

"Stop it, Carmine," said Immediato. "Carmine loves John Wayne. Be warned. Ante up. Sorry, Urs. Carmine's got this thing about John Wayne. It's like a religion or something."

"I would have guessed Marlon Brando," said Connor.

"I should be so lucky," laughed Immediato, knowing full well that Connor was referring to Brando in his role as Don Corleone in *The Godfather*. "You know, they got a Corleone social club up in Yonkers. I don't now if those guys are just stupid or if they have brass balls because they own the city. We shot some scenes for *Bada Bing* up there. We had to invite a few of the Yonkers gavones as a way of saying *grazie*."

"Perhaps you should explain to Dwerg where Yonkers is?" asked Urs.

"North. Just over the Bronx city line," said Immediatio. "Fourth largest city in the state. No one in Manhattan knows it exists."

"I know Yonkers," said Dwerg. "And Spuyten Duyvil, the Bronx, Harlem, Gansevoort, Staten Island, all the old Dutch places when the city was New Netherlands."

There was a knock at the door and two men in polo shirts, numbers on their sleeves, walked in. New players. They were followed by Straparola, wearing a big smile on his face.

"Connor, cash out. There a beautiful babe downstairs asking for you."

"Really?"

"Yeah, really. I could hardly believe it myself. And she's got red hair. Seventina is keeping her company but we better hurry down there before every guy in the hotel hits on them."

Derga.

Chapter Fourteen

Derga! The sight of her made Connor wonder if he was falling for a woman who was out of her mind. It was not a thought he cared to entertain completely sober.

"Let's have a drink," he said, placing his arm around her waist and steering her toward the Gershwin's bar. Straparola threw him a nod from a nearby table where he sat with Seventina but otherwise did not attempt to join them. Connor was not surprised when Derga ordered a glass of merlot. It was a red drink after all and it matched the red cotton sweater and claret-colored jeans she wore. The red-eye patch was a constant he was learning to ignore. *She probably drinks cranberry juice in the morning. I should be so lucky to find out.*

"A Pernod and water, thanks," said Connor to the barman.

"Pernod?" asked Derga. "That's French, isn't it? Have you been to Paris?"

"Once," replied Connor. "But I actually developed a taste for it before that. I used to write reviews of new video releases for a magazine that no longer exists and paid horribly. There was this French black& white movie made in 1965 called *The 317ᵗʰ Platoon* and directed by Pierre Schoendoerffer. It's about the French experience in Vietnam before the U.S. involvement there. Four French soldiers and a band of Laotians are ordered to retreat from a remote mountain base following the fall of Dien Bien Phu to the Communists. Among the few essential supplies they carry into the jungle is an icebox of Pernod that takes four guys to carry. I figured any drink worth that much trouble is worth trying."

"Dien Bien Phu?" said Derga. "I'm afraid I'm not familiar with it."

"It was a battle back in the 1950s where the French lost their colony and it is the reason the French distrust Americans."

"I don't understand."

"After World War II, the U.S. told the French they had no need for bombers as the U.S. would come to their aid if their ally ever needed that kind of air support. Fast forward a few years to Dien Bien Phu where the only weapon that could have held back the Viet Cong horde was bombers. The French asked for the bombers but the U.S. didn't keep its promise."

"And they still hold a grudge?"

"Yeah, well, it was a big blow to national pride. To make matters worse, among the 10,000 prisoners taken at Dien Bien Phu were a lot of Algerians who eventually returned home to start their own revolution against French rule. That conflict divided France, led to years of terrorist attacks on French soil and a presidential assassination plot. From the French perspective, all those years of bloodshed would have been avoided if the Americans had kept their promise at Dien Bien Phu. That's how I met Straparola."

"I'm not following you."

Connor smiled. "I advanced my theory regarding the decline of Franco-American relations at a Francois Truffaut Film Retrospective at the Angelica Theater downtown. Straparola was there trying to pick up French women. He said I was full of crepe so to speak but he liked the fact it was pretty original crepe. We've been friends ever since."

Derga chuckled. "I'll have to see this film sometime."

"Sorry, I'm a bit of a history buff. The director, Schoendoerfffer, was at Dien Bien Phu. It was a real turning point."

Derga face lost its smile and she took a sip of wine. "We may have reached a turningpoint as well."

"Not quite," said Connor. "I need to know one thing before we get there."

"Yes?"

"What's your last name?"

Derga laughed. It was a deep, throaty, sexy laugh that sprinkled him with the promise of intimacy. "My apologies. It's Learmont. Derga Learmont."

"Ryan Connor," said Connor in mock seriousness. "Now that's what I call a turning point."

"Seriously, though." Derga then told Connor of her encounter with Lt. Gomez, the Iceman.

"It sounds like you put him off the scent," said Connor, when she had finished.

"No. I blew it," said Derga. "I knew too much about something I claimed to know nothing about. That's not the worst of it, though."

"No?"

"The Iceman will file a report. I'm worried that it will attract attention." Derga's eyes left Connor's face and she stared blindly off into the distance.

Connor touched her hand. "Hey, stay with me. Whose attention?"

"Medea." The word was almost a whisper.

"Who's Medea?" asked Connor. "Wait, wait. I know. Some villainness in that film about Jason and the Argonauts, wasn't she?"

Connor smiled but Derga just stared back at him as if he was mad.

"C'mon," said Connor. "Tell me. Turning point, remember?"

Derga hesitated and Connor raised his eyebrows in encouragement. When she spoke next, her voice was low and Connor had to lean forward to hear her. "Medea has ties to certain elements within the intelligence community. Medea will learn of my interview with Lt. Gomez and send the Nephilim."

"OK. Back up," said Connor, raising both his hands. "Why would anyone other than Gomez be interested in you?"

"Let's just say the name Learmont is known to Medea from past associations," said Derga. "When my name is linked to the artifact you so blithely carry around in a sock, it will arouse Medea's interest."

"Are you wanted for any crime?" asked Connor.

"What?" asked Derga in surprise. "No. Of course not."

"So there is no real reason for you to fear Medea—whoever that really is--or the Iceman," said Connor. "The worst that is going on here is that Customs will slap me with a fine and take away my old comb."

Derga stared at Connor. "You're not getting this. I'm worried about you. This could be much more serious than a fine."

"And these other guys? What did you call them? The Nephilim?"

"Yes."

"They are not really in the picture either, are they?"

Derga waited a beat before replying. "You may know your Yeats but you've neglected your Bible."

"My Bible?"

"Yes. C'mon. Take me to your room now," said Derga. "This is a hotel. There should be a Bible in your room."

"Ah, yeah. There was one in the drawer when I moved in. I guess it's still there." *I hope.*

Connor threw some money on the bar and followed Derga to the elevator. Straparola threw him a smile and a thumbs up. *This is a first. A beautiful woman wants to come to my room to read the Bible. Hallelujah! But how ethical is it to bed a woman who may not have taken her meds today?*

Connor opened the door to his room on the 13th floor just down the hall from the entrance to the roof deck where tomorrow's premiere of *Bada Bing* would take place.

"You left that little dagger of yours at home, right?" he asked.

"I'm really sorry about that," said Derga as she entered the room. The room wasn't large and the furniture was sparse—a full-size bed paired with a small end table, a bureau, a two-shelf legal-style bookcase filled with film directories, DVDs of classic films, a few history titles and volumes on Yeats, and a small café table with two chairs sought to separate themselves from walls painted a lime green.

Derga walked over to the end table, opened a small drawer and removed a Bible. The good book's bedside placement in hotel rooms was universal. Derga took a seat at the café table and Connor plopped down across from her. She passed the Bible across to him.

"Genesis. Chapter six, verse four." she said.

Connor found the passage. "The Nephilim were on earth in those days and also afterward when the sons of God came into the daughters of men and they bore children to them. These were the mighty men of old, the men of renown."

"What does that sound like to you?"

Connor thought for a moment. "A mingling of races? Some kind of hybrid being?"

"Numbers 13:33."

Connor flipped through the pages until he found the passage. "And there we saw the Nephilim (the sons of Anak, who came from the Nephilim) and we seemed to ourselves like grasshoppers and so we seemed to them."

"Your thoughts?"

"OK, so the old Hebrews were either really short or the Nephilim were really tall."

"In ancient Hebrew, Nephilim translates as 'the fallen ones.' When the Bible was translated into Greek, it was written as 'gigantes.'"

"Are you trying to say 'gigantes' became 'giants' in English? That the Nephilim are giants?"

Derga didn't reply. Connor cocked his head sideways. "And you believe that the Nephilim still exist and are out there kicking ass?"

"There are not that many left," said Derga. "Keep in mind that populations were much smaller than those of today. The Neanderthals, for example, numbered maybe 50,000 worldwide at their peak and they lived for centuries. As for the Nephilim, most were killed ages ago in a war the record of which only exists in legend. The remainder found homes where they could for better or worse. Goliath and his brothers made the mistake of supporting the Philistines, for example, against the Israelites. One became a Roman emperor. But their numbers continued to decline. Or so we think because these days they take steps to hide themselves. We're not sure of their numbers. Those that exist today vow vengeance against the deenee shee and to save those the deenee shee would take. The deenee shee call them hunters. Some call them the cucculatti…"

"Giants shouldn't be too hard to find," interrupted Connor.

"Harder than you think," said Derga. "They take drugs to curtail their growth and remove identifiers like a sixth finger on each hand. Now they are the size of an average basketball team although they tend to be more muscular."

"OK, back up," said Connor. "Why are the Nephilim bent on killing the deenee shee?"

Derga sighed. "It's a tragedy, really. The Nephilim are the offspring of deenee shee and human women. The Nephilim used their knowledge of deenee shee ways to jump start human civilization. And for that, the Nephilim were punished because now humans posed a threat to the deenee shee. For the Nephilim, it's as if their own fathers turned against them."

"And who are Nephilim saving exactly?"

"They seek to save those the deenee shee would take," Derga repeated.

"The deenee shee." said Connor. "I know that name. Or something like it."

Connor stood up and went to the bookshelf where he grabbed a slim volume of poetry by Yeats called "The Wind Among The Reeds." It was first published in 1899. He sat down again and opened the book.

"The host is riding from Knockarea and over the grave of Clooth-na-Bare."

"Yes, I know it," said Derga. "It's a poem called 'The Hosting of the Sidhe." Different spelling but the same, nonetheless."

"Are you saying the deenee shee and the sidhe are one and the same?"

Derga remained silent.

"They're the Tuatha De Danaan of Irish myth. You're talking about fairies. You know that, don't you?"

"If you know your Yeats, you'll know he wasn't talking about little, cute creatures with wings," said Derga. "That's a lot of nonsense Shakespeare made up just to make people feel good. The English minimize that which they fear the most."

Derga was right, Connor knew. Yeats wrote about the Sidhe as if they were life-sized entities. And Yeats never mentioned anything about wings. He'd never really thought about this aspect of Yeat's work before but now he recalled an essay on folklore Yeats had penned. He had used the term deenee shee as well. He read another excerpt from the poem.

"Away, come away:

> *Empty your heart of its mortal dream.*
> *The winds awaken, the leaves whirl round,*
> *Our cheeks are pale, our hair is unbound,*
> *Our breasts are heaving, our eyes are agleam,*
> *Our arms are waving, our lips are apart;*
> *And if any gaze on our rushing band,*
> *We come between him and the deed of his hand,*
> *We come between him and the hope of his heart."*

"It sounds like Yeats got a good look at them, doesn't it," said Derga. "Maybe even had a chat with them. Poets are the best reporters of the unbelievable and Yeats may not have been the best of them. You should read James Clarence Mangan. Oh, he was in the thick of it. Critics think poets are using metaphors or some deep symbolism. And sometimes they are. But a lot of the times they're not Do you remember Yeats' poem "The Stolen Child?

Connor did.

> *"Come away, O human child!*
> *To the waters and the wild*
> *With faery, hand in hand,*
> *For the world's more full of weeping than you can*
> *understand."*

Derga nodded. "Well, the Unseelie Court doesn't waste time on sweet talk. They just take you."

"They are kidnapping people? Why?"

"To breed," said Derga. "The deenee shee cannot reproduce on their own. They need humans."

"And why hasn't anybody noticed?"

"Oh, people have noticed for centuries but no one listens," said Derga. "The stories are there. Every culture has them. The Arabs called them the djinn. In Norway, they're called the Huldrefolk. The Hebrews thought they were angels. Pick a country and there is a name for them. Nowadays, people talk about alien abductions. They are half right but nobody is going to outer space."

"So you think the Unseelie Court is behind all kidnappings."

"Of course not!" Derga was beginning to lose patience with him. "Only a small percentage. They take them from different places at different times. Preferably people no one will miss. They leave behind a string of unsolved disappearances. No one puts it together. Other than Medea."

"Where are these people taken?"

"Away."

It took a moment for it to click. "You mean away like in the Irish sense. Like in a Yeats sense? Fairyland?"

"Think of it as another dimension," said Derga.

"And this added dimension is invisible, I'm guessing?"

"Yes," said Derga. "Think of it like this. Imagine the world as you know it covered in clear bubble wrap. The deeneeshee live in those bubbles."

"How many bubbles are there?"

"I don't know," said Derga. "I do know that to get from one bubble to another, you often must pass through the space we are in now."

Connor ran his hands through his hair. He got up and opened the top draw of the bureau and picked up a brown wool sock. He pulled out the silver comb and laid it on the table in front of them. "What this got to do with anything?"

"I believe your comb belongs to a woman of the deenee shee—a banshee to be more precise," said Derga. "It's very important to her. Every banshee story always mentions the comb. There is more to it than meets the eye."

"A banshee? That's a bit of stretch."

"I know it's a lot to take in. Welcome to my world."

"Thanks."

"Look, I'm really worried about you," said Derga. "There is another Irish verse by Seoirse Bodley that speaks of the banshee.

'Don't touch my comb,

> *My one and only,*
> *Lay no hand on it.*
> *Steal it,*
> *Pick it up,*
> *I'll come get it.*
> *Burn, burn all I*
> *Touch.'"*

"Shit," said Connor. "I'm not familiar with Bodley but that sounds more than a little scary."

"You should memorize the whole thing. Look, I'll keep an eye on you," said Derga. "I've checked into a room directly below yours—I asked at the front desk which room was yours. If anything comes for you in the night, climb down the firescape. I'll leave my window unlocked."

Derga stood up and leaned over him. She kissed him lightly on the lips and Connor felt a bolt of electricity flow through his torso, continue down his leg, and reach into his toes. "I'll do everything I can to help," she promised as she left the room.

Connor sat in silence for a few minutes. He looked at the door, trying to imagine the sight of a banshee bursting through it. He shook his head and took out his cellphone.

"Yo, Connor! What's up?" said Straparola. The connection was a little noisy but he could hear Straparola chuckling.

"Strap, I'm in deep shit."

"Yeah?"

"She's hot. She's sexy. I like her."

"But?"

"She's completely bonkers."

"I hate when that happens. Tell me."

Connor recapped his conversation with Derga. When he finished, Straparola couldn't help himself. "Giants, fairies, and spies, oh my!" he sang.

"Thanks, Dorothy," said Connor. "Let's leave the *Wizard of Oz* out of this. The field is already too crowded."

"OK. I'll check out this Medea thing and see what else pops up under Learmont."

"Thanks. How are things going with Seventina?"

"Great! She's sane at least." Straparola hung up but Connor heard him laughing for a few minutes more.

Chapter Fifteen

They struck a bargain of sorts because a couple often attracts less attention than a man or woman alone. They sat together--she in a fashionable little black dress and he in black suit with grey pinstripes with a black shirt closed at the neck--at a small table near the door of a small, well-worn jazz club called Cleopatra's Needle located on Broadway at 92th Street on Manhattan's Upper West Side. The club was named after a 3,500-year-old, 70-foot red granite obelisk brought from Alexandria, Egypt, to nearby Central Park in 1880. She glanced out the window onto Broadway and noted the absence of pedestrians. It was moving toward 3 AM and the young black woman on the stage tucked into the corner to the right of the club's horseshoe bar was finishing up a song called "String of Pearls."

That's just what the Heer of Dunderberg is collecting.

She looked over at her companion. He was studying the singer with an intensity that was within inches of a drool. She was glad he was distracted. He didn't talk much and when he did, his words were drenched in a Low Dutch accent that made her strain for comprehension. He preferred it over the old tongue, he said. Whatever the language, he had a way of getting his meaning across. Two men, a white, balding bass player and a black bearded guitarist, accompanied the singer. She doubted they would be a problem.

190

"Thank you and good night," said the singer when she had finished the number. "You've been a wonderful crowd."

She wouldn't have called it a crowd. The tables surrounding them were empty and the applause came entirely from the bar, a U of singles lingering in hopes of a late night hook-up that might develop into a relationship that would extend past breakfast. One young, Latino brunette, she noted, seemed to have found an older Sugar Daddy who looked surprised that he attracted any notice at all.

The singer left the stage followed by her two back-up musicians. They were headed for the door and the bass player already had a pack of cigarettes out. *Smoke break*. Then they would return for their instruments and their take of the night's proceeds.

"You have a wonderful voice," she said to the singer as she walked by.

"Why thank you, honey," said the singer in a voice that dripped with sweetness and a hint of the Old South. The smile lasted only as long as she reached the door.

She waited a moment before looking at the Heer of Dunderberg. He nodded and they rose together and went outside.

The singer and her two musicians were standing near the curb. Both men were smoking cigarettes. The singer was there for the comraderie.

The Heer of Dunderberg stood near the door, unobtrusively blocking the exit so no one could exit the club until they were done. There was no foot traffic on the sidewalk and the street was clear of nearby cars She took a few steps toward the trio.

"I just wanted to say how much I enjoyed your performance," she said.

The singer smiled politely and the two men, who were standing nearly shoulder-to-shoulder, nodded their heads in acknowledgement.

"Have you been singing long professionally?" she asked.

"Just a couple of years," said the singer. "Of course, they near threw me out of the home cause I wouldn't stop singing." The singer laughed, her voice now sounding more bittersweet.

"Oh, I'm sorry."

"That's all right, honey. It wasn't your fault. Besides, I got the feeling when I sing those old Billie Holiday blues tunes."

"Say, could you spare a cigarette?" she asked.

"Not me," said the singer. "I'm trying to quit. Which means I bum them off these guys."

"Me too," she said. "My date doesn't smoke, though. And they're so good after a drink."

The bass player produced a pack of cigarettes and she took one. The guitarist supplied the light from a book of matches, flicking the match against the striker in a one-handed maneuver that showed off his dexterity.

"Thanks," she said. "Nice move."

The guitar player smiled in a way that said lighting a woman's cigarette was a prelude to foreplay. The bass player and singer smiled in a there-he-goes-again sort of fashion. *Everyone's smiling. That's good.* She pursed her lips and blew two smoke rings in quick succession in the direction of the two men. The smoke rings expanded until they looped themselves over the heads of the two men. Both looked up and smiled at the trick. She sucked in her breath sharply as her hands warmed up and she brought them together in a circle with the fingertips red hot. The smoke rings dropped around men's necks and contracted, becoming a solid black ring that tightened like a noose to cut off each man's air supply. They fell to the sidewalk with burn marks around their necks.

The Heer of Dunderberg leaped before the stunned singer could scream, clasped a gloved hand around her mouth, picked her up and stepped into the street. The singer passed out almost immediately. *He's used a sleeping scent.* Almost as if on cue, a yellow taxi rolled up with the trunk lid popping open as the car stopped. The Heer of Dunderberg bundled the singer into the trunk and shut the lid. She slid into the back seat and the Heer of Dunderberg entered the car through the other door and sat next to her. The car sped off, blending into the Manhattan night, heading south on Broadway. It was over in seconds.

"Where will you take her?" she asked, curious, using Gortigern.

Her question was answered in Low Dutch. She wondered why the Heer of Dunderberg wouldn't use the language that bound them. She didn't think she'd ever get an answer.

"Up the North River, he says," said the driver, running his hand over his bald head. "That's the old name for the Hudson."

"Wherever." Without knowing the local geography, the answer was meaningless. "Remember now. Tit for tat."

"Tomorrow night. The Gershwin Hotel," said the driver. "I already scouted the place. Saw your comb. Guy named Ryan something was waving it around. There's a movie premiere with a party on the roof. I have a name you can use to get in. You'll have to look fancy."

"Don't worry. I'll look the part." With that, the black dress she wore changed into white. "All it takes is a little glamour."

Inside her mind, she frowned. She wasn't sure she really needed the Heer of Dunderberg's help to retrieve her comb. But when he had suggested that she helphim, she had given her assent even though she knew the Seelie Court most likely would not have approved. She didn't like it much either. Abductions always ran the risk of attracting the attention of hunters. But she needed to keep the Heer of Dunderberg close. If for some reason she couldn't retrieve her comb, then her only way home might be through The Unseelie Court. That would a desperate course of last resort.

The Cornet of Horse lay out on the bed with his feet dangling over the end. His eyes were closed but he wasn't sleeping. He was thinking and listening to the Old Voices of the hunters who had come before him. One of Lt. Gomez's men had tailed Derga Learmont to the Gershwin Hotel, reporting that she had booked a room at the weekly rate. Convinced that Derga Learmont was somehow connected to this latest appearance of the deenee shee, the Cornet of Horse had checked into the Gershwin later that night, noted the absence of any cat odor and asked for a room as low to the ground as possible, accepting one on the fourth floor. The night clerk, her eyes wide at the size of him, had expressed regret at the lack of king-sized beds. *Very considerate.*

"Any cats?" he'd asked.

"Oh, no, sir!" the night clerk had replied. "We are vermin free!"

"That's not what I meant."

"Oh, I see. You're allergic?"

He left the question unanswered and headed for the elevator. It was small and narrow.

A couple walking in after him thought about getting on with him but then saw how little space was actually left and decided to wait. Upon entering the hotel room, he took the usual precaution of laying down some cat poison by the windows. There were always strays to consider.

And now he was second-guessing himself.

This morning's principal case sheet developed by NYPD's Major Case Squad had done it. He had accessed the principal case sheet, a terse compilation of the previous day's felonies, using the powerful laptop that now occupied a nearby table. The laptop used

MEDEA-developed software that could surreptitiously access other computers via the power line, an entry point left unguarded by computer security types despite the fact that power lines had been shown to be able to carry data years before. The Cornet of Horse half chuckled to himself. MEDEA actively discouraged the use of power lines as data carriers and sabotaged the efforts of various companies seeking to bring the technology to people's attention, even buying up inventories of new powerline data devices when necessary for stockpiling in a MEDEA warehouse located in one of the hundreds of bland industrial parks that littered Florida. MEDEA might not stop use of the technology indefinitely but they could slow its adoption.

The item that had gotten his attention was the report of woman's possible disappearance from a jazz club on the Upper West Side. Two men who had been with the woman were dead and the cause of their death was telling. If the two men had been shot or stabbed, he would have passed over the report. *Not their style.* But asphyxiation with burn marks around the neck was another matter. *Yes, they've done that before.* If the two men had died of strokes, though, he'd have been surer. That was a favorite method of theirs. Doctors diagnosed the deceased as having died of a sudden, massive stroke, which, while unfortunate, was perfectly natural. They never considered the possibility that stroke victims were sometimes murder victims. It was understandable, though. Fairy darts left no puncture marks, just a small blue blemish that was easily overlooked. The fairy dart was unreliable in that it didn't always kill but it often left those who survived slobbering fools. *Pray you are not that lucky.*

So was the woman truly missing? Had she been kidnapped along with the others? Or had she just fled the scene of the crime? Could she be the killer? Not likely. Witnesses had reported that a man and a woman had left the club just prior to the incident. NYPD was canvassing the area for more information.

There are two together.

What do we know of them?
The female has not been encountered before.
Be sure. Remember the compact with the sorcerer Pope!
But the Heer of Dunderberg we know.
How did he escape Pollepel?

The Old Voices were growing more distinctive as their interest in the current hunt accelerated. There was the strong tone of Aenotherus, loyal bodyguard to Charlemagne and he thought he recognized Pier Gerlof Doria, leader of the Black Heap, mercenaries who had fought the Hapsburg Empire. The Dutch aspect of the hunt was of interest to him. Sometimes, he wished he knew how many Old Voices there were and that he could summon them individually. But it didn't work that way. It was like he had been given a radio without a tuner.

Pollepel was now called Bannerman Island, he knew. General Washington had issued the order for a prison to be built there but no prison had ever been constructed. But nearby West Point had become a military academy for the army, the location chosen so that an eye would always be kept on the island even as officers were trained for other wars. If the Cornet of Horse was honest with himself, he had to admit that he hadn't given the Heer of Dunderberg much thought in the intervening years even after Washington had formalized their relationship in 1789 after his inauguration, mostly for the benefit of future presidents. The Cornet of Horse didn't exactly answer to the United States government but the Cornet of Horse still felt like he was acting under orders, or at least with the authorization and consent of the first president, a man revered as the father of his country. In his book, executive privilege extended to dead presidents.

The Cornet of Horse's eyes flickered toward the long black case resting atop the room's lone bureau. It looked like the kind of case a musician --a trumpet player perhaps--might carry. Inside the case were two long, black daggers made of iron. His back-up weapon was five-inch iron blade hooked like black fang, better at slashing than stabbing. It was small enough to conceal on his person and he took it out of his sheath. The handle was like a slim bit of wrought iron folded into the proper shape with the blade extending from it in one solid piece. The blade end was black with small hammer marks on it from when it was hand forged so long ago.

He wondered then if he had adopted the right course of action.

Follow Learmont, they all agreed.

Learmont. The name sounded familiar.

"Have we heard her name before?" he said aloud.

No answer.

The Cornet of Horse sat up and typed a few commands into the laptop until the video from the hotel's security cameras appeared on his screen. *Sometimes the hunter must wait for the hunted.* Yes, he would see them when they arrived and then he would strike. With luck, two more of the enemy would be consigned to oblivion. The only question to answer in the interim was how good was room service?

Chapter Sixteen

Anthony Immediato dug an elbow into Connor, whose eyes had strayed upward toward the golden spectacle of the Met Life Building, and nodded in the direction of six twenty-something guys sporting zippered leather jackets, swept-back hair, and gold chains around their necks, dressed in marked contrast to the dark blue suit, white shirt, and pale blue tie Immediato wore.

"Fucking *gavones* from Yonkers," said Immediato. "The Tumbledown Boys, they call themselves. Can you believe that shit? They name themselves after a strip mall on Central Avenue. What is happening to Italian youth?"

Connor shrugged to a sip from the bottle of Peroni beer in his hand.

"Yeah, I don't know either," continued Immediato. "*Marone*, it's like we're in our own dead-end time warp. You know, I was born in Italy. Italian is my first language. But I've been here since I was a teen-ager. That was 20 years ago."

Connor nodded.

"So I'm back in the old country a few months ago and I'm talking to this old lady about nothing, you know. And you know what she says to me? She says 'You speak the antique Italian very well.' We're fucking dying over here. We're cut off. Italy is moving on without us."

"It's hard to believe, "said Connor, trying to sound sympathetic.

"The whole Italian thing--I mean our thing--in this country is for shit. Look at Little Italy. It's down to two blocks. We're surrounded by the Chinese. In fact, they've taken over. We're making payoffs to them. We're nothing but front men for the Chinks. Have you been up to Arthur Avenue in the Bronx lately? We owned that street. Now half the Italians there are Mexicans. And then a black man beats us to the White House. I got nothing against him but an Italian should have been in there ahead of him. You know what I mean? Bad enough we're decades behind the Irish."

"To President Kennedy. Cheers." Connor took another sip of beer.

"Yeah, lemme get a drink and I'll join you," said Immediato. "Fuckin' Tony Soprano was the worst thing that ever happened to us."

"Good TV show, though," said Connor.

"When your shit shows up on TV you're done because it means no one is afraid of you anymore. It's like when you see a bad neighborhood in a film. Then you know it's safe. They'd have been scared shitless to film there when it was a bad neighborhood. All those expensive cameras would have disappeared. No one ever filmed in my neighborhood." Immediato was already moving away. "You don't see TV dramas about the Mafia on Italian TV. They're on the news. That's all I'm going to say."

Connor watched Immediato edge his way through the rooftop crowd as he headed to the bar. The lights had come back on while the end credits for Bada Bing were still rolling. He saw the film's producer smiling and talking as if he was a major Hollywood player instead of a man facing a murder indictment for his role in eight gangland-style slayings. An *Esquire* writer Connor had met earlier in the evening hung on the producer's every word as he gathered material for a profile in the magazine. The producer stroked his little mustache as he offered up what he thought were great insights about how film mirrored reality. Nearby, a few actors who played bit roles opposite Tony Soprano were lighting up cigars. The secret to their success was that they were not acting; all they did was be themselves. They and the other guests—about 50 in all--seemed happy which meant Connor should get his money for hosting the event without too much trouble. Still, he couldn't wait for the evening to be over. He didn't want to think about how many of these guys were packing but he had noticed tell-tale bulges around the ankles and under the jackets of a few guests and that made him nervous. And too many were wearing their shirts out over their pants, another tell. He spotted Seventina and Derga huddled together talking. They both looked stunning but Derga looked conservative in her form-hugging red pants suit compared to Seventina's strip-club fashion sensibility. Seventina had almost induced an unscheduled intermission when she left in mid-film for a visit to the ladies room. He noticed a few of the Yonkers guys eyeing the women appreciatively and began to wonder where Strapaola was and why he seemed to have abandoned his assigned shepherd role. Fortunately, there were other women around— mostly young women with a few acting classes behind them—so Derga and Seventina were not the only eye candy available.

"The movie sucked."

Connor turned to find Strapaola standing behind him.

"Just keep it to yourself until I get paid," said Connor.

"Did this guy make pornos before this?"

"Don't know. Don't care. It's just a gig."

"Did you ever wonder why a small magnet can exert a more powerful force that the entire gravitational pull of the Earth?" asked Straparola.

"What? Are you drunk?"

"No. Not yet, anyway."

"So what's with the question from out of left field."

Straparola considered the question. "Ah, yes, a baseball reference. I'm not so good with the stick-and-ball sports."

"Okay. Here it is in plain English. What are you talking about?" said Connor. "I thought you said you'd run cover for Seventina and Derga while I did my mingle-thing."

"Derga is what I'm talking about," said Straparola "I did a little homework. It seems Derga's description of a fourth dimension is not so different from that of an eminent physicist at MIT, who, by the way, is a pretty good-looking babe in her own right."

"You can't be serious."

"You haven't seen her picture. Lisa Randall is her name. Beauty and brains is her claim to fame," continued Straparola. "She wondered why gravity is such a weak force. After much consideration and mathematical noodling, she postulated the existence of a fourth dimension where gravity is stronger. It's pretty complicated."

"Bottom line me."

"We're bumped up against another dimension. Gravity there is stronger than here. Derga's fourth dimension is plausible in theory."

"I'm not sure if that's good news or bad news," said Connor.

"I know what you mean," said Straparola. "Then there is the Measurement of Earth Data for Environmental Analysis."

"Huh?"

"Think acronym," said Straparola.

"What?" said Connor. "Wait. MEDEA?"

"Yes," said Straparola. "In the early nineties, MEDEA pops up in connection with the de-classification of some satellite images of the Arctic. MEDEA is identified as a group of scientists, mostly geophyscists, working with unnamed intelligence agencies operating in the national interest. The name pops up again a few more times but after 1999, there is nothing."

"So they don't exist anymore? Good."

"That wouldn't be my take on it," said Straparola "My guess is they've gone black."

"What do you mean?"

"The secret world. Black ops. Black funding. Do you know that half the budget for the U.S. Air Force is black? And that's just the tip of the iceberg. MEDEA just disappears from public view. No "thank you" for their work. Nothing. That's a dead giveaway. MEDEA went deep. Way deep."

"You're starting to make my head hurt, said Connor. "How do you know this stuff?"

"I'm not at liberty to say."

"Sources," said Connor. Sometimes, Connor bumped into a wall past which only Straparola lived.

"The thing is MEDEA sounds very similar to another secret organization that dates back to at least World War II and the atomic bomb project," continued Straparola. "It was outed during the Vietnam War. It is called 'Jason' and it is basically a group of scientists who advise the government on all matter of topics. Jason still exists but it's practically in mothballs. What the acronym means I've no idea. But I don't think it matters. The acronym is the key. That's the recognition signal. Someone's got a thing for code names based on the work of Euripedes. You know who he was, right?"

"There is a famous old movie called *Jason and the Argonauts*. That's him, isn't it?"

"His story. Euripedes was a Greek playwright who died in 406 B.C. Get this. There is a legend that says Euripedes was killed by a pack of fairy dogs. They're white with red-tipped ears. It must have been ugly."

"Really. Do you think MEDEA and Jason are the same thing?"

"No. In Euripedes, Jason survives and gets the golden fleece only because the sorceress Medea bails him out every time he gets in a jam. She's the one who puts the dragon guarding the golden fleece to sleep. I think MEDEA is higher up the food chain than Jason."

"You mean more secret than Jason ever was."

"Exactly. And by implication, more powerful. At the very least, MEDEA seems to have satellites at its disposal. Maybe MEDEA is a replacement for the now very public Jason organization. Or maybe MEDEA existed all along and Jason was like some kind of subsidiary. Black shit gets very complicated."

Straparola paused to let Connor digest the information he had given him so far and then continued. "Which brings us to Learmont. A rare sort of name, it appears. It happens to be the last name of a guy widely known as Thomas of Ercildoune."

"Never heard of him," said Connor. "Sounds old-fashioned."

"He was a bit before your time. He was also called True Thomas which is a corruption of his original moniker: Druid Thomas."

"A Druid?"

"It gets better. It seems Thomas of Ercildoune—that's in Scotland—is famous for running off to marry a fairy queen. A redhead, apparently." Straparola paused. "That was in the 13th century."

"You don't seriously believe Derga is on the level, do you?" asked Connor.

"You have to admit the level of detail is impressive."

"I'm beginning to miss my last botched date. OK, the fun's over. Give it a rest. So the girl is a little whacked. Get over it."

"I'm just saying." Straparola shrugged and looked away. "Whoa, where did that chick come from?"

Connor swiveled his head in the direction Straparola was looking but all he saw was a wall of suits. "Where?" Connor was leery of uninvited guests. They tended to drink the bar dry before they got around to harassing legitimate guests. The hotel had a man just outside the door to the roof checking names against a guest list but this late into the program, security often got lax.

"Those fatheads got in the way," said Straparola. "Wait until they move. She's worth checking out. She's a woman you don't want to wake up next to."

Connor's attention, however, was drawn to the approach of Seventina and Derga. Seventina's breasts jiggled as she walked and they looked like they were about to spill out of some complicated strap-thing masquerading as a dress. Male eyes followed the two women as they walked, enjoying the show. *Packaging matters.* Straparola slid next to Seventina and put an arm around her, perhaps in an attempt to keep things in place.

"You two are turning into tonight's feature presentation," said Connor.

Seventina giggled.

"Very smooth, movie man," said Derga with a smile. She stood smiling at him and Connor enjoyed the moment. Derga looked back at him, sending an unspoken message that Connor hoped he was deciphering correctly. Suddenly, something behind Connor caught her attention and Derga smile faded and her face paled.

"Girl, are you all right?" asked Straparola "You just lost enough color to paint a house."

Connor looked over his shoulder but could not see anyone or anything that might be upsetting. He turned back to Derga. "What's the matter?"

Derga gripped him tightly by the arm. "Something bad is going to happen," she said almost to herself. Then she looked hard at him. "Where's the comb?"

"In my pocket," said Connor. "Feel." Connor took Derga hand and laid it against the outside of the black blazer he was wearing. He felt Derga press her fingers against the comb. "It's nice and safe."

Connor looked over at Straparola as he gathered Derga into his arms. *OK, somehow a switch got flipped. This is where she loses it.* Straparola got the message or at least the gist of it and he shrugged his shoulders helplessly. Then he too spotted something over Connor's shoulder that brought a look of concern to his face. Connor twirled with Derga to look behind him but saw nothing. Whatever or whoever it was, the crowd had moved to block his view.

"Connor!" said Straparola into his ear. "It's that woman I saw a moment ago! She's with some guy who looks fucking dangerous and they're both eyeballing you. Four o'clock! Quick!"

Connor turned his head sharply to the right and caught a glimpse of two figures looking at him before they were blocked from view. One of them was wearing something green and he looked around trying to pick that color out off the crowd.

"There," said Derga suddenly and Connor saw them as well. At first glance, the woman seemed attractive but upon closer inspection, Connor saw there was something about her face that gave him the creeps. Her skin was drawn back tight over her cheekbones and her hair was pulled back tight as if to deliberately create a skeletal look. It looked like a California Botox treatment gone really bad. She wore a strapless moss green gown with small brightly colored wings embroidered along the side from the waist down. The hem of her gown shimmered like it was made from some kind of phosphorescent material. As Connor watched, she raised a long silk-like veil above her head, gripping it with two hands so that it billowed like a canopy above her head. She stared straight at Connor.

"Thief!" she cried and the sound was like the sob of a woman at a funeral.

"What the hell?" asked Connor. "Is she yelling at me?"

Connor felt Derga shiver. For a fleeting instant, he hoped this was a practical joke but that wish evaporated as he looked into his accuser's eyes and saw the malice there.

"Banshee!" Derga's voice was almost a whisper.

The veil swirled and then Connor saw her escort and a hollow pit formed in his stomach. He was dressed in what would be called downtown black, complete with knee-length duster, but the clothes looked so sinister on him that they must have been designed in hell. His eyes were as black as his clothes and devoid of warmth. There was no other word for him other than dark. It wasn't that his skin was black although Connor couldn't really put a name to his skin tone. It was more like something you felt rather than saw. He was a dark sensation.

"Who's the guy?" Connor managed.

"I don't know," stammered Derga.

"This lack of detail really bothers me, you know," replied Connor, dryly.

"Thief!" shrieked the banshee. A few heads turned in her direction but people hadn't yet determined that Connor was the focus of her rage. One of the guests reached out to the banshee— what he intended Connor didn't know—but before he could touch her, the banshee made a quick flinging motion and the man's face turned pale and he clutched at his heart.

"He's having a stroke!" one of his companions yelled.

Stroke or not, Connor was sure the banshee was the cause of the man's troubles.

"Fairy dart!" said Derga.

The banshee was armed.

Connor was just beginning to think about heading for the exit when the hotel security man stationed at the door came barreling onto the roof like a man on a mission. Connor almost breathed a sign of relief until he realized that the man had been propelled through the door and was struggling to keep his feet, a battle he lost as he careened into a chair and didn't move again. A second figure came through the door, stooped at first and then straightening into the biggest man Connor had ever seen. It was more than just his height that impressed. It was his depth, his girth, the size of his arms and hands, and finally just his presence. He dwarfed even the steroid-enhanced mob muscle that now stood slack-jawed and rooted like potted plants. The big man kept moving, sweeping back a cloak that he wore in lieu of a coat. His arms criss crossed in front of him in a blur and then Connor saw two long daggers with black blades that seemed to absorb light.

A woman screamed.

It was Seventina.

The big man kept coming.

Chapter Seventeen

Connor felt like he had been dropped into another world without moving a muscle. Everything was the same but now it was different. It was like some wizard had uttered a magic word like *abracadabra* and pulled back the transparent curtain that revealed a new reality. Before him was a whirl of motion amidst people too stunned to move.

The whirling began with the dark man as soon as he heard Seventina scream. The dark man moved just in time to dodge first one, then a second, dagger thrust at him. The big man who had barreled into the film premiere was a killer. The dark man then did an impossible spine-breaking back flip and landed on top of the bar behind Connor. The big man leaped after him but the dark man jumped again. The big man landed on the bar to the sound of a loud crack and the bar crushed beneath his weight, sending him sprawling. The dark man, meanwhile, landed softly in front of Seventina who opened her mouth to scream again but no sound came out of her mouth. The dark man reached for her but Derga threw her body between them.

"Pudidum!" said Derga, her voice full of command.

The dark man looked at her in surprise. There was a heartbeat's hesitation and then he tapped Derga on the forehead. Derga collapsed into the dark man's arms and he threw her over his shoulder. The he did the same to Seventina. Both women were now hanging over the dark man's left shoulder like two rolled up rugs.

"No!" yelled Connor.

But the dark man was too quick. Despite the weight of the two women, he effortlessly leaped again, this time onto the wall surrounding the roof deck, gently landing on the ledge that overlooked the street. Behind him there was nothing but empty air and a long drop.

For a fleeting, horrible second, Connor thought the dark man intended to leap to his death, taking Derga and Seventina with him. But Connor had not been watching the dark man's female companion who now appeared with the hotel's emergency water hose in her hands. The water came on just as she reached the wall and she aimed the hose so the water streamed down onto the street below. Connor watched as the dark man put his hand into the water and swirled it in a tight spiral. The water froze to form a circular ice slide and without a moment's hesitation, the dark man jumped onto the ice slide still carrying Derga and Seventina. The woman shrieked, making him wince, and for a moment, he thought it was a sound of despair but she leaped after him and they all vanished from view.

Connor rushed to the wall and looked over the shoulder-high ledge, with Straparola beside him. He couldn't believe his eyes. The dark man, an unconscious Derga and Seventina, and the woman were slowly spiraling down the ice slide toward the street like they were on some amusement park ride. The slide melted behind them as they descended. Off to the side, a small half-circle of red, yellow and blue bands shimmered in the misty spray created when the cascading water hit the sidewalk below.

"What the fuck kind of hit is this?" said a voice that sounded both outraged and disgusted. Immediato, Connor realized. It all happened so fast that half the guest list was just now remembering they were armed and guns started to appear in fists.

Connor turned and ran toward the roof deck door to find the big man there ahead of him. The big man ran through the door and glanced toward the elevator. A LED indicator on the side panel indicated the elevator was on the second floor and the big man headed for the stairs.

"Service elevator!" yelled Connor.

Connor stepped past the guest elevator and over to a dingier-looking elevator used by the staff. He pressed the button on the side panel and the doors swung open. He had guessed right. The service elevator had been last used to bring wine up from the bar and no one had used it since. This was an old-style freight elevator and Connor had to slide a gate open to get in. The big man was on his heels and Straparola piled in breathless behind him. Connor swung the gate closed behind them and slammed the lever forward from 13 to 1. With a lurch, the elevator descended. They were jammed in pretty tight.

Connor looked up at the man whose head grazed the top of the elevator. His black cloak was embroidered with a black design of three interlocking pyramids that rippled at the slightest movement of its wearer. The cloak hung around the big man's body, obscuring the clothes beneath and it was held in place by a gold clasp etched with a figure of a horse and rider in military garb. *Cavalry.* Connor glanced down. The big man was wearing riding boots. Connor looked up again. The big man wore his hair close cropped and the eyes were filled with murderous intent even as his face betrayed frustration.

The big man scared Connor and Connor noted that Straparola looked a few shades paler. *The enemy of my enemy is my friend.* He must have heard that line in some war movie.

"Who the fuck are you and who the fuck are they?" Connor believed if you rarely cursed, then cursing would be shockingly effective when you did it, particularly if you said it in a demanding way. This time, Connor was wasting his breath. The big man looked at Connor like an extra on a film set that talked when he wasn't supposed to. The big man then looked at Straparola who kept his mouth shut, having decided a non-speaking role suddenly suited him.

The elevator doors opened and Connor's stomach dropped when he saw they weren't in the lobby. A maid stood looking at them, eyes wide and mouth opened. Behind her, Connor could see the head of Marilyn Monroe, blond hair against an orange backdrop. It was a large Andy Warhol painting that hung on the wall of the third floor. Straparola pressed the button for the doors to close and the elevator descended again, only to stop once more on the second floor. The elevator door opened. Elvis Presley stood facing them, large as life, with a six-gun in his hand and a holster on his hip. Actually, there were three of them. Warhol again. The artist had overlapped three separate black & white images of Elvis to create the painting on the wall. The original image was a still from Flaming Star, a 1960 Western. There was no one else. Whoever had pressed the call button must have decided to use the stairs.

"Fucking Elvis!" muttered Straparola as he frantically pushed at the control panel buttons and the door closed, more slowly than it ever had before in Connor's mind.

They reached the lobby and the big man ripped the gate open before Connor could touch it. The big man raced across an empty lobby and onto the street with Connor and Straparola right behind him. Derga and Seventina were nowhere in sight and neither were the dark man and the woman. A big puddle of water covered the sidewalk, all that remained of the ice slide.

"Shit! Where are they?" said Connor.

The big man said nothing but pulled the two long black daggers out of their scabbards at his waist, sweeping the cloak back over his shoulder as he did so. Connor followed the big man's eyes and noticed a group of four, small men walking from the east in their direction. They were dressed in outfits that seemed vaguely naval: white, tight-fitting T-shits and bell-bottom pants and gun-metal boots. Each wore a red knit cap on each head, although some of the caps looked more mottled than others. They had the musculature of young men but their faces were lined with age. And they wore gloves whose metal fingers were curved like the talons of eagles.

"Redcaps," said the big man as calmly as if he was bird-watching "They dip their hats in the blood of their victims. You better start thinking outside the coffin."

The big man retreated a dozen steps, still facing the redcaps. Connor and Straparola backed up even farther, trying to put the big man between them and the redcaps.

The redcaps charged, their taloned hands raised, and the big man braced himself. Just then, a group of men came charging out of the Gershwin Hotel, inadvertently placing themselves between Connor and the oncoming redcaps. *The Tumbledown Boys!*

Their name became their epitaph. The Tumbledown Boys had enough time to raise their fists—one was quick enough to draw a pistol—before the redcaps mowed them down. The redcaps' talons ripped into the throats of some and tore off the faces of others in a single stroke. Blood quickly mixed with the water on the sidewalk and the Tumbledown Boys screamed together like a church choir headed for hell. The pistol came spinning out of the melee and landed at Straparola's feet, a finger still wrapped around the trigger. The melee became a massacre in a matter of seconds. A redcap doffed his hat, soaked it into the blood of the first Tumbledown Boy to die, and then put it back on his head. The redcap saw Connor and Straparola staring at him and the big man waiting for him. The redcap straightened his clothes and took a few strides in their direction with an air of unfinished business about him.

Connor nearly lost his hearing as two pistol shots exploded beside him. The redcap coming toward him staggered and fell to his knees with two holes in his chest. A white liquid bubbled from the holes. *They bleed white!* Connor turned his head and saw Straparola standing next to him with the pistol in his hand.

"Good shooting," said the big man. "A bullet won't kill them but it does slow them down a lot."

The big man turned and raced west away from the redcaps who now appeared to be feeding. Straparola looked like he was about to puke but Connor pulled him, forcing him to run.

"They'll disappear when they hear the police sirens," said the big man, over his shoulder. "They are living out on that deserted island in the East River where the insane asylum used to be. Never go there. They have your scent now."

Connor didn't know where the big man was going and didn't care. All he wanted to do was put a lot of distance between himself and the redcaps. They followed the big man across Fifth Avenue, heedless of traffic. Car brakes screeched behind Connor and he glanced over his shoulder. Straparola was still there. They made eye contact.

"Where did you learn to shoot a gun?" yelled Connor.

"Dad was in the military," gasped Straparola. "Didn't I ever mention that? Childhood trips to the shooting range? Big fun. Not."

The big man was fast for someone his size and was already a half block ahead of them when he turned into a garage.

"He's got wheels!" yelled Connor.

The car nearly ran them both over as it came thundering out of the garage. Three headlights, one dead center between the other two, blinded Connor. *What car has three headlights?*

"Take us!" yelled Connor.

"Why?" said the big man from somewhere behind the head-lights.

"He's got my girl!"

"Mine too!" said Straparola.

The engine revved and both Connor and Straparola jumped a bit, thinking the car was about to roll over them.

"Let's go, Romeos! In case you didn't notice, the bitch is after you and I'm after the bitch and her new boyfriend. You ride with me. Maybe you'll be worth your weight in bait."

Chapter Eighteen

Sometimes Lt. Gomez de Suarez wished he had never left Cuba but those moments were quickly followed by the memory of a prison cell in Havana. He had been a young artist in Cuba but for reasons he never understood, his art was deemed subversive by the communist authorities. A couple of exhibitions had both led to a month long incarceration where he was questioned about all manner of things unrelated to art. Then again, his interrogators weren't exactly art critics but abstract paintings open to interpretation were dangerous in their eyes. In retrospect, he was lucky to only have been beaten a few times, assaults that were administered as part of routine questioning rather than any actual malice. Then suddenly, he was tapped for a cultural exhibition of new Cuban art at a gallery in New York City. Elated, he said goodbye to his family at the Rancho Boyares airport, expecting to return home in a few days with stories of his success. At the gate, he viewed the Russian airplane he was to board with a mix of alarm and excitement as he had never been on an aircraft before. His name was called and he was handed a one-way ticket with a stopover in Mexico by an airport official who wore the same cologne as his prison interrogators and was told not to come back. His goodbyes to family and friends were final, he realized.

On opening night in New York City, he bolted from the gallery and walked into a neighborhood police precinct station and asked for asylum. To his surprise, the New York City art community warmed to him, an embrace that eventually led to a New York University scholarship where he studied art history. As a Cuban refugee fleeing communism, he was fast tracked for American citizenship. Upon graduation, he had joined ICE, a federal agency promising good pay, job security, and rapid promotion for multi-lingual people. He also felt a debt to the country that had taken him in. With his art history degree, ICE put him to work stemming the flow of illegally imported cultural artifacts, a racket worth millions of dollars that often had links to terrorist funding operations. Mostly, he tracked down ancient artifacts like those plundered from the Iraqi museum in Baghdad during the war. But getting a promotion also meant participating in the round-up of illegal immigrants for deportation, actions he had performed as part of a variety of task force groups over the years and where his ability to speak Spanish was viewed as tool that helped reduce the threat of violence against officers. He took some comfort in that but also was conflicted. He often felt like the last guy to buy a house in a good neighborhood, one who was intent on shutting the door behind him. It was a thought he didn't share with colleagues but it was an ongoing internal debate, usually held over a cold glass of cerveza. Hard-core criminals aside, the rounding up illegal aliens who were only trying to improve their lives did bother him. Some politician said that every deported illegal immigrant created a job for an American worker but he didn't buy that. Most of the jobs held by illegals no American wanted. The reports on his desk were often troubling. One current case involved the deportation of a seven-year-old boy born in Canada sent back to his country of birth even though his mother was an American citizen. A case like that should never have been prosecuted in the first place. Now it would take of years of bureaucratic wrangling and untold hardship for the family before the obvious injustice and heartless stupidity of it all was rectified. The system was full of similar cases and they were never sorted out promptly. He remembered a deported restaurant owner in Buffalo who made the best tacos in the city, said his customers. He had no problem tracking down potential terrorists and violent criminals but his zeal flagged when it came to finding what his superior officer called undocumented economic immigrants. The worst was the raid on the kosher meatpacking plant filled with illegal Latinos workers in Wisconsin, an assignment forced upon him because of his fluency in Spanish. Over a hundred workers had been arrested on site, all of them from somewhere in Latin America. The effect on the wives and the children, many now born in the United States, was heartbreaking. Fathers separated from mothers. Fathers and mothers separated from children. One woman from Guatemala noted his name.

"You are one of us," she cried in Spanish. "Why are you doing this? All we want is work."

Lt. Gomez de Suarez, like many Americans, didn't have an answer. Immigrants had helped make the country into the powerhouse it was. Stop immigration and the country would lose its muscle and much of its brains. If there was any country that should have a welcome mat at the door, it should be the United States.

"Where is your family from?" asked one of the arrested men, also speaking Spanish.

"Cuba."

"You're lucky you are from Cuba. Otherwise, you'd be one of us."

"Screw him," said another, also in Spanish. "The Cubanos always thought they were better than us even when they sent Che Guevara into my country to preach revolution. And the ones in Miami are even worse. They only help themselves."

The words stung. Lt. Gomez de Suarez was sorry he spoke Spanish fluently at that moment. He felt worse when he later learned that the plant was targeted not so much for the illegals but

217

for numerous suspected health violations. The raid was the quickest way to shut the plant down and to gather evidence regarding the decidedly non-kosher food preparation. The reality, he feared, was that the roundup of illegals was a means to an end, a headline-grabbing bonus for the regional agent-in-charge.

The deputy chief was aware of his feelings on the immigration issue—it divided the entire agency—and generally kept him off such cases if he could help it. The trouble was that if an agent screwed up and let someone off the hook he shouldn't have, that agent would be out of a job. Illegally imported artifacts normally didn't have a career-ending risk associated with them. An illegal alien who turned out to be a terrorist intent on mass murder was another story.

All this was background noise in his mind. But it was why priority one was the mysterious woman he'd lost on the Triboro Bridge. In his mind, she was definitely a potential terrorist and if she engineered some catastrophe after escaping his custody, his career was over. There was also the matter of jurisdiction and any possible laurels her arrest might bring. So far, he had managed to keep the case on his turf. If he labeled her a terrorist then the FBI would take over as the lead investigative agency and grab whatever acclaim there was to be had. *That's not going to happen.* This was still a case of illegal immigration. His report stated that she'd come off that freighter in Rockaway although he suspected that might not accurate. He was still the special agent in charge of this case and the FBI was out of the picture, at least for now.

And then there was the other woman. Something about Derga Learmont and this Irish artifact kept grabbing his attention. Lt. Gomez had assigned a man to tail Derga and the agent had reported that she had checked into the Gershwin Hotel on 27th Street. *Not exactly five-stars.* He should have left it at that and pulled the tail. But instead some instinct had moved him to keep an agent parked outside the hotel ever since. *I hope no one calls me on this.* Resource allocation was the topic of endless seminars at headquarters.

So far the tail on Derga Learmont had yielded nothing, Learmont hadn't left the hotel. *Did that mean she was expecting Ryan Connor to meet her there? But would a beautiful woman like her stick around for an entire day waiting for a guy to show up? Not likely. Maybe he was already in the hotel before Learmont got there? He should ask the agent on site to check the hotel register for Ryan Connor's name. But would the inquiry tip off Connor that he was being watched? One of the hotel staff might give him the heads up. And then he's off to the races. And I've already lost one suspect. Better to watch and wait.*

Lt. Gomez stood up from behind his office desk and walked over to the coffee maker positioned atop a cheap, metal credenza backed up like a suspect against the far wall. He poured some coffee into a paper cup and drank it black. *Will I be able to dictate events or will events dictate to me?*

The phone rang and Lt. Gomez knew this last question was about to be answered.

"Gomez."

"LT, you're not going to believe this."

"Try me." Gomez recognized the voice as belonging to the agent on site at the Gershwin Hotel. *What was his name again? Roosevelt.*

"That mystery woman you're looking for just walked into the Gershwin. She's with an unidentified male. Sorry, I didn't get a good look at him. You think she's going to meet Learmont? It can't be a coincidence."

"I'll be right there," said Lt. Gomez. "Don't do anything. But call me if either leave the hotel." *There it was. A connection between Learmont and the woman. Screw the FBI.*

Lt. Gomez parked his car on the corner of Madison Avenue and 27th Street in front of an Art Deco office building dating from the

219

1920s. This part of city was one of the few areas that didn't have some fancy real estate tag like Soho, Noho or Dumbo. One wag, however, had christened it DoNeNo which stood for Down Near Nothing but not even that name had stuck. He walked west on the south side of the dimly lit street for a few parked car lengths to where agent Roosevelt sat behind the wheel of a boxy, tan sedan. The car was parked diagonally across the street from the hotel entrance. Lt. Gomez opened the front passenger door as music from the car radio died in mid-song and slid in next to Roosevelt, who nodded a greeting. Lt. Gomez looked him over. *Middle-aged white male counting the days to retirement, probably living in suburban New Jersey.*

"Any movement?" asked Lt. Gomez.

"No, sir."

"Good. Back-up is on its way. We won't make a move before they arrive."

"She's a tonk?" Lt. Gomez knew the word was an abbreviation for "Territory of Origin Not Known." It also was a word that U.S Border Patrol on the Mexican border used to describe the sound a massive Maglite flash light makes when it hits someone in the back of the head. These days much smaller flash lights were standard equipment but the term lived on past its shelf life. He wondered if Roosevelt had been a head basher. Lt. Gomez grunted in a way that could mean yes or no or even I don't know. But Roosevelt was the talkative type.

"Pretty funky hotel," commented Roosevelt.

"You live in Jersey," asked Lt. Gomez.

"Uh, yeah," said Roosevelt, somewhat perplexed by the question and wondering if some sort of Jersey put-down was coming his way.

"Thought so," said Lt. Gomez. "I got a place in Hoboken. River view."

"Morristown."

Suburbia. "Frank Sinatra was born in Hoboken, you know that?"

Roosevelt nodded.

"You like Sinatra?"

"Yeah, sure," said Roosevelt.

"I hate the guy," said Lt. Gomez. "The Mafia singer. Him and that short prick Springsteen are the only music played in the whole state. You hear them everywhere you go. There should be more singers from New Jersey just for the sake of variety."

Agent Roosevelt blanched. He had muted the sound when Lt. Gomez opened the car door but the dashboard display screen clearly showed Springsteen's "Born to Run" was to still playing. And for a Jersey guy, hating Sinatra was like hating the Pope.

"Relax," said Lt. Gomez. "I'm just winding you up. I don't live in Jersey. Watch the hotel. You don't need a soundtrack for the job."

Roosevelt exhaled deeply, wondering if he'd ever listen to music in a car again, and tried to focus on the hotel entrance. In the sideview mirror, he glimpsed a black horse pulling a black carriage with red trim making the turn onto 27th Street from Madison Avenue.

"That's odd," muttered Roosevelt. "The horse trade doesn't come this far south generally. They stay up around Central Park where the tourists are."

Lt. Gomez was about to turn in his seat to check out the horse and carriage when a waterfall appeared in front of the Gershwin Hotel with a huge splash on the sidewalk. Both men peered upward through the windshield of the car to see the source of the water. As they looked up, the water twirled into a spiral and then solidified to form a circular slide of ice. A man, carrying two obviously unconscious women slung over each shoulder, was riding the slide like it was some kind of amusement park attraction, descending from the darkness above. Another figure also was riding the slide, coming fast behind the man.

"Holy shit!" exclaimed Roosevelt.

Both men were rooted to their seats, expecting the riders of the slide to be dashed to the sidewalk. Instead, the man, dressed in black, leapt nimbly from the slide even though he carried two women, one with long blonde hair and the other with long red hair.

"That's Derga Learmont!" said Lt. Gomez.

Even as he spoke, the second rider--a woman--landed lightly on her feet with no more trouble than a child hopping off a slide at a playground. The ice slide quickly dissolved behind her, creating a widening puddle on the sidewalk that spilled into the street.

"And that's my Jane Doe!" added Lt. Gomez, reaching for the car door handle. But to his astonishment, the black horse and carriage with red trim halted to pick up the four figures and then headed toward Fifth Avenue at a gallop.

"After them!" ordered Lt. Gomez.

Roosevelt shook his head to clear it of the sight he had just witnessed and turned the key to start the car's engine. Nothing happened.

Roosevelt looked at Lt. Gomez dumbfounded. The horse and carriage were already across Fifth Avenue.

"Try it again!

Roosevelt followed orders and still nothing happened. The third time proved the charm and the engine started. Roosevelt pulled out into the street and headed toward Fifth Avenue in pursuit. Roosevelt flicked on the siren and a hidden bank of yellow, red, and white lights front and rear flickered in a random, horizontal pattern of blocks like some kind of alien Morse code.

"Go! Go! Go!" yelled Lt. Gomez, slapping a red light onto the dashboard. The traffic light was with them as they flew across Fifth Avenue and Roosevelt accelerated toward Sixth Avenue, their flickering red light bouncing off the buildings and illuminating darkened sidewalks as they passed.

"Can you believe that stupid carriage driver picked them up like some kind of regular fare?" said Roosevelt. "I'll bet that driver is an illegal. Shit, I'll bet they're all illegals.

Lt. Gomez's mind was elsewhere. *Who in their right mind would use a horse and carriage as a getaway vehicle?*

The street was luckily devoid of traffic at this late hour and they were at Sixth Avenue in an instant. But the light here was against them and they had to slow to avoid intersecting traffic headed uptown.

"They're turning down Seventh!" shouted Lt. Gomez. "Heading downtown!"

"This horse-fucker knows the neighborhood," muttered Roosevelt. Lt. Gomez did as well. The Fashion Institute of Technology loomed ahead on Eighth Avenue which ran uptown. And a metal guardrail closed off 27th Street on the west side of Eighth so traffic couldn't continue straight through. There was take-out sandwich joint on the corner he liked called Manhattan Heroes.

Roosevelt gunned the car the length of 27th Street and turned hard onto Seventh, both men expecting to see the horse and carriage almost in front of them. Instead, they made a woman in denim shorts, a black jacket and a big black bow the size of Mickey Mouse's ears in her white hair nearly jump out of her heels before she scampered back to the safety of the curb. Then they glimpsed the back of the black carriage making a right turn onto 23rd Street.

"Damn!" cursed Lt. Gomez.

Roosevelt accelerated and they spun onto 23rd as pedestrians ran from the crosswalk, and they narrowly missed hitting an oncoming bus. Unlike 27th Street, 23rd Street was a major four-lane crosstown thoroughfare. Lt. Gomez peered ahead and saw the carriage crossing Ninth Avenue.

"Jesus Christ, Roosevelt!" screamed Lt. Gomez. "Can't you catch a fucking horse!"

"Lieutenant, I'm driving as fast as I can but I can't close on them."

At Eighth Avenue, the car swerved to avoid a man clothed in a woman's flowery dress looking forlornly at the horse and carriage disappearing into the west.

"Take me! Take me!" they heard the drag queen shouting as they drove by. Other men, some holding hands, gaped from the sidewalk. This was Chelsea and this section of Eighth Avenue was the main street of the city's gay community.

"Go! Go!" shouted Lt. Gomez and Roosevelt pushed the gas pedal to the floor.

"They're headed for Chelsea Pier!" shouted Roosevelt.

Chelsea Pier was a mix of restaurants and recreational sporting facilities on the Hudson River interspersed with numerous multi-million yachts and sailing vessels that offered trips out into the harbor and around the Statue of Liberty.

"You think he's got a boat?" asked Roosevelt.

"Shit!" The question reminded Lt. Gomez that he hadn't called in the pursuit. In truth, he had thought that they'd be able to catch a horse and carriage long before any backup could arrive. *But who knew a horse would be so hard to catch?* Lt. Gomez grabbed the microphone of the two-way radio mounted between the two front seats.

"Dispatch! Officers in pursuit of two, possibly three, suspects entering Chelsea Pier. Suspects are in a horse-drawn carriage. Request backup. Request NYPD send uniforms to the scene. Also notify Harbor Patrol."

"Roger that," said a slightly garbled voice. "Be advised Harbor Patrol has no boats in the vicinity."

"Shitheads!" said Lt. Gomez.

They drove across the West Side Highway and into Chelsea Pier and saw the horse and carriage outlined by a streetlight, standing in a little plaza between a sailing sloop and an outdoor skating rink. They stopped the car behind the carriage and let their headlights bathe the scene in light. The driver of the carriage sat still with his back straight, seemingly oblivious to their arrival. The horse seemed to be following the driver's lead and stood unmoving.

Roosevelt cut the siren and both men got out of the car with guns drawn.

"Raise your hands!" yelled Lt. Gomez to the driver who instantly complied. Lt. Gomez couldn't see inside the carriage. He motioned to Roosevelt to approach from the left while he took the right. Gingerly, Lt. Gomez worked his way along the length of the carriage and as he approached the middle of it, he could see inside. Derga Learmont lay unconscious across one seat, her head on the lap of a blonde woman who sat with her head tilted back and her eyes closed. Sitting opposite them was the woman he been looking for since she had escaped his custody on the Triboro Bridge.

"Let me see your hands!" yelled Lt. Gomez. The woman extended her hands and as she did so something slammed into his back, pushing him forward into the side of the carriage. His head hit something metallic and he fell to the ground. He heard a shot fired and then a scream before he passed out.

When Lt. Gomez came to, it seemed like only seconds had passed but the black horse and carriage were gone. In its place, there stood a yellow taxi cab. Lt. Gomez could see the taxi was empty. The driver was looking over his shoulder, getting ready to pull out into traffic. There was something about the driver, though, that looked familiar.

"Hold it!" he meant to shout but his voice only managed a croak. His pistol lay next to him and he grabbed it. He fired a warning shot into the air and the driver braked, rear red lights flaring, and twisted in his seat to look at him as if he was surprised to find him alive.

"God-damn right,' he croaked. He waved his pistol up and the taxi driver raised his hands in the air behind the wheel. Lt. Gomez finally got a good look at the driver and was struck by the single black line of hair that went straight across over his eyes.

"Who the fuck are you?" asked Lt. Gomez

"My name is Dwerg" said the driver. "I'm a legal alien. Just like Sting. You know, the British singer. I swear it."

Dwerg's eyes shifted right. Lt. Gomez turned, expecting another assault. Instead, he saw the huddled form of Roosevelt on the ground. He went over and checked for a pulse and found one. Lt. Gomez did a quick check of Roosevelt. *At least he's not bleeding.* Roosevelt was unconscious but seemed all right otherwise.

"This has nothing to do with me," said Dwerg. "I just do transportation."

Suddenly, a car with three headlights--*some kind of antique for chrissakes*--swerved into the plaza like cavalry coming to the rescue, lighting up the area like the noonday sun. The driver's side of the car opened and a huge man got out. *Some kind of cop.*

Two more men got out of the car but they struck Lt. Gomez as being more tentative in their approach. They didn't look like cops of any kind. Both had worried looks on their faces but one looked like his worry lines ran deeper.

"Lemme guess," said Lt. Gomez. "Ryan Connor."

Chapter Nineteen

"L t. Gomez de Suarez, isn't it?"

Blood trickled down the side of Lt. Gomez's face from a small cut on his forehead but he seemed oblivious to it. "Lt. Gomez will do. Do I know you?" he asked.

"You sent me the bulletin about the state trooper killed on Whiteface Mountain."

It took Lt. Gomez a moment to remember. "Medea? You're Agent Medea?"

Agent Medea? Connor's mind was thrown into confusion. *Is MEDEA a secret organization or just a man? Clearly, not everything is a figment of Derga's imagination but could she be right about some things and wrong about others?* The ride to Chelsea Pier had been too brief to obtain any answers. Derga's kidnapping and the encounter with the redcaps were still too fresh for him to formulate any big picture questions for the big man now being addressed as Agent Medea. Straparola, meanwhile, had become instantly enthralled with the technology Agent Medea had access to. Yes, that is a rear-mounted jet engine powering the car, Agent Medea had acknowledged. It's a Czech-made Tatra. And he was tracking the kidnappers using a handheld device that registered Kaluza-Klein particles—that were quickly dissipating, by the way. Straparola got the implied message and let Agent Medea drive. A red flashing light popped up from a hidden compartment in the dashboard as the siren began to wail. Their bodies pressed back into the leather seats as the car accelerated and the next thing Connor knew was that they were pulling into Chelsea Pier.

Agent Medea, if that was his name, didn't respond to Lt. Gomez's question. Instead, he posed one of his own. "Where are your suspects?"

"How do you know about them?" asked Lt. Gomez.

"We just came from the Gershwin," said Connor. "We were on the roof."

"I see," said Lt. Gomez. "We were parked outside the Gershwin when we saw the four suspects exiting the building…

"Some exit," commented Straparola. "And then there were the redcaps. Believe me, they weren't looking to carry your luggage."

"Redcaps?" asked Lt. Gomez.

"Two suspects. Two victims. You were watching the Gershwin?" interrupted Connor. "Why?"

"We were looking for you, actually," replied Lt. Gomez. "We have a report about an Irish artifact that you might have brought into this country illegally."

"Continue," said Agent Medea. Connor was grateful for the interruption.

"The suspects fled the scene in a horse-drawn red carriage," said Lt. Gomez. "Somehow, we couldn't catch up to them. I can't figure out why. We caught up to them here. As we approached the carriage, someone jumped me and I was knocked out. When I came to, my partner, Roosevelt here," Lt. Gomez nodded toward the unconscious man lying on the pavement, "is dead and the red carriage and horse were gone. Instead, I'm left with a taxi cab. But I think the driver is the same."

Lt. Gomez walked over to the taxi and inspected a door hinge. "There is blood here. I'll bet it's mine even if it doesn't make any sense."

Agent Medea nodded and walked over to the taxi where the driver still sat behind the wheel.

"Out of the car, baldy," said Agent Medea.

The driver complied. "Am I under arrest?"

"I ask the questions." Agent Medea reached out and grabbed the driver with one hand and flung him through the air. The driver stayed airborne until he hit the wall above the entrance to a nearby shuttered French restaurant called Café des Amis and fell to the ground. Agent Medea calmly strolled over to the driver and stood over him.

At that moment, a loud roar split the air and they all turned to watch a sleek-looking motorboat take off from across the pier and head for the open water of the Hudson River.

"That's a MAS 28!" said Straparola. "It's a luxury version of an Italian Navy torpedo boat. We'll never catch it."

Connor's heart sank. The women were on that boat. Derga was getting beyond rescue. As was Seventina. Connor glanced at Straparola He looked anxious.

Agent Medea turned his attention back to the taxi driver and Connor took his first real look at the man.

"Isn't this the guy from the card game last night?" said Connor to Straparola.

"You're right!" said Straparola. "What was his name again?"

"Something Hungarian or Czech, I think."

"Dwerg" croaked the man on the ground. "Dutch. I'm a legal alien."

"Yeah, just like Sting," said Straparola.

Agent Medea picked up Dwerg and propped him against the restaurant door.

"Nephilim," said Dwerg, spitting the word out like a curse.

Nephilim! Derga had mentioned that word as well, recalled Connor.

"You're just a transporter. Don't make this any worse for yourself. Just answer my questions," said Agent Medea.

Dwerg said nothing. Agent Medea took Dwerg's hand in his and squeezed. Connor heard bones breaking. Dwerg screamed.

"The compact with the sorcerer Pope doesn't cover you," said Agent Medea. "Who are we chasing?"

"The Heer of Dunderberg," hissed Dwerg.

"Very good. You answered the test question correctly. Where is he going?"

"Pollepel."

Agent Medea let go of the driver and he fell to the pavement, clutching his shattered hand.

"Dunderberg? Pollepel?" said Lt. Gomez. "This guy must be on drugs. I never heard of any such places around here."

Connor looked at Straparola. "New to me," said Straparola and pointed toward Agent Medea. "Never shake hands with that guy."

Agent Medea walked toward his car. "Coming, Romeos?"

"Where to?" asked Connor.

"After the Heer of Dunderberg. To Pollepel."

Connor and Straparola looked at each other. "We're with you," said Connor.

"Can we catch him?" wondered Straparola..

"Yes," said Agent Medea. "If we hurry."

"Hey, wait a minute!" interjected Lt. Gomez. "I'm going too."

Agent Medea hesitated. "That may not be wise."

"Listen," Lt. Gomez was adamant. "This Heer of Dunderberg or whoever he is drew first blood. I want mine."

"The Heer of Dunderberg will not submit to arrest," cautioned Agent Medea.

"That's his fucking problem," said Lt. Gomez.

Agent Medea sighed and nodded.

Their conversation was interrupted by the arrival of a police car. "Call an ambulance and hold that cab driver," yelled Lt. Gomez, pointing at the figure of Roosevelt and waving his badge. He turned back toward Agent Medea. "We're taking your wheels, I guess. What the hell kind of car is that anyway?"

"It's an old Czech model," said Agent Medea.

"A classic import. Tell me all the paperwork on it is in order."

Agent Medea drove up the West Side Highway, ignoring the ridiculous 25-mph speed limit that no one ever heeded. The jet engine of the Czech-built Tetra started to purr and Connor was settling in for what he anticipated would be a long ride. Wherever Pollepel Island was, he knew it wasn't local. But then Agent Medea abruptly turned left at 45th Street and rumbled into the parking lot for the *USS Intrepid*, a 40,000-ton, World War II era aircraft carrier that was now a floating museum.

"Where are we going?" asked Connor. "Shouldn't we be chasing this Heer of Dunderberg guy instead of visiting a museum."

"Flight deck," said Agent Medea as they all climbed out of the Tetra.

A pair of heavily armed security guards closely examined a pass produced by Agent Medea and then waved them through. The

Intrepid had been recently renovated to the tune of $115 million and Connor suddenly got the idea that those funds had been spent on more than just some new exhibits. Agent Medea bounded up a steel staircase two at a time and Connor hurried to catch up. They crossed a metal gangway and went aboard.

Connor had been to the *Intrepid* once before for a film magazine's awards ceremony. The large cavernous spaces that formerly housed squadrons of fighters now often hosted various corporate shindigs after hours. The *Intrepid* was still a draw for event planners looking for a unique location for a special event although it hadn't yet stooped to hosting bar mitzvahs and children's birthday parties. The only downside was the lime green paint job on the walls, a color thought least likely to promote seasickness, he recalled, remembering the lecture he had heard at the awards ceremony. The only problem was the color made you want to puke.

"They used to call this 'The Ghost Ship'," said Connor, remembering more details from the lecture.

"Why's that?" asked Lt. Gomez.

"Seven bomb attacks, five kamikaze strikes by suicidal Japanese pilots, and one torpedo hit," said Connor. "A lot of men died on board her but she always returned to service."

"It figures. A ghost ship," said Lt. Gomez. "This whole night is spooky."

"This was the ship that recovered the Mercury and Gemini space capsules back in the early days of the space program," piped in Straparola with the science angle. "She retired in 1974."

"Not completely," said Agent Medea. "It makes for an excellent surveillance platform and as you'll discover, it offers a fast way to get out of town."

"I wondered why President Bush paid a visit here," muttered Straparola

Agent Medea led the way through a door with a posted "No Admittance" sign and straight into a waiting elevator. Connor had the sensation he was taking a ride to the roof of an apartment building. But instead of landing on rooftop tar, they ducked through a narrow hatchway to stand on the carrier's flight deck. Connor remembered that the last missions launched from the carrier had been during the Vietnam War. *Looks like there is going to be one more.* Connor stared at the silhouettes of various aircraft parked on the flight deck as exhibits. In addition to U.S. planes, there were British, French and Polish fighter aircraft on display. The most remarkable aircraft was the long, dark shape of the A-12 Blackbird that had flown spy missions at the edge of space for the U.S. Central Intelligence Agency. A white tent hid one of the old Space Shuttles from view but everyone in New York knew it was here. Above them the ship's call sign, "11," was lit up brightly enough to illuminate the flight deck.

"That's the biggest pause button I've ever seen," joked Straparola. His voice betrayed how worried he was, however.

Agent Medea steered them away from the planes toward a portion of the flight deck farthest away from shore where two helicopters were parked. Agent Medea stepped up to one, a battered-looking Black Hawk, and slid open the passenger compartment's door. "Don't worry. It's supposed to look like a museum piece but it is fully operational. Get in."

Connor, Straparola and Lt. Gomez quickly strapped themselves into their seats while Agent Medea squeezed his big frame into the pilot's seat and flipped a series of switches that started the rotors revolving. "Headsets on," shouted Agent Medea as the engine noise increased and the rotors spun into a blur. With a jolt, the helicopter lifted forward off the flight deck and quickly turned north up the Hudson River.

"You have impressive resources, mi amigo nuevo," said Lt. Gomez.

"Hooah!" yelled Straparola.. "Now this is flying!"

Connor had to agree. He had been on helicopters before and the experience had left him slightly unnerved each time. On civilian helicopters, it seemed all that lay between you and the ground was a thin sheet of metal flooring where your feet rested uneasily. Connor was of the opinion that helicopters were still an unperfected invention. But riding in a Black Hawk was a whole different experience. Connor felt his body being pushed back into his seat. The sheer power, size, and speed of the Black Hawk made Connor feel invincible. He half expected to hear a "Die Valykrie" soundtrack from one of those military movies like *Apocalypse Now*. Connor looked around the cabin. *A dozen men could fit in here easy.*

The Black Hawk swooped to hug the eastern shore line and Connor momentarily found himself staring into the black waters of the Hudson. The helicopter straightened and went low and Connor could see little whitecaps in the water as they rushed by. The helicopter flew parallel to the West Side Highway but unlike the roadway, they didn't rise to meet the brightly lit George Washington Bridge that spanned the Hudson to link New York and New Jersey. Instead, they flew under it and Connor's heart skipped a beat.

"We're flying under the radar for sure," said Straparola. Connor could hear him clearly through his headphones. "What's our air speed?"

"About 180 mph," answered Agent Medea. "There are extra fuel tanks hidden away so range is not a problem."

"We should be able to catch up to that Italian torpedo boat," said Straparola.

"Hopefully," said Lt. Gomez. "I couldn't catch a fucking horse.'

"Glamour," said Agent Medea.

"Que?"

"Think of it as very old school camouflage," explained Agent Medea. "It was always a taxi."

"Madre de Dios!"

"Definitely not," said Agent Medea.

The helicopter zoomed up the river, the lights from houses on both shores marking the borders of their flight plan. The twinkling lights of a tugboat headed downriver shone ahead and then behind them. Within minutes, they were flying by the Tappan Zee Bridge, the last major span over the Hudson River. Connor noticed a lighthouse striped like a barber's pole in red and white just north of the bridge. It marked the location of Sleepy Hollow, where a headless Hessian horseman had once roamed, filling the hearts of the descendants of the early Dutch who had settled the area with terror. More than a few of the villagers had been cut down by the headless horseman's sword, according to the tale written by Washington Irving in 1848. Connor had enjoyed the film version of the story made over 150 years later.

But where is Dunderberg and Pollepel?

As if he was reading Connor's mind, Straparola was attempting to find out the answer to that question on his own. He found a flat-panel display screen and was busily pushing a variety of control buttons.

"I've got a GPS-based map in front of me but I'm not finding any reference for Dunderberg or Pollepel," complained Straparola.

"You won't," said Agent Medea.

A blaze of lights appeared on their right, illuminating massive walls in the shape of the letter H that worked their way upslope from the river. *Sing Sing.* Originally built in 1825, Sing Sing was still an intimidating sight even in the moonlight. Connor had seen many of the 1930s gangster movies that featured the notorious prison and its electric chair. The great actor Jimmy Cagney had coined the phrase "sent up the river" as a euphemism for Sing Sing and it had become a universal slang for being sent to prison. In real life, hundreds of prisoners had been executed there, including, in 1953, the spies Ethel and Julius Rosenberg who allegedly had handed over the secret of the atomic bomb to the Russians.

"You see that mountain that juts out like a sore thumb into the river up above Peekskill?" asked Agent Medea.

Straparola consulted the map. "Got it. It juts in from the west. But the mountain is called Thunderbird on this map."

"Yes," said Agent Medea. "Think of it as a phonetic cover-up to mask past associations."

"Pretty lame," said Straparola

"Real estate developers seem to like it," said Agent Medea. "But that's Dunderberg. It marks the approach to the Heer of Dunderberg's domain."

"Heer?" asked Lt. Gomez.

"Low Dutch," said Agent Medea. "It means 'gentleman' but he is anything but."

"You know this guy?" asked Lt. Gomez.

"I'm acquainted with his sheet," said Agent Medea.

There was silence as they waited for Agent Medea to elaborate but he didn't.

"What about Pollepel?" asked Connor.

"The original name for Bannerman Island," said Agent Medea. "It marked the northern edge of his domain. But he seems to have expanded his horizons of late. But that's where we'll find him."

"You think there is a chance we can rescue Derga and Seventina without running into him?" asked Connor.

"No," said Agent Medea. "Understand this. If we can save your girlfriends, that's great. But this is not a rescue mission. She is not the primary objective."

By the glow of the flat panel display, Connor saw Straparola make a fist and then extend a middle finger. Connor smiled but doubted Straparola could see his face in the darkness.

"I don't care who you work for but this better be a rescue mission," said Connor. "Otherwise, what's the point?"

"Damn right," said Straparola.

Silence. Agent Medea wasn't one for arguing.

Another big cluster of lights appeared on the right and the helicopter banked away from them toward the middle of the river.

"Indian Point,"said Straparola. "I'm sure we don't want to get any security people there nervous."

Indian Point was a nuclear power station used to generate electricity. They flew by in silence, like penitents walking by a church. Indian Point might not be a holy spot but inside there was power next to God's.

Peekskill flew by as did the West Point Military Academy. Dunderberg became visible as a darker mound outlined against a dark sky. The Hudson River narrowed considerably and the shorelines seemed to press in.

"Coming up on Pollepel," said Agent Medea. "There is a powerboat anchored there."

The others looked down but could see nothing in the blackness. The moon hung low, looking like a small light left on in the window of a faraway house. Connor remembered the poem about Yeats' cat.

Black Minnaloushe stared at the moon,

For, wander and wail as he would,
The pure cold light in the sky
Troubled his animal blood.

Then another thought entered his head. Rosaleen! He hoped that she was all right and in his mind's eye, he could see her in a hospital bed in Sligo General. *Focus on Derga for now.*

"I can't see a thing," said Connor. "Can we land there?"

"No," said Agent Medea. "The island is too small and rocky. We'll put down in Beacon. We'll get a boat there."

"Lemme guess," said Lt. Gomez. "We sail at dawn."

Chapter Twenty

Technically, the boat was stolen but the Cornet of Horse put the thought out of his mind as he steered away from the dock at Beacon into the waters of the Hudson. The helicopter had touched down in a dimly lit park near the dock. The pier was well away from the town center so their arrival attracted no immediate attention and it was too early for any commuters to be gathered at the train station they passed as they walked from the park to the pier, a distance of less than a quarter mile. The absence of witnesses was a bonus as he jimmied the lock of the only building of note, a rundown shack belonging to Riverkeepers, a not-for-profit group that championed a cleaner Hudson.

The Cornet of Horse had quickly found the keys to a 25-foot motorboat docked nearby and the group had quickly boarded.

"It won't match that Italian torpedo boat in a race but I guess it will get us where we're going," said Straparola.

The Cornet of Horse said nothing in reply. His three companions were now spread over two benches below deck in the boat's cabin. They knew him as Agent Medea and that was good enough for now. Maybe forever. Lt. Gomez and Straparola had closed their eyes and appeared to be sleeping. Only Ryan Connor sat with his eyes open, staring off into space. The Cornet of Horse pushed the throttle forward and the boat picked up speed. There was only one other boat on the river, a small craft hauling in a rare catch—a sturgeon that looked to be eight feet long and 200 pounds in weight. The fish had spawned in the Hudson for 15,000 years but were rarely seen since they stayed away from shallow waters. The fish kept to the deep, where strong currents running both upstream and downstream protected them. They lived at the bottom of the river like giant ghosts.

Again to Pollepel Island.
Another island assault.
But nothing like Vineta.
Thank the sorcerer Pope!

The Voices reveled in the victory of Vineta like it was yesterday even though the battle had been fought over a thousand years ago. But the Cornet of Horse couldn't fault their satisfaction. Today, no one even knew Vineta existed even though it had rivaled Constantinople in beauty at the time. The sorcerer Pope had been as good as his word. Vineta had been the last major campaign in which the armies of man and sidhe had fought each other on the battlefield. And while Vineta was ultimately a victory, it was also a reminder of how insidious the foe was.

Vineta had begun as a small settlement on an island in the Baltic off the coast of Germany, growing in size and stature as the inhabitants reclaimed land from the sea to build an impressive port city surrounded by thick walls with 12 gates that controlled access to its streets. Ships from as far away as Greece and Arabia traded there. The city became known as the home of accomplished goldsmiths who produced items of superior beauty and craftsmanship. Golden towers, in fact, soon sprouted over the battlements, reflecting sunlight that could be seen by ships miles away.

The secret of Vineta's success had been well kept at the beginning. Men and the sidhe had come to an accord. Men achieved wealth with the help of sidhe arts. In return, their sons and daughters lay down with the sidhe for no sidhe could reproduce without human help. The male sidhe needs a female host while the female sidhe needs a human seed. The Cornet of Horse didn't fully understand the biology involved because no sidhe had ever been captured for study.

But as the years passed and the inhabitants of Vineta felt increasingly secure behind their walls, the sidhe grew brazen and openly walked the city's streets. A sidhe king, Oberon, assumed the throne of Vineta and it was noted that his reign exceeded the lifetime of most men. And that's when the rumors started. Pagan beliefs reigned supreme, giving rise to all kinds of stories--some true, some not. Vineta became a refuge for those not welcome in their own lands and a symbol for those who couldn't get there. The Nephilim, meanwhile, discreetly investigated and learned of the sidhe presence. But Vineta was simply too large a nut for them to crack on their own.

The big mistake was the issuing of a decree that banned all mention of Christianity within the walls of Vineta. For the sorcerer Pope in Rome, it was a challenge to papal authority that could not be ignored.

There was another reason.

The Cornet's of Horse's mind skipped a beat. That was a new Voice. One he had not heard before.

I am The Morhalt.

He shook his head slightly like he was trying to get rid of cobwebs. Many of the Nephilim were found by a priestly order, secretly embraced by the church and renamed the cuculatti, the cloaked ones. They had been led by a Nephilim who made his home in Ireland.

I am The Morhalt.

They were given a mission: conduct a holy war against the sidhe in Vineta. With a huge treasury behind them, the cuculatti gathered a horde of Danes, supported by the more disciplined troops of a Polish prince, and descended without warning upon Vineta. With God on their side and the promise of all the booty they could carry, the army created by the cuculatti was unstoppable. The sidhe, to their credit, fought well. The memory of the last sortie by the sidhe host leapt into his mind. They had been a sight to behold. The Voices remembered the poem written that day by an anonymous hand and by now he had it memorized.

White shields they carry in their hands,

> *With emblems of pale silver,*
> *With glittering blue swords,*
> *With mighty stout horns*
> *In well-devised battle array,*
> *Ahead of their fair chieftain,*
> *They march amid blue spears*
> *Pale-visaged, curly-headed bands.*

The Cornet of Horse shuddered at the memory. Each blue sword had cut down a dozen Danes.

No wonder though their strength be great,

> *Sons of queens and kings one and all,*
> *On their heads are*
> *Beautiful golden yellow manes.*
> *With smooth comely bodies,*
> *With bright blue-starred eyes,*
> *With pure crystal teeth*
> *With thin red lips.*

Another memory. The Polish prince had cursed when he saw the crystal teeth and had vowed to send them all to hell, horses as well. Afterward, the prince and his remaining men had sailed away to Greenland with the surviving Danes. The idea had been Rome's but the Cornet of Horse appreciated its genius. Rome even sent a bishop along to mind them. All of those who knew of the fate of Vineta were effectively banished.

Good they are at man-slaying...

He shuddered again. There was more to the poem but the Cornet of Horse didn't want to remember any more. In the end, their numbers had overwhelmed the sidhe. The gates were breached, the city was put to the torch and the inhabitants—*oh, those many thousands*—slaughtered like godless beings deserving of nothing else, especially the Lord's mercy. For good measure, the dikes were destroyed and the sea reclaimed its territory. The name of Vineta was erased from every map by order of the sorcerer Pope. Priests banned all mention of the city's name in their sermons and any who persisted in speaking of the city suffered excommunication or worse. A few loudmouths were even dispatched by the cuculatti. The message was clear. Vineta became shrouded in legend, an Atlantis of the North, its exact location unknown.

"So what about those redcaps?"

The Cornet of Horse snapped out of his reverie snapped out of his reverie in the blink of an eye. *The tone of voice is forced. Too casual. He's trying to maintain control. Good.*

He shrugged and the brown leather messenger bag he had retrieved from the helicopter shifted on his back. "When blood is spilled, the danger is past. Once they dip their hats in blood, they quickly return to wherever they come from."

"They were summoned by the Heer of Dunderberg?"

"Or the woman with him."

Connor hesitated and he glanced out across the black water before he spoke again. "Derga. The one with red hair. I haven't known her long. In fact, I barely know her at all. But there is something about her...my life hasn't been the same since I met her."

"We'll do our best to get her back," said the Cornet of Horse. *Have to keep him in the hunt. Focused.*

243

Connor nodded. "The woman who took Derga is a banshee. Or at least that's what Derga said."

"I am familiar with banshees. But I don't really understand this one's part in all this."

"God, you speak of banshees like they were some well-known species of dog or something," Connor paused." I think she's after me. I have something she wants."

The Cornet of Horse was surprised. "You mean your girl is a hostage? What do you have to trade?"

Connor reached into his pocket and pulled out the sock containing the comb.

"Nice sock," said the Cornet of Horse.

"I get that a lot." Connor pulled the comb out of the sock and held it up for inspection. The comb seemed to suck in all available light and it gleamed in the night air.

"Very interesting," said the Cornet of Horse. "I suspect it is more than a mere bauble."

"I'm getting that feeling too." Connor put the comb away.

"That's good, you know," said the Cornet of Horse. "If you have something they want, it means they won't vanish. We can still get your girl back. Or at least there is a chance. The Dutch named the place Pollepel after a girl named Polly who was rescued from the island. It can be done."

"Where would they disappear to?"

"That's hard to explain."

"You don't know."

"There is a lot I don't know," said the Cornet of Horse. "Years can go by without an incident. Then there is a flurry of activity that we're never able to anticipate. We're always on the defensive. The waiting is the hard part. And maintaining continuity. Recognizing that one incident is connected to another over the span of years or that the enemy is the same in one place as it is in another even if it has a different name. It's only now that we can really monitor the whole world."

"Satellites?"

The Cornet of Horse nodded. "Still, our enemy is hard to find and hard to kill."

"What do you know about the Heer of Dunderberg? He is no stranger to you."

"The Native Americans were already scared of this place but it was the Dutch who named him when they colonized New York. He wreaked havoc with their ships and left a sugar-plum hat atop a broken mast as his calling card. This is where the notorious ghost ship of legend, *The Flying Dutchman,* disappeared with a hold full of settlers. In my opinion, that was a kidnapping that maybe didn't go as planned."

"Damn!" whispered Connor.

"Then things went quiet for a few years until the Revolutionary War when he made his presence felt again. The Americans laid a *chevaux de fries*—a chain of 106 log boxes anchored with stones and spiked with pointed metal poles that rose to just below the water line—across the river just below Pollepel to stop a British fleet coming upriver. The Heer of Dunderberg thought it was something designed to keep him in check. At least that's our guess."

The Cornet of Horse made a slight course correction before he continued. "There was a battle and the Heer of Dunderberg tipped the scales for the British who dismantled the *chevaux de fries*. The British ships sailed by unobstructed and created havoc. They burned 300 buildings in nearby Kingston to the ground. At first, the Americans thought they had been betrayed Benedict Arnold-style but they later discovered the truth. General George Washington secretly assigned a certain Dutch-American Major to hunt down the Heer of Dunderberg. That was the beginning of your government's involvement. The Major believed he had trapped the Heer of Dunderberg in a cave on Pollepel. The Major and a small group of specialists piled a ton of rock into the cave and told everyone they were building the underground prison but there had been a cave-in. The Major even filed a report with his superior officer, Major General Heath, to that effect so he could bring masons in on the job. The prison was never built, of course, but it wasn't a prison for men they were trying to build."

"It didn't work."

"No. The Major's mission ultimately was a failure. Although that didn't become clear until much later. It seems the cave was not the access point. Or maybe it is only one of several. I don't know."

"Access point?"

"Gateway, if you prefer. West Point was fortified to monitor the area even as it later churned out new officers for the Army. It's a dual-use facility at times."

"So you want me to believe this whole thing has been going on for hundreds of years?"

"For us, yes. For them, no. A long time for us is a short time for them. The physics is complicated. One day there equals seven years here. It's like how you count dog years differently than you count years for humans. Times passes at different speeds. It's much like a river where the current flows at different rates depending how close to shore you are,"

"I see. Well, actually, I don't but I'm trying to." Connor paused. "Your name isn't Medea is it?

"What gives you that idea?"

"Something Derga said."

"She is more interesting than she appears, it seems."

"So your name isn't Medea."

"I'll answer to it for the time being. That all right with you?"

"You're going to have to do better than that."

"No, I'm not," said the Cornet of Horse, as he pulled back on throttle. "Not today. Boots and saddles. We're almost there."

"We're awake," said Straparola from below deck "Say, you wouldn't know where I could find a cup of coffee?"

Chapter Twenty-One

S he watched as the Heer of Dunderberg bent over the figure of the redheaded woman laying on one of two sofas in the boat's cabin. He swept back the hair that had fallen over her face and studied her red eye patch. The woman's red clothes was disheveled and torn in places. The blonde woman unconscious beside was in a similar state. The boat swayed slightly and she heard the boat bump against the side of the dock to which it was tied. The sound was slightly muffled below deck by the luxurious carpeting inside the cabin of the MAS 28.

The Heer of Dunderberg looked at her and then pointed at the redheaded woman's lips.

"Pudidum," he said.

For a moment, she looked at him uncomprehendingly. *He prefers Old Dutch and suddenly he uses a word from the Old Tongue?*

"Pudidum," he repeated.

"Pudidum? She said 'Pudidum?'"

The Heer of Dunderberg nodded.

"She spoke the Old Tongue? How can that be? Is she one of us?"

The Heer of Dunderberg shook his head and then went out on deck. She heard him step onto the dock. *How can she know the Old Tongue?*

She began to despair, an emotion almost too easy to embrace after all the deaths she had witnessed over the years. Losing her comb had been like tying a needle to a thread and then watching as gravity unwound the thread from the spool in a downward spiral that ended with the point of the needle embedded in the floor. She had never counted on the Nephilim appearing. *And now the Nephilim was on their trail!*

She wondered if she should flee and leave the Heer of Dunderberg to face the Nephilim alone. But she would be no closer to retrieving her comb if she did that. She glanced at the redheaded woman. *The man who stole my comb will come after her.*

For a moment, her spirits rose. Then another thought occurred to her. For some reason, she couldn't see the holder of the comb and that bothered her. She always knew where her comb was but it seemed that as long as it was in this man's possession, its location was a mystery to her. *When he comes for the girl I'll get it back. There was a big problem, however. The Nephilim will come as well.*

She shivered and went up on deck. The sharp lines of the MAS 28 looked like they could cut paper. There were only two black leather seats with long curved backs on deck and she settled into the one behind the steering wheel. From this standpoint, the 28-foot boat tapered before her like a spearhead. From here, she could see that the dock led to a wooden staircase that climbed the side of a cliff until it disappeared over a ledge. She could sense a big structure of some kind farther away to her left but couldn't make out the details in the darkness. The Heer of Dunderberg was nowhere in sight.

She heard a noise below deck in the cabin. *The redheaded woman!*

She would appear to her as an old woman, an unthreatening persona that may lead to the redheaded woman taking her into her confidence. With a murmur that invoked the power of glamour, she changed her features into that of an old crone wearing a gray dress. With a deliberately unsure step, she went below.

The redheaded woman sat cross-legged on the floor and stared at her as she entered.

"Where am I?" she asked.

In English, she noted. She answered in kind. "On a lovely boat, dearie. And what would your name be?"

"Derga."

"And a lovely name it is as well."

She could see that Derga was eyeing her suspiciously.

"I know you for what you are," said Derga.

"And what would that be?"

"An old woman in appearance only," said Derga. "What is it you want? What is it you want of Connor?"

Ah, the transporter was right. That is the thief's name! "He has something of mine."

"The comb!"

She laughed to hide her surprise and the cackle echoed off the walls of the cabin. *She knows!* "And I have something of his."

"I wouldn't go that far."

"He'll come for you nonetheless. Tell me, how is it you speak the Old Tongue?"

"Who said I did?" asked Derga, defiantly.

"Pudidum."

Derga countered with a question with of her own. "And where is your lord and master?"

For a moment she bristled. A small sound of crickets escaped her lips. Then it passed. *She is deliberately trying to bait me.* "Now you wouldn't want to upset an old woman. I might have a stroke."

"You're more likely to cause one," said Derga. "He's of the Unseelie Court, for certain. I didn't take you for one of them."

She's very clever. She's trying to drive a wedge between us. Or see if one is already there. Still, it was something to consider. Would her actions have repercussions in the complicated politics of the deeneeshee? Will my King hear of my activities? I have been weak, sucked into following the agenda of the nearly wordless Heer of Dunderberg. Now I'm trapped in a current of unfolding events.

"Unseelie Court? My, aren't you the smart one."

"What if I can help you get the comb back? Connor doesn't know what he has. I can convince him to return it."

She has seen my weakness. She hopes to split us apart. This isn't going as well as I had hoped. "So, dearie, tell me. Who are you?"

Derga didn't reply.

"I can make you wish you told me. You wouldn't want to lose your other eye, now would you?"

Derga's one eye blinked twice in quick succession.

*That struck a chord. But…*She hesitated…*the note doesn't ring true somehow. Something else lies there. Something hidden.*

They were interrupted by the sound of heavy boots boarding the boat in the light of the breaking dawn. They looked up to see the Heer of Dunderberg carrying the body of a young unconscious black woman. He glared at Derga and she backed away. He put the black woman on the floor and she noticed the woman's hand

and feet were bound. Without a word, he exited and reappeared a moment later with another unconscious body, a young white woman with blond hair.

"Now we have four," she said. "How nice."

The Heer of Dunderberg reached into a pocket and produced a mallet with a hard rubber head. "I believe this is something you use from time to time," he said as he handed it to her. "It was in the boat's toolbox."

"A beetle." She grasped the mallet in her hand. This one was different, of course. The beetles she was familiar with had wooden heads. Long ago, women would use them at the river's edge to beat the dirt out of their clothes while they were washing their garments.

"You don't expect me to clean your clothes, do you?"

The Heer of Dunderberg put his finger over his lips. He was listening to something far away. Then she heard it too. It was the sound of an engine. Another boat was approaching.

"Nephilim!"

The Heer of Dunderberg nodded and then there was a streak of red racing toward the door. The Heer of Dunderberg gave the red streak a slight push and Derga crashed into the cabin wall and slumped to the floor. The Heer of Dunderberg picked up Derga and laid her across the bodies of the other women.

"Does she run from us or the Nephilim, I wonder?" she said.

He turned toward her and made a horizontal motion with his arm as if he was covering something up. She understood his meaning and reached inside her dress for her gwynn. She unfolded it and laid it across the bodies of the four women. The four figures would be invisible to human eyes.

The Heer of Dunderberg pointed at her face and shook his head.

She agreed. *This is no country for old women.* With another murmur, she transformed herself back into the form with which he was familiar and for a moment she thought he looked pleased. Then he beckoned her to follow him off the boat.

I hope he doesn't have any funny ideas.

Chapter Twenty-Two

"You think this guy is like some kind of Indian tortoise that lives to be 250 years old?" Straparola whispered. "That's nuts."

"I don't know what to think," said Connor, turning to look in the direction of Pollepel Island. The dawn light made the island increasingly visible and Connor couldn't believe his eyes. Towering over the island was the ruins of a massive brick castle, complete with turrets and crenellated towers. Moss, vines, and other types of creepy vegetation clung to the base of castle walls and grew up around patches of stucco. As their boat drew closer, Connor could see large letters near the top of the castle wall.

"Bannerman's Island Arsenal," read Straparola aloud.

Connor took in the castle and the surrounding mountains that lined both shores of the river. "It feels like we're in the Scottish Highlands."

"Bannerman was Scottish," said Agent Medea. "He was a descendant of the MacDonald clan. His branch of the family was re-named Bannerman after one of his ancestors captured an English banner in battle for Robert De Bruce."

"Who?" asked Lt. Gomez.

"He was a famous Scottish king excommunicated twice by the Pope," said Connor. "You ever see the movie *Braveheart?*

"Missed it," said Lt. Gomez. "Mambo Kings is more my speed."

"Bannerman?" asked Straparola. "Isn't he the father of the modern army/navy store?"

"You amaze me, Mr. Straparola," said Agent Medea.

"Fast search engine," said Straparola, holding up his cellphone.

Agent Medea smiled. "Bannerman bought up military surplus left over from the Spanish-American War and other conflicts for resale. He built this castle to store it all. That's why it's called an arsenal. Rifle, machine guns, mortars cannons, ammo, clothing—he could outfit a regiment."

"But that was over 100 years ago," said Straparola.

"Yes," said Agent Medea. "Bannerman worked on the castle until his death in 1918."

"Right on the home turf of the Heer of Dunderberg," said Connor.

"Deliberately so," said Agent Medea. "It was to be the fortress that kept the Heer of Dunderberg bottled up."

"Looks like things didn't work out," said Lt. Gomez.

"Bannerman possessed a power that died with him. That's when this place became vulnerable. The powder magazine was blown up in 1920," said Agent Medea. "Then the ferry sank in 1950."

"What kind of power?" asked Connor.

"I don't know exactly," said Agent Medea. "The Scots are notorious for cutting their own deals. I suspect Bannerman had an arrangement with those who wanted to keep the Heer of Dunderberg in check."

Connor looked toward the eastern shore and guessed it was at most 1000 feet away.

"The worst incident occurred in 1969," said Agent Medea. "The castle was torched. It burned for three days." He had hoped that if the Heer of Dunderberg was involved, he had perished in the flames. Clearly, that wasn't the case."

"There's the MAS 28!" said Straparola as they approached the dock. The Italian powerboat look deserted.

"Looks like no one is on board," said Lt. Gomez.

They approached the MAS 28 from its stern and as they touched the dock, Lt. Gomez leapt off the boat and onto the dock. Drawing his pistol, he stepped onto the MAS 28. Connor could see him peering into the cabin.

"I don't see anyone," called Lt. Gomez.

Straparola jumped onto the dock and tied the boat down. Connor moved to follow Straparola.

"Wait," said Agent Medea, grabbing the canvas bag he'd brought on board. He opened the zipper and produced what Connor at first thought was a knife in a scabbard, although the hand was square rather than rounded. Agent Medea handed it to him and Connor pulled the blade out of it scabbard and was surprised to see it was a black-bladed machete, but of a type he'd never seen before.

"Spesnatz survival tool," said Agent Medea. "Russian special forces. You can use it as an ax, a shovel, a wire cutter—whatever you need. For our purposes, it's the high iron content that matters. Iron is the only thing that kills our enemy. The blade has lots of iron in it. The only downside is that it tends to rust so keep it dry."

Agent Medea eased past Connor and stepped onto the dock. Connor slid the machete into its scabbard and attached it to his belt.

"Maybe you'll get lucky," said Agent Medea.

"The castle reminds me of some of the old armories in the city," said Straparola. "It's all brick like that one on Park Avenue they use for antique shows."

"Or the one on Lexington Avenue that's the home of the Fighting 69th," said Connor, referring to the storied regiment founded by Irishmen in the American Civil War.

They had climbed a wooden staircase that led up from the dock and followed the side of a cliff until it reached the summit 68 steps later. They had landed at the rear of the castle, Connor saw, and now a narrow dirt path led toward the front entrance. The castle was even more impressive than it first appeared. It followed a line up a hill and a second tier rose above the first, making the entire structure the equivalent of an eight- or nine-story building. Roman-looking columns supported the upper levels and while Connor was no architect, it was clear that a mix of architectural styles were all in play so as to give the castle a unique look. Finials the size of cannonballs lined the ramparts. The entrance to the castle was a wide stone staircase that led up to an arched drawbridge. Underneath was a fake moat that turned into a road that led to a sally port and continued east toward the harbor. The main door was on the third level, marked by a coat of arms above the entrance.

"Wow!" said Straparola. "There are no right angles for the walls. They are all parallelograms."

"That seems weird," said Connor.

Connor heard Lt. Gomez mumble something in Spanish. Or is he praying?

Connor looked to the east where a small mountain rose in the distance. He took a few steps forward and noticed some steps in disrepair that led downwards. From here, he could see that walls had been built out into the river to create a sheltered harbor. A tower, a few hundred feet away, was all that remained of the harbor entrance but the walls extended to turn right to continue along the island's south side.

"It must have been beautiful," said Connor.

"A monument to the futility of positional defense," said Agent Medea.

Connor climbed the sixteen steps that led up to the bridge. Little puffs of green grew along the sides of each step, as if dropped by passing maidens. At the top of the steps, he looked across the causeway to the main entrance. Lying just past the entrance in the shadows were three long forms.

"There is something here!" said Connor.

His three companions joined him and they walked across the bridge together. The bundles were wrapped in deep red blankets, they saw, and had been laid side by side.

Lt. Gomez stepped forward and unwrapped the first bundle. Inside was the body of a young woman with blonde hair.

"Oh, God!" said Straparola.

Lt. Gomez unwrapped the second bundle and found the body of a young black woman.

"Damn!" cursed Connor. He knew what the third bundle contained. He had been too late. Lt. Gomez unwrapped the third bundle and a shock of red hair spilled out. Connor averted his eyes and they filled with tears.

"Seventina, I'm so sorry," said Straparola

"I don't think they've been dead long," said Lt. Gomez.

"God, this is awful," said Straparola..

Connor felt rage and sorrow. Rage directed at the one who had killed Derga. And a deep, deep sorrow that he had known her for so short a time. Connor knew something had gone out of his life that could never be replaced. *I was falling on love with her!*

And then there was Seventina and a young, black woman he had never seen before. *Someone's daughters.* There would be people who would miss them as well.

Lt. Gomez took a few steps away from the bodies and searched the surrounding area for any evidence. Agent Medea quietly stepped forward and examined each body. A look of disgust mingled with frustration came over his face and he kicked the body of Derga so hard it lifted off the ground, then rolled like a tumbling log and disappeared down a hole in the floor where it landed with a loud thud in the basement below.

Connor felt like he had just been punched in the stomach and all the air had left his body, leaving him incapable of making a sound.

"Jesus Christ!" yelled Straparola.

"What the fuck are you doing?" shouted Lt. Gomez.

They all looked at Agent Medea in horror, like he was some demon desecrator of dead bodies. Agent Medea stared back at them.

"They're husks," said Agent Medea.

"What?" asked Connor in a wheezy voice.

"Husks," repeated Agent Medea. "Biological copies. Not clones. They are something less than human because there is never any life to them. I don't know how they make them but if you examine the body closely..."

Agent Medea reached down and snapped the arm off the black woman.

"Shit!" screamed Straparola.

…you'll see that the bones are not bones at all. They are just stiff, hollow tubes made from something like cardboard covered in a kind of cellulose material that looks like skin, touched up with a bit of glamour," finished Agent Medea. "All these women are still alive."

Chapter Twenty-Three

Connor found the Heer of Dunderberg playing cards. After the shock of finding the husks, they had agreed to split up and search the island. Agent Medea, as they thought of their large companion, took the lead as taskmaster, assigning himself the job of searching the castle while Lt. Gomez would pick his way around the old powder magazine and check the harbor area. Connor and Straparola would inspect the original Bannerman house on the other side of the island. Bannerman had used the castle mostly as a warehouse, choosing to live with his Irish bride in a separate structure nearby. Most of the rocky western part of the island was undeveloped so the search area was not a large as it first appeared.

Connor and Straparola walked single file up a narrow, winding, nearly overgrown path that led to the Bannerman house. They had not progressed very far when they discovered that the trail split in two. One path, steeper than the one they were on, looked as if led directly up to the house, even though it wasn't visible from where they stood. The second path was more like a continuation of the one they were on and appeared to wind around the south side of the island. From where the stood, they could also see twin towers that marked the entrance to the island's small harbor.

"Now what?" asked Straparola.

"We split up," answered Connor. "Why don't you head straight up and I'll circle around on the south side."

"You think that's wise?"

Connor shrugged. "I think both trails will wind up at the house. We'll be within earshot of each other. If you see anything, yell like crazy."

"Count on it," said Straparola. "It won't take much to set me off. Those husks freaked me out."

"Me too. I thought Derga and Seventina were history."

Straparola looked around from left to right. "And there is poison ivy everywhere. You know, those husks would never stand up to today's autopsy procedures and DNA analysis. But then again, a lot of families don't like autopsies. If the cause of death seems obvious, then an autopsy wouldn't be done. And why would you analyze the DNA of a corpse if you thought you were sure of the identity? Those husks were really good copies."

"Promise me that if you see something that looks like me lying around, you'll do a thorough check before pronouncing me dead."

"Man, don't go there," said Straparola "but that goes ditto for me. And don't let anyone kick me either."

"See you on the other side," said Connor, heading down the trail toward the south side of the island. Straparola watched him until Connor disappeared behind some overgrown bushes.

Connor walked along the narrow path as it curved gently toward the ruins of a straight line that was the old south harbor wall. After a few minutes, he came to a narrow stone staircase that led down to the water. The top stair bore the inscription "wee bay steps." *The stairs must lead to a landing for small boats.* Through the trees, Connor could see another small tower just offshore that appeared to mark the western boundary of the island. Connor stuck to the trail he was on and soon came to the remains of a garden at the bottom of a cliff. Looking up he could see part of a building. *The house.* A stone staircase on his right seemed to lead up to the house but Connor was more troubled by two other features before him. Directly ahead and built into the side of the cliff was an arched doorway that had been completely sealed up. But on closer examination, Connor noticed brick debris lying on the ground in front of it. A small rectangular slit had been cut out of the bottom of the doorway. The brick debris in front of the slit suggested someone had cut their way out, pushing the brick out ahead of them.

And then there was the dark opening in the side of the cliff slightly above him and to his left. It was obviously a cave and there were 13 steps leading up to it. The cave opening was wider than it was tall and a ledge of rock hung over the opening, hiding whatever might be in there in total darkness.

Okay. That's worth investigating but there is no way I'm going in there on my own. We'll come back to that.

Connor climbed the staircase on his right and soon came to a landing where he found a small round brick and stucco structure that was probably an old storehouse. But from here, he could see the Bannerman house at the top of another flight of stairs. The house looked bigger than he expected and reminded him of a small temple like he had seen once in Italy. The house was modeled along the same lines as the castle but the Roman columns that lined the entryway were much more prominent. A round turret stood at each corner of the house.

Connor climbed the stairs and approached the entryway that faced north. He then walked around the eastern side of the house where he found a large patio with a magnificent view of the Hudson. Storm King and Breakneck mountains dominated the western shore. It was a remarkably pristine scene, looking as beautiful as the day Henry Hudson first saw it from the deck of the Half Moon those long centuries ago. It was no wonder that 19th century painters flocked here in such numbers that their art became known as the Hudson River School of painting.

And then there is the dark side of the river. The Flying Dutchman and the Heer of Dunderberg. What really happened to Rip Van Winkle who, legend said, vanished into these nearby mountains before reappearing decades later? Had the author Washington Irving known more than he could tell, hiding the facts behind the thin veil of fiction?

Connor shook his head to clear it. He was questioning everything now, looking at every strange story with a new perspective. *Thanks, Derga.*

Connor turned away from the river to look back at the house. From here, he could see that the west side of the house was actually an open gallery. The second floor featured more castle-like touches including the type of slits that medieval archers used to fire arrows down upon the adversaries. There were also two round openings in each of the corner turrets he couldn't explain but looked big enough for cannons. Yeats sprung to mind unbidden and Connor recalled how the Irish poet had turned the word "castle" into a symbol of oppression.

Do the Scots feel the same way about castles? Certainly, Bannerman didn't.

Connor shook off the poetic thread that had entered his head and approached the house for a closer look. Connor stood in a doorway and surveyed the interior. It was in ruins but the fireplace was still there and some panels on the wall hinted of some decoration. The interior space was ample and would rival modern multi-million dollar homes. Connor twisted his body so he could see all the way through the house.

Where's Straparola?

Connor peered cautiously into the interior of the ruined Bannerman residence and tried to gauge whether a stray brick was likely to fall on his head if he proceeded further. The floor was strewn with rubble and it looked as if whatever was going to fall down had done so long ago. He tried to imagine the fire that had destroyed the house and the castle in 1969 but such an inferno was beyond his imagination. He had seen big fires on the television news, of course, but he had never seen a really big blaze up close—nothing bigger than an apartment building going up in smoke due to faulty wiring. *Certainly not a fire that burned for three days and devastated an entire island.*

Connor entered the house through what may have been a window at one time and picked his way toward the center of the room until he stood in front of the old fireplace. Doing a small turn, he surveyed the room, noting the bay window that would have given the occupants a wonderful view of the river. The sound of a crackling fire made him jump and he turned back toward the fireplace and saw with astonishment flames licking around three logs. A cloud of smoke billowed toward him and momentarily encapsulated him. His eyes smarted and he squeezed them shut until he felt a light breeze on his face that told him the smoke must be clearing. He opened his eyes and discovered everything had changed.

The room had been transformed into what it once must have been. Rough brick walls were now plastered over and framed pictures of the Scottish countryside decorated the walls. Above the fireplace hung a sword upon a shield and above it was an inscription: "Jehovah is my strength and my shield." The shield had a coat of arms divided into four quarters—a sailing ship, an ordinance pot, a grappling hook, and a hand holding a banner. A clock that wasn't working stood on the mamtel. In front of the fireplace were two wicker chairs with an oval butternut rug between them. The rest of the room was bare except for a small table set against the far wall. It was as if someone had just moved out and had left behind a few pieces of furniture they didn't care about.

"Welcome to the Craig Inch Lodge."

Connor felt the hairs on the back of his neck rising and they stiffened like needles when the Heer of Dunderberg walked into the room. Connor's hand instinctively reached for the hilt of the machete at his waist. The Heer of Dunderberg shook his head as if surprised at such bad manners and motioned Connor toward the two chairs.

He's not planning to kill me. At least not yet.

The Heer of Dunderberg picked up the table and placed it between the two wicker chairs and sat down. He motioned for Connor to sit as well and Connor felt compelled to do so. Connor felt his mind going numb around the edges, as if his senses were being dulled somehow. He fought off the feeling and focused on the Heer of Dunderberg.

He is the only thing you can be sure is real.

Connor considered the thought again.

Maybe.

Close up, the Heer of Dunderberg had features that seemed to hint at some inner darkness. His hair was black but it was the dark eyes that dominated his face. The cheekbones were very pronounced as if sculpted purposefully as a resting place for his eyes. The Heer of Dunderberg was dressed in a tuxedo minus the tie and wore a round white hat that looked vaguely like a fez without the tassel. *It's like he's just come in from a formal night out and is about to have a nightcap by the fire.* The odd item on his person was a slender silver trumpet about 18 inches long with a bell around six inches in diameter attached to his belt with a lanyard. The trumpet was engraved with letters and images but Connor couldn't see any of them clearly.

The Heer of Dunderberg opened the single table drawer and extracted two small glasses and Connor wondered if the Heer of

Dunderberg was a mind reader. From inside his tuxedo jacket, the Heer of Dunderberg produced a small flask and poured a green liquid into each glass.

Absinthe. That really messes with your head. Or maybe it's worse than absinthe. Eat or drink fairy food and you'll remain with them forever, wrote Yeats. Shit!

"The Craig Inch Lodge. That's what Bannerman called this pile of bricks. His ancestor performed well at the Battle of Bannockburn under Robert de Bruce. That's how they became Bannerman. A bit of the St. Andrew's Cross flag presented by De Bruce himself. Then known as Bannerman forevermore. You have to know your enemies."

The Heer of Dunderberg picked up his glass and made a toasting motion. When Connor didn't move, the Heer of Dunderberg shrugged and emptied the glass in one gulp.

"Pudidum," said the Heer of Dunderberg.

Connor held his breath and said nothing.

"I am curious how the woman with the red hair knows this word," said the Heer of Dunderberg. His English was thick with a strong Dutch accent.

"Derga," said Connor as if he had been poked and then clamped his lips shut. *Is she dead to me or alive? Which way to play it? We found her husk. Should I let him think I think she's dead? If he thinks I think she's dead, will that keep her alive?*

"Rest your brain," said the Heer of Dunderberg. "The Cornet of Horse is not so easily fooled any longer, I know. Those husks are for men's eyes, not his." He paused. "It is the cursed Cornet of Horse again, isn't it?"

"The Cornet of Horse?"

"A name he hasn't revealed to you yet, I see." said the Heer of Dunderberg. "The giant hasn't told you very much, has he?"

267

"Giant?"

"Yes. Giant. Like in your Bible. Like the one killed by David with the slingshot."

"Goliath?"

"Yes. Not so big perhaps as Goliath. But of the same race."

"That's a little hard to believe."

"So am I. But here I am."

The Heer of Dunderberg frowned and Connor felt goose bumps all over. "Have you known Derga long?"

"No."

"More there than meets the eye," said the Heer of Dunderberg. "Drink to her health."

"That looks a bit strong for me, thanks."

The Heer of Dunderberg smiled. "Don't take drinks from strangers, eh? But I know so much about you. You like to play cards, I understand.

The Heer of Dunderberg reached into the desk drawer and produced a deck of cards with blue spirals on the back. "You have something a friend of mine desires. Wants back, in fact. Perhaps we should play for it."

The comb. "I'll trade it for Derga," said Connor.

"It is of no interest to me personally. My acquaintance shall retrieve it in her own good time. The Cornet of Horse is all that restrains her for the moment. She's afraid of the hunters. She doesn't have the history with MEDEA that I do." He paused. "Perhaps I say too much? No matter. MEDEA remains a secret to all. You understand?"

Damn, there is a third side to all this and I'm on it. And I'm on the weakest part of the triangle.

"Please let Derga go," said Connor. "Let all the women go."

The Heer of Dunderberg ignored Connor's plea. "I would like to learn this game you call '25'". The Heer of Dunderberg passed the deck. "Deal."

The taxi driver who came to the Gershwin Hotel. That's how he knows. Connor looked at the deck of cards. Are we playing for Derga's life? Is that what he's thinking?

"It's not really that good a game with two people," said Connor. "It's better with five or six players."

"Deal." The tone of voice was threatening.

This is crazy. "Okay, okay. Each player gets five cards. It's basically a trump game."

"Spades."

"That'll work," said Connor. "The highest trump is the five of the trump suit. In this case, it's the five of spades. The next highest card is the jack of the trump suit. Here is where it gets a bit tricky. The third highest card is always the ace of hearts. Then it's the ace of trumps, followed by the king, queen, ten and so on down the line, skipping the five."

Connor stopped and looked at the Heer of Dunderberg, who nodded.

"Each trick is worth five points," continued Connor. "The first one to reach 25 wins. It's all about how you play the hand that is dealt to you even as you consider how others play the hand that is dealt to them and how it affects you. It's kind of like life."

"Hence my interest,' said the Heer of Dunderberg.

Connor suddenly remembered a story written by Yeats. The hero Red Hanrahan was on his way to see his fiancé, Mary Lavelle, but had been tempted into a game of cards by a mysterious old man. During the course of the game, a brown rabbit had appeared from the cards the old man held, followed by a pack of hounds that chased the rabbit. Red Hanrahan had followed the hunt and soon found himself in front of a big shining house. A sweet voice bid him enter and he discovered a beautiful queen sitting on a throne with four grey-haired old women sitting at her feet. The old women had attempted to test Red Hanrahan to see if he was worthy of their queen but he was unable to speak. Red Hanrahan fell into a slumber. When he awoke a year later, Mary Lavelle had left Ireland and he never saw her or the queen again.

"Deal," commanded the Heer of Dunderberg.

"Are we playing for Derga's life? Is that it?" demanded Connor. "I won't play cards for someone's life."

The Heer of Dunderberg reached across the table and took the cards from Connor. He dealt five cards to each of them face down. "Perhaps the bet is your life. Or maybe it's just about whether you'll see her again or not. Look at your cards."

Reluctantly, Connor obeyed. He tried to keep his face devoid of emotion but as he examined his cards, he was relieved to see the ace of hearts. There were no spades. *Not good.*

The Heer of Dunderberg threw down a five of spades and Connor placed a king of clubs down. The Heer of Dunderberg took the cards and placed them to the side. He then put down a jack of spades.

Connor's heart sank as he put a three of diamonds on the table. *Ten points behind!*

The Heer of Dunderberg put an eight of spades on the table. Connor trumped with the ace of hearts. *Yes! Finally!*

Connor looked up at the Heer of Dunderberg in triumph but his excitement faded when he saw the Heer of Dunderberg holding a brown rabbit in his left arm. The rabbit leaped onto the floor and disappeared outside.

"Shall we follow the hunt?" asked the Heer of Dunderberg.

Connor pushed himself harder into the chair. *I will not get up!*

The Heer of Dunderberg gazed thoughtfully at Connor. Then, unexpectedly, he laughed. It was a sound that hurt Connor's ears.

"Pudidum! Yeats! Ha!" said the Heer of Dunderberg. "It's good you remember that story. My little joke."

Connor looked at the Heer of Dunderberg in surprise.

"Yeats is a name known here and there, like some others," said the Heer of Dunderberg. "But you are right. This game is better served with more players. Perhaps we shall find some."

With those words, the Heer of Dunderberg threw his cards at Connor's eyes and Connor reflexively closed them. When he opened his eyes again, a moment later, the Heer of Dunderberg was gone and Connor was sitting on a small pile of bricks in front of the ruined fireplace.

"Connor!" yelled Straparola. "What the hell are you doing sitting in there?"

"Marked deck, I'll bet," mumbled Connor angrily as he got to his feet. *Did that really happen or is this guy just messing with my mind?* Connor looked around. There was jack of spades lying on the floor. He let it be.

Chapter Twenty-Four

W ho knew he could talk so much?
She had stood unseen in the shadows just outside the
house in the ruins of the old gallery. A small touch of
glamour had made the interior of the house look like it once had,
albeit perhaps in its more Spartan days.

A trap, he'd said, for the hunter. But the hunter had not appeared.
The thief had entered the trap instead and she had not sprung it.
Her comb would have been buried in a pile of rubble. The thief
would have been killed, surely, but she would have been at the
hunter's mercy while she shifted through the rubble for her comb.

*And then what does he go and do? He plays cards with the
thief! And chats him up! All this talk of Yeats! The poet had agreed
not to speak of what he'd seen directly. But the thief admires Yeats.
The horrible little driver with the single eyebrow had been right.
But what can be done with that knowledge? She needed to think.*

She stamped her foot in frustration and fury and then stole
a look inside the ruined house. The thief stood there talking to
his thief-friend accomplice. She pulled back her head. The hunter
must be nearby as well.

"Watch the northern approach. Let the hunter through. Delay
any others," he had said.

She had found a hiding spot halfway down the trail that led up to the house. She stepped behind a round brick structure that may have been either an outhouse or some kind of storage facility and waited. It wasn't long before she heard the sound of footsteps approaching. Her pulse quickened. It must be the thief. The hunter would not make so much noise approaching the house. She closed her eyes and willed her features into a form men found appealing.

She waited until the hard crunch of shoes on gravel was almost upon her and then stepped out onto the trail and faced disappointment. It was only the thief's assistant. He was bent over, his head in darkness, peering into the shadowy entrance of the round brick structure. Bits of brick lay strewn at random.

"Talk about shitting bricks," he murmured. He straightened and turned almost in one motion and nearly bumped into her. She stared at him while his eyes went wide behind his glasses. *What awaste.*

"You're beautiful," he said. She had him where she wanted him. She opened her mouth slightly, sending air over her uvala, felt them beginning to vibrate in time with her flicking tongue and then pursed her lips to blow him a kiss.

But he was quicker and smarter than she gave him credit for. Or more frightened. He was racing back down the trail. Her kissed miss, exploding into ground and shrubbery and releasing the high pitch whine of crickets. He ran faster.

She let out a small scream of frustration. He was effectively out of sound range. She wouldn't chase him. He was probably running back toward the hunter and she had no desire to confront the dreaded Nephilim. She took the mallet from her waist and flung it after the fleeing man. The man stumbled slightly, however, and the mallet went sailing past his ear, pulverizing a nearby ruin of brick wall. The man covered his head and scooted out of sight around a bend in the trail.

She clenched her fists. The missed throw suddenly made her feel skittish. *I don't like this island. I feel like the one who is trapped.*

She was still standing in the shadows when she felt his presence.

"Come," whispered a voice behind her. She turned to face the Heer of Dunderberg. *He's gone back to his monosyllabic ways. Is this something he does just around the females?*

"I should never have gotten involved with you!"

"Likewise," he hissed.

"I'm getting my gwynn," she said. She's taken only a few steps when she heard him whisper again.

"Careful."

She stopped. The hunter was somewhere between her and the boat. She didn't want to face the hunter alone. She'd heard stories. For the feeneshee, the various roads to oblivion were rarely taken but the hunter waited on one of them.

"We have to get back to the boat," she said. "I need my gwynn and you need your catch. The trap failed."

The Heer of Dunderberg nodded and stepped past her. She followed onto a trail that wound in a westerly direction away from the house and the castle, passing a small bridge that led to the undeveloped portion of the island, before it looped back toward the staircase that led to the dock.

"There is someone there," she said as they approached the stairs. *It's the policeman from the beach.*

The Heer of Dunderberg took her arm in his and continued walking like they were a couple out for a stroll. It was only a matter of moments before Lt. Gomez spotted them. He was holding a pistol and he now pointed it in their direction.

"Police! Just hold it right there," said Lt. Gomez. "Keep your hands where I can see them."

The Heer of Dunderberg kept walking and she followed his lead.

"I said stop right there!"

The Heer of Dunderberg stopped two paces in front of Lt. Gomez and before she knew what was happening, he spun her around like she was doing a slow twirl in a waltz. Lt. Gomez's eyes shifted in her direction and as they did, the Heer of Dunderberg spun like top in the opposite direction. His foot reached out and kicked the pistol out of Lt. Gomez's hand and it dropped to the ground.

It was as she was regaining her balance that she saw him--*the hunter*—leaping out from the dense underbrush, two long, dark blades in his hands, racing toward the Heer of Dunderberg. He looked huge. She believed now the old stories she'd heard that the hunters were of giant blood. He had the strength, the power, to kill them both.

She managed a small cry of alarm and maybe it was enough to warn the Heer of Dunderberg or maybe he'd heard the crashing of the underbrush or maybe he'd expected it all along. But as those horrible black blades descended upon the Heer of Dunderberg, he stepped under them and grabbed the hunter by both wrists. For what seemed an age, they stood there, locked in a contest of strength until all at once the Heer of Dunderberg seemed to collapse under the force of the attack. But it was a ruse, she saw, as the Heer of Dunderberg planted a foot into the hunter's midsection and propelled him over his head through the air. The hunter landed with his face in the dirt.

She darted forward and Lt. Gomez stepped in front of her to block her path. She pushed against his shoulder with her hand and smoke rose from his clothes. *Scorched!* He screamed in agony and surprise and lurched backwards, lost his footing and tumbled over the railing for the stairs. Somehow, he grabbed onto it with one hand, saving his life in the process because the fall to the rocks below would surely have killed him.

She didn't wait to see what happened next. She hurried down the stairs toward the boat, not looking back. From the sound on the stairs behind her, she knew theHeer of Dunderberg was right behind her.

She didn't look up toward the stairs until she reached the boat. The hunter had not followed them. He was pulling the policeman to safety. The Heer of Dunderberg gunned the engine and the boat began to move away from the dock. As she watched, the thief and his accomplice arrived at the head of the stairs. With a curse, she went below deck and ripped her gwynn off the four bound women and tucked it safely away. She glared at Derga and then pulled her to her feet and dragged her above deck where she could be seen. With her red hair blowing in the wind, the thief would have no doubt as to whom she was and who had her.

He'll come after her and I'll have another chance.

The Heer of Dunderberg pointed the boat up river. They were headed north. Their pursuers by now were clamoring on board their own boat to give chase. The Heer of Dunderberg fingered a silver trumpet that hung for a lanyard looped into his belt. There were words from the Old Tongue engraved upon it and an image of a river that was most likely the one they were on, she guessed.

"What is that?" she asked.

It was as if her question had decided it use. "It's my speaking trumpet," said the Heer of Dunderberg as he put the trumpet to his lips. "Pardon my Dutch." The mouthpiece of the trumpet was wider than one that might have been on a musical instrument, she saw, allowing the Heer of Dunderberg to move his lips as he spoke into it. She didn't understand his words but the effect on the water was immediate as it began to churn. A large fish—it was longer than she was tall and looked like something born an eon ago-leaped out of the water and then loudly flopped back into it with a sound that echoed off the mountain walls. A mist began forming over the river to the rear of their pursuers. The mist moved with a mind of its own, slithered toward the boat behind. She saw there were forms inside the mist, tumbling head over heel as they closed to the gap on their pursuers, who now realized they were being pursued themselves. She could see them pointing. They too saw what was inside the mist.

The pursuing boat veered toward the shore but not before the leading edge of the mist reached them. Ghostly tendrils turned into fingers that tried to grip the boat from behind to slow it down. More fingers hung onto the sides trying to tip the boat over. Heads became visible and she guessed they were moments away from those figures inside the mist turning into solid forms. Imps, she realized, just as they seemed to lose their grip on the boat, letting it escape.

"They are getting away," she said in the Old Tongue.

The Heer of Dunderberg shrugged. "It was a gamble. Those imps abide at World's End, the deepest part of the river where I have sent many a ship. Alas, their range is limited. They are not very effective coming north of the island. If our pursuers had been in the Race, that narrow section of the river below the island, they would not have escaped."

The Heer of Dunderberg paused. "Do you know that captains still tip their caps when they're sailing the Race? I respect their respect."

"But why didn't you kill the hunter?" she demanded.

The Heer of Dunderberg considered her before he spoke and when he did it was if he was pulling words out of a dictionary one by one. "The outcome was far from certain. And if I killed him what would I do for entertainment?"

"Entertainment? You can't be serious."

"The ultimate game. He helps me keep my edge."

277

She sighed in frustration. "Just so you know…" she paused and the Heer of Dunderberg looked straight at her. For the first time, she felt like she had his full attention. "I hate that hat you're wearing."

"Pudidum," said Derga.

She had almost forgotten about the red-headed woman. She smashed her forearm into Derga's face and Derga collapsed onto the deck, unconscious once more. It was said redheads felt pain more intensely than other people. She hoped it was true.

Who knew she could talk so much?

Chapter Twenty-Five

"I heard Chuale in concert once," said Lt. Gomez from his hospital bed, looking at the three of them. The hospital gown he was wearing was the same light green color as the walls. It covered a white bandage on his shoulder. On a table that swung over his lap was a barely touched meal. "He was the greatest mambo player of his time."

The Cornet of Horse nodded. He had saved Lt. Gomez's life back there at the top of the stairs and Lt. Gomez knew this, of course. Lt. Gomez had been rambling for at least 30 minutes, telling Cornet of Horse things about himself as if to let him know that saving his life had been worthwhile. It was like learning the provenance of a piece of ancient art. A number of cultures had the same rule, he recalled. If you save a man's life, you're responsible for it.

Inwardly, the Cornet of Horse admonished himself. He had been weak. And not just with Lt. Gomez but with the other two as well. With Lt. Gomez, he could kid himself that the interest was purely professional even if it was not a relationship of equals. For Connor and Straparola there was no excuse or rationalization that was justifiable. He glanced at the two of them, standing on the other side of the hospital bed. He should have cut them out of this operation at the first opportunity. It was Connor's interest in the redhead that had done it. He needed to be clear about her. She had some connection to the feeneeshee but was she one of them or something else? Connor obviously had feelings for her. The thought reminded the Cornet of Horse that it had been a long time since he had felt close to another person. Would Connor become a friend?

You should kill them all now, said one of the Voices. *But first find out if they have sisters and then rape and kill them as well.* The Cornet of Horse recognized it immediately. It was the Voice most filled with hate and it belonged to Harpin de la Montagne, dead for more than 1500 years and still filled with bitterness. It was a wonder that Harpin had waited so long to make himself heard. Harpin was a self-made chevalier in an age where the aristocracy didn't appreciate the ambitions of those lacking noble blood. Harpin, in a rage over a series of perceived slurs, kidnapped the six sons of a local lord, slew two outright, and besieged their castle with the other four in chains. Harpin told the lord he could save his remaining sons if he handed over is daughter to become a whore for his army. Naturally, that didn't go over well but before Harpin could carry out any further executions, a champion named Yvain arrived on the scene with his pet lion. The lion bit Harpin, infecting him with the dreaded disease. Yvain hunted Harpin down and in his weakened state, Harpin lost his head to Yvain's sword. No one mourned him. The Cornet of Horse wished they'd cut out his tongue before they killed him. Maybe that would have kept him quiet.

Do you think they'll be your friend? They'll turn on you in the end and they'll kill you. Remember Jack? A so-called friend who became a serial killer. Cormoran, Blunderbore, Galligantus. That Welsh idiot. And more. He killed us and he became famous. Jack the Giant-Killer. Kill them before they kill you.

The Cornet of Horse blinked hard. It was difficult to handle Harpin's venom and harder to ignore it.

The lion killed Harpin. Not a man, said another Voice. It was Silvius Brabo, the Roman general. *Harpin was infected. Those who Jack killed were also infected. I too am a giant killer. I would have killed them as well.*

The Cornet of Horse knew the story. Brabo had killed an infected Droun Antigonus. The madness that gripped Droun's mind had caused him to prey on passing ships from his base near present-day Antwerp, severing and eating the right hand of sailors who were unable to pay his toll for passage. Brabo had severed Droun's right hand before killing him. A statue of Brabo clutching the severed hand of Droun stood in the main square of Antwerp. Most people paid it no heed.

Harpin had to die. He would have begun eating people very soon after the bite. Some wondered if he had been infected even before the lion bit him.

And then Harpin again. Fuck them.

"What are you thinking about," asked Straparola, interrupting the Voices.

"Cats," said the Cornet of Horse.

"Like them?"

"Hate them."

Straparola raised an eyebrow butLt. Gomez carried on like he hadn't heard them. "You know, they used to say I looked like the Cuban actor Andy Garcia," he said. "He's a big mambo fan too."

"I can see the resemblance," said Connor. "I liked him in *The Untouchables.*"

"Yeah," said Lt. Gomez. "He was good in that. But wasn't his character Italian? Garcia is Cuban. My family is Cuban. I am Clemente Gomez de Suarez. I was named for an ancestor who was a brigadier general in the Cuban War of Independence against Spain. I was named after our hometown Suarez. Fuck Castro."

Perhaps it was the medication used to treat his wound that had loosened is lips. Or maybe it was the near brush with death. It had been a near thing. The town of Beacon, once a forgotten factory town of brick buildings, was going upscale with galleries and antique shops lining a long straight main street that was bringing people back to the river. With that had come a surprisingly modern community hospital capable of treating Lt. Gomez's wound, even if the burn mark in the shape of a hand had raised some eyebrows.

Lt. Gomez had run out of things to say about mambo and Cuba and there was a long silence.

"I'm so sorry," said Lt. Gomez eventually. "I can't believe I missed her on the boat. I swear she wasn't there when I looked. None of them were."

Connor nodded.

"They were there," said Straparola. "But our eyes couldn't see them somehow."

He's a smart one.

"And who knows where they've gone," said Connor. "That detector thing of yours has lost his trail. Right?"

He's talking to you. He even sounds like Jack.

"Temporarily, I hope," said the Cornet of Horse.

"Where do we start looking?" asked Connor.

The Cornet of Horse considered the "we" part of the question before he answered. He could walk out of this room and leave the three of them behind. One was hurt. The other two had no transport. It would be the wisest thing to do.

Jack's back.

"There has been some unusual activity recently in the Adirondacks Mountains," said the Cornet of Horse.

"Hey, wait," said Lt. Gomez. "That state trooper. I sent you the report of his murder. Some bastard ripped his heart out. Are you saying that bastard and our bastard is the same bastard?"

"What trooper?" asked Connor..

"A state trooper sees this guy kidnapping a girl," said Lt. Gomez. "He gives pursuit. Car chase. The trooper's body is found on top of Whiteface Mountain with his heart in his hand. The girl and the perp haven't been found. Just vanished off a mountain with one road up and down."

"Sounds like our guy," said Straparola.

"Yes," said the Cornet of Horse. "It would seem the Heer of Dunderberg now sees the entire length of Hudson River as his theater of operations."

"Tear of the Clouds," said Straparola "That's a small lake that's the source of the Hudson River. It's in the Adirondacks. Makes sense."

"Can you pick up his trail?" asked Connor.

"Of course, he can," said Lt. Gomez. "Obviously, he's been monitoring the area. He must have someone on the ground there already."

"Correct," said the Cornet of Horse. "And other assets have become operational recently as well."

"You're watching from the air," said Lt. Gomez. "No, wait. You've got a bird."

"A bird?" asked Connor.

"A satellite," explained Straparola.

"You guys must have some budget," said Lt. Gomez.

They're putting things together quickly now.

The door to the hospital room opened and the doctor who treated Lt. Gomez on arrival entered.

"How's the patient?" said the doctor. He was tall, thin and blonde, dressed in white and wearing a stethoscope around his neck like a badge of office.

"Fine," said Lt. Gomez.

"Good," said the doctor. "You sustained a most unusual injury—a second-degree burn in the shape of a hand. Care to tell me more about it?"

"Doc, what did you say your name was again?" asked Lt. Gomez.

"Booth. Dr. Anthony Booth."

"Right. Thanks for fixing me up. But now listen closely. You saw my badge. I'm in the middle of an investigation involving national security. Do you see where I'm going with this?"

"Please," said the doctor. "You don't have to treat me like an illegal enemy combatant."

"Exactly," said Lt. Gomez. "So like the little kids say: zip it, lock it, put it in your pocket."

"Understood," said the doctor, taken aback.

"Good. So I'll be leaving sooner than later."

"I'd prefer to keep you here for observation…"

"Not happening, Doc."

The doctor nodded and left, closing the door behind him. Lt. Gomez glared at the doctor's back until he was gone. "Shit, that doctor was looking at me like I was his next paper in some medical journal. Probably descended from the guy who shot President Abraham Lincoln."

"Whiteface Mountain," said Connor. "You think that's where Derga is?"

"Or somewhere nearby," said the Cornet of Horse.

"Yeah," said Lt. Gomez. "He's not going to be standing on top of the mountain waiting for us. He's got to a have a hidey-hole nearby."

"Lieutenant, I'm not sure you should be moved out of hospital," said the Cornet of Horse.

"You get me out of this bed or I'll have you all busted," said Lt. Gomez.

" For what?" objected Connor.

"I'll think of something."

"Just when I thought you were my friend," said Straparola.

"But more to the point, Agent Medea, I got an illegal alien who's probably a terrorist of some kind running around with a cop killer. There is no way I'm not coming with you."

"I don't think his name is Medea," said Connor.

"Whatever," said Lt.Gomez. "Find my fucking clothes."

"Can I have your juice?" asked Straparola. "You know, that bitch nearly clobbered me with a mallet? The experience has left me a little dry in the mouth. And I'm not inclined to go boating on the Hudson again anytime soon. Damn imps, for crying out loud,"

Connor didn't want to discuss the imps in the river mist. He could still see their ghastly faces. Connor opened a wardrobe where Lt. Gomez's clothes were hanging.

"We'll wait in the hall," said the Cornet of Horse.

"Yeah," said Straparola. "I'm not ready to see you naked."

"Take the damn juice with you," snapped Lt. Gomez, gripping Connor by the arm to prevent him from leaving. Connor had little choice to hang back while the others left.

285

"By the way," said Lt. Gomez. "Why don't you hand over that little artifact you're holding for safekeeping."

Connor hesitated.

It'll be just between us girls."

Connor reluctantly reached into his pocket and pulled out the sock containing the comb.

"Nice sock," said Lt. Gomez as he took it from Connor's hand. He held the sock for a moment then handed it back to Connor.

"I just wanted to see how you felt about it. I have a feeling you should hold onto it."

Chapter Twenty-Six

The world below Connor was like an old black & white movie, a rolling forest of deep blacks and light grays that covered the Adirondack Mountains. Then the cloud passed and color returned like a cinematic revolution. Connor looked down from the helicopter window at the passing trees, mostly pine sprinkled with white birch. Off to the right was a black ribbon dotted with reflections from cars traveling north to Montreal.

Connor looked over at the hulking figure of the pilot, wondering for the hundredth time just who he was.

"Agent Medea," said Connor. "We keep trying to give you a name but they seem to slide off you. It might work better if you gave us one."

For a few seconds, Connor wondered if he had been heard. The engine noise was deafening and all four wore headphones with a microphone attached. But he wasn't sure if it worked. The pilot had been having a running conversation with someone ever since they'd left Beacon but Connor had not been able to overhear any of it.

"No, it wouldn't," said a voice in his ear. "We're bearing left. Hang on."

The craft veered away from the highway, heading west. The mountains were higher now and topped with stony outcrops. A waterfall appeared briefly, the water falling like a line drawn by a silver pen. Then it was gone. In the distance, he could see a half dozen lakes looking like puddles left after a heavy rain.

"We can't just go around yelling 'hey, you' anytime we're trying to get your attention," said Connor. "That's not going to work very well."

There was no immediate reply and Connor began to think he'd been brushed off.

"Cornet of Horse."

"What?" said Connor.

"That's what you can call me."

"The Heer of Dunderberg calls you by that name," said Connor.

"How do you know that?"

Connor shook his head as if too clear it. "I heard it in some kind of dream."

"Is that a rank?" asked Lt. Gomez.

"It is the one I liked the best."

"Pity the mount," mumbled Straparola. "Must have been a goddamn Clydesdale or something."

"We're here," said the Cornet of Horse and the helicopter descended onto what appeared to be an empty field in the middle of nowhere.

They walked along a narrow, wooded trail for about 50 yards until they came upon a dirt road covered with a carpet of browning pine needles. The Cornet of Horse turned up the road with purpose, his stride carrying him ahead of the others.

"Where are we?" asked Lt. Gomez.

Straparola looked up from his phone. "GPS app says we're near St. Hubert's."

"Thanks," said Lt. Gomez. "That really helps a lot."

"St. Hubert is the patron saint of hunters. Looks to be a small hamlet around 20 miles from Lake Placid," continued Straparola "You must have heard of it. Two Olympics. The second one in 1980 was the Miracle on Ice. We beat the Soviets in hockey. Won the gold medal."

"Do I look like I follow hockey?" said Lt. Gomez.

"It was made into a movie," added Connor.

"What's a Cornet of Horse?" asked Lt. Gomez.

Straparola consulted his phone. "Third and lowest grade of cavalry officer tasked with carrying the colors."

"Interesting," said Lt. Gomez. "That would imply superior officers."

"So what do you make of him?" asked Connor.

"You mean his size?" replied Straparola. "He's nearly seven feet tall and built like a brick shithouse. No sunken chest. Arms and legs proportional. Big muscles. Rules out some kind of genetic disorder. He's the real deal."

"Which is what exactly?" asked Connor.

"A giant." replied Straparola..

"Get real," said Lt. Gomez. "There are lots of basketball players his size."

"Not with his mass," said Straparola. "I mean the guy just breathes density. My guess is he weighs well over 300 pounds."

"So he takes steroids or something," said Lt. Gomez.

"Maybe," said Straparola. "But he moves quicker and is more limber than the average dude doing supplements. I'm sticking with giant. Given everything else we've experienced lately, I'm not ruling it out."

"Ho, ho, ho" said Lt. Gomez

Straparola looked annoyed but Connor smiled at the reference to the Green Giant, an advertising character whose face appeared on boxes of frozen vegetables.

"I thought you were the science guy," said Connor.

"Giants are not unknown to science," replied Straparola. "It's just that we all think there is something medically wrong with them. Well, maybe not all of them."

The Cornet of Horse disappeared around a bend in the road and as they in turn rounded the curve, they caught sight of him approaching the entrance of a large building constructed from logs. Connor couldn't tell exactly how big it was because, except for the entrance, trees surrounded it on all sides. Standing in the doorway was a well-tailored bald Asian man with one of those hospitality smiles that looked like it was applied every morning with some kind of device.

"Welcome to The Needle," he said. "My name is Ivan Ho."

"No. Two words. Ivan and Ho. My parents were big fans of Elizabeth Taylor and they met at a screening of *Ivanhoe*. It has been my burden to bear ever since," explained Ho.

"Sorry," said Connor.

"I've come to terms with it and it makes for a good story. Please call me Ivanhoe. Everyone does. It's like they can't resist it."

"Well, if it was me I'd be pissed at my parents but it's your call," said Straparola.

"And you're called 'Strap."

The Cornet of Horse had called ahead.

"Only by my friends. So what is this place? Some kind of hotel? "

"More like an exclusive club," replied Ivanhoe.

"For who?" asked Straparola.

"Members."

"Anyone we would know?" asked Connor, sliding in between Ivanhoe and Strap before their relationship deteriorated beyond repair.

"I'm not at liberty to comment about current members," replied Ivanhoe. "I can tell you that Franklin Delano Roosevelt was a frequent guest although he came here most often when he was Governor of New York and less so after he became President."

"So you're saying everything after the 1940's is what you would call 'current.'"

"That is correct. Please follow me," said Ivanhoe.

They walked up two slate steps and followed Ivanhoe through a circular vestibule into a great room with two giant fireplaces at each end, both ablaze. Beams crossed the ceiling and rich Persian rugs covered the floors. A leather couch and chairs were arranged around the nearest fireplace while a long wood dining table slightly obscured the one farthest away. Smaller table and chairs were situated around the room, all made from twigs and bark.

Connor had expected the room to be empty but was surprised to see five men in combat fatigues sitting at the dining room table, each one intently looking at the screen of a portable laptop computer. The soldier nearest him was bald except for a narrow strip of hair that ran from the front to the back of his head in a style Connor recognized as belonging to the Mohawk Indians. The four others, he quickly noticed, wore their hair cut military-style short but each sported a long braid of hair that ran to the middle of their backs. One wore a camo pattern baseball hat. All of them had black eyes with even blacker eyebrows as straight as hyphens. Connor also noted a pin on each of their shirt collars. A solid white pine was featured in the center linked to the outlines of white rectangle and a white box on both flanks, all set against a purple field. They all looked up at the Cornet of Horse and nodded in greeting.

"Anything?" said the Cornet of Horse.

One shook his head.

"Mohawk, Oneida, Onondaga, Cayuga, and Seneca," said the Cornet of Horse. "Tuscarosa is on guard outside."

"I didn't see him," said Lt. Gomez.

"That's the idea," said Ivanhoe.

"Those are the names of the Six Nations of the Iroquois Indians," said Connor. "I remember that from school."

"Also known as the 'Haudensounee,'" said the Cornet of Horse. "The People of the Long House have been native to this area for centuries."

"Not exactly your average lacrosse team," said Connor. The Iroquois were already playing the game when the first colonists arrived in North America, sometimes using the heads of their enemies for a ball. Connor remembered reading about the sport when the British had refused to recognize their tribal passports for an international tournament in the UK some time back. The Irishman in him always took note of the perfidies of the old enemy.

Connor's comment elicited a chuckle from the group, breaking the ice.

"A representative from each nation has been part of this unit for generations," said the Cornet of Horse. "We don't use given names."

Straparola had noticed the pins on their shirt collars as well. "There are six nations but only five symbols on those pins."

The Mohawk spoke up. "They represent the original five tribes of the Iroquois Confederacy. The Tuscarosa joined later. That's why Tuscarosa gets guard duty all the time."

The other Iroquois chuckled softly at the old joke.

"The white pine symbolizes the Onondaga on whose land the treaty was signed. The square on the left symbolizes the Mohawk, Keepers of the Eastern Door, while the square on the right is for the Seneca, Keepers of the Western Door. The two rectangles are for the Oneida and Cayuga."

The Iroquois collectively projected an aura of calm and a feeling Connor could only describe as depth. Connor felt like he was in the presence of something far older than the America he knew. He was a white man and a newcomer, if not an outright trespasser. His people were Irish immigrants but he had only thought of that in relationship to the older white Protestant stock that had founded the United States. They were immigrants as well but that knowledge only became personified in the presence of the Iroquois. He realized that he felt strangely uncomfortable and he was not pleased with himself for having that feeling. Was it guilt? He and no one he knew had ever caused a Native American harm but somehow he felt responsible for those who had. And, Connor realized with a tinge of regret, he had rooted for the cowboys in all those bad western films he had seen as a boy.

He now noticed that there was a New York Yankee logo emblazoned on the front of the baseball cap worn by one of the Iroquois.

"Yankee fan?" Connor asked the wearer. Oneida.

A nod. "You?"

"Lifelong, especially against the Red Sox." Connor didn't think this was the time to admit he usually fell asleep by the third inning of baseball games unless he was seeing it live. The game was often slow and boring but its languid pace somehow meant that all was safe in the world. Baseball induced dozing.

"Hate the Red Sox."

"What's the difference between the Red Sox and the Yankees?" interjected Straparola. "When the Red Sox lose, it's an act of God. When the Yankees lose, it's a financial problem."

Guffaws all around. "The joke does illustrate the difference between a Boston founded by religious Puritans and a New York founded by Dutch merchants."

"That's too deep a thought for baseball," said Connor, getting smile all around.

Ice broken.

"So what do you guys do normally?" asked Oneida.

Straparola spoke up: "Science journalist, film festival director, and federal agent," pointing at Connor and Lt. Gomez in turn.

The Iroquois glanced at each other but said nothing.

"So can we get back to finding the girls," said Connor, perhaps more sharply than he intended.

"That's what we're doing now," said the Cornet of Horse, nodding toward the Iroquois.

"What are you looking for?" asked Lt. Gomez.

Tell them nothing! said a Voice. Harpin again. Bitter as always.

"A tell-tale sign," said the Cornet of Horse cautiously.

"What exactly?" asked Lt. Gomez.

Inform them, said another Voice the Cornet of Horse recognized as Salvius Brabo, the Roman general. *It's a sound move strategically.*

Brabo was smarter than Harpin, the Cornet of Horse decided. "Are you familiar with M-brane theory?

Connor and Straparola looked at each other.

"I see that you are," said the Cornet of Horse.

"No, not all of us," said Lt. Gomez quickly. "What is it? Some kind of surveillance tech?"

"Hear me out." said the Cornet of Horse. "M-brane theory posits the existence of parallel universes. Think of our universe as a bed sheet flapping in the wind. Alongside of it is another bed sheet, also undulating in the wind. When the two bedsheets touch each other, a connection between dimensions called a wormhole is made. A lot of the time the two sheets hit each other in the same spot. Gravitational force isn't spread out evenly. It's stronger in some places than others. Ireland, for example, is a particularly strong point. So are the Adirondack Mountains. Sometimes the hits seem random, moving around much the same the way magnetic north shifts location. All these points of contact seem temporary but recurring. We don't know how to predict those points of contact. The Other Side does."

"Like a shifting layer of bubble wrap," said Connor. "That's what Derga called it."

The Cornet of Horse gave him a long look. "She's well informed."

"Give me a break," interrupted Lt. Gomez. "You're telling me we're chasing kidnappers from another dimension?"

"Or from a previous universe," added Ivanhoe. "The points of contact may be Hawking Points.

"You mean like those named for the great cosmologist Stephen Hawking?" interjected Straparola. "I thought those were in deep space." Straparola noticed the puzzled looks on many faces.

"Sorry," said Connor. "I saw *The Theory of Everything* film with Eddie Redmayne but I may have missed that."

"Hawking Points are anomalous points in space that don't fit into the known scheme of our universe," explained Straparola. "Hawking thought they might be evidence of a previous universe, maybe even gateways of some kind."

"It's a minority view but the points where the Other Side comes and goes seem to emit very low levels of the same type of radiation that the Hawking Points in deep space do," continued Ivanhoe. "If that's the case, the laws of physics that apply here may not be applicable there. That means the Other Side may be capable of things that we can't even imagine. Truth is, we don't know anything for sure."

"OK, I'm not buying this but let's say I do," said Lt. Gomez. "Why can't we just follow them into their dimension or universe and bust their asses? Where is it exactly?"

"Well, if we stick to the M-brane theory, it's closer to you than your own clothes but we don't know how to get there," said the Cornet of Horse. "The laws of physics appear to be different between dimensions. Wormholes occur all the time but they're very small-- microscopic. The Heer of Dunderberg and his kind seem to be able to stabilize and expand a wormhole or a Hawking Point if that's what it is--something that would take the power of our entire planet for us to accomplish. The best guess is that they are able to harness what's called dark energy."

"What's that?" asked Connor.

"It's a quantum mechanics thing," piped in Straparola. "Essentially, it is a way of creating energy from nothing. Or at least nothing you can see. It's all based on harnessing the movement of sub-atomic particles between universes."

"You mean there's more than one parallel universe?" asked Lt. Gomez.

"At least eleven," said Straparola.

"Ah, man, this is all bullshit," said Lt. Gomez. "The bottom line is that you don't know where the fuck these guys are from but you have to catch them before they leave town. Otherwise, they're out of your jurisdiction."

"That's one way of looking at it," conceded the Cornet of Horse.

"So how long have these bastards been running their kidnapping ring," asked Lt. Gomex.

"For hundreds of years," said the Cornet of Horse.

Lt. Gomez looked hard at the Cornet of Horse. "OK. I get it. Some kind of goddamned religious cult engaged in human trafficking…"

The Cornet of Horse shook his head.

…or something like it," continued Lt. Gomez. "How are we going to catch them? There's a lot of mountain out there."

"Very true," said Ivanhoe. "The Adirondack Park is the biggest in the country and it practically covers the top half of New York State. And hardly anyone lives here. There are parts of the Adirondacks no one has walked through since the Civil War."

Ivanhoe walked over to a wall map that showed the Adirondack Park's boundaries marked in blue. "And then there is this area here." He traced a line with his fingers.

"Blue Mountain Lake to the north, Indian Lake to the east and the West Canada Lake to the west form what local forest rangers have dubbed The Triangle. At least 10 hikers have disappeared without a trace within The Triangle in the last 50 years."

"You mean like the Bermuda Triangle?" asked Yacobuzio.

"Correct," said Ivanhoe. "The rangers noticed the similarity to disappearances to that area."

"You think our guy has been snatching these people?" asked Lt. Gomez. "That makes him one very old kidnapper."

"It may also explain why none of my people ever lived here in the High Peaks," said Mohawk. "There are old stories about warriors who went into the mountains and never returned. We hunted here but no longhouses were built."

"And how do we find him?" asked Connor.

"We have that satellite I mentioned," said the Cornet of Horse. "It has a new sensor on board."

Lt. Gomez smiled. "Now you're talking."

"It's not clear whether it's an indication of a wormhole or a by product that's caused when it is used but in any event a specific type of particle called Kaluza-Klein is associated with the phenomenon. A sensor aboard an orbiting satellite is able to detect these particles and give us a general location. We can use handheld devices to pinpoint the location more exactly."

"The bad news," said Connor, "is that if you detect the particles it may mean they're already gone."

"I won't try to fool you," said the Cornet of Horse. "That's very possible. So we're going to take a gamble. We're going to position ourselves near Whiteface Mountain. We have reason to believe they're in that general area."

"Because of the state trooper that was murdered there recently," said Lt. Gomez, remembering the report he had seen about it. "A woman was kidnapped from a ski lodge and the state trooper who went in pursuit was found with his heart in his hand but with no sign of a wound. The kidnapper and the woman disappeared."

"Particles were detected within that same time frame," said the Cornet of Horse.

"So what do we do now?" asked Connor.

"We put a surveillance ring around Whiteface Mountain. One man will remain here to monitor satellite data. It'll be in place by morning. Then we wait and hope we can get to wherever they are quick enough."

"Why does this feel like a long shot," said Connor.

"Don't worry," said Lt. Gomez. "This is basically an illegal immigration issue. You're lucky I'm here."

I knew he was an idiot. It was the Voice of Harpin. The Cornet of Horse laughed.

Connor shivered. There was something in that laugh that made Connor wonder if the Cornet of Horse was slightly mad.

Chapter Twenty-seven

S he didn't like riding around in a stolen vehicle, particularly when she had stolen it herself.

The Heer of Dunderberg had driven the motorboat north up the river to a small city called Albany that billed itself as the capitol of New York although she found that hard to believe after seeing the metropolis at the mouth of the Hudson River. There were a lot of dome-shaped buildings and others with Roman-style columns that reminded her of the government buildings she had seen in Dublin years ago. They cruised along the river until the Heer of Dunderberg tied up at an abandoned pier at sunset.

The Heer of Dunderberg climbed out of the boat and beckoned for her to follow. At least he had stowed his awful hat somewhere. And the trumpet had vanished as well. She suspected it was collapsible and stored in a pocket. She shot back at questioning look.

"They're not going anywhere," he said.

She assumed now their captives below deck were somehow incapacitated so they would remain unconscious. Some class of fairy dust, she guessed, developed by the Unseelie Court. "Where are we going?"

"We need different transportation," he said.

The Heer of Dunderberg walked like he knew where he was going and within minutes they were across the street from a restaurant called the Rusty Knot. "Put on your gywnn and go over there and get us the keys to a vehicle big enough for our cargo. Something big, black and preferably with tinted windows."

"I don't know how to drive," she said.

"Just get the keys."

She donned her gwynn and strode over to the parking lot and as if on cue, a large, black vehicle with the words Cadillac Escalade emblazoned on its bumper drove in. A burly man with a ponytail got out and locked the door with his key fob. She let him get almost to the door of the restaurant before she hit him with one of the tiny darts she kept in a pouch inside her dress. He collapsed into the door with a thud, foaming at the mouth. She moved quickly and removed the keys from the man's pocket, retrieving the dart at the same time. She turned back toward the vehicle and saw that the Heer of Dunderberg was already waiting. She opened the SUV's door remotely and the Heer of Dunderberg slid in behind the wheel. She opened the passenger door and gave him the keys.

"Always the gentleman, I see," she said.

The Heer of Dunderberg sneered as the engine started. A customer leaving the restaurant had found the vehicle's owner and was calling for help. No one noticed the Cadillac slowly leaving the parking lot.

"He'll be in hospital for at least a week," she said.

They returned to the pier and she used her gwynn to cover their cargo as the women were moved from the boat to the SUV, lowering the rear seats and laying the women side by side. Then they drove north.

They followed the highway for a few hours and traffic thinned the farther north they went. By the time they reached Exit 30, cars were few and as far between as the exit signs. They left the highway and drove west, slowly climbing until they abruptly started downhill, passing a waterfall on her right. The mountains here were taller than the ones in Ireland and different somehow. To her eye, it seemed as if the rock was bubbling up from below, pushing older stones out of the way. *The things people don't see.*

They drove through a few small villages. In one she noticed a red phone booth and it suddenly hit her how rare they had become. She had noticed how everyone carried their own phone these days so the phone booth told her how remote they must be that the owners didn't even bother to come and remove it. At a junction they made a left and then another right shortly thereafter. Eventually, they came to a dirt road and she caught a glimpse of lake. They bumped along until they came to a stone bridge she knew immediately had been glamoured. The bridge appeared to be impassable with trees growing out of the dirt covered roadway. The Heer of Dunderberg drove right through them and they parted as if they were alive. Of course, the trees weren't really there but the illusion was convincing, she thought as she looked back over shoulder.

When she turned her head forward once more, she saw the house. It was a Swiss-style chalet built on a slope with decks on the second level. The house looked to be about 40 years old but was in good condition. Mostly the house was brown but the slates on the deck were painted a French blue.

"The people who own this place come only during the summer," said the Heer of Dunderberg.

They climbed a flight of wooden stairs up to a porch to the front door. The door opened onto a small kitchen that led into a large living room with a view of Whiteface Mountain in the distance. The walls and ceilings were fashioned from knotty pine planks and

302

the room was furnished in the twiggy Adirondack style. But her eye was drawn to the pair of large, red leather easy chairs in front of the fireplace. A Persian rug covered the floor and the far end of the room was dominated by a striped sofa. A staircase led up to a small loft and a bedroom. But rather than go upstairs to explore, she was quickly mesmerized by a three-dimensional wood carving of a forest scene hanging on the staircase wall. The carving was of a log frame cabin by the shores of a lake, with a rowboat in the foreground that seemed to jump out at her. She reached out instinctively to touch it, running her finger along the fine line of the prow. Curious, she took the carving off the wall and examined it, surprised to learn from the inscription on the back that it had been made in Finland in 1959. The artist's name meant nothing to her but he had been talented. The scene was very much like her present surroundings and she had assumed the carvings were of local origin.

Things are not always want they seemed. A good reminder.

She hung the carving back on the wall.

A reminder. She closed her eyes for a moment and was suddenly seized by a clear vision of where her comb was and in whose hands it lay. The vision baffled her while also filling her with joy. *Why could she only see it now and not before?*

"I know where they are," she said. "I have to go."

"Good," said the Heer of Dunderberg. "We'll go together."

"I want to go alone," she said, fearing his presence might complicate things and jeopardize the recovery of her comb.

"So be it," he said. "If you wait until dark, I can prepare a little diversion that might make things easier. You're going into the lair of the hunter. You'll need all the help you can get."

She nodded her assent although she had to admit to herself she didn't trust him.

"You really can't go home without it," he said. "The comb, I mean."

She hadn't discussed the comb with him or told him why it was so important. *But he knows of it anyway.* She looked into the darkness of his eyes and saw the Unseelie Court. *He is like the devil men fear.*

"No. I can't."

And that's how she found herself outside an animal shelter shortly after sundown. She had entered what was basically an oversized storefront wearing her gwynn an hour before closing and was amazed to discover rooms packed with cages full of cats-over 200 by her estimation. A sign on the wall noted that this was the only no-kill shelter for indoor cats in the county—that explained the overflow conditions. When the two employees had left for the day, she had waited for the car to pull away and then simply unlocked the door from the inside. The Heer of Dunderberg appeared as if on cue, carrying two large, black sacks.

The Heer of Dunderberg opened the cat cages and stuffed the animals hissing and spitting into the sacks, nine into each one, with no regard to color other than skipping over one that was black. The sacks became wriggly things that bulged in a new spot every second.

"Why cats?" she asked.

"You'll see," he said. "Nine is a good number. As are multiples of nine. Cats are supposed to have nine lives. They're going to need every one. Let them loose as close to the enemy's abode as you can. The cats will keep them busy."

"You skipped the black one."

"I want them to be seen in the dark."

They left by the front entrance and tossed the squirming sack into the back of the SUV. She sat in the front seat and closed her eyes, focusing on her comb.

"Go east," she said after a few moments. They drove for some distance, taking a side road that skirted the town of Lake Placid until two monstrous ramps appeared before them, structures the Heer of Dunderberg described as ski jumps but she showed no interest in them so he didn't explain further.

They were close now, she knew, as they drove east on a skinny road called Route 73 that slipped between mountains. They passed through two small towns called Keene, and Keene Valley. At a small hamlet called St. Hubert's she felt the hairs on her neck tingling and she motioned for the Heer of Dunderberg to stop. She could find her way on foot from here.

"Don't forget the cats," he said.

"I still don't understand."

"You'll see. The hunter hates cats."

She must have looked as uncertain as she felt.

"Just do it."

She gave him a sharp look but went around to the back of the vehicle. She donned her gwynn and then opened the cargo door and grabbed the sacks of cats, tucking them underneath her gwynn so it too was out of sight. The sacks squirmed in every direction and holding onto them was tricky. Slowly, she walked forward until she saw a structure with lights on inside. She focused on the nearest window and was amazed to see her comb in the hands of a swarthy looking man she recognized from Bannerman Island. He was talking to someone else in the room that was out of view. She could read his lips.

"Well, the truth is that I don't know if a crime has been committed," said the man. "There is no complaint as of yet. If there is one, I know how to find you. In the meantime, you might as well hold onto it."

The man extended his hand, the one holding the comb and another hand appeared to take it. She could have screamed right there and was nearly set to just crash through the window and recover it herself when she heard a noise to her right. Another man was approaching and she could see he carried a rifle of some sort. *A guard!* The cats reacted to the noise as well and a pair of them in the sack hissed loudly. The guard immediately tilted his head and began mumbling into a device on his collar.

Within seconds more armed men poured out of the house. She counted eight in all. Five were armed with the same kind of rifle as the guard while the rest had drawn pistols. Now seemed like a good time for a diversion and she let loose the cats, The cats poured out of the sack in a tumble of colors and scooted away from her as fast as they could. She did the same, moving to her left away from the cats and the armed men.

The cats made a beeline for the house and were instantly spotted by the men.

"Open fire!" said a voice.

The night exploded in the flash and noise of weapons fire. The rifles fired automatically, she saw. The last rifle she had seen close up used a bolt for loading and fired one bullet at a time. These produced a wall of bullets. The cats tumbled in the air as the bullets found them. The men were expert marksmen and she realized the diversion wouldn't last long. She slipped quickly behind the men and through the door, keeping to the wall as she entered a large room with beams overhead and a fireplace at each end. The sound of a heavy footfall approaching from another room gave her pause. *The hunter!* She quickly moved down a hall and into a bedroom. She was now uncertain of her next move. She was loathed to confront the hunter and all those men. She would wait in the dark, invisible to their eyes, until an opportunity presented itself. She tried to focus once more on the comb but no clear image of it appeared in her mind. The gunfire had ceased and the men were returning to the great room.

"Mohawk, Oneida," said a voice she knew instinctively as belonging to the hunter. "Check the perimeter."

"You just blew a bunch of cats to hell," said another voice. *The thief!* "What was that all about?"

"A diversion, I suspect," said the hunter. "We need to check all the rooms."

"Yeah, but why did we have to shoot all the cats?"

There was no reply. She would have liked to hear the answer to that herself. *A weakness of some kind.* The Heer of Dunderberg knew what it was but hadn't told her. *Why not?* She didn't know the answer and it made her uneasy. The hunter's footsteps receded and she dared to open the door a crack. The remaining men had disappeared into other rooms but the small movement of the door had attracted the attention of the thief. He was coming her way. She backed up against the far wall opposite the door. The bed was to her right and a window was to her left. She stood ready to spring at him as he entered the room.

The door slowly opened and the thief stood there holding something to his eye.

"What's that?" said a voice behind him. She couldn't see the other one yet but she could take both of them easily.

"A stone with a hole in the middle," said the thief. "Derga gave it to me. She said if I look through the hole, I'll be able to see the Deeneeshee."

Her eyebrows raised in surprise. *Derga must be the woman with red hair.*

It was all becoming too dangerous for her. The hunter was too close. She lunged but not toward the thief. She crashed through the window and she guessed she'd been seen because she heard him cry out even before she smashed through the glass. She was through the window so quickly the broken glass didn't touch her. And while she had left the thief in her wake, she scarcely realized where she was going. The next thing she knew she was practically on top of one the men she'd seen earlier. In her surprise, she bumped into him without intending to and while she was still invisible, the man knew she was right in front of him. He was already in a firing position but before he could pull the trigger, she swept back her gwynn and screamed into his face at a frequency beyond the hearing ability of men. That didn't save him. The man clasped his hands to his ears, dropping the weapon. She couldn't be sure but sometimes their eardrums ruptured. Sometimes not. But at such close range, her victim would suffer major tissue damage. She heard a small cry of agony as she stepped around him and ran for the woods, kicking up a whirlwind behind her.

All of her kind created a sound like a swarm of bees in flight when they moved quickly and she realized that she had made a mistake even before the punishment for that error was upon her. As she reached the trees, a black blade came out of the night and she only just managed to swivel her head at the last moment or it would have skewered her right eye. She had made it easy for him to track her and that carelessness had almost ended her existence. She swerved and that move saved her as she felt another blade slide past her abdomen, leaving a thin cut in its wake. He was in front of her, a large, dark shadow with arms moving to strike again. Without thinking, she jumped into the air as the blades sliced the air below her, spinning forward as she pulled her gwynn around her disappearing from sight. The blades stabbed at the air but didn't find her. She landed on the ground in a crouch and remained still, less any movement betray her, hoping the darkness would help conceal her. There were stories that hunters could see through a gwynn. She didn't know if the stories were true but this wasn't the time to test the veracity of the tale.

All was quiet. She tried to spy her attacker but he was likely using the trees to hide himself. Then a moan reached her ears from the man she had encountered earlier.

Then she heard the voice of her attacker, speaking in some kind of gibberish that sounded like a saw hacking its way through wood. *Zamzummin.* She didn't know the language but recognized it at once from stories she'd heard about the enemy. And she didn't need to know the words to understand the message. He would kill her on another day.

She heard footsteps moving off in the direction of the moan and when she judged that it was no ruse, she moved off, careful not to leave a whirlwind in her wake. She reached the road where she had left the Heer of Dunderberg and got another surprise.

The Heer of Dunderberg was nowhere to be seen.

That's when she screamed. The air filled with a high pitch whine that sounded like thousands of crickets. But she kept it under control. Only a few nearby tree trunks cracked.

Chapter Twenty-Eight

A loud moan escaped from the lips of Seneca and Connor shuddered. Seneca's face was a mass of purplish boils that had swollen his eyes shut. All of his Iroquois companions were crowded into a bedroom where the stricken man lay.

Connor couldn't bear to look anymore and returned to the great room where he found Straparola and Lt. Gomez slumped into a pair of leather wingback chairs. Straparola looked very pale while Lt. Gomez looked stunned. A scrapping noise made Connor look outside where he saw the Cornet of Horse and Ivanhoe under the light of an exterior light. They looked as if they were firing up an old-fashioned coal-burning barbecue. It hardly seemed like meal time.

Connor flung open the door. "Are you serious?"

"Very," said Ivanhoe. "Seneca has been blasted. We're working on a cure."

The Cornet of Horse ignored them both and worked a bellows to make the coals hotter.

"It's called *esane,*" continued Ivanhoe."

The Cornet of Horse nodded and Ivanhoe reached down for a pitcher of water that had been at his feet and removed the lid. The Cornet of Horse reached into the barbecue pit wit a pair of tongs and extracted one of the hot coals. He said some words in a language Connor didn't recognize but that sounded like a saw cutting through wood. He then dropped the hot coal into the pitcher. The Cornet of Horse repeated the process until the water was in the pitcher was bubbling and that's when Ivanhoe slapped a lid on top.

Ivanhoe rushed back into the house with the Cornet of Horse and Connor following. Straparola and Lt. Gomez roused themselves from their chairs and followed them all into the bedroom.

"Make a hole," commanded the Cornet of Horse. The Iroquois parted and Ivanhoe knelt by the stricken man and poured some of liquid into Senaca's mouth, holding his head up so the man could swallow. Seneca made a gagging sound that made Connor wonder if he wasn't being poisoned.

"It's a cure for all manner of Deeneeshee afflictions," said the Cornet of Horse, in way of explanation. "But no one ever said it tasted good. He should recover."

"And those boils?" asked Straparola.

"They'll fade away," said the Cornet of Horse. "He'll be as handsome as ever."

"He was never handsome," said Mohawk.

The joke wasn't that funny but they all laughed, mostly in relief that their comrade seemed to be out of danger.

"Let's clear the room and let him rest," said Ivanhoe.

They all re-entered the great room and Straparola and Lt. Gomez reclaimed the wingbacks while the Iroquois checked their weapons.

"I almost had her," said the Cornet of Horse. He opened the front door and stepped outside. He didn't look like he wanted company. Ivanhoe, for his part, unobtrusively went back to the bedroom to check on Seneca.

"Shit, those look like those new South Korean smart weapons" said Lt. Gomez, nodding at the Iroquois. "They fire a standard 5.56mm rifle round but the humdinger is the 20mm explosive shell with some kind of tracking chip in it. Even if you're hiding behind a wall, a shooter can airburst it over your head, turning you into hamburger. It's also got a thermal night vision infrared scope. But the design here looks slightly different." Lt. Gomez paused for a moment. "And I don't think it's legal to import them."

"No worries," said Mohawk. "They're ghost guns."

"Ghost guns?" asked Connor.

"We buy individual components off the Internet. All perfectly legal since only the receiver housing the trigger and magazine section is actually regulated. We make our own receivers from blocks of aluminum using a high end 3-D printer. Then assemble the weapon ourselves. No serial numbers. Untraceable. Ghost guns."

"Nice to have deep pockets," said Straparola.

Mohawk shrugged and glanced toward the Cornet of Horse. "Not my department."

"Do you do any custom work?"

"Sure. That's the fun part actually." Mohawk pointed toward what looked like a machine pistol hanging off Oneida's hip. "The receiver on that one is basically from a standard AR-15 hunting rifle. You just jam a clip into it like you would the rifle. But the modified design is more effective for close quarter combat and offers the benefit of more ammo without reloading. Plus the ammo magazines are interchangeable between the rifle and the pistol.

"Damn," said Lt. Gomez.

Connor hoped he would never have to use one. "I was wondering where I could get a cup of tea," he asked.

Straparola pointed at a pair of swinging doors off to the side of the room.

"Want a cup?" asked Connor.

"Coffee would be better," said Straparola.

"Ditto," mumbled Lt. Gomez.

Connor followed Straparola's outstretched arm through a swinging door and into a kitchen that would have been impressive in any restaurant. There was an impressive array of pots and pans, long expanses of shiny steel surfaces for preparing meals, and industrial looking burners and appliances. Connor found a kettle to boil some water and a tin of English breakfast tea. He then saw the coffee maker and eyed it warily. He was too embarrassed to admit it to anyone but he had never used a coffee maker and had no idea how it worked.

The water boiled and Connor added some milk from the refrigerator to his tea. He took a sip of the hot liquid and eyed the coffee machine. The kitchen door opened and Oneida walked in and went right to the coffee maker and turned it on.

"Hell of a night," said Connor.

Oneida nodded as he busied himself with making the coffee.

"You OK?" asked Connor.

Oneida shrugged. "It's tough. I won't kid you. I thought we were going to lose Seneca. I've known him a long time. But then you've got big troubles of your own. Those women are close to you?"

"Yeah," said Connor slowly. He paused. He didn't want to dwell on the women at the moment. What he wanted was a momentary distraction to keep his mind off them, at least until he finished his tea. "So where are you from?"

"Caledonia," said Oneida. "In Ontario," he added when he saw the blank look on Connor's face. "There is a reservation there. We were on the wrong side of your American Revolution."

"Canada," said Connor. "This is becoming a real international operation."

"You're right," said Oneida. "But I don't consider myself Canadian. I belong to the sovereign Iroquois nation. We have our own passports."

"Well, I want to thank you for your help," said Connor. "But I really don't get the connection between you and the big guy out there in the other room."

"We call him Dehotgohsgayeh. He helps us fight against Shagodyowehgowah, ruler of the false faces. It has been that way for generations. Only he can teach us how to fight certain enemies."

"Like the one we face now."

"Yes." said Oneida. "Besides, it's good training for our next war."

"You mean the war against terrorists?"

"No, I mean fucking Canadians. They keep stealing our land. They pay only lip service to the old treaties. Ontario, and Quebec was once ours. I'm not saying we're going to take it all back. But now they want what little we have left. We're surrounded by subdivisions. We're going to have to fight them one day soon. And suburbanites are going to die."

Connor didn't know what to say and Oneida knew it.

"We're not just about casinos, lacrosse, and tax-free cigarettes," added Oneida, before pouring some coffee into his cup and departing. He drank it black, Connor noticed. Oneida paused at the door and looked back. "Sorry. Canadians just piss me off."

"I didn't think anyone was mad at Canadians."

"Oh, there are," said Oneida. "New Yorkers are pretty cool, though. At least they are letting the tribal police patrol the Hogansburg Triangle."

Connor face was a blank.

"Up by Akwsesane."

Connor nodded, feigning understanding lest he be considered a complete idiot. There was a whole First Nation landscape he was unaware of. *A Native American freedom fighter. Scalped Canadian suburbanites. What next?* Connor looked around the kitchen. Right now, his cup of tea tasted pretty weak but he didn't see a bottle of anything stronger.

Oneida passed Straparola in the doorway, one leaving as the other entered.

"Find any coffee?" asked Straparola.

Connor nodded toward the coffee maker and Straparola poured himself a cup. He took one sip and scowled.

"Needs a little help." Straparola opened a pair of cabinet draws directly in front of him.

"Aha!"

"What is it?"

"Looks like alcohol which is good enough for me." Straparola pulled out a decanter with a greenish liquid inside. "Crème de menthe, maybe. I knew this Bulgarian babe who used to mix it with anisette. Looked nuclear. It was awesome but two was too many."

Straparola found two glasses and poured a measure into each one.

"Slainte!" said Connor as he downed the contents of the glass in one gulp.

"Whoa, wait up! You're too fast for me," said Straparola.

"Definitely not crème de minthe," said Connor. But then his eyes widened in alarm. Connor felt his legs weakening. Then someone turned off the lights and everything was quiet.

The feeling only lasted a moment, or so it seemed. Then the lights came on but there was still no sound. He was no longer at The Needle. He was walking south on the Grand Concourse in the Bronx. The boulevard was modeled on the Champs-Elysee in Paris. He was walking on the west side of the street. On the opposite side was Poe Park. He could see the small white cottage where the gothic writer Edgar Allen Poe had lived for a few years in the 19th century. The Bronx had been a rural outpost of New York City back then. Connor remembered seeing some of the classic movies that had been made from Poe's stories in the 1960s. He had liked *Tales of Terror*, a trio of stories that featured Vincent Price, Peter Lorre and Basil Rathbone—all directed by Roger Corman, who later achieved fame for his zombie movies. *Poe would have loved it. Nevermore!*

Kingsbridge Road was behind him and he crossed 193rd Street. He turned his head to the right and glimpsed an entryway into St. James Park before his view was blocked by a white brick apartment building. He looked forward again and continued walking, unable to stop himself. A white Victorian that was the local branch of the Knights of Columbus came up quickly and then a matching pair of red brick apartment buildings.

There was still no sound and Connor realized he was in a dream. People walked by, heading in the opposite direction. A boy walked by with the latest edition of the *Journal-American* with its distinctive red line under the banner, the only splash of color on a black & white page. Among them, he realized, was a man he recognized as his father, although he appeared much younger than any real memory he had of him. His father was going to work. He worked as a freight conductor on the railroad. Iron Mike, his friends called him as testimony to his durability. He never missed a day on the job sick, worked double and triple shifts without complaint and had been recognized for an unblemished safety record.

All this went through Connor's mind in a flash. He was walking faster now, already at the next corner now, crossing 192nd Street. He glanced right down the street. Some boys had drawn a skully board on the blacktop and were flicking wax-filled bottle caps from square to square—thirteen in order and thirteen in reverse—while trying to avoid or be hit into the dead zone around the center box that cost the player a turn. On the sidewalk, another group of boys were lined up for a game of Ace; King, Queen, slicing the pinkish ball –a Spaldeen--up and down the line of sidewalk squares with an open palm, the loser being demoted and the Ace controlling the serve.

On the Grand Concourse, some boys and a pair of tomboys were squatting over a steel grating, fishing for coins with chewed bubble gum wrapped around a string. The subway train ran under the Concourse and a whoosh from underground sent the kids' hair straight up. Halfway down the next block was the apartment building his family had lived in when he was a very young. The next corner was Fordham Road. The Grand Concourse slipped beneath it and rising on the other side in a straight line toward Yankee Stadium another 30 blocks south. Baseball was just a short subway ride away.

But it was the bar on the corner now that drew his attention. It was called The Raven. He had never been inside. Everyone said it was the local mob hangout. The Irish didn't drink there, that was for sure. The door was two steps down and Connor saw his hand on the doorknob, turning it and pushing the door open into the dark.

He must have blinked because now he was inside a well. It was bit gloomy but he knew it instantly. It was the fresh water well on his uncle's farm in Sligo. He was standing on a stone ledge, a pool of black water extending outwards to lap at the stone wall some fifteen feet away. He turned slowly and as expected, saw the stone steps that led upward in a slow curve. He climbed the steps. They were damp and slippery. He came up on a field with low stone walls running around it. It was a typical Irish day, cloudy with the threat of rain more of a certainty than a possibility.

He headed off in the direction of his uncle's farm house and passed it at a brisk pace, turning down a tree-lined boreen barely wide enough for a donkey and cart, his four-wheel-drive vehicle, his uncle had said with a smirk but that was a later memory. The path led to the ruin of a house on a paved road. The thatch roof was long gone. This was the house where his father had been borne and his father before him.

There was a man waiting for him in a beautiful green car. It was a classic with big fenders and white sidewalls on the tires. He climbed in like he had been expecting it.

Chapter Twenty-Nine

"Stop your fidgeting," said an Irish male voice. Connor could hear again but it was what his eyes saw that seized his mind.

"My family is from up that road," said Connor.

"Are ye all right?"

His head felt out of sorts but the road was anchoring his mind. An empty two story that once belonged to a family called Kennedy and was stilled called 'the Kennedy house" by the locals even though no one had lived in it for decades. It stood like a big guardhouse next to a thin one-laner that rose slightly for a half-mile before disappearing.

"Nothing much up that way from the look of it," said the driver, a man with a square head topped by a mix of light and dark blonde curls and wearing a dark blazer.

"Right you are," said Connor, even though he knew there was a bachelor cousin living there in a house that smelled of stale tobacco and wet dog.

Connor didn't recall the driver's name although in fairness, they had only met a few hours before, being thrown together for a long journey in the Delahaye they were driving. Connor had driven an earlier leg so now he was in the passenger seat. *How do I know that? Where are we coming from?* Connor couldn't remember that either. *Fuck me and the existential questions.*

The Delahaye was gorgeous green. The car was the epitome of elongated elegance with a hood that was half the length of the car. Big front fenders curled over white-walled wheels. It was a cabriolet but they were driving with the top up. A long vertical grille flanked by a pair of big round headlights announced their coming. The Delahaye was the automotive pride of France—at least Connor thought so--created by the legendary car designer Henri Chapron. A Delahaye was the perfect mix of elegance and minimalism.

From the late 1940s! And how do I know who Henri Chapron is?

"What year is this?" asked Connor.

The driver shook his head. "Are ye asking about the car or the date?" The driver shot him a look. "Do you need some hair of the dog?"

Connor took in the clear acrylic steering wheel, suddenly realizing he wasn't sure how they came to be driving the Delahaye on a road toward Sligo town. That was the first clue, noted some part of his brain, that all was not as it should be.

"Dog?" asked Connor.

The driver laughed. "Don't tell me you can't recall the name of the dog?"

Questions answered with questions. All Connor wanted was answers that might make his headache go away. *How did I ever partner up with such an annoying prick?*

The second clue came as they drove into Sligo town as night fell. The town was lit up in warm amber like a Hollywood version of some pre-war European town, an effect that seemed right and wrong at the same time. Like if it hadn't been that way, it should have been. A dark spot of British colonialism appeared in his mind and then vanished under the glare of an oncoming streetlight.

The Delahaye cruised past a large cul-de-sac that opened into a large square with numerous small row houses jammed together and a few shops like a grocer's and a butcher's squeezed into small storefronts. As they drove by, Connor spotted an older woman leaning against a metal balustrade. She was wearing a brown sweater and a large beige shirt. Her hair was mousy brown and parted on the side so that her hair rose higher on one side of her head than the other.

"That's my aunt!" yelled Connor, but by that time they had rolled past.

"Reverse! Quick!"

The driver cursed under his breath, glanced into the rear view mirror and spun the car backwards into the square, nose pointed forward for a quick getaway should the need arise. Connor leaped out of the car but his aunt was gone. Aunt MayAg. Short for Mary Agnes. Something tripped in his mind. She was long dead.

A young girl of about 11 years with long blonde hair was crossing the square.

"Are you a Connor?" he called, running toward her. She didn't answer but Connor was close enough to grab her by the arm in an attempt to slow her down. But she shrugged him off without a look and ran into a small pub he hadn't noticed before.

Connor followed her in, ten paces behind. The door opened onto a long hallway with a double wide opening on the right that led to a long, dark bar of polished wood. The customers were all men, standing silently over pints of Guinness. One man sat by himself at a small high table in profile to Connor, a youngish man with a long neck, a prominent Adam's Apple, and black hair that looked like the only water it had seen was rain.

The blonde girl had vanished but there was a staircase at the back and Connor climbed it two steps at a time up to the second floor—no, the first in this country—where there was a kitchen of gleaming steel but it stood empty. The stairs went up another flight and Connor was surprised to discover a seamstress factory with two rows of tables with giant spools of thread above them. This too was empty.

Defeated, Connor retreated down the stairs. But as Connor was heading down, a massive man was heading up, dressed in a long, thick sweater that came down to the top of his knee-high Wellingtons, black hair and black beard that seemed all at one with angry blue eyes.

"Are ye the one interfering with the wee girl?"

In the man's mind, Connor was already guilty. The question was a formality.

"No, No!" Connor held his palms up in surrender. "I'm a relation. I think."

The big man wasn't buying it and stepped closer, fists clenched.

"I'm looking for the Connors," said Connor. "I thought she was one. I'm a Connor."

"You're no fooking Connor I've ever seen before."

"I have ID," said Connor, reaching for his wallet.

The man snarled and stepped forward.

"My wallet," said Connor, slowing his arm movement. Connor removed his driver's license and extended it. The man examined the document like a bouncer, and then threw it on the floor.

"Fook off." The tone said Connor was not yet guilty but not yet innocent either. The man turned to thunder down the stairs. Connor retrieved his license and followed him out, returning to the square to find it full of people in what felt like a carnival atmosphere. He found himself standing beside a man that looked his Uncle Tom. His dead Uncle Tom.

"What's going on?" asked Connor.

"Everyone's out taking a gander at the car. One like that doesn't drive in here every day. A Delahaye, I'm told, by some instant expert. Never even heard of it before today." The man paused. "But it looks something the gentry would drive. Are you here to fetch Dolores?"

"I don't know."

"Weren't you told?"

"No."

"Well, let's get it sorted." His uncle look-alike wrapped a beefy hand around Connor's elbow and maneuvered him across the square to a house with a wrought iron railing and a staircase that led up to a first or second floor entranceway, depending on what country he was in mentally. A woman in a tight blue sweater and black skirt stood in the doorway.

"Dolores," said the look-alike uncle. He went inside, leaving Connor to her like it was the next step in some initiation.

"Here is the femme fatale of the film," said some movie critic inside Connor's head. Long dark raven hair, a bust that could not go unnoticed, a slim waist, and long legs under a pencil skirt.

Connor didn't know if she was a relation or not. He hoped not. Dolores looked like she knew but wasn't saying, waiting to see how much of an ass he'd make of himself. Or not.

"I can't stay," said Connor, thinking that's all he wanted to do. He glanced toward the Delahaye and she followed his eyes and noted the driver waiting. The crowd had backed off a few steps and driver and car stood unmolested. Dolores looked back at him and Connor felt like he was on the verge of dissolving.

"What year is this?"

"Not the best line I've ever heard," said Dolores. "But not bad." She paused. "OTR, are we?" she said.

On the run. "It's not like that," said Connor.

"Of course not," she said in a tone that said it was.

Connor now himself wasn't sure. He stole a glance at the Delahaye. *Were there guns in the boot? The trunk in another country. Maybe he was on the run.*

"I'll walk you down," said Dolores, taking his arm and raising the heat everywhere else.

They reached the car and the passenger door swung open. Connor slid into the sea and closed the door, rolling down the window as fast as he was able. Dolores leaned over, all red lips, deep eyes and a deeper cleavage.

"You're always welcome here," she said.

Connor nodded and looked over at his driving colleague. The man was mesmerized.

"Go on, now," said Connor quietly. The words broke the spell. The street was clear. They sped into the night, heading north, and Connor closed his eyes so no other image could compete with his last look of Dolores. But a blast of the car's horn forced him to open his eyes again only to find himself flat on his back.

Connor raised himself on his elbows in time to see a very large man detach himself from a group of sword-carrying men marching in formation. The man, at least seven feet tall, wore a white linen shirt, dark breeches and a tunic fringed with silk set off by a blue cloak. The large man was upon now and picked him up by the throat with a six-fingered hand.

Connor looked his captor in the eye and saw that something in his own caught his captor's attention.

He could still hear but the only sound he heard was like a buzzing noise that sounded like a swarm of bees. Then it changed timber slightly to sound like a saw cutting through wood. And it was coming from him. His captor looked at him in surprise and then made a similar buzzing sound. At first he could make no sense of it but then the buzzing seemed to change frequency and he was able to discern words.

"Again. Who are you?"

"Connor."

"No, it's not. You smacked your head and now you're possessed."

"Who are you?"

"Aenotherus, bodyguard to Charlemagne, King of the Franks. You already know that."

"Are you a giant?"

"I am. But you're not. That we knew already. But suddenly you speak the language of the giants."

"Where am I?"

"Reims. Where else? To whom do you swear fealty?"

"No one."

"Wrong answer. I need a name."

"Charlemagne?"

"You don't sound convincing. Where do you live?"

"New York."

"Sounds Saxon. That won't make you any friends around here. Worse, the man I know to be you lives in Aquitane. Once more. To whom do you swear fealty?"

Connor threw out the first name that came to him. "The Cornet of Horse."

"Never heard of him. Doesn't seem like much of a title. But at least it doesn't sound like the devil. So maybe there is hope for you. Now, I'm going to smack you in the head. It will either reverse the damage or kill you."

Connor looked at a massive fist of Aenotherus. He counted the six clenched fingers again. His eyes widened. "Wait! What kind of medicine is that?"

"Bad medicine but it's all we got. Sorry we don't have a priest available. And most never survive an exorcism anyway. Say a quick prayer if you're able."

"But I'm not possessed. I'm speaking the same language as you."

"That's the real problem, isn't it? Like I said, I'm a giant and you're not."

Aenotherus punched Connor in the middle of the forehead. His vision started to go dark around the edges. He thrashed. Something snapped and his vision cleared. He was back in The Needle.

"Are you with us?" asked the Cornet of Horse. He was bending over Connor with a look of concern.

"I'm sorry," said Ivanhoe, who was kneeling beside Straparola,, holding a bag of ice to his friend's head. "I should have put that stuff under lock and key."

Connor groaned. "What kind of moonshine was that?"

"Call it my private stock," said the Cornet of Horse.

"It's all yours," moaned Connor. "I'll never touch that drink again."

"Do you remember anything?" asked the Cornet of Horse.

"Aenotherus, bodyguard to Charlemagne. He punched me in the head."

The Cornet of Horse nodded. "The drink contains an ingredient that lets you access the memories of your ancestors. Aenotherus is known to me. It would seem you accessed the memory of an ancestor that had met an ancestor of mine."

"What ingredient?" asked Connor.

"It's grown on a small Greek island," began the Cornet of Horse. "It's a recipe that has been in the family for a long time."

"You drink it regularly?" asked Straparola.

The Cornet of Horse shook his large head. "More so in the past but rarely these days." *There was no need. The Voices in his head were stronger than ever. But the drink was still useful if he needed to find and focus on a single Voice for an extended period.*

"Whatever you're doing will have to wait," said Oneida suddenly re-appearing in the doorway. "You'd better get in here."

The urgency in Oneida's voice was like a shot of adrenalin. Connor and Strapaola were quickly on their feet, following everyone into the great room. Dawn light was creeping in the through the windows but everyone was absorbed by the light coming from the display screen of a laptop computer. "I've got KK particle readings all over the summit of Whiteface Mountain," said Mohawk.

"The bitch was the diversion," said the Cornet of Horse. "He was a step ahead of us."

"You mean he's gone?" asked Connor.

"Shit," said Lt. Gomez.

Connor's heart sank. All hope of rescuing the women now seemed to have evaporated. Connor heard the distant sound of a whump-whump that may as well have been the Heer of Dunderberg jeering in triumph but part of him recognized it as the sound of helicopters.

"Choppers," said Oneida.

"At my suggestion, elements of the 10th Mountain Division are conducting training exercises around Whiteface today," said the Cornet of Horse. "They're simulating a rescue mission in the Afghanistan mountains. The hope was that all the activity might keep our enemy away from that location. But it looks like we're too late."

Then he heard a cry that sounded like a war whoop coming from behind him. They all turned toward the sound. Straparola, Connor realized, had been sitting in front of another laptop all this time. Straparola looked up to see everyone staring at him like he had gone mad.

"Sorry, I got caught up in the moment," said Straparola. "Must be the company. But I think I found something."

"Explain," commanded the Cornet of Horse.

"Take a look at this display," said Straparola, as everyone crowded around him. "I have no clue as to how to run the software you guys are using. But what I do know how to do is access commercial satellite space imagery. I've been comparing photographs of this area last year with imagery taken more recently. It seems someone ordered up some shots in connection with another Winter Olympics bid for the entire Adirondacks region."

Straparola hit a few keys on the computer and two images appeared side by side. "The picture on the left shows a bridge leading to a house in a small clearing. The more recent picture on the right is of same coordinates but now all you see is trees."

"Trees don't grow that fast," said Ivanhoe.

"Glamour," said The Cornet of Horse, making it sound like a curse and Connor suddenly flashbacked to his encounter with the Heer of Dunderberg on Bannerman Island.

"But it's too late," said Lt. Gomez. "He's gone. And so are the women."

"Maybe not," said the Cornet of Horse. "I believe he can take only one at a time."

"You sure?" asked Connor.

"No," said the Cornet of Horse. "But that has been the pattern in the past."

"So if we're quick, we may still be able to save at least one," said Lt. Gomez.

"And if we're lucky," said Oneida, "maybe the 10th Mountain Division will force that prick to keep his head down."

"Do not wait to strike till the iron is hot but make it hot by striking," said Connor.

"William Butler Yeats," said Straparola for the benefit of the Iroquios,

"We know who he is. Dead Irish poet." said Oneida. "One of the few to ever talk to a Deeneeshee queen."

"What did she tell him?" asked Lt. Gomez.

"She told him to back off and mind his own fucking business," said Oneida. "Or else."

"She must have really liked his poems to give him a warning like that," said Mohawk. "Practically unheard of."

"Usually, they just kill you," added Cayuga.

"Some say Yeats got it on with her," said Oneida and Connor recalled that Yeats had written a small work called Dhoya about a liason between a human and a fairy.

"Like Thomas of Erceldoune in the Eildon Hills in Scotland," continued Oneida.

"Oh, yeah," said Mohawk. "He's the guy who shags the queen until she's batshit ugly and then they travel to the Other Side where her beauty is restored. Our man Tommy comes back prophesying about Scottish independence and then skips back to rejoin the queen when the authorities show up looking for him. Still a wanted man, I hear. The English have long memories."

"When was that?" asked Lt. Gomez.

"Early 1300s, I think," said Mohawk.

"Crap," said Lt. Gomez. "I thought you were talking about the last Scottish referendum."

"No, this is more Robert de Bruce, like the film *Braveheart,*" said Mohawk. "I love the Scots. There is some kilt in my bloodline."

"Derga's last name is Learmont," said Connor.

"No shit?" said Mohawk.

"What?" asked Ivanhoe, speaking for other puzzled faces.

"Same last name as Thomas of Ercildoune," said Mohawk.

Of course, said The Voices.

"So she still has her looks?" queried Ivanhoe. "That means she hasn't had sex with anyone, right?"

"No, man. it doesn't," said Mohawk, fixing Ivanhoe with a glare. "And it's none of your business."

"Hey, I'm not that interested," insisted Ivanhoe, bringing a palm up. "I'm just trying to follow the thread."

Connor's mind drifted back to that moment at the Metropolitan Hotel in Manhattan when Derga had slipped her hand down her pants and then traced a wet finger around his lips. She had marked him in some way, he realized. *There was a promise in that. An invitation. Or was it a spell of some kind? Didn't matter.*

"So where is this house?" asked Connor.

330

Chapter Thirty

"I still don't get the thing with the cats," said Connor. "Why were we blasting them to kingdom come?"

"Yeah," said Straparola. "You guys need a couple of dogs."

A Voice whispered. *Why can't we get a decent-sized hound like Orthos, the one Eurythion had?*

Another Voice. *"That bastard Tristan killed me and gave my fairy dog Petitcrieu to that bitch Isolde."*

A third. *"The white dog with the red tips on its ears? You had no business owning a fairy dog in the first place."*

The Cornet of Horse said nothing, ignoring the bickering Voices but considering a reply, even as his eyes watched the road ahead. They were traveling in two vehicles toward where they hoped to find the Heer of Dunderberg even though the presence of KK particles on Whiteface Mountain suggested he may have already vacated the area. Still, there was a chance the women could still be rescued. Mohawk was in the driver's seat next to him while Connor and Straparola sat in the rear. Lt. Gomez and the four other Iroquois were in the second vehicle, a matching brown Jeep SUV. Ivanhoe, along with a recovering Seneca, remained at The Needle to handle communications and monitor the computer systems.

"Are you familiar with zoonoses?" he asked finally.

"No," said Connor, even as Straparola took his phone out of his pocket and began looking for an Internet connection.

"It's the name for a range of diseases that can be transmitted from animals," said the Cornet of Horse. "I am particularly susceptible to one transmitted by cats called toxoplasma gondii and the results are fatal. Toxo acts upon me like Alzeimer's—my brain will rot until I becoming a slow-witted fool. It rewires the brain."

"Yes?" said Straparola as he poked his finger around the display screen on his phone.

The Cornet of Horse continued. "For me it's like being infected by rabies from an infected dog. I would become slow and dim-witted once the incubation period is over in 23 days. Worse, I become a anthropophagic."

"Anthro-what?" asked Connor.

"Maneater,"said Mohawk, eyes firmly glued on the road.

Connor and Straparola looked at each other, eyebrows raised.

"That's a pretty extreme reaction," said Straparola, looking down at the display screen on his phone. "Toxo is a tiny protozoan that's pretty harmless in most adults, although kids are vulnerable. You might get some flu-like symptoms and a case of the shits. It does lie dormant in the brain, though, which is kind of creepy."

Straparola paused while he caught up on his reading. "Still, there is a scientist in the Czech Republic who thinks toxo can trigger schizophrenia and attention-deficit disorder. Oh, you'll love this. This same guy thinks toxo makes infected women more friendly and reckless. He thinks it's a major cause of traffic accidents involving women. It probably explains all of my dates as well."

"But cannibalism?" asked Connor. "What is that about?"

"Morose, suspicious, jealous, maybe. It seems to affect men and women differently. But there is nothing here about eating people."

"It's the stone I can carry," said the Cornet of Horse. "Certain ethnic groups are more susceptible to some diseases than others. It's like that for me, one that I share with my kind." He glanced at the GPS navigation screen on the dashboard. "We're almost there."

"Excuse me," said Connor. "My kind?"

"Genesis. Chapter 6, verse 4," said the Cornet of Horse.

Straparola tapped the phone's screen. "There were giants on the earth in those days, and also afterward, when the sons of God had relations with the daughters of men, who bore children to them. These were the mighty men who were of old, the men of renown."

Straparola took a breath. "Also known as the Nephilim. Depending upon your translation. So toxo turns you into one of those dopey giants from folklore?"

"I knew it," said Connor. "As fucked up as that is, I knew it. Derga's not nuts. And now that I know it, I have to worry about not becoming lunch."

"So I'm thinking about Homer's Odysseus when he was attacked by the Laestrygonians," said Straparola. "You know, that gang of giant women who sank his fleet and ate the crews, leaving Odysseus with just the one ship he escaped in."

"One of the worst infections ever," said the Cornet of Horse.

"And the Cyclops?"

"Infected as well. That was in Corsica. By the time Odysseus arrived there, Polyphemus was the last one left. His vision was mostly gone. He could only see out of one eye."

"Odysseus gouged out that good eye to get away after the Cyclops ate six of his men."

"As Homer said."

"I used to like cats," said Straparola.

"I'm a dog lover," chimed in Mohawk. "But Seneca is allergic to dogs. Gets hives. That's why we have no hounds."

"We're here," said the Cornet of Horse. Mohawk brought the SUV to a stop and the second one rolled up behind them. Mohawk and The Cornet of Horse opened their doors and got out, with Connor and Straparola following a moment later. Straparola's focus was still on his phone even as Lt. Gomez and the other Iroquois joined them.

"Nephilim. Straight out of the Bible. How sick is that?" said Straparola as Lt. Gomez came up to join them.

"That was a name Derga had used,' said Connor.

"What are you talking about?" asked Lt. Gomez.

"The big man says he's a giant and if a cat bites him, he may eat us," said Straparola

Lt. Gomez stared at them both. "You been drinking at a time like this?"

"No booze. I swear," said Connor.

"Smoking some shit, then." Lt. Gomez shook his head and turned away from them to consult with the other Iroquois. The Cornet of Horse looked at Connor but then talked into a microphone hooked around his ear. "Comm check. Ivanhoe. All clear?"

"Clear, said Ivanhoe in his ear. All the Iroquois had a similar ear mike.

The Cornet of Horse turned away to observe the Iroquois checking their equipment but he could hear Straparola's next words were well enough. "Well, now we know why Jack became the giant killer. The giant was eating people."

Fee fi fo fum! I smell the blood of an Englishman! That was like saying grace before dinner for Cormoran!

The Cornet of Horse shuddered. Zoonoses was the only thing he feared.

"It's no joke,"said Mohawk in a whisper. "Ask Tuscarora about Deadoendjadases. He was a man-eater. It took 800 warriors from three clans to kill him. Or so the legend says. This was all before the white man showed up, of course." He paused. "I think the Jack story is bullshit. He had to have had help."

He did. From a Deeneeshee.

The story was burned into his brain and the Cornet of Horse found himself speaking of it like it was a case file. "Cormoran had been infected and decided to live in a cave with all the swag he'd taken from the Deeneeshee in battle. The Deeneeshee were what fairies were called in those days. Cormoran on a murdering spree and was eating people and cattle alike from the surrounding villages. Among the victims was Jack's father. The Deeneeshee gave Jack a drinking horn full of liquid nectar that he used to lure Cormoran into a camouflaged pit. Jack killed him with a pick axe that caved in Cormoran's skull."

He killed more than just Cormoran!

"Once Cormoran was dead, the Deeneeshee helped Jack with other treasures. One was a Cloak of Darkness that made the wearer invisible," continued the Cornet of Horse. "The other items included a Deeneeshee sword that can cut through almost anything, shoes that made the runner swifter, and a cap of knowledge that made the wearer smarter. The last item, we suspect, is some type of remote audio set-up that essentially let the Deeneeshee whisper into Jack's ear. With those tools at his disposal, Jack became an exterminator of those who had been infected".

Galligantua.Thundell, Blunderbore and his brother.

There were others as well.

"What happened to all that special gear?' asked Straparola.

"Disappeared when Jack died," said the Cornet of Horse. "Probably reclaimed by the Deeneeshee. They don't let their stuff out of their hands for long."

Connor and Straparola exchanged a look that didn't escape the Cornet of Horse's notice but there was a clamor inside his head.

And don't forget Blunderbore's wife! The treasonous bitch. This last comment the Cornet of Horse recognized as coming from Harlin de la Montagne.

The last remark was unkind. Everyone knew Blunderbore had to be stopped before he killed again. And yes, there was a certain amount of resentment that Jack received aid from the Deeneeshee who were more than happy to make Jack into a tool of their own. But the truth was that Jack had done what they couldn't do themselves, kill one of their own. Jack had remained a friend until his untimely death. He glanced at Connor. He had the makings of a friend. Maybe as good as friend as Jack had been before and after he had become a giant killer.

He killed seven of us!
We were as good as dead anyway!
Focus on the mission at hand!
Remember the compact with the sorcerer Pope!

The Voices were at odds with one another. The Cornet of Horse banished all thoughts of Jack from his mind. They were parked alongside a paved road at the juncture where it was met by an unpaved track wide enough for the vehicles to enter. There was an old tennis court with rotten nets a few yards up on the left followed by a creek bank that continued as far as he could see. On the right was a wall of trees. If there was trouble, there would be no room for the vehicles to maneuver.

"We walk from here," said the Cornet of Horse. "Mohawk, you have point." No need for him to keep spinning old Indian tales, even if they were true. It would just make everyone nervous.

Mohawk wasn't stupid, though. "Me and my big mouth," he grumbled. He knew why he was the point man.

The Cornet of Horse mentally reviewed what he knew of the area. It was basically an Adirondack pipe dream called the Ausable Acres. Forty years ago, a developer had bought a large tract of forest with a river, the AuSable, running through it with the idea of developing second homes for the wealthy. He had even built an airstrip—out of site somewhere to the southwest—to make access easy. Things hadn't quite worked out as he planned. The few Swiss style chalets that had been built wound up in the hands of retirees and some avid skiers. Whiteface Mountain was within sight, perhaps just five miles distance. The wealthy preferred to be nearer their own kind in Lake Placid, some 15 miles away on the other side of Whiteface. But for the Heer of Dunderberg it was a perfect location.

Mohawk took the lead, kicking up a little dirt as he started to walk. The other Iroquois followed him, walking along the edge of the road two abreast. The Cornet of Horse followed with Connor, Strapaola and Lt. Gomez bringing up the rear.

Oneida slowed his initial pace and drifted backward until he was abreast of Connor.

"What kind of films?" Oneida asked.

"What?"

"You run a film festival?"

"Shorts."

"How long are shorts?"

"For us," Connor paused. There really wasn't an "us" but it always seemed better to make the Empire Shorts seem bigger than it was, a thought he rationalized by including gig freelancers who designed the poster, for example. "Under 20 minutes but the best ones are half that."

Oneida nodded. "What's the hardest part of the job?"

"The programming. We have a two-hour slot that fits into a theater's daily schedule. Normally, we have about 10 short films. The trick is to show them in an order that makes it look like a coherent program. We're making films play together when they weren't designed to and we have to make it an experience the audience remembers and tells other people about because we have no money for advertising."

"So 'plays well with others' is a festival criteria even though the filmmakers can't take that into account. They are all making films independently."

Connor nodded. "There's the rub, as Shakespeare would say."

"Shakespeare hid the truth," replied Oneida. "He gentrified the fairies to make them more acceptable to an urban audience. He gave the fairies manners and elegant speech. He made them less deadly and even mildly helpful at times. In the process, he erased the old stories. And that's where the truth lies."

Oneida suddenly stopped, pulling Connor to halt as well. "You can't handle the truth! Son, we live in a world that has walls and those walls have to be guarded by men with guns." Oneida paused. "I have a greater responsibility than you can possibly imagine!"

Connor, initially taken aback, saw a glint in Oneida's eyes.

"Jack Nicholson?" ventured Connor. "*A Few Good Men.* 1992."

Oneida smiled. "Okay, you're the real deal. I wish I could impersonate Jack's voice. But he's spot on here."

They found what they were looking for at the first left hand turn about a mile down the road.

"The Bridge of Trees," said Oneida. It was a small stone bridge that crossed the stream that had been on their left the whole time. The road surface of the bridge was covered in a thick layer of dirt. Trees about the width of a man's arms had sprung up out the dirt, growing to a height of 15 or 20 feet high and effectively blocking the crossing.

"Glamour or just some really good fertilizer?" asked Oneida.

"A little bit of both, I think," said the Cornet of Horse, nodding at Cayuga and Mohawk. The two men stepped forward, pulling out machetes that had been scabbarded on their hips and began hacking at the wood until they had cleared a narrow path across the bridge.

"I've got some vehicle tracks over here," said Mohawk, when they had crossed over the bridge. "Not very old."

Cayuga looked at the tracks and then at the trees on the bridge. "Man, that shit must grow fast."

The shadow of a flock of birds flashed across the sky, vanishing without a sound, caught the Cornet of Horse's attention. *Quiet. Too quiet. Like they used to say in those old westerns before things went sideways. I'm ready.*

"I guess that means we're in the right place," said Connor. The world was no longer quiet. "What's that buzzing sound?"

The sound had started out low but was increasing in intensity until it sounded like there were thousands of bees in the woods around them.

"Bees?" asked Lt. Gomez.

The Cornet of Horse said nothing. It wasn't bees. It was a familiar sound that meant they were on enemy territory. He tried to see everything at once, looking for a point to focus on. The forest had changed from one big mass of brown and green to a series of individual trees that seemed to judge him as he walked by each one. The light had shifted as well. Everything looked gloomy. He looked up. High overhead he could see bits of a French blue sky. Then a low growl reached his ears and he froze. The terrain ahead was flat but off to the right was a slope that marked the beginning on oversized hill called Mount Hamelin. The sound seemed to come from that direction. He looked up at the summit. Rocky. It was strange that a mountain in the Adirondacks should have the same name as the German town from which the legendary Pied Piper of legend had spirited away all the children.

A low growl somewhere unseen.

"You hear that?" said Onondaga.

"If I didn't know better, I'd say that was a cougar," said Mohawk.

"What do you mean?" asked Lt. Gomez.

"They were killed off around here over 100 years ago," said Mohawk.

"Flush it out," said the Cornet of Horse. Some 50 yards ahead, a long shape of some kind materialized and then disappeared among some trees. The two men sprinted forward and they were soon lost to sight. After a few minutes, they heard shots. Then silence.

"Cayuga, come in," said Oneida into his ear mike. "Onondaga, respond. Over."

Oneida shook his head.

"Ivanhoe come in. Over."

Oneida shook his head again. "Comms down."

Unbidden, Mohawk, Oneida, and Tuscarora advanced in the direction of the gunshots, forming a triangle as they progressed.

At first, the Cornet of Horse was inclined to let them go in support of Oneida and Mohawk but then he grew uneasy. So did The Voices.

Some kind of trap?

"Wait," commanded the Cornet of Horse. "Oneida, you come with us. Mohawk and Tuscarora, collect the other two and meet us at the house."

Oneida led them over a landscape dotted with slabs of granite rock interspersed with bits of shrubbery. They saw nothing and heard nothing but the sounds of their own footsteps and the non-stop buzzing whose source couldn't be identified.

Too easy.

The Cornet of Horse silently agreed. Maybe that mysterious cat was the lone sentry. Or maybe it had nothing to do with any of this—just a stray mountain lion that had migrated east.

Not likely.

Again, the Cornet of Horse silently agreed.

Suddenly, the front door of the house flew open and the Cornet of Horse raised his weapon.

"Derga!" cried Connor.

The Cornet of Horse recognized her but didn't lower his weapon. "Are you alone?"

"Seventina is here but she's not conscious," said Derga.

Connor and Straparola rushed forward and climbed the front steps in two bounds. Connor paused for a second and then threw his arms around Derga in an embrace.

"I can't help myself," said Connor into Derga's hair. "I thought we had lost you."

Derga aqueezed him back. "Thank you."

Straparola edged by Connor and Derga and disappeared into the house.

"Where is the Heer of Dunderberg?" asked the Cornet of Horse.

"Not here," said Derga, her head resting on Connor's shoulder. "There were two other women as well. They're gone too."

"Damn!" said Lt. Gomez. "What about his partner? The woman."

"This is Lt. Gomez from ICE," said Connor.

"We've met," replied Derga. "She's not here either. I don't know where either one of them is." Then she whispered into Connor's ear. "Who are your new friends?"

"Iroquois," said Connor. "They work for the big guy. I'll explain later. Is Seventina okay?"

"I don't think she's been harmed," said Derga.

"Shit!" cursed Oneida.

They all looked at Oneida but quickly realized he was looking back behind them. Coming toward them were the rest of the Iroquois. But only four were walking. The fifth—and they soon saw it had to be Onondaga even though his face and upper body was covered by a green poncho--was being carried on an improvised stretcher by Cayuga and Tuscarora. They all looked very pale.

"Report," said the Cornet of Horse softly.

"Mountain lion," said Cayuga. "It was nothing but a blur. Ripped his throat apart before I could even bring my rifle around. I got off a few rounds but it was too late to save him."

"Hit anything?" said Mohawk.

"I must have," said Cayuga. "I couldn't miss at that range. But the animal acted like I wasn't even there and then it was gone. I've never seen anything that fast."

Straparola appeared the door with his arm under Seventina. "I kissed her and she woke up. I'm a god-damned Prince Charming!" Both their faces were beaming until they saw the remains of Onondaga and their smiles died.

"Killed by a mountain lion that's not supposed to exist," said Lt. Gomez.

One that was meant to for you. A cat is a cat.

One little bite is all it would take

"I get it!" shouted the Cornet of Horse. All eyes were on him. "It was after me."

Take command!

"We need to go," said the Cornet of Horse, lowering his voice. He looked at the two women who were still dressed in the clothes they had worn when they were snatched from the Gershwin Hotel. Seventina seemed to read his thoughts.

"We're a little overdressed for a romp in the woods," she said.

"I'm not complaining," said Straparola with a smile.

"Try to keep up," said the Cornet of Horse.

"We can walk barefoot," said Derga and both women promptly took off their heels and held them aloft.

"But too expensive to discard," added Seventina, showing the shoes red soles before realizing the gesture was lost on all the men.

The Cornet of Horse turned away and looked at the Iroquois. "Cayuga, you have the point."

The Cornet of Horse and Oneida fell in behind Cayuga. Mohawk and Tuscarora picked up the body of Onondaga and followed them. Everyone else filled in behind the body like it was a funeral procession.

They had only gone a short distance when the rock came to life. Cayuga was just about to step on one of the granite slabs they had passed earlier when a grey hand seemed to morph out of the stone and grab Cayuga by the ankle. Cayuga yelled as the hand rose up to become an arm. Then a head appeared, looking like something that had been chiseled by a stone mason. It was like someone rising from a startled slumber. In a moment, the stone figure was on its feet, holding Cayuga by the foot like a trophy. Cayuga tried to keep his balance, hopping on one foot while his other was held firm. Cayuga screamed in pain and that's when they saw that Cayuga's leg was turning into stone as well.

"Stone Coats!" Mohawk's voice was almost a whisper but everyone heard him. More of the granite slabs began to change shape, becoming man-sized stone figures cut so it appeared they were wearing knee-length coats with boots. The Cornet of Horse counted six in all. By the time he finished counting, Cayuga was dead, turned to stone and standing like some kind of garden ornament. Then the figure of Cayuga seemed to melt into the ground, becoming a granite slab.

Everyone was stunned into shocked silence until Seventina screamed as the Stone Coats took a step forward and then another, walking in unison. The party backed up as the Stone Coats moved forward.

Lt. Gomez unholstered his pistol and fired a round at the leading Stone Coat. It bounced off the stone figure and ricocheted away. The bullet didn't even cause a chip. The Stone Coats took another step forward.

"No firing!" said the Cornet of Horse. "The ricochets will just bounce off and hit us."

"What are Stone Coats?" asked Straparola..

"I just know the name from old stories told round the campfire by the elders," said Mohawk. "All they say is that the Stone Coats are why we moved out of these mountains back before the white man's arrival."

"How come you didn't mention them before?" asked Connor.

"Man, I didn't believe that old story!" said Mohawk.

"What do we do?" asked Seventina.

"The old legends say the blood of a menstruating woman will dissolve them," said Mohawk. "I don't suppose…"

Derga and Seventina shook their heads in unison.

"Well, they don't look too fucking fast to me," said Lt. Gomez. "I say we run. I'm sure as shit not going to try to arrest them."

"If we cut through the trees, we can flank them and get back to the Bridge of Trees," said Oneida.

"Go!" said the Cornet of Horse. "Oneida watch our backs. I'll take point."

They ran away from the Stone Coats at more of a trot than a run, their pace dictated by the body of Onondaga and to a lesser degree, the women running barefoot. The trees didn't help either as they had to weave in and out to go around them. Some of the branches were leaving scratches. The occasional sharp intake of breath behind said as much.

He could hear the Stone Coats now walking in the distance behind him. The good news was that Stone Coats weren't sprinters. But then maybe that wasn't such good news after all.

They are herding you like beaters in the hunt.

He conjured up an image of the Bridge of Trees in his mind but didn't recall seeing any stone slabs in the vicinity that might start walking of their own accord.

That leaves the big cat.

He felt a sense of panic rise in him and was surprised by the sensation. He fought it down even as he acknowledged the cause. To have his brain slowly rot away and then turn into a man-eater was a fate he couldn't face.

Out of the corner of his eye, he though he saw a shadow moving amongst the trees to his right. It was a blur but it looked like it was headed toward the Bridge of Trees.

It will be there before you.

You're fucked.

That was the Voice of Harpin.

"Nice of you to join us," said the Cornet of Horse.

"What?' asked Connor.

"The mountain lion wants to attack us as we reach the bridge," said the Cornet of Horse.

Connor reached out and pulled the Cornet of Horse to a halt.

"You'd better let me go first then," said Connor. "It's you it's after."

"Let's say you're right." said Lt. Gomez. "I'll take the right side and Straparola will be on your left with the Iroquois as our rear guard. We'll just escort you over the bridge like a prisoner in custody."

The Cornet of Horse looked at them, a protest on the tip of his tongue. But he never aired it. He was the biggest and strongest among them but they were his equal when it came to courage. And he respected that.

Tactically speaking, he's right.

"All right," said the Cornet of Horse. "But let's see if we can give ourselves some breathing room."

Oneida stepped forward. "I'll take the right flank.

The Cornet of Horse and Oneida opened fire simultaneously, spraying each side of the bridge with bullets. Tree branches spun into the air and the noise alone should have made any animal nearby flee in terror.

They stopped firing on a signal from the Cornet of Horse.

"Stone Coats still coming," said Mohawk.

"Let's move!" yelled the Cornet of Horse and they trotted forward en masse. The Cornet of Horse watched the forest for any sign of the big cat but saw nothing. He couldn't help but notice that the hands of both Connor and Straparola were shaking a little as they ran. The bridge came up on them fast and the Cornet of Horse stopped and spun around.

"Ladies, after you please. Then bring Onondaga."

The rest of them formed a loose skirmish line while the others crossed. Nothing moved and the Stone Coats seemed to have vanished as well. The buzzing sound was gone too, like a bad headache that had just dissipated.

"Smart mountain lion," said Mohawk. "It's not suicidal."

"It seems so," said the Cornet of Horse. They rose as one and crossed the bridge. On the other side, they regrouped.

It won't cross the water.

"Madre de dios!" said Lt. Gomez. "What the hell was that all about?"

"Too many things are occurring for even a big heart to hold," said Connor, bending over and breathing hard, reaching for a line of Yeats to steady himself.

"Scary shit brings out the Yeats in all of us," said Straparola. "Are we okay here?"

"Yes," said the Cornet of Horse.

"You know, I was half expecting that female horror show from last night to be here," said Connor.

"She was," said Derga. "You just missed her."

Chapter Thirty-One

Derga opened her eyes to find herself lying on a Persian rug looking up at big, triangular-shaped window filled with an expanse of blue sky, treetops, and a distant mountain with what appeared to be a castle at its summit. The view threatened to monopolize her mind and made her painfully aware of the blank space in her memory. To close your eyes in one place and to open them in another was wildly disconcerting. And it made her feel very vulnerable. The idea that someone could move you around at will and without explanation made her feel like she'd lost control of her own life.

And now she remembered who had done that to her. With a start, she sat up, looking for him and ready to run in the opposite direction. But he wasn't there. She sighed with relief. At this point, she couldn't even give him a name.

And where am I?

The castle on the mountain threw her. *Europe?*

She turned her head slightly and saw Seventina lying unconscious on a striped couch of greens and browns and Derga half-stumbled over to her.

"Seventina! Wake up!"

But Seventina looked like she was in a coma.

348

The she remembered they had been four. *Where are the other two?*

Derga noticed stairs leading up to a bedroom. She went up them quickly but found the room empty. She came downstairs and found the master bedroom. Empty. She checked the basement. There was no one there.

She returned to the couch and sat beside Seventina, shaking her. No response.

"I guess I'll have to find a prince to wake you up."

That made her think of Connor and Straparola. *Where are they and are they still alive?*

Dark thoughts came unbidden and she didn't know if they were true or false. *The banshee has her comb. Connor is dead. And maybe Straparola too. And what's in store for us? Two women gone and two to go. To be dragged before the Unseelie Court and slated for breeding.*

She shook her head, knowing those last thoughts were not helping matters.

They had to leave. *But where to? I have no idea where I am? And what if we run out the front door straight into his arms?*

That's when she heard the front door open.

Her eyes darted around the room and she was surprised to see an iron poker next to the fireplace. That told her the house had been once occupied by humans. Deeneeshee wouldn't have touched it. Frantically, she jumped over to the fireplace and grabbed the poker, holding it point first in front of her, hoping he'd impale himself as he rushed toward her. But when she looked up, it wasn't him. It was her.

The banshee looked like a walking cinder that had just left hell. Her face was the color of ash and her long hair was a mix of black, grey and white streaks. Her clothes were charred black and she smelled of smoke. For a moment, Derga was struck speechless but then she found her voice, retrieving it from somewhere deep inside her where it had gone to hide.

"Where is he?"

The banshee made no reply but her eyes flared like flames and Derga surmised the two were not the partners they once were.

Derga tried another tack, wondering if talking wouldn't even work. "Did you find your comb?"

The banshee hissed, growing angrier. Derga realized it may have sounded like she was mocking her. *I have to speak carefully.* Derga waved the poker in front of her. A banshee didn't like iron.

Derga tried to think things through, even as fear climbed up her spine and made her legs weak. *He's left her. She doesn't have the comb. She can't get back without it. And if he's left her, he's not going to help her get back.*

The banshee glanced at the prone form of Seventina, dismissed her as a threat, and returned her gaze to Derga.

"I can help you get back."

The banshee gave her a look that was at once incredulous and disdainful.

"Listen to me. I am Derga Learmont. I am a walker between worlds. I answer to Reverend Kirk and the Red Man."

The banshee took a step back. The names meant something to her. *Good!*

Derga lowered the poker as a sign of good faith. The banshee did nothing, waiting for her to say more. *Talk about trying to put a genie back in the bottle!*

"I know a way back. But I have to stop him. We must save the other two women."

350

The banshee waved her arm as if to say it was too late and she didn't care about them anyway.

"I have to try. Where is he?"

The banshee pointed out the window toward the castle on the mountain.

"Will you help me?"

The banshee stood there, brooding and steaming at the same time.

"You don't want to go back with him by way of the Unseelie Court. Trust me."

The sound of voices in the distance grabbed their attention. The banshee spun around, walked to the front door and peered out. Derga could tell she didn't like what she saw. The banshee turned to face her and Derga raised the poker. The banshee, she realized, was about to speak.

"Death comes."

With a shriek that made Derga wince, the banshee turned and vanished out the front door.

Of course, Derga didn't tell them all that. For one, they already knew that her kidnapper, the Heer of Dunderberg, had been to the castle on the mountain that turned out to be a weather station on Whiteface Mountain in the Adirondack Mountains of upstate New York. And he was probably on his way there again. Connor filled her in on their adventures on their way back to a place they called The Needle. She wished they'd go straight to Whiteface Mountain but the men insisted on the need to get more ammo. As Derga listened to Connor, she realized she was touched by the effort he'd made to rescue her.

He's a special one.

But Derga put whatever murky and complicated feelings she had toward Connor into a box in her mind to be opened later. They understood that there was still a chance to rescue the other two women. But it seemed likely that one of the women was already away. She hoped they were wrong but she was impressed by their use of KK sensors and its implications. The hunters must be well-funded to be able to develop such a technology.

The Seelie Court will be interested in that.

But it was clear that saving the two women was not the primary mission for the Cornet of Horse and his Iroquois team. For him, it was all about the Heer of Dunderberg.

Derga understood that for she knew what he was. She had never met one before but she knew he was a hunter of the deeneeshee. She had been told of them. Their hatred of the deeneeshee began ages ago when the bride of the giant Orion had been taken. Orion had been their leader. She had thought it just an old story but now she realized there was some truth in it. She wondered if the Cornet of Horse saw any distinction between the Seelie and Unseelie Courts. Or was his motto: *Death to all deeneeshee?*

"Something odd here," said Ivanhoe from the table where he had been looking at his laptop. "It looks like we just lost one of our landlines." Ivanhoe swiveled in his chair to face everyone. "We have two landlines and a power line. The landlines are more reliable than wireless service around here, especially in bad weather. We have two landlines for operational redundancy and a backup generator for power." he explained for the benefit of the Needle's guests. "Can someone go outside and check the lines?"

"I'll go," volunteered Connor and headed for the door.

"I'll go with you,' said Derga, following Connor. A knife hung in its sheath by the door and Derga grabbed it on the way out. *If something is being cut, I may need to cut back.*

They stepped outside and quickly located the black cables attached to the side of the house and their eyes looked upward to follow the black lines through the trees to the nearest pole that supported them in their stretch to another pole on the road and beyond. One was already hanging slack and they could see where it had been cut as a great length of it lay on the ground. Definitely cut.

"That would be one of the landlines," said Connor. "The power line looks fine but there is some kind of big stick that seems to be weighing down the other landline."

Derga could see the stick. The part closest to them was thickest. It split at the back, two branches slightly curved and flaring outward. Somehow, this configuration allowed the stick to balance itself horizontally on the wire, even as it swayed slightly.

Derga grew suspicious. She wondered if she should chance a look with her covered eye. *Well, there is more here than meets one eye.* She drew the knife as a precaution, a movement that drew Connor's attention and his eyes widened as she reached up and pulled away her eye patch for a quick look. The Heer of Dunderberg had sent another threat their way. She covered her eye again quickly. The thing on the wire hadn't noticed her looking at it. If it had it might have attacked her right away.

"What?" asked Connor.

"A wood dragon. I saw one once before in a forest in Austria."

"A wood dragon?" The tone in his voice told her he didn't quite believe her. "An invasive species then? Or something from a toy shop?"

"The former, I'd say. If you still have that stone with the hole in it, have a look."

"I keep thinking of it as a coin."

Derga turned away as Connor began searching through his pockets. There were a few ways to deal with a wood dragon. They were mostly a nuisance but you still had to be cautious around them. This one was about average sized, about a yard long. A pair of small talons up front provided a grip while the rear branches were more like legs that could bend and stiffen as needed for balance as it moved from tree to tree, mostly out of sight through the upper canopy. The eyes were like little burls set high like a crocodile and the mouth worked much the same way, although it didn't open as wide and its teeth were made of wood so it would be a while yet before it chewed through the cable. That gave her time to make a weapon, one that could reach the wood dragon.

A long straight branch that looked like it would make a good quarterstaff rested on a nearby woodpile, destined for fireplace kindling, she guessed. She grabbed it and began stripping the bark off in long strips with the knife.

"Holy shit!" Connor had found the rock with the hole in it. The branch was bare now and she used the point of the knife to etch lines, whirls and curves into the round wood--words no would recognize as such for they looked like lines left by insects that had once lived beneath the bark. In medieval times, it would have been called a spell, sealed with a drop of her blood pricked from her skin while she cut the thin end of the staff into a point so it could be used as a spear. The thicker end could work as a cudgel. A weapon imbibed with blood from the Other Side made killing something from the Other Side easier. *That was one thing the hunters didn't know. Otherwise, there would have been stories of them poking holes into the deeneeshee.*

"It's chewing on the cable!"

"I know," said Derga. Connor was taller than Derga so his greater height volunteered him for the extermination job. "Catch!"

Connor turned in time to catch the spear tossed toward him around its midsection. Derga made an upward stabbing motion.

Connor put the stone in his pocket and stepped down off the small porch, slowly advancing toward the wood dragon until he stood directly beneath it. He held the staff with the pointy end high and thrust upwards. And missed. The wire looked as if it had vibrated slightly, shifting the wood dragon like it had been moved by a gust of wind. Still, it didn't fall. Connor thrust again and again, missing every time.

"Whack it on the back legs!" yelled Derga.

Connor backed up a few feet and then ran forward, leaping into the air and swinging the hard end of the staff overhead like a sledgehammer. There was the satisfying sound of contact being made and the wood dragon fell to the ground. Connor jumped toward it, swinging the staff down time and time again until pieces of the wood dragon broke off and it lay splintered at his feet.

The door behind them swung open in the midst of Connor's battering and the Cornet of Horse and Straparola stepped out of the house. They watched Connor take a few last blows to the wood dragon and then he stopped.

"Why are you hitting a stick with a stick?" asked Straparola. "Are you going nuts? I swear, I think we're all suffering some kind of collective psychosis.'

"A pest the Heer of Dunderberg sent," said Derga. "It's not what it looks like."

The Cornet of Horse eyed her with her look that said: *Neither are you.*

She wondered now about her own safety. Already she had seen the Cornet of Horse look at her with a question in his mind. Now he seemed to be ready to answer that question in his mind. Strictly speaking, she wasn't deeneeshee but if her relationship with the deeneeshee became clear to him, then might he think her a target as well? For now, he was focused on the Heer of Dunderberg but what about afterwards?

And now they were speeding toward what she guessed would be a confrontation between the Heer of Dunderberg and the Cornet of Horse. *How to handle that? Assuming I can? Should I just let them kill each other and hope they succeed? And what about the banshee?*

She knew these thoughts would still occupy her mind hours later as they drove through the small village of Wilmington and over a small, stone bridge that spanned the Ausable River. She had seen the live street view photos on the Internet. There was a small building with a New York State Police sign out front but there was no sign of any troopers. The few cars on the road all turned left at the intersection past the bridge, no doubt headed for a nice restaurant meal in the town of Lake Placid. They wouldn't make that turn. Instead, they would drive straight on, past a small, children's amusement park with a pint-sized roller coaster and some overfed reindeer that advertised itself as the workshop of Santa Claus.

Oh, if only all fairy tales were lies.

Chapter Thirty-Two

The pine trees stood close like fellow mourners clothed in green and shadow black. They all stood in a small clearing amongst the trees just a short walk from The Needle. In keeping with the Iroquois custom that decreed all those who died violently must be buried immediately, Onondaga lay in the ground before them. In time, perhaps a decade from now, his bones would be disinterred and returned to his people where he would be honored as a Pine Tree Chief in a special ceremony.

Cayuga, turned into a granite slab by the Stone Coats, was another story. The Cornet of Horse wasn't sure because of its secretive nature, but Cayuga's death would likely involve one of the curing groups the Iroquois used to deal with the spirit world. *Most likely the False Faces.* He remembered seeing the grotesque masks they wore. Each mask represented a spiritual being they hoped to control. Sometimes it didn't work out so well which is why he knew what would come next.

The Mohawk caught his eye. "You will start us with the words?"

The Cornet of Horse nodded. "You are thinking of the two kinds of weather from which you must protect the grave of your loved one," he began. "So throw some grass on the grave to protect it from the hot rays of the sun."

Oneida stepped forward with a sack of grass cuttings and smoothed them over the grave.

"And place a flat board on it to protect it from the cold rain."

Tuscarora stepped forward with a pine plank and laid it vertically on the grave.

"During your sorrow, you have allowed your mind to dwell on the great loss which you have sustained," he continued. "You must not let your minds dwell on this lest you suffer from serious illness."

He saw Connor, Straparola, Lt. Gomez, and Seventina glance toward him.

They think that I am insensitive but I am in keeping with Iroquois tradition.

Derga, he noticed, kept her eyes on the grave. *She knows more than she says. She is more than she appears. Not Deeneeshee but not quite not either.*

Oneida continued the observance. "When a person is in deep grief, the tears blind his eyes and he cannot see. By these words we wipe away the tears from our eyes so that we may see again."

Now it was the Seneca's turn. "When a person is mourning the loss of a loved one, his ears are stopped and he cannot hear. By these words, we remove that obstruction so that we may hear again."

From Tuscarora. "When a person is mourning, his throat becomes stopped so he cannot breathe well nor consume food that the Creator has given him to eat. By these words, we remove that obstruction so that we may breathe and enjoy our food."

And now it was for the Mohawk to finish. "Since our brother has died, the light has dropped from the sky. We now lift up the light and replace it in the sky."

His mind wandered. An end brought thoughts of the beginning.

It was all about the feet. His true nature was there for anyone to see, at least for anyone who looked closely at a certain pediment that had once adorned the Old Athena Temple in Athens.

Curse the Athenians! said one of the Voices. *We fought to keep their so-called gods out of the affairs of men!*

And to stop them from kidnapping our women, said another.

And thanks to man we lost the fight! said the first. *A mercenary named Heracles who shot us with poison arrows. Don't forget that! 23 dead!*

He tried to shut the Voices out of his mind and contemplated his feet, sheathed in custom made boots. Funny how modern man rarely thought about his feet, except perhaps for some rich women concerned about fitting into a high-priced heel. How many people today would be able to identify a Greek, Roman, Germanic, Egyptian, or Celtic foot simply by looking at it. The differences were significant. That's what happens when everyone wears shoes, something his kind counted on.

For the ancients, feet were a big part of the story. Think of all the idioms about feet that had entered the language. People who didn't like each other when they met got off on the wrong foot. Explorers set foot on new lands. Victors placed their foot on vanquished foes. People got footholds in new careers. Scared people got cold feet. An admirable person with a flaw had feet of clay. And the seriously ill had one foot in the grave.

Demons were revealed by their feet. Their feet were turned the wrong way or they had feet that belonged to animals like goats or horses. Or they had web feet like duck or geese. The Queen of the Night has talons for feet.

His feet were like those that came before him. Thick and wide. A little toe as big as a man's thumb. And they were on display at the Acropolis Museum in Athens. Most people didn't look at them, their eyes drawn to the figure of Athena, wearing her leather coat full of poisonous snakes.

His ancestors lay defeated before her. Unlike Athena, however, their figures were not intact. Of one, only a foot remained. Others were missing their heads and others their arms.

Still, anyone looking closely might make some interesting observations. If you imagine the supine figures standing upright, they would be about the same height as Athena, an admission in his mind that the sculptors knew they were on equal footing.

He half-smiled at his own joke.

Athena, even accounting for her femininity, was built differently. Her adversaries were heavily muscled around the abdomen and thicker of bone. The thighs were massive tree trunks and the shoulders were broad.

But feet told the story. Athena's feet were long and tapered like those that came to be associated with royalty. The feet of the defeated were massive by comparison.

Fuck Athena and her pretty feet! Where do you think Heracles got the poison from? She's a murderess! She herself killed Enceladus!

He raised an eyebrow. That was a Voice he hadn't heard before. Was that Aristaios, still defiant. Syceus, the other survivor, had yet to raise his Voice.

The victors wrote the history, of course, but he knew the Gigantomachy, as the Athenians called the ancient war against the Olympians, had been a disaster. The Athenians had exaggerated its significance, naturally, to inflate their own importance and their claim to Athena's patronage. Strictly speaking, it was a local power struggle involving just a few extended families from around nearby Pallene.

Lessons had been learned, however. Heracles, aided now by a band of men, turned into a relentless bounty hunter, pursuing those who had retreated when Porphyrion, the eldest head of the family and the strongest, died. And there had been regrettable events, like the rape of Hera, adding fuel to the hunt. Only Aristaios escaped, digging into the Mt. Etna in Sicily like a dung beetle to hide for years in the lava tubes beneath the mountain. He, like many others, wore a small beetle tattoo on his calf to honor him.

Eventually, Aristaios had sought refuge in the north, finding brethren in places like Istria, Cornwall and places in between.

The Athenians, though, wouldn't let it go. The story of the Gigantomachy, told and retold over the centuries, meant they were a defeated people and fair game for all those who came after. They had always lived in small family groups but now it became a matter of survival. They were forced to live in remote places and walk the earth discreetly to avoid being hunted down, rarely, if ever, gathering in groups so that even if discovered, their existence could be explained as freaks of nature that belonged in a circus. Any chance at rehabilitation was often thwarted by the atrocities committed by those who succumbed to the effects of zoonoses. Sometimes, of course, an individual would shine in the limelight.

Goliath of Gath!

Maximillan!

Charlemagne!

But not very often. And now it was actively discouraged.

And there was the soldiering, especially the glory days in Prussia in Regiment No. 6 during the War of Austrian Succession and the Seven Years War. They had come from all over the world back then. Desired. Sought after. Presented as gifts to a Prussian prince. Some had come reluctantly, of course, always wary of becoming involved in the affairs of men. Some had come in chains. 3,861 in all. It was the last time so many had been together.

Hohenfriedberg, Rossbach, Leuthen, Hochkirch, Liegnitz, Torgau.

Some had died in battle in those places.

Prussia's defeat by Napoleon had put an end to it, at least as far as large army units were concerned. Centuries had gone by.

"But we fight on," he said aloud.

The remaining Iroquois looked at him and he could read their intentions. They blamed the Heer of Dunderberg, the Deeneeshee woman, and evil spirits in general for the loss of their comrade. They wanted another crack at them. They were all Pine Tree Chiefs, a designation awarded them by their tribe for bravery and expertise in war. The Cornet of Horse blamed himself. The mountain lion had been there for him. Its bite would have introduced a toxic zoonoses into his bloodstream, one that would have rotted his brain like a deadly version of the Mad Cow disease that affected humans.

Being different has its drawbacks," said one of The Voices in a soft, almost mocking one.

"I am in your debt," said the Cornet of Horse to the Iroquois. For a moment, he felt like he was speaking for all Americans. The Iroquois Confederation had been in place before the arrival of Columbus and it had been the inspiration for the alliance of like-minded states that eventually became the United States of America. Ben Franklin had said as much. The American Indian was an exemplar of the spirit of liberty they so cherished. But the Iroquois chose the wrong side of the American Revolution, rightfully anticipating the future westward expansion of the country that meant the loss of their lands. The Iroquois disappeared from the minds of Americans. Now, two more were gone. But they would not be forgotten.

"Just so you know," said Derga. "I'm coming with you."

That meant Connor would be coming. Straparola would follow him. And Lt. Gomez was still thinking of making an arrest. The Cornet of Horse smiled.

"I'll just stay at the Needle and help Ivanhoe," said Seventina. "I really don't want to get near that bastard again."

She's the only smart one here.

Chapter Thirty-Three

S he sat motionless between two big grey rocks and watched
the road. There was no one to be seen but she wore her gwynn
anyway. They would all be coming soon as the twilight
approached and she didn't want anyone to see her before she saw
them. Yellow tape across the castle entrance fluttered in the breeze.
That won't stop anyone.

In truth, she didn't know why she was here, high up on this
mountain with its scarred white face and a castle on its summit.
But she did know one thing. *This is where the Heer of Dunderberg
will leave this world for mine.* Not that the knowing of it would do
her any good. His path wouldn't take her where she wanted to go,
of that she was almost certain. She realized now that from the start
he had looked into her mind and he knew she would never follow
him to the Unseelie Court. *He knew it before I knew it myself but
used me for his own purposes nonetheless.*

She shuddered, imagining herself before Nicnivin, his Queen,
with her mane of feathers black as a crow's. She was beneath
her notice, really, but there was no sense in chancing it. Slipping
through the Unseelie Court unnoticed would be like hoping for a
blessing from a priest.

Still, all the players would be here soon enough. The hunter
and his allies, Connor and his friends, and the red-haired woman

who had been a captive all this time. The hunter promised death but she might have to risk it to get next to Connor. Would he give back the comb willingly? She couldn't return without it. And what role did the red-haired woman have in this—she who held out the promise of aid? Her mind hadn't held so many uncertainties in a long time.

A sound pulled her out of her own thoughts. A figure was crossing the road, down below the castle where trees lined either side of the road. The figure was too far away to make out any details but whoever it was looked to be on the smallish side.

A child?

The figure disappeared among the trees. She made no move. *A child is no concern of mine.*

She heard the rumble of approaching vehicles before she saw the headlights. They stopped in front of the castle, at the entrance to the courtyard that lay beyond, aligning their vehicles so that no one could pass. She counted nine: the huge hunter and four warriors dressed in camouflage, the red-haired woman, Connor and his two friends. She was too far away to hear every word they said but she could tell a lot from their movements. The hunter, curse him, posted his four warriors in front of the vehicles like sentries. Then the hunter disappeared with Connor's two friends to inspect the courtyard behind them. Connor and the red-haired woman stood together near one of the vehicles.

What was her name? Ah, yes. Derga.

She could see from here there was an attraction between them just by the way they looked at each other.

And where was the Heer of Dunderberg? He is nearby. Waiting for the right hour of the day. Passing between was easiest during the hours of dawn and sunset. He'd make a move soon. Some one of them will likely die. Would Connor's death help her retrieve the comb? I can't kill him myself. But if he should die by the hands of the Heer of Dunderberg? And what of Derga? Would her death be helpful or not?

She clenched her hands in frustration, not daring to move lest she be spotted somehow by the hunter who had now rejoined Connor and Derga. As had Connor's two friends.

A shout from one of the sentries made her re-focus her attention on the scene in front of her. The sentry was pointing down the road, drawing the attention of the others. She looked down the road as well and saw what appeared to be a child, dressed in a long, pink coat standing with its back toward them.

Another sentry shouted but the child didn't turn. Instead, the child took one step, then another, towards them, walking backwards, as if he was recoiling from something farther down the road only he could see.

The two sentries who'd shouted began to trot toward the child, weapons ready, in an apparent effort to shield the child from that unseen threat. The light was failing now and whatever was further down the road must be hidden by the darker shadows thrown down by the surrounding trees and rocks. Yet, she was puzzled because she could not sense any presence that might threaten the child.

Suddenly, the space in front of the child was filled with a bright light, as if the child had switched on a powerful lantern. She could see the figure of the child alternately silhouetted and then half disappeared as the child turned and tossed a glowing orb into the air. It was then she saw that the child was no child at all. While child-sized at about three feet tall, it possessed an oversized nose, ears, and fingers. Its skin was a smooth grey with tufts of white hair about its head. It looked like a pint-sized old man that had an ugly demon for a father.

Something from the Unseelie Court. But what?

The sentry nearest to this little creature looked up at the shining orb floating above him. He never saw the tiny hand crossbow now in the creature's hand. And he never saw the tiny bolt that pierced the soft skin under his chin and bore a tunnel into his brain. His weapon fell to the ground before him, a clatter on the black tarmac before a softer crumple. There was no doubt he was dead. She keened softly for him, more out of reflex that genuine sorrow although she felt a touch of that. But then she saw Derga react as if she had heard her and she thought she now might have to shift positions to avoid being spotted.

All these thoughts came in the few seconds before the orb pulsed and released fingers of white energy that reached out to sizzle one of the vehicles, then touch the other sentry who'd come forward. Derga, Connor, and the others were spared, although they were all lying prone to escape any further attacks.

"Tuscarosa! Mohawk!" She heard the names shouted by one of their comrades but she didn't know which one was which but one was surely dead. The other looked only slightly injured.

"A pukwudgie," said a voice behind her. The Old Dutch accent told her who it was.

She shouldn't have been caught unawares but she was.

"They really hate American Indians," said the Heer of Dunderberg. "And giants. I found them not far from here in Connecticut, hiding and hating. Seems like a local Indian tribe talked a giant into beating on them years ago. The pukwudgie were murdering, kidnapping, and raping at every opportunity. Hard to believe such small beings were such big trouble. But we both know it can happen. The giant killed a lot of them, in fact, but a few survived. They want to get even but they like the casinos the tribes run there now. With their grey skin and short stature, they fit right in by looking like near-dead retirees with osteoporosis. So they enjoy out-of-state excursions involving Indian blood-letting. Sometimes they bring me an Indian girl from the casino, one that mistreated them in some way. One girl, I recall, didn't refill drinks quickly enough."

"I liked it better when you were a bastard of few words."

She turned and raised her hand to burn him but he shifted his weight so that some large bundle, cinched at the top, was now between them. A black hand with painted nails popped out of the bag and the Heer of Dunderberg pushed it back in.

He glanced quickly at his burden. "Thanks again."

It was the black woman from Cleopatra's Needle. The singer. His gratitude stung for there was none in his words.

"Don't say I never did anything for you." He nodded toward Connor and Derga. "He's all yours. When you're done, hide the redhead some place I can find her. But only if she's still alive."

She shook her head. "I can't attack him."

He understood the reason immediately. "A geas. You can do him no harm. I should have known. Things were getting more complicated than usual. Just don't let him know." He paused. "I'd still like the redhead, though, if it's no trouble."

One of the two remaining sentries rushed forward to aid the fallen ones while the second aimed a weapon to cover him. The Heer of Dunderberg waited until the sentry had moved past them and gave her a last look, one that told her that her troubles were her own. He jumped out onto the road and with the black woman over his shoulder, ran toward the hunter. A long blade appeared in his hand and he swung it like a saber as he passed the hunter who barely avoided the slash but sunk to one knee with the movement. The Heer of Dunderberg kept running and disappeared into the courtyard beyond. Within moments, a soft glow emanated from the courtyard. With a roar, the hunter regained control of his legs and went after the Heer of Dunderberg. The others peeled themselves off the road and followed. All except for the sentry who had by now ascertained that his two comrades were dead.

The pudwudgie, meanwhile, had disappeared.

He was fast and he carried a burden like it was no burden at all.

Connor saw the long blade appear in the Heer of Dunderberg's hand and his eyes widened in shock and alarm because until now, it had never occurred to him that the Heer might be armed. The blade sliced the air like a saber and he sensed the large figure beside him dip to one knee to avoid the cut.

It was the gap the Heer needed and Connor was reminded of the way a rugby player carrying the ball followed his line of blockers, scooting through the hole they created to gain yardage. Only in this instance, the Heer of Dunderberg charged through the hole created by his blade on a dead run. The bundle, Connor now saw, was the size of a duffle bag and what was inside it must be very light since it seemed to cause the Heer of Dunderberg no strain at all. Or the Heer of Dunderberg was a lot stronger than he had thought.

Option two is the more likely bet.

A roar next to him grabbed his attention and the giant—*how else now to think of him—rose and spun in pursuit.*

Connor wasn't so quick, stealing a glance down the road where he could see Seneca kneeling over his fallen comrades. The little man who had attacked them was gone. Seneca looked back in their direction and shook his head.

"What was that?" he said aloud, not really expecting an answer.

"Pudwudgie," answered Seneca. "Don't worry. I know where to find the little bastard. He's as good as dead."

Oneida sprinted forward to join Seneca. Connor sprang to his feet and chased after the giant with the others. Lt. Gomez paused to draw his pistol. Straparola held a rifle like he knew what to do with it. The Mohawk had his gun held ready as well. They all followed him. Derga hung back at a safe distance, a decision Connor welcomed even as he realized that he had no idea where his weapon was. The Heer of Dunderberg might try to take her again.

Connor ran on. The castle was a high mass of grey stone. A gallery on the left and right allowed vehicles to enter and depart from the courtyard beyond. In between was a slight larger tower with slits shaped like an inverted cross high up on the second level. There were windows on either side where a café served visitors in the summer months.

Connor veered right and raced through the gallery, a pair of arches on his right. He emerged into the courtyard, taking in the scene without slowing. The Heer of Dunderberg stood poised atop the stone wall with a bright sphere full of rainbow colors in a circular pattern forming behind him, He faced the giant who stood warily before him, feet braced, iron blades in each hand, ready for an attack. It was like traveling back to a medieval time. All he needed was some armor.

The Heer of Dunderberg looked ready to oblige but needed to get rid of his burden first. He swung it around like an Olympic athlete readying a hammer throw, pivoting to send it flying into the sphere over his shoulder.

Except it never got that far. *There is a woman inside the bag!* Connor found an extra burst of speed and launched himself into the air, colliding with the duffel bag. He wrapped his arms around it like an exhausted boxer holding onto heavy punching bag, falling backwards onto the stone floor.

The impact knocked the breath out of him and he heard himself gasping for air, the sound mixing with that of a cry from inside the duffel bag. His brain caught up to his instincts and he realized he was right. One of the women kidnapped by the Heer of Dunderberg was making the noise.

The Heer of Dunderberg was looking down on him with surprise. For a moment, Connor feared he would come down off the wall to retrieve the duffel bag and the prize inside. A louder humming sound filled his ears—words he didn't understand—and the giant rushed by him, heading straight for the Heer of Dunderberg.

Connor braced himself for the clash but the Heer of Dunderberg reacted differently than he expected, spinning backward like an acrobat into the sphere behind him, moving out of reach. The giant didn't stop at the wall, however. He planted a large foot onto the top of the wall and used it like a springboard to follow the Heer of Dunderberg. They both vanished beyond the wall out of sight. The sphere disappeared like it was being sucked away, collapsing in an instant, the loss of its light making Connor blink furiously to re-focus.

Connor lay looking at the spot where they had been, trying to process it. Finally, he twisted around to see his companions rooted to the stone floor. They all had the same look of shock on their faces, one that must be on his as well.

But then the look on Connor's face began to change and the others could see it. It was a look of alarm. Their eyes shifted toward him.

All except Derga's.

She wasn't there.

Chapter Thirty-Four

Dwerg couldn't get the taste of vomit out of his mouth and it colored everything he saw. He was in Tarrytown, an oversized village 25 miles north of Manhattan on the eastern shore of the Hudson River. It was a sleepy place. Nothing exciting had happened here since the American Revolutionary War in the 1770s. The British spy Major John Andre had been hanged in town for aiding the American traitor Benedict Arnold. Dwerg had seen the statue in the center of town commemorating the grisly event. And just a stone throw's north, the Headless Horseman had romped through Sleepy Hollow clad in his Hessian uniform in pursuit of Ichabod Crane. The tale had been penned by Washington Irving who had lived just south of Tarrytown in a cottage called Sunnyside.

The Headless Horseman was famous, Dwerg knew. He had appeared in a movie with the star Johnny Depp and he'd been in a television series named after Sleepy Hollow. They sold little souvenirs showing the headless horseman riding his black horse in the shops in Tarrytown. Pretty good for a headless fairy bastard properly called a dullahan.

Irving also had written about the Heer of Dunderberg but no movie had been made as far as Dwerg knew. Maybe they'd make a film involving the Heer and some actor would play Dwerg.

That would be something. Maybe they'd let him handle the transportation.

Dwerg laughed to himself. Wishful thinking.

Right now he was focused on getting the taste of vomit out of his mouth. He was standing on the train station platform on the edge of town, down by the river. A gust of wind wrapped itself around him and he opened his mouth wide, hoping the wind would help clean out his mouth. The station was in the shadow of the Tappan Zee Bridge, a massive span that linked Westchester County with the town of Nyack on the far side of the river. Dwerg had heard the name of the bridge had been changed but he liked the Old Dutch name best. The road over the bridge was called Interstate 87 and if you were traveling by car, it was the fastest route back to New York City from the Adironadacks.

Dwerg wanted to spit into the river but it was too far away even though he was standing on the southbound side closest to the water. He contented himself with sending a big glob on the train tracks below him. The taste of vomit wouldn't go away. The wind here was brisk and for a second he worried that his spit would blow back at him. The wind got inside his shirt, making it inflate like a bellows.

The sound of a horn in the distance alerted him that a train was coming into the station. The people on the concrete platform began clustering in little groups at regular intervals, knowing exactly where the doors of the train would open. Dwerg watched these veteran commuters board the train. Most, he noticed, went quickly to specific seats as if assigned by some invisible reservation system. These were people who liked to sit in the same seat day after day. If you sat in their favorite seat, they'd be almost sitting in your lap before they'd notice you. Dwerg noted the seating configuration. On the far side of the train, there was a pair of seats in each row while on the side closest to him, each row held three seats. Every other car had a restroom.

The doors closed and the train exited the station and Dwerg noted that it picked up speed very quickly. By the time the last car went by—there were seven in all—he could feel the draft it left behind.

Dwerg looked at his watch. The next train was his.

At the moment, the platform was empty of people and Dwerg eyed the free bench a few feet away. His legs begged him to sit but his butt was still tender. The thought made him clinch his ass cheeks tight. The vomit taste in his mouth grew sharper and he spat again. He hated the way the Heer of Dunderberg contacted him from wherever he was when he needed Dwerg. It was always in the shower and Markova never saw it coming. The bathroom would fill up with a grey mist in a second, as if the door to a smoky room had just been opened. A thin black thread of smoky wind, stronger than the surrounding mist, would emerge, undulating like a snake and shooting into his anus before he could clinch his ass cheeks together.

Dwerg knew what was inside him. It was a gand. Certain travelers he had assisted used a gand as a forerunner to an attack, using it to ensure their victims were unable to defend themselves. The Heer of Dunderberg had modified a gand so it could be used as a communications device, albeit one way from a place he's rather not go. That wasn't a place where they used phones.

The gand entering his body forced everything inside him upwards and he puked on the shower's walls with such force that it hit the tiles like it was coming from a hose. The force of it raised him on his toes but as the flow dissipated, he fell to his knees, head sagging as the last dregs of vomit dripped from his mouth. Most of the time, the water would be running when these attacks occurred so most of the vomit would be washed away quickly. The inside of his body felt purged of whatever had been there and his brain would tingle like it was being pierced by hundreds of pins.

That's when the Heer of Dunderberg spoke to him. No, that wasn't quite right as he didn't have a memory of specific words. But there would a moment of clarity when he understood what the Heer of Dunderberg wanted of him.

Dwerg spat again and wondered if it would be better to take it in the mouth rather than in the ass. At least, things would exit the way they were supposed to. But the choice wasn't his. It could be worse. Once he'd seen a gand inflate a gagged victim's body so that it exploded. Very messy.

Dwerg allowed himself a small smirk. It was almost worth the discomfort to learn that the Heer of Dunderberg had lost the bitches. Somehow, the redhead and the banshee were now a pair and the Heer was angry enough to want them both eliminated. Naturally, it was better to make their murder look like an accident. And there was nothing like a big accident to hide a small killing.

Dwerg rubbed his hand over his bald head. The incident at the Gershwin Hotel and its aftermath had been an untidy affair. He'd been arrested but someone had blown some kind of dust up a judge's nose and he'd been released on bail. He wasn't sure whom to thank but obviously someone in the "community" was on the ball and had acted quickly. Dwerg wondered if it was time for a new identity and a whole new look. It'd be nice to get his hair back.

Dwerg wondered what sort of dust had been used on the judge and the thought made him finger the small metal dispenser in his pocket. He was sure the dust supplier was the same one he used. The grey industrial-looking dispenser was small enough so that he could wrap his hand around it and use his thumb to press the white button that would discharge its contents. He'd picked it up on his way to Tarrytown at a warehouse in the Bronx run by Sandee, a long-legged woman who claimed to be a former dancer before her mother's retirement from the sand trade. Dwerg guessed most of her dancing had been at strip clubs in the outer borough of Queens rather than at the ballet-loving Lincoln Center downtown but he kept his opinion to himself. Sandee had met him at the door of the warehouse, pistol in hand, mumbling something about sand mafias stealing whole beaches as an apology once she recognized him.

"Did you know the Arabs are building skyscrapers in Dubai with sand from Australia?" she whispered, shaking her head in disbelief. "Mark my words, sand soon will be as precious as water."

Dwerg thought her slightly mad but Sandee knew her business. She produced everything from kits for making those multi-colored sand jars that every kid made at least once in their life to unity jars used by new-agers in wedding ceremonies. Then there was the more specialized products pulverized into tiny dust particles made from jinn-infected sand from Bir Tawal, an 800-square-mile no man's land between Egypt and Sudan. Ostensibly, the Bir Tawal lay unclaimed by either country due to a 100-year-old border dispute but the truth was neither country was eager to claim a dry, seemingly uninhabited country of mountains and sand that had been a jinn refuge for centuries. Both countries discouraged visits to the area but Sandee's semi-annual trips to Bir Tawal kept a few local officials—mystified as to why anyone would want to harvest sand from there—in comfort above their pay grade. Sandee's arrangement with the Bir Tawal jinn was never discussed but Dwerg had noted a few lamps of the type that made Aladdin famous in her Bronx warehouse and wondered if there was some kind of transportation angle in play. Dwerg had never moved jinn lamps himself. That business was handled exclusively by Lalla Mirra, king of the djinn in Morocco. But maybe the king was losing his grip. *File for future reference.*

To the untutored eye, the sand of Bir Tawal looked like the sand found across the Sahara. But Sandee had shown Dwerg Bir Tawal sand magnified 300 times and it was an incredibly varied with a variety of colors and shapes: tubular, hooked, ridged, swirled, starred, transparent.

"This isn't the normal small, rounded grains you find in the Sahara," Sandee explained. "That stuff doesn't bond well in concrete. You need more angular grains for building. It sounds nuts but that's why the Arabs have to import sand."

Sandee would sort through the Bir Tawal sand and combine the grains for a desired effect, drawing upon recipes that had been developed over hundreds of years. The knock-out dust had been around so long it was legendary—a low dose version had once been used to put unruly children to sleep, a practice that gave rise to the legend of The Sandman, one of Sandee's ancient forebears. Dwerg had used Sandee's combustible dust once but only reluctantly, as explosions tended to attract lots of investigators and were getting harder to conceal as accidents. Sandee also made a thinking dust that made some people mad if not used properly, a dust that could enhance the senses, and red slightly radioactive dust that was popular before the invention of Viagra.

For this job, Dwerg favored an electrostatically charged dust that adhered to walls and ceilings. It also didn't work right away which was good when you wanted a little time delay. Sandee called it TD dust just for that reason. Afterwards, all that remained were some tiny grey flecks that looked like paint chips. She could even color the TD sand to match an interior. The only risk was that the TD dust was so fine that it sometimes became clumpy in the dispenser. Sandee had put a marble inside the dispenser to reduce that risk. She knew her sand.

The real trick was calculating the time delay part of the equation. The effect produced by the TD dust was temporary. It would make its victim lose his concentration without actually knocking him unconscious. Everyone knew what it was like to zone out momentarily. TD dust stretched the moments into minutes. But calculating the time between activation and cessation was tricky because it was a bit imprecise. It could last anywhere from between 15 and 20 minutes, depending upon the amount the victim inhaled. Dwerg had consulted the train schedule. The train took 18 minutes to travel from Tarrytown to Spuyten Duvil. So the TD dust should be effective within the required window of time.

Spuyten Duvil was the key. The name was Dutch for "Spitting Devil" so naturally the Heer of Dunderberg was fond of the place as a spot for mayhem. Spuyten Duvil took its name from a now paved-over creek known for its treacherous currents that spilled into the Hudson River. And while the creek had been tamed by cement, it still lent its name to the area, with multiple bridges connecting it to Manhattan.

Spuyten Duyvil probably would have been drawn a blank in most people's minds if it wasn't the name used for the local train station, reached by descending down a hill to a spot on the river bank. While the bridge over the Harlem River for cars loomed high over the train station, a bridge used solely for trains heading toward Penn Station on Manhattan's west side operated at almost water's edge. Trains alternately heading for Grand Central in midtown Manhattan veered to the left, slowing to crawl in order to navigate a tight turn that followed the Harlem River inland from the Hudson River. If the train missed the turn, it would wind up in the river.

At least that was the plan. Dwerg wondered if the Heer of Dunderberg was involved in a 1882 train crash at Spuyten Duyvil that killed 10, including a state senator that was the likely target. The air brakes failed to work and while the train had managed to stop, it was rammed from behind by a later train. There had been other accidents here as well, including a recent freight train derailment. But the wreck in 1882 was the most famous. Dwerg did his homework. Transportation was his specialty.

The minor calculation was determining the arrival of the redhead. It had been a good guess on his part that she would dump the car she'd fled the Adirondacks in. And for a New Yorker, taking the train was almost as natural as hailing a taxi.

It had been a simple task to place a phone call to a few of the taxi services upstate, asking for professional help as it were. Dwerg identified himself as a taxi driver in Manhattan in need of assistance—a fare was coming in from upstate but the client had neglected to say whether she was arriving at Penn Station or Grand Central. And she wasn't answering her cellphone. Penn Station meant it was an Amtrak train coming from Montreal while the Grand Central destination meant it was a more local train probably originating in the state capitol of Albany. Could they help by keeping a lookout for a hot-looking redhead with an eye-patch?

A request like that was taxi porn. Within minutes, dispatchers in towns up and down the Hudson River were radioing their drivers, mostly males who began fantasizing about encounters with their stick shifts even as they sat behind the wheel of an automatic model a hot chick wouldn't get into on a dare. Hot chicks take limos or use a private car service but most taxi drivers were in denial about that—just like they had been in denial initially about ride-sharing services. Hot chicks didn't take them either after a few bad incidents. But every taxi driver knew who the private drivers were and a fare like her would soon be spotted.

It wasn't long before a dispatcher in Albany called in. She's been seen and salivated over by a score of drivers operating out of the Albany train station, waiting for fares from the raft of supplicants and politicians visiting the state capitol. They couldn't have been more helpful. Yeah, she was hot. The eye-patch was kinky sexy. She was on a train bound for Grand Central. They told him the departure and arrival times. She was in the fourth car. The conductor had a boner already.

But here was the odd thing. Some said she was traveling alone. Others said she was traveling with another woman who was pretty good-looking herself. Others said the companion was a dog looks-wise or a scary looking bitch. Garbled radio transmissions perhaps but Dwerg sensed the banshee he'd picked up in Central Park was with her.

A blast from the train's horn signaled its imminent arrival. Like all the commuters on the Tarrytown station platform, Dwerg checked his watch. This was the one.

Dwerg had initially positioned himself at the northern end of the platform where the train's last car would stop. Now he began walking toward the opposite end of the station as the train slowed. The train's passenger cars were all silver with a blue stripe down the middle running parallel to the windows. The locomotive, slightly taller than the cars, was silver as well, with a blue stripe and a smaller red one around its midsection. The locomotive pushed the train from the rear because there was no place on the line to switch the engine to the front. So the locomotive pulled the train heading northbound and pushed it heading southbound. But even though, the power for the southbound train was at the rear, the engineer sat in a small compartment in the front car, controlling speed from there.

Dwerg scanned the windows as the train came in just in case she'd changed her seat, But no, there she was in the fourth car. She looked like she was sitting alone on the far side of the car with an empty seat beside her. Dwerg figured the other one must be sitting there wearing her gwynn.

He quickened his pace and moved along the back of the platform, keeping as many commuters as possible between him and the train lest his movement attract her attention. He noticed there were at least two policemen on board the train but that was no cause for alarm. The police wouldn't be prepared for an attack that didn't look like an attack. The train came to a stop and there was a long pause that worked to his advantage, allowing him to close the distance to the front of the train. He was almost there when he heard the ding-dong chime that signaled the opening of the train's doors. This wasn't like Europe where passengers often opened the train doors themselves. Yeah, he knew his transportation.

A number of people exited the first car and Dwerg saw that the engineer had already dropped the little window of his compartment and was peering back down the train line behind him. Engineers worried that they would get underway with someone stuck in a closing door. They also worried about being incapacitated somehow while they were underway. A "dead man's switch" required the engineer to keep constant foot pressure on it while moving. The dust would put the engineer into a daze but he wouldn't move. It would be like he'd fallen asleep at the wheel of a car, foot still on the gas pedal.

Safety is a vulnerability. That was one of Dwerg's operating mantras and he repeated it to himself as he approached the engineer's compartment. All too often, he'd learned, the safety systems designed to protect something were vulnerable. In this instance, he'd be taking advantage of another safety feature that worked only half the time. The locomotive was equipped with an audible alert that emitted a tone every 45 seconds, requiring the engineer to acknowledge it with a press of a button within 15 seconds. But when the train was traveling southbound, the alerter was all the way at the other end of the train from the engineer. He'd never hear it. The engineer looked to be about 50 with a girth that nearly matched his age. The engineer's hairline was in full recession and the face looked well-fed and heading toward jowly. A pair of bushy greying eyebrows inched upwards as Dwerg approached.

"Does this train stop at Spuyten Duyvil?" asked Dwerg.

"No. This is an express. Next stop Grand Central."

"Oh."

"Next train should be a local, though."

"Thanks," said Dwerg. "Hey, is that door behind you supposed to be open?"

"What?" The engineer tucked his head back into his compartment and swiveled his head and body away from Dwerg to check the door. Dwerg extended his clenched fist, pointing it upwards inside the compartment and pressed the plunger. A mist of fine particles floated upwards and adhered to the ceiling as Dwerg withdrew his hand.

The engineer swiveled his bulk back toward Dwerg. "The door is fine…" he began but stopped as he saw Dwerg walking away from him.

"Fucking joker," the engineer mumbled as he felt something tickle his nose. The engineer waved at the air in front of his face. He closed the window and another ding-dong chime signaled the closing of the train's doors.

Dwerg turned his back to the train as it left the station and looked out across the Tappan Zee. This was where the Hudson River was its widest—so wide that the Old Dutch colonists had seen fit to call this part of the river a sea. He listened to the sound of the train departing and when the rattle grew dimmer, he checked his watch. The express train would be making a local stop very soon.

Chapter Thirty-Five

S he sat on the train next to Derga although to passersby, it looked like Derga was sitting alone. Derga said it would be better if she wore her gywnn since anyone looking for them would be searching for two women traveling together.

The gywnn had certain other advantages. Unseen and at Derga's request, she had removed a wallet from a woman's bag in Albany, extracted some strips of green paper Derga said was money and then returned it. Derga had used the money to buy a ticket at the station ticket window as well as some food. Derga said as long as she wore the gwynn she wouldn't need a ticket.

At first, she'd been terrified of this machine that moved on rails. The idea of confining herself in a large container as it hurtled along was unsettling. Gradually, she became used to the speed and the slight side-to-side motion as the train headed south back towards New York City. She wasn't keen on returning to the big city with its crowds of people and never-ending concrete. It wasn't a comfortable place.

A door at the end of the end of the compartment slid open and a man wearing blue trousers, a lighter blue shirt and a hat with a badge on the front stepped through, stopping at each seat. Passengers handed him a piece of paper or one encased in a wallet or pictured on a phone screen.

Click click.

The man had some device in his hand and used it to punch holes in sliver of paper that he stuck into a slot at each seat.

"Tickets!" It was a word spoken in a low tone. A priest of some kind? She had some experience with priests over the years. *They want death all to themselves.* She watched Derga perform the ritual. His name was Conductor, according to the badge on his hat. He passed without a glance her in direction.

The train traveled along the eastern bank of the Hudson River and when she saw the water, her mind drifted back to Lough NaSool. What a safe, small world that had been.

Early on, she'd caught of glimpse of the island in the Hudson where the Heer of Dunderberg had been. The brick castle went by in a flash and she tensed for a moment, wondering if he was somehow there and could see them passing by so close. But nothing happened and she calmed herself.

They rode in silence as Derga advised. She noticed some people around them with wires coming out their ears who seemed to be talking to themselves. Perhaps Derga could do the same and no one would notice.

She'd like to hear more from Derga. She said she knew how to get her back. But she couldn't imagine how that was possible without her comb. When strummed like a harp, it unlocked the door between here and there.

"My comb?" The sound was a whisper curled into a tight cone aimed directly at Derga's ear so only she could hear it.

In a low voice that sounded like a prayer: "Ryan Connor is a stubborn man but I will not harm him over this. Remain quiet."

Her eyes widened and she nearly fell into the aisle. *I have been such a fool!*

She gathered herself and cursed her stupidity.

All this time, she had been thinking of him as Conor, a common first name in Ireland. But it was his surname they had been using. Connor. A shortened version of O'Connor. It all made sense now.

He is O'Conchobhair Sligigh.

O'Connor Sligo. A branch of the O'Conchobhair. Kings of Connaught, the kingdom in the west of Ireland now called one of the four provinces. Two had been High Kings of Ireland. The family tree formed in her mind, lines going back centuries like branches of a massive oak. Lords of Carbury. Lords of Sligo in later years. The names rolled through her mind all the way back to the first one in 1181, Brian Luighnech Ua Conchobhair.

I can't touch him.

No one with royal Irish blood could ever be harmed or interfered with. No wonder she found him difficult to track. His blood was like her gwynn, making him practically invisible to her. Hurt him? It was her sworn duty to warn him when death approached. The cry of the banshee. They called her a messenger of death. And that was true. But for royal blood it went one step further: the cry was a lament that someone was beyond their protection.

There were no more kings in Ireland, though. All that had disappeared with the Easter Uprising in 1916 and the subsequent creation of the Republic of Ireland. It was doubtful that Connor was even aware of his royal bloodline. Her mind dove back through history. It had been worse for them. The O'Connor Sligo had been dispossessed of their lands by Cromwellian invaders from England in--1610 was it? Time flew for her. Many of the O'Connor Sligo had left Ireland, although such were their numbers that there is still plenty of O'Connors in Sligo. But the last recognized chief of the name died in Brussels in 1756, a lieutenant general in the Austrian army. She had keened for him. The O'Connor Sligo had been Catholics so the British erased all traces of them. No wills. No deeds. No public documents. There had been one, James, who started a newspaper in the 1790s. The British didn't like its tone and wrecked his printing office. James and all his immediate relations had been forced to flee to Norfolk, Virginia in 1794. She had keened for James from afar in 1819. He died as a newspaper editor in America.

And this descendant of the O'Connor Sligo has my comb and there seems to be no way of getting it back from him!

She wanted to scream. And for a second, she did, catching herself when the nearest passenger grabbed his ears in discomfort. The effort made her feel more frustrated.

She had been stupid to lose it in the first place. But who would believe that it would wind up in the hands of an O'Connor Sligo, a bloodline she was powerless to act against. It was a rule issued by the Seelie Court. And you didn't break the rules. Of course, she had done just that in trying to retrieve her comb. But there were big rules and there was no forgiveness for breaking them. Attacking an O'Connor Sligo was a big rule she couldn't break. All the rest might be little rules. She hoped.

It's all a slippery slope.

The comb was lost to her. The Seelie Court would not be pleased. She didn't know what would happen to her when she returned. She's never heard of a comb being lost before.

What a mistake!

And she'd been stupid to fall in with the Heer of Dunderberg. *Another mistake.*

But Derga said there was still a way back for her. There was a door in Rome. But she'd say no more about it. Rome! A city full of priests that hated her on principle. She hoped she wasn't about to make another mistake, trusting this woman. She had already made too many.

She let herself drift, encouraged by the rocking of the train. It seemed to have a rhythm of its own, a pulse of sorts, beating faster as the speed of the train increased. It was as if the train sensed it somehow would come to life if it went fast enough.

But then the train slowed like it was coming back from the brink of birth. It was stopping at a platform and there were people standing on it, waiting to come aboard. A sign on the platform read "Tarrytown." A few people rose from their seats and moved toward the doors, clutching bags of different sizes, shapes, and colors. A man glanced back in her direction but his eyes were on Derga, she realized. Then he turned away to face the door. An old understanding surfaced in her mind. Derga didn't travel unnoticed, particularly by members of the opposite sex.

Something familiar outside the train caught her attention, a figure moving parallel to the train. She strained to get a better look but there were people in the way. The train came to a stop and a loud ding-dong chime startled her. The train doors opened. People got on and off but none were familiar. She suddenly felt like she should get off the train but she couldn't see what alarmed her. She twisted in her seat to see forward. Derga felt the movement and put her arm on the seat back in front of her, boxing her in.

"Easy," Derga whispered.

The word made her uneasy. It was something said to a donkey or a horse when the animal was alarmed. And donkeys and horses knew when to be scared. Something wasn't right. She waited, tensing up. She half-expected the Heer of Dunderberg to board the train and attack them both.

But nothing happened. The ding-dong chime signaled the doors closing. The train moved out of the station, gathering speed as it went. All she could see was a man named Conductor stopping before each passenger, checking their tickets and double-clicking a slip of paper for the new passengers. She looked out the window and that's when she saw a lone bald-headed figure walking back along the station platform, a figure that abruptly turned his back away from the train.

He wasn't fast enough. She saw his face. And she recognized him. The carriage driver who'd found her in the park.

And here he was looking for her again. *Did he know she was on this train?*

Yes, he knew. That's why his back was turned. He didn't need to look at the train because he already knew.

So why was he letting them leave?

They were in danger.

She squirmed again, looking up and down the length of the train as far as she could see, wondering where the danger would come from and how it would present itself.

"Be still," whispered Derga. No one could see her but she guessed Derga was worried about any noise she would make.

The train picked up speed and she waited. Still nothing happened. *Was the danger waiting for them at this place called Grand Central Station? Then why was the coachman waiting for them at a place called Tarrytown.*

No, the danger was imminent. She was sure. But what was it?

"Do we stop again?" she asked.

Derga looked her way, her eyes pleading for silence. But before Derga could say a word, a short man sitting across the aisle wearing a jacket that read "Yankees" across it breadth raised himself up in his seat and half-turned their way.

"Next stop is 125th Street," he said. "This is an express train to Grand Central but it stops at 125th Street first. You know—in Harlem. They never tell you that until you're almost there."

Derga smiled her thanks.

"I don't know why they do that."

Derga shrugged.

"Yankee fan? We'll be passing the Stadium."

"Red Sox."

The man noted Derga's red hair and the red-eye patch.

"Figures," he said, slinking back down into his seat.

Harlem? Now she had two places to worry about. And who was this man anyway? She hadn't even noticed him before. She rose from her seat and looked down over his shoulder. The man was staring down at a tablet. On it was a photo of a man in uniform hitting a ball with a long stick. Not hurling, though, the old Irish game. There was no curve on the end of the stick, honed down to the thinness of a blade. She eyed the other passengers more closely. Some were dozing, some were reading and others were staring blankly in front of them. *I wish I had a hurley in my hands right now.*

Another train heading in the opposite direction made her heart leap with the noise because it was unexpected, a silver blur of horizontal metal with dark stripes on its side. She had almost raised her voice to it in a reflex action. It was only a thing, she reminded herself, not a threat. *Unless you got in its way.*

She was becoming more tense. She fought the urge to cry out but a moan escaped her lips. A few people looked her way with puzzled expressions. Derga was now alarmed. She knew. Death was approaching. She could feel it. The train went faster and the side-to-side rhythm increased. She stood there unseen but ready to act against whatever appeared. The train headed back to the brink where it could take on a life of its own.

And it did.

It began with the screech of metal on metal as she felt the wheels underneath her lock in a desperate attempt to stop. The world roared and it all went sideways with a back-breaking jerk. The windows opposite her shattered as the side of the train hit the ground. Dirt and gravel poured into the car like it was being sucked in. Rocks flew through the air. Branches on the outside made their insistent way inside. Metal crunched and folded. Bodies tumbled and one woman disappeared out the window. A man was thrown into what had been an overhead luggage rack and had the presence of mind to hook his hand into the rack to hold his position. Others wrapped their arms around seats, hugging them to keep from moving until the seats themselves dislodged and sent them crashing. A red jet of liquid pierced the air as someone's artery was severed.

She was lucky she was already standing. As the car tilted, she reached up with one hand to grab the overhead rack while simultaneously grabbing Derga by the arm just as Derga began to fall out of her seat. For anyone looking at Derga, it would appear that she was suspended in mid-air without any support.

No one was looking. Most of them had their hands over their faces to protect themselves. Others were toppled over. A few had limbs that were bending the wrong way. A couple didn't move and she could tell they were dead. Those still alive were moaning or screaming, the sound of their voices melding with the screeching of the train. What she'd thought of as a bid for life by the train had turned into a piercing cry of death. It was a sound she knew well.

The coachman had tried to kill them. She didn't know need to know the details of how he'd gone about it. She knew he'd caused the wreck. She looked around the train and saw the pain he'd caused. *All to get at them.* A soft keen escaped her lips to join the cries of those around her.

Derga found some footing on the armrest of a now sideways seat. The train was slowing but the car suddenly lurched sideways so that it was perpendicular to the tracks. Finally, it came to a stop. She could hear water lapping nearby. They were just short of the river.

Derga stretched to reach a red lever on the side of the window and pulled it, releasing a locking mechanism. Then she pulled a long black snake of rubber from around the window and discarded it like it might bite. The window came loose a little and she pried it the rest of the way, letting it slide away behind her out of the way with a sharp thud.

She didn't wait for Derga to go first. She swung her body upwards like a gymnast and slipped out the window onto the side of the train car. Derga followed her moments later, spitting dirt from her mouth, and they both stood up to survey the scene. The train derailed a 100 yards short of the Spuyten Duyvil station. In the distance, she could see that the train tracks curved in one direction but also split to head over a low bridge that looked like it swiveled to let passing boats through. Her train had sought a third way. The first car was still upright but only feet from the river. The second, third and fourth cars had followed the first but they were all tipped over on their sides, with the fourth lying across the tracks. The fifth car had detached somehow so the rest of the train was off the rails but still on the track bed.

People were pulling themselves from the wreckage and spilling out onto the ground. A wail of sirens sounded in the distance. She noticed an old, narrow, rusted metal bridge overhead that led down to the river but the last few steps were gone, leaving only a frame that hung over the rocky riverbank. This place was already a wreck.

"God's bones!" said Derga.

"Are you all right," she asked.

"Yes. But look at all these people."

"We need to leave. The Heer of Dunderberg is behind this. I saw his man at the Tarrytown station. He'll be coming to check his work."

Derga looked in her direction and then back again at the disaster in front of her. "OK. You're right." Derga paused. "How do we get off this?"

"I'll catch you. Look down in a few seconds."

She jumped from the side of the car and landed on the ground, knees slightly bent. She looked around but no one was her looking her way. The car blocked the view of her from the station. She took of her gwynn and folded it away.

She looked up to see Derga staring down at her.

"Jump!"

And Derga did. A leap of faith, she realized, as she caught the woman and steadied her upright. Inwardly, she was pleased that Derga had trusted her. It had been a long time since anyone had done that.

"Nice catch," said Derga. "I didn't realize you were that strong."

Derga swept her hair back from her eye. "Let's go. Toward the station. From there we can get out onto the street."

Together, they crossed the tracks and ran toward the station. Already, a small crowd was forming on the station and the overhead walkway that crossed over the tracks. They clambered up some steps onto the platform and the people there gave way before them.

"Are you okay?" someone asked.

"Yes," said Derga and kept walking.

"Don't jump into a taxi," she said. "It could be his man at the wheel."

Derga nodded. The road next to the station was at the bottom of a hill and she could see it curved upwards toward the left. They'd only got about halfway when she heard a loud hum. She stopped and looked behind her. She couldn't see anything but the sound didn't stop. It sounded threatening.

"What is it?" asked Derga.

"That hum."

"Cars," said Derga. "Look up. That's the Henry Hudson Parkway over your head. The bridge crosses the Harlem River. That's the island of Manhattan on the other side."

She looked up and saw the bridge high above her. It looked massive from this angle. It stretched across the water onto the opposite shore and seemed to be imbedded into a hillside covered with trees.

"Inwood Park," said Derga following her gaze.

"It looks like a giant clasp that keeps Manhattan from floating away."

"You sure you're okay?"

"Yes."

"You're really that new to all this, aren't you?"

"Lough NaSool doesn't change much. We like places that don't change. Or change only as slowly as we do."

Derga resumed walking and they were soon at the top of the hill. But it turned out to be just the beginning of a longer climb as the road rose again in a long steady climb. Vehicles with sirens blaring and red lights flashing sped past them, headed downhill.

"I know where we are," said Derga. "Follow me."

They turned right and kept walking toward and then through a forest of red and white brick towers of varying height. People walked in and out of them and she guessed they lived in them.

"You're not new to this, are you?" she said to Derga.

"I've been doing this sort of thing for a while."

"But you're not like me," she said. "Who are you then?"

"I work for the Red Man," said Derga.

"I've never met him but I've heard stories."

"Some of them are true," said Derga with a smile.

"So you're like…"

"We try to make sure things don't get out of hand."

"Yes, but we don't normally try to kill each other," she said. "You're in between. No one at court will care if you live or die. You're fair game."

"There is that risk."

"Will I get my comb back? I can't take it from a Connor."

"Perhaps its more trouble than its worth," said Derga gently.

She felt rebuked. It was another sensation that she'd not felt in ages and she nearly drowned in it. Then there was another feeling, even worse. Remorse it called itself.

Eventually, they came out on a street full of small shops. At the end of the street was a green structure elevated above the street.

"That's where we're going," said Derga. "The subway."

"Subway?"

"It's a train that runs underground, although up here it's elevated. When it gets downtown into Manhattan, it's underground."

She stopped, forcing Derga to halt as well.

"Another train?"

Chapter Thirty-Six

Connor walked with ghosts and he knew them well. Sean Thornton was one's name. Another was called Red Will Danaher. And there was the small one named Michaleen Oge Flynn. There was a whole village's worth of ghosts walking with him, around him. But Connor was only interested in one, the ghost of a beautiful red-haired woman named Mary Kate Danaher, sister of Red Will.

In his mind's eye, Connor could replay the scene in which Thornton first sees Mary Kate.

"Hey...is that real?" says Thornton. "She couldn't be." Connor was wondering the same about Derga. It had been two weeks since he'd lost her on Whiteface Mountain in New York. There had been no word from her or about her. Some instinct told him to return to Ireland and a film festival there had been on the docket all along. So he went.

Connor stood outside Ashford Castle in the county of Mayo in west of Ireland taking in the landscape where the Oscar-winning film *The Quiet Man* had been shot. Connor, like most Irish-Americans, had seen the film on television at least once a year around St. Patrick's Day for most of his life. Derga wasn't as fiery a character as Mary Kate Danaher, perhaps Maureen O'Hara's most famous role. O'Hara's red hair made him think of Derga and that was no fault of his own. In Ashford Castle and the nearby village of Cong, it was hard to think of anything else but the film as the local economy was built around servicing the tourists who came to see the place made famous by the movie. But as far as Derga was concerned, Thornton's remark could be his own. Sean Thornton, a haunted American boxer, was returning to the land of his birth. Thornton had been played by John Wayne, that icon of American westerns. John Ford, known for the same, had been the director. The film was essentially a western made with fists rather than pistols. Most thought the film was a low-brow, sentimental, romantic comedy. But Ford, whose real name was Feeney, was a genius and the real story flew over many people's heads. *The Quiet Man* was subversive film that went counter to the American dream, being the rare immigrant movie about a man happy to leave the United States. Connor wondered what Wayne would make of Derga. Connor was sure he'd approve. But then she might be just as real as Mary Kate Danaher.

"Oh, the kisses are a long way off," said Mary Kate to Thornton. It felt like that was something Derga had forgotten to say or had been just about to. *Was there an unsaid promise on her lips? Had that been real?*

Cong had turned *The Quiet Man* into an industry, an achievement all the more remarkable in that the film had been released in 1952. Cong, standing in for the fictional village of Innisfree, had been making a living off it ever since. A small whirlwind captured Connor's attention but it disappeared as quickly as it came. Connor's eyes wandered toward a middle-aged couple walking diagonally away from him. Americans, he could tell at a glance, given their soft shape and the track-suit leisure wear they wore. The wife clutched a plastic bag from The Quiet Man Museum, a white-washed thatched cottage made to look like Thornton's ancestral home. No doubt they were headed toward Pat Cohan's Pub that had been seen in the film. It would be a pint of Guinness for the man and a glass of the same for the wife as she wouldn't like the taste of it but would have a sip of it to say she did. It was all in the spirit of the film, even if the exterior had been a shop at the time and the interior was a replica of a Hollywood set. Quiet Maniacs. The village was full of them.

The Quiet Man was the film most responsible for American's view of Ireland. The film idealized Ireland as some charming class of third-world country with rural greenery and natural beauty, pubs, balladeers, donkeys, and devout Catholics. Neither the Irish Republican Army nor IT whiz kids working for the likes of Intel, the computer chip maker with a plant outside Dublin, could put a dent in the image. In this small village in the county of Galway, modern Ireland didn't exist. People came here to see the Ireland of their imagination and to sing old songs like *O Danny Boy, Toora Loora Loora, and The Black Velvet Band* in the pubs at night. U2, Ireland's most famous rock band, didn't make the play list.

Ashford Castle had a little more going for it from an authenticity standpoint. The first stone had been laid in 1228 by the De Burgos, descendants of Charlemagne, who then proceeded to break the backs of the O'Connors who had run things in this part of the world until then. Ruari O'Connor, some said, had been the last true king of Ireland and Connor supposed there was a royal drop of blood in his veins mixed in with the vast amount supplied by his less exalted ancestors. It wasn't something he'd ever given any thought to. The world was full of Connors.

Ashford Castle was certainly a grey place. A bridge of grey stone spanned a small river that may have doubled as a moat. At the far end, a grey stone guard tower with a big A carved into the upper deck spanned the roadway. Lord Ardilaun, otherwise known Sir Arthur Edward Guinness, had laid claim to the place in the 19th century, floating in on proceeds gained from sale of the national beverage. Guinness added to the castle's expanse, becoming a structure built more with decoration than defense in mind. Ashford was a status symbol of its time. Today, it was a luxury hotel of grey stone.

Connor muscled his way through the hotel lobby of dark wood and Persian rugs as politely as he could, trying to find a gap amongst a crowd of Quiet Maniacs wearing Notre Dame sweatshirts touring the premises. Some had the "Fighting Irish" university slogan emblazoned across their chests. Red Will Danaher, who had been quick with his fists in The Quiet Man, probably would have embraced them.

Ashford had different classes of customers. One was Americans—Quiet Maniacs to greater or lesser degrees in search of old ballads and some ethereal connection to a place their ancestors had once fled. Sadly, if seemed that if you stayed in Ashford Castle, it meant you'd lost all connection to Ireland. It meant you didn't know where your family was from and you'd no idea if there were any relatives still living. If you did, you'd be off staying with them. Connor had learned that much at the bar in Ashford Castle. The Guinness was quite good, though, and was the only reason for being at the bar. That and it was a short stroll to his room with its oak panels and canopied bed. You woke up feeling a like a lord. It gave you a sense of how the other half lived back in the day. They lived well.

The other class of customers were Brits touring places in Ireland they used to own or think they did. Reliving the days of Empire in their own minds when they brought civilization to the country with the same zeal cowboys did for Native Americans, conveniently sidestepping the less savory issues associated with running a conquered country. They were easy to spot, keeping their eyes averted, the confidence of Empire gone, worried that they may be laughed at or scorned in equal measure by the locals. Yeats said it best, thought Connor. For the English, their home was their castle. For the Irish, a castle was as symbol of oppression. That's why the Irish burned so many. Connor wondered if modern visitors saw the ghosts of the millions who had died in the Great Famine of the 19th century.

And in a category of their own were the celebrities who stayed at Ashford Castle. Presidents, princes, actors like Brad Pitt, and even John Lennon. The photos were on the walls. But Quiet Maniacs as well at the end of the day.

All these thoughts went through Connor's mind like the background score of a film. Foremost on his mind was distribution. Theater revenue, he had begun to realize, was best in smaller markets that attracted vacationers—places like Jackson Hole, Wyoming, or Naples, Florida. Cracking the big cities was difficult as they were dominated by movie chains and potential audiences had a lot of other entertainment options to choose among. But he had luck in alternative locations like museums that had a ready-made audience of members. That had led him to contact libraries and in very small markets, they had been very responsive since libraries were often the only purveyor of culture in their areas.

Connor headed down a flight of stairs to The Dungeon Bar, now closed to the public for the opening reception of the event Connor had come to attend, the Cong Film Fleadh. The room was already packed with people, drinks in hand. Banners with coats of arms ranging from Burke to O'Brien hung from the red walls and the curved ceiling sported chandeliers that a musketeer would have been thrilled to swing from. A suit of armor stood by the door, visor down in anticipation of mayhem.

Connor headed toward the serving bar in the back of the room, edging his way carefully past a woman carving the air with her hands as she talked with a man who seemed nervous about being hit accidentally, keeping his distance but leaning in toward her at safe intervals when her hands were immobile.

"A pint of the black, thanks," he said to the barman who topped off one in waiting and handed to him. Properly done, pouring a pint of Guinness was a seven-minute affair so bartenders at events like this kept a small production line going to keep up with demand. Connor took a quick sip, savoring once more just how much better

Guinness tasted in Ireland than it did anywhere else. A pint of Guinness would make you believe in magic because once it left the island and traveled over the water, it lost something intangible in the taste. Many of the other attendees, he noticed, were drinking red wine, a drink more in fashion among the many Irish keen to show their international sophistication.

Connor spotted a familiar face across the room but getting there was like swimming through a Joycean stream of Irish consciousness.

"I've just been excommunicated," said a voice to Connor's left.

"Jesus, Plunkett, how'd you manage that?"

"So you know I'm living over in Berlin now making the odd film for quite some time. The Catholic Church there takes a tithe out of your wages. And if you can believe it, this was Adolf Hitler's idea, thinking it would make the Church less popular like. But the war ends and the Church keep the tithe. They like the new revenue stream. I refused to pay it so I've been excommunicated so I have. They sent me a letter."

"So what you're saying is that you're willing to risk eternal damnation for the sake of a few bob."

Connor smiled and squeezed by.

"That's a load of bollocks!"

"Listen to me now. He's a gombeen, a geebag and maybe worst of all, dry shite."

Two voices, one female, incredulous. Man trouble. Something Yeats said comes to mind: for every conversation between two people, there is a third unseen. *A lot harder to interpret now, isn't it?*

"I'm starved with the hunger."

"Will we go for a scoop first?"

"I'd eat the back door buttered."

Three going the other way. One male with a hard brush.

An old bald head with speckles holding court. "When I was a wee lad, it was a fine day if I had two and six in my pocket, sweets on my mind and an ass to get to get me there." A smack of the lips like he could still taste it. "Jakers! You don't look that old." A reply from a listener, a young woman with long black hair down one side of her head and a coiled braid on the other.

"Irish independence is a temporary condition." The words gave Connor pause and he glanced over at the speaker, tall man with a mane of white hair and bushy eyebrows a nest of crows would call home. The partition of North and South was always the elephant in the room, a subject tactfully danced around in most social events but here was a man having a go at it head on, talking to a pair of men half his age. "That's what those bastards in Parliament think. 100 years on our own but 800 years under the Crown before that. Mark my words. Brexit will give them an excuse to take Ireland back. No hard borders, they say, like it's a good thing. Do you think we Irish would have the same rights under English law as we do under European? We have been there before. Just wait: one act of terror in England that can be traced through Ireland and they'll jump us in the name of security. Sure, the streets of Dublin are already crawling with MI5 and 6 Brits."

Another male voice talked into his ear. "Where's the jacks?"

Connor nodded toward the door behind him. "To the right of the stairs."

He turned slightly to find a glass of red at close quarters, with slightly chubby female fingers firmly clasping the stem.

"What's the craic?" said Fiona Campbell, with a broad smile on her face. Rosaleen's film-friend from Dublin, met in Sligo in what seemed like ages ago.

"Fiona! How wonderful to see you!" The familiar face had found him. Connor was only half-surprised to see her. As the mother hen of the Dublin film crowd, he'd guess she be here.

"And how's your dear cousin Rosaleen?"

Not that she didn't know. "Much better, thank you," said Connor. "I had a quick look in at her on the way here. She'll soon be in fine form."

"The poor creature," clucked Fiona.

"Yes, it was awful. Rosaleen tells me you dropped in to see her once or twice. Thanks for that.

"It was the least I could do," said Fiona. "Still searching for shorts?"

Connor nodded. "I don't know if there will be much here but like Woody Allen says: 90 percent of life is showing up."

"And 10 percent of the time it's worthwhile," Fiona said. "There will be a lot of people talking shite. Be warned. Anyone who says they've had a word about their film project with Gabriel Byrne, Liam Neeson, Colin Farrell, or Brendan Gleeson hasn't had a word with them at all."

Connor chuckled. The four were among the most famous of Ireland's horde of actors. "Don't worry. I'll make short work of them."

Fiona smiled. "Fair play to ye, Ryan Connor. Slainte."

"Slainte," replied Connor with a clink of his pint to her wine glass.

"Oh, Christ. Here she comes to give you the once over," said Fiona in a half-breadth.

"Fiona!" said an older woman who looked to be in her seventies. She wore a pale blue gown and a massive necklace worn like a collar that seemed designed to keep her head on her shoulders.

"How lovely to see you. It's so lovely to be in Cong. People say that the greenery in the south looms much larger and brighter than in the Black North. But I don't know why they say that. My late and very much older husband always said the Black North is just as green. Someone needs to put that idea on screen."

She turned toward Connor and not waiting for an introduction. "Don't you think so? Emma Lord of the West Tyrone Film Board."

"I couldn't say. I'm Ryan Connor, Empire Shorts. New York." Connor recognized the coded language for what it was. The Black North referred to the Protestant North, most specifically to The Royal Black Preceptory, an order of anti-Catholics more extreme than even the more famous Orange Order from whom they recruited. It was her way of letting you know who she was.

"Empire Shorts. That's a fascinating idea!" said Lord. "How lovely to meet you."

Then she turned and walked away.

"You've been found wanting," said Fiona. "She's been searching for years for a producer to tell the Black North story 'properly' as she says. What she doesn't understand is that everyone already knows the story and there is nothing proper about it."

Fiona paused. "It's a bit sad really. The West Tyrone Film Board is just herself. Her late husband made a fortune selling carpets."

Connor suddenly sensed a stirring in the crowd, the kind that usually signals the arrival of a celebrity.

"Jesus, Mary and Joseph," said an accented male voice behind him. "Will you look at that red-haired colleen!"

"Bean rua," said another man's voice in Gaelic. "Dearg te!"

Before he saw her, Connor knew who he was talking about.

Derga walked through the Dungeon Bar, people moving out of her way without having to be asked. Heads swiveled in her direction

403

and Connor heard whisperers trying to fathom who she was. A few men just ogled silently. She was wearing a loose red blouse that only encouraged male eyes to wander to the tight red skirt that clung to her hips and molded itself to her legs. The red eye patch was the real crowd stopper, though.

Derga stopped in front of him and now women were eyeing him as well, wondering what there was about him that attracted her attention. Truth was he was wondering that himself. *Play it cool.*

"Quite an entrance," said Connor. "Everyone thinks you're a movie star from some foreign film they can't remember."

"You really know how to make a girl's head spin."

"I'd say you're far better at spinning heads than I am."

"You'd be right. Can I steal you away?"

"Not much chance of me saying no is there?"

"No," said Derga.

"Great fucking dialogue," said Fiona. "What film is this?"

"Thought I dropped you?" asked Derga.

Connor didn't reply.

"I'm here to pick you up again."

"How did you find me?" asked Connor.

"There have been eyes on you since you arrived in Ireland but no one knows quite what to make of you."

"Who are you?" asked Fiona. "Really?" She looked around. "Is someone shooting this with one of those new tiny cameras? Am I in this?"

"What eyes?" asked Connor.

"Notice a small whirlwind, did you?" said Derga.

Connor's raised brow revealed his surprise.

"They thought you'd made them and backed off. But you missed the big guy tailing you. One of the Joyces. Notre Dame sweatshirt. Trying to pretend he's an American. He outside now making everyone nervous. But it looks like he is here just for surveillance."

"Joyces?" asked Connor.

"As in Joyce Country," said Derga, a little impatiently.

"Not James Joyce, the writer of *Ulysesses*? Stream of consciousness and all that?"

"No. Joyce Country. Galway. Home of the Joyces. Giants who moved there from Wales in the 14th century."

"Even I know that," said Fiona. "Not that I would know one to see them. And the fairies are in the film as well? Ah, wait now. Joyce Country. That's over by Leeane where Jim Sheridan filmed *The Field* with Richard Harris back in 1990. Sheridan's one of Ireland's best directors. Should have won an Oscar for that one. Are you doing a remake? I can see it now: Bull McCabe on a ghost estate going stark raving mad fighting the bankers for possession of an empty shell of a house. It'll make small potatoes out of the original."

"Just when I think you know something, you know nothing at all," said Derga.

"Oh, I'm using that!" said Fiona.

"Where we going?" asked Connor.

"What's the release date?" said Fiona. "Has shooting started?"

"Rome," said Derga. "I've a car waiting to take us to Shannon Airport."

"You're driving?"

"No. One of the Dullahans."

"A Dullahan?" asked Connor.

"A Dullahan?" said Fiona. "Sweet Jesus. Are you telling me Dullahans are like Uber drivers now with a ride-sharing app and all?"

"Who's your friend?" asked Derga.

"Derga, meet Fiona."

"She seems to know something after all," said Derga.

"Ah, no," said Fiona, with a shake of her head that started her whole body trembling. "I don't know a thing, especially about Uber-Dullahans. And I don't want any shite app for them either."

"Fiona, it's just a taxi," said Connor.

Derga nodded at Fiona, grabbed Connor by the arm and led him to the door before Fiona could get her mouth working again.

"Away, he is," said Fiona, finally. She was dumbfounded. *Never in my life did I think I would say that. Away with the fairies was something my grandmother used to say about people that weren't around anymore. Or those who had come back with their minds addled.*

Chapter Thirty-Seven

S he watched the thief and Derga get into the car. She eyed the thief carefully. He was dressed in jeans and a blue shirt with thin white stripes. Over the shirt was a black blazer. And in his hand he carried a brown leather bag of the sort human doctors used to carry in the old days when they traveled by horse. He looked well-rested. She saw him peer curiously at the dark, tinted windows but she knew he wouldn't be able to see through them. Not that it mattered from her point of view as she was wearing her gwynn. It was, perhaps, unnecessary at the moment but it had become like a second skin these past two weeks. But few people would want to lay eyes on the Dullahan driving the car. A tinted partition between the front and rear seats meant no one in the back could see him either.

Just as well. The Dullahan's head was on a round rotating tray centered on the dashboard above an emblem that looked like a three-pointed star inside a circle. The head was hairless and had a greyish color. The head looked like a cabbage gone bad. The rest of the Dullahan's body was dressed in a black suit and a white shirt. He wore black leather gloves and his hands were on the wheel.

The Dullahan's right hand reached over and spun the tray so that its face now looked at hers. He could see right through a gywnn, she knew, but she wasn't wearing it for his benefit. The eyes were red flickers. A finger placed itself over the Dullahan's lips in the universal sign for silence. One of his fingers pressed a button on the dashboard and she could suddenly hear the conversation in the seats behind. The Dullahan winked. Out of the corner of her eye, she noticed a little black box attached to the Dullahan's jacket. It blinked red. She wondered what it was for until she remembered that a Dullahan always had to be in contact with its head. Otherwise, the head couldn't control the body. In the old days, the Dullahan was always holding its head in its hand. But things were different.

The Dullahan noticed her interest and his fingers fiddled with another button on the steering wheel. Then he pointed to a display on the dashboard. "Bluetooth," read the display. She nodded but was inwardly confused. *What did an old Danish king have to do with it?*

"I was expecting a taxi with the name Dullahan on the door," she heard the thief say.

The Dullahan smiled. That's a first. A Dullahan with a sense of humor. Let's hope he doesn't smile too often.

The hand rotated the tray so the tray so the eyes were facing forward and she felt herself exhale. The Dullahans were very useful but that didn't mean she liked looking at them. *With luck, I'll never see one smile again.*

The car pulled away and she looked at Ashford Castle somewhat wistfully. She wasn't that fond of it for it had been the home of the enemy of the O'Connors to whom she was tied. Still, it had stood for centuries in one form or another and had become a landmark of sorts for her. Most places changed so quickly she sometimes wondered if she was in the right place at all after returning to a spot she hadn't been to a while.

She didn't like cars that much either. They were like rolling coffins you could sit upright in. She had keened for more than one who had died in these wheeled things. But she knew they were more discreet that the horse and carriage the Dullahans used to drive. Invariably, the Dullahans had been a careless in years past, giving rise to hair-raising talesof specters driving in the night carrying the souls of the dead. *But what would you expect from a figure that drove around with his head in his hand.*

For her, the Dullahans were a transportation option, particularly when humans were involved. She watched as the hands of a headless body expertly turned the steering wheel as they drove away.

Her attention was caught by a large figure wearing a blue top with gold letters emblazoned across his chest that spelled out the words "Notre Dame." There were other people wearing something similar but she recognized him for who he was. One of the Joyces, the local hunters. The sight of him made her shiver slightly. He would try to follow, she knew, but that would be pointless. The car had its own gywnn which the Dullahan would engage at a moment of the Dullahan's choosing. A slight shimmer in the window view would be all that a passenger noticed.

A voice from the rear snapped her to attention.

"Are the kisses a long way off?" asked the thief, his voice very human, very male.

There was a silence and she wondered if she'd have to listen to the sounds of love-making. If things went that way, she'd get the Dullahan to mute the sound.

"Do I look like Mary Kate Danaher to you?" replied Derga. Her voice was sultry, she thought. It was a little lower in register than most human females and there was a slight accent from an English spoken long ago. "If you think you're going to drag me by the hair somewhere or beat me with a stick, you'd better think again. And the only way you're going to spank me is if I get to spank you as well."

"You don't approve of John Wayne's courtship rituals?" offered the thief.

Brazen of him.

"Hardly," said Derga. "I took a walk around the village before retrieving you. If anyone has noticed that times have changed, it's me."

There was another long silence. She didn't know what a film was. She thought some more about Derga's voice. It was like listening to a translation of English into English, the first arranged differently from the second. She could tell where Derga was making the changes, substituting words, altering pronunciation, re-constructing sentences. Her brain thought in the first even as she talked in the second. The first was much older than the second.

"Do you have her comb?"

Her breath caught. Maybe there was hope.

"I left it in America."

And her spirit sank. The comb was in his possession. She would have sensed otherwise. *Why does he keep it?*

"It would have been easier if you had the comb."

"Where is the lovely girl?

Lovely? Ah, wait. He thinks I'm about so that's why he says he hasn't my comb. He probably gave Derga a wink when he said it.

"Up front with Dullahan. They're old friends. She doesn't want to be too near you at the moment."

True.

"So what's in Rome?"

"A way to get her back to where she belongs."

"It doesn't involve the Pope, I presume."

"No. I'll tell you more when we get there."

She was nervous about going to Rome. Too many priests. But Derga insisted it was the only way she knew how to get her back without the comb.

There was another long silence and then the thief spoke. "I'm a little nervous. Well, maybe not nervous. Uneasy. Why did you disappear?"

"Because your burly buddy would have killed us," said Derga. "He's a hunter. It's what they do. It's what they've been doing for a long time."

"Can't it be stopped?"

"No. Too many have died along the way." She heard Derga exhale deeply. "It started long ago and there will never be an end to it. Frankly, I'm not sure he would have killed me but he was beginning to suspect that I was in league with his quarry. Not the Heer of Dunderberg. But with her. She would have been his next target. And I think he'd have targeted me as well."

"He vanished as well," said the thief. "I've no idea where he is."

"He knows where you are, though. The Joyces are proof of that. It'll take him a while before he figures out we're in Rome."

Because the whole car had its own bit of glamour that made it hard to track. She left that part out.

"I left the others behind. I knew the lieutenant wouldn't follow me out of the country. Straparola stayed with Seventina although he wanted to come. I told him it was all film festival business. That I just needed to get back to work. But I knew you'd show up."

"Feeling alone?"

"A little."

She could almost hear the thoughts whirling in Derga's brain. "Your friend might be useful."

"He worked in Rome for an English-language newspaper for a couple of years. He knows his way around the city. I'll text him."

Her acute ears picked up the small sound of fingers tapping something hard. There was a pause, then more finger tapping, another pause, more finger tapping. It was like listening to some tiny creature learning how to play the drums. Irritating.

"Seventina says she can get him on a plane she's crewing this evening. He wants to know where he should go when he lands."

"Someone will meet him at the airport."

More irritating tapping.

"Feel better?" asked Derga.

"Yes," said the thief. "I mean it will be nice to have my friend there but I like that you're okay with him being there."

"We are here."

The Dullahan flicked a switch on the door beside him and she heard the door beside her click. The Dullahan gestured with one hand, indicating she should open the door and get out.

She followed the Dullahan's instructions. The thief and Derga were already out of the car. There was a mist in the air so typical of Irish days. She slammed the door shut and the noise made Connor turn in her direction. His eyes widened. *He doesn't see me but he knows I'm here.*

She walked around the back of the car and stood next to Derga and the thief, who was still looking at the car. The driver's side window rolled down very quickly and a hand waved before the window rolled up again. The Dullahan pulled away, leaving them standing in front of a small building with Derga and the thief.

"Shit!" exclaimed the thief.

"What?" said Derga alarmed.

"Just play it cool, boy, real cool." The thief snapped his fingers a couple of times.

"What are you doing?"

"You never saw *West Side Story*? Sharks versus Jets? I fell in love with a girl named Maria. The musical?"

"I don't understand."

"When the driver's side window rolled down, I could swear the guy driving didn't have a head."

"Don't be silly," said Derga. "A Dullahan always has his head with him."

"I meant on his shoulders like the rest of us."

"Sorry," said Derga. "I thought you knew what a Dullahan is. He's a bit like your American Headless Horseman legend. He's the original."

"I've heard of him but seeing one makes it totally different. So what does he do? Drive with one hand while he holds his head in the other?"

"He used to but I've made some technical improvements. I assure you he drives with both hands on the wheel these days."

"Maybe you should assume I know nothing from this point onwards."

"That might be best," said Derga. "Just don't start snapping your fingers every time you see something strange. It's mostly better to stay quiet. Don't start losing it on me. Shall we walk?"

"Go, man, go but not like a yo-yo, schoolboy." The thief looked around him. "Sorry, the film is stuck in my head. Somehow, I thought we'd be arriving at the main terminal."

"We're taking a small private jet," said Derga. "It's a dead leg. In fact, all our air transportation has been arranged by Seventina. She is a handy person to know. But I asked her not to mention it to Straparola for the time being."

The thief raised an eyebrow.

"Bondage binds."

The thief nodded his understanding. "I think I like the term 'empty leg' better," he said. "Very posh and very discreet, I see. I was wondering how we were going to handle an airport with her in tow."

"Tow?"

"I suppose being invisible helps a lot," he added.

"My friend, you'll see us walk through a machine that's there for security reasons." She knew Derga was now addressing her but she spoke in English rather than her own language so the thief understood as well. She preferred Derga speaking English anyway. She had trouble understanding Derga sometimes when the red one spoke her language. *You'd think Thomas the Rhymer would have taught her better. He's been with us long enough, since the days of Robert de Bruce. But I shouldn't be so harsh. Her mother takes no notice of her or so it is said. "I trust you'll have no difficulty in finding your way around that."*

They entered the small building and she stood a small distance away while Derga and the thief conversed with various people in different uniforms. She shuddered as a green and white monstrosity with wings soared overhead with a shamrock emblazoned on its side, creating a loud noise that made the windows in the building vibrate. She almost screamed herself, her mouth opening, about to get caught up in the sound. *It would feel so good to get lost in it.* But she restrained herself. She let loose a small keen, one that got smothered in the surrounding noise. But it made her feel better.

She followed Derga and the thief onto the tarmac toward a smaller plane, looking almost pencil-thin compared to the bigger one that had flown overhead. There was a small staircase leading up to the interior. She hesitated. She didn't like the idea of being trapped inside. But she had to trust Derga.

414

She watched as Derga let the thief go ahead. Derga paused at the bottom of the stairs, as if taking one last look around. There was a gap now between her and him. That was her cue. She slipped in ahead of Derga and mounted the stairs.

Chapter Thirty-Eight

There are still a few places left for the old gods in Rome.

Connor considered the thought as he walked briskly past the towering white granite Egyptian obelisk outside the Basilica of Santa Maria Maggiore, one remarkably similar to the one called Cleopatra's Needle in New York City's Central Park. Connor bounded up the wide steps toward the church's entrance gates, circling around a scavenger seagull with red-rimmed eyes. The cathedral was an impressive pile of columns, arches and statues with one of Mary holding the Christ child towering above the rest. Taller yet was a bell tower that dominated the surrounding streets, its height accentuated by it and the church's construction on a small hill. Unlike most of the other massive cathedrals in Rome, this one seemed under-visited with no throngs of tourists entering or exiting the spot. Still, that didn't mean the area was deserted. The constant buzz of scooters was already hurting his ears. Connor marveled at the ability of modern Romans to steer a scooter, make a phone call, and gesticulate a free arm for emphasis while they talked to someone unseen, all without crashing. Most people, he noted, were dressed in the latest fashions, a habit, he guessed, developed in a city where so much was old.

Once inside the massive church doors, Connor could see the half-expected ornate marble floors and columns but he was surprised at how his eyes—indeed his entire head—angled upward of its own accord as if he had lost control of himself. Above him, on both sides of the central nave or hall, a row of large windows cast their light on a panel of illustrations that Connor recognized as being from the early life of Jesus, Mary and Joseph, the Holy family.

"Magnificent, isn't it?" said a familiar voice, coming up from behind him.

Connor turned with a smile on his face. "Strap!" he said, embracing his friend. "I'm so happy to see you!" Straparola had made no concession to Italian fashion and wore his black suit, tie and white shirt.

"I got your text," said Straparola, as if that was sufficient reason to fly half way around the world. "What's going on?"

"It's complicated," said Connor.

Straparola nodded. "So is this cathedral. It was built in the fifth century by Pope Sixtus III after the Council of Esphesus agreed that Virgin Mary was the Mother of God. Seems like a simple thing now but they argued about it for hundreds of years."

Straparola pointed upward to the panels. "This church is like a history of Italian art. Bernini, Fontana, Michelangelo—they all have made a contribution here over the centuries. Over by the altar, there is supposed to be a piece of the Holy Crib where Jesus was born. Imagine that? But for me, one thing stands out. You see that panel, the one with the boy who looks about 10 years old and with a halo around his head? That tells the story of Jesus converting King Aphrodisius who sheltered the Holy Family in Heliopolis when they had to flee to Eygpt. When I was growing up Catholic, no one ever mentioned what happened to Jesus in Eqypt. He flees to Eygpt as a child and shows ups in Jerusalem as a 30-something. Nothing in between. Certainly no one mentioned Aphrodisius."

Connor nodded. Aphrodisius was new to him.

"What I find interesting," continued Straparola, "is that panel depicting the Holy Family and Aphrodisius is the only episode in the life of Jesus that is not sourced from either the Old or New Testament."

"I'm not following," Connor said.

"Bear with me. Our eyes gravitate toward Jesus because he is familiar to us. But maybe the panel is really about Aphrodisius whose name marks him as a follower of the Greek goddess Aphrodite, in fact. So he predates Christianity. To make a long story short, the Egyptian Aphrodisius winds up in Beziers, France, where he is the local bishop. One day, Aphrodisius is walking down the road with his camel." Straparola shook his head at the wonder of it. "A bunch of pagans cut off his head but instead of dying, Aphrodisius picks up his head and walks off with it."

"A Dullahan," gasped Connor. "I think I just met one in Ireland." Connor gave Straparola a quick summary.

"The French call them cephalophores. In Beziers, they mark the feast day of Aphrodisius by parading around a camel wearing a fabric that says 'I am reborn from antiquity' and 'We are numerous.'"

Straparola grasped Connor by the arm. "My point is that these beings we have been dealing with have been around for a long time and there are more of them than we think. The stories about them are already out there but we chose not to believe them. I am guilty of it myself. One of my ancestors is Giovanni Francesco Straparola. He lived in Venice. He was writing about this stuff 600 years ago. I didn't remember until I was on my way here. I've been doing some homework. These creatures can be dangerous, as we know. Aphrodisius turned some locals into stone just for bad-mouthing him."

Connor nodded. "I get it. What happened to Aphrodisius?"

"Disappeared into a cave. His cover was blown. But if you start digging, you can find references to about 140 cephalophores in France alone." Straparola paused. "You know it's like Albert Einstein once said: 'It's entirely possible that behind the perception of our senses, worlds are hidden of which we are unaware."

"Einstein talked about fairies?"

"Who knows? No one knew what Einstein was talking about most of the time anyway. But keep in mind we and the ancient Neanderthals existed at the same time and some interbred. Most of us have Neanderthal genes. And who did the Denisovans mate with? Us? Neanderthals? Both? Anyway, my point is that the idea of multiple intelligent species sharing the planet has happened before. It may have never ended. We just don't know about them. And I'm guessing they don't want to be found because we would probably kill them if we were aware of them."

Connor vaguely recalled reading about the Denisovans. They were named after a cave in Siberia where a few bits of their bones had been found. But next to nothing was known about them.

"So what's this all about?" Straparola broke into his reverie.

Connor looked at Straparola and then reached into his pocket, pulling out a sock.

"You're kidding me," said Straparola.

"Derga says the comb is some kind of key that the banshee uses to get home. I have to give up the comb willingly so she can go back to wherever it is she goes back to."

"Wouldn't that be a good thing?"

"I guess. But my gut is saying that if I give up the comb, I will never see Derga again. I will be become a wandering Aengus."

"And who is Aengus?

"Aengus is a guy the poet Yeats wrote about. He caught a glimpse of a glimmering girl 'who called me by my name and ran and faded through the brightening air.' He spent the rest of his life looking for her. I can't explain it but I feel that if I keep the comb I still somehow have a hold on her and I will see her again. If I lose it, I lose her. Frankly, I think Yeats was writing about himself."

There was another reason, Connor realized, and maybe it took standing in a church for him to admit it to himself. The comb was evidence that Something Else existed, even if he didn't fully understand its workings. The comb was like a religious medal kept by the faithful to remind them that there was more to this world than what they could see.

"OK," said Straparola. "I guess you're in love. So if we're not giving up the comb, what are we doing?"

"This sounds crazy, I know. I'm supposed to open a magic door that will get the banshee back to wherever it is she comes from."

"Magic door?" repeated Straparola. "Not so crazy. I know exactly where that is. But no one has ever opened it. Or that's the story at least."

"I just want you to have my back in case things go badly."

"Done," said Straparola, opened his jacket to reveal a holstered pistol.

Connor looked at him in surprise.

"Hey, I'm Italian. I know some guys."

"What are you going to do with that?"

"Me? Nothing." Straparola removed the pistol from its holster and handed it to Connor. "It's for you."

Connor took the pistol in his hand. It was black, about a foot long overall with a four-inch barrel and was heavier than he expected. It had a curved grip that fit into hand easily. It looked vaguely familiar as well.

"Webley revolver," said Straparola. "Old favorite of the Irish Republican Army back in the day. Range is about 50 yards. Two options: just pull the trigger and start shooting or cock the hammer back for a more measured shot. No recoil to speak of. Six rounds with .38 caliber bullets so they'll knock a man down. If you haven't hit what you're aiming at by then, I figure you're pretty much dead anyhow."

Connor remembered the gun now. A scene from *Michael Collins*, the Liam Neeson film about the Easter Uprising in Ireland, flashed through his head. Then a catalogue of images from other old war movies followed. "This gun belongs in a museum."

Straparola shrugged. "I got it from a retired antiques dealer. Sorry, it was the best I could do. Let me give you the holster."

Connor wasn't keen on accepting the gun. One thing he had learned living in New York City was that people who carried guns tended to get shot. And then there was the matter of carrying a weapon in a foreign country. The local *Polizia* and *Carabinieri* would surely take a dim view of it if he was caught with a pistol.

Straparola read his mind. "Remember those short guys with the red hats back in New York?"

Connor holstered the Webley.

Chapter Thirty-Nine

It was dark, in the late hours, so there was no one around as the Cornet of Horse approached the black SUV, smaller than the big ones common to the USA and sized more for Roman streets. It was parked just up ahead of him and he quickened his gait, anxious to get inside the vehicle before any curious eyes appeared in the windows of the oversized alley that passed for a street here. He had to admit they'd picked a good location. The neighborhood was a warren of alleys where the locals spoke their own dialect. The *trasteverini* had a them-and-us attitude—especially toward their fellow Romans on the other side of the Tiber where most tourists frequented—since the first century when it was populated by the descendants of slaves. If a local took you in, the neighbors would keep quiet and maybe keep watch more vigilantly.

The window on the driver's side rolled down and he stopped in his tracks. Even in the rough light provided by the street lamps, he recognized the barrel of a pistol equipped with a silencer. The gun wasn't pointed his way, he realized, even as he heard the whisper of a bullet being fired. He looked in the direction the pistol had been aimed. A dead cat—an orange tabby—looked like it had been pinned to the wall below a window of a café. The pistol disappeared and the window rolled up. All very casual. He walked up to the passenger side door, heard the door click, and let himself in.

"Just making things safe for you," said the woman behind the wheel. She was a large woman but it was all well-defined muscle. "And me." She smiled, with her lips parted, and he could see the double row of teeth. She was old school. Her people had learned their skills fighting everyone from the Venetian Empire to the Nazis.

He nodded. Shooting cats on city streets, even at this hour, wasn't a great idea but there was little point in making an issue out of it. She was from the other side of the Aegean Sea in Istria. She was from one of the old families near Montevun and while she wasn't strictly part of the organization, the Cornet of Horse had known her a long time. She was a relentless hunter.

"I hate Rome," she said.

"Don't we all."

"Florence too. That statue of David really galls me. Goliath was a dope. Killed by a slingshot. What an idiot!"

He had seen the statue of David and wondered if the look in David's eye was the same as when he killed Goliath. Here comes the rock, said David's eyes, unsure if a stone from a slingshot would be enough.

The Romans killed Maximus, said one of The Voices. *A general murdered by his own troops.*

Another Voice: *With his son!*

A smaller voice: *Maximus was one of us. Curse them!*

Maximus had been a general of a Roman legion and had fallen prey to cutthroat Roman politics. Everyone had left Italy after that. And everyone had agreed to a new directive. Keep a low profile lest they discover we are different and hunt us down. The world isn't as big and empty as it once was. There are too few of us. Do not become prominent in the affairs of men, although in recent years some found basketball hard to resist but worked hard to stay in minor leagues that garnered less attention. Idly, he wondered why Maximus wasn't speaking for himself. Perhaps he disagreed but chose to remain silent on the issue.

Don't forget Reprobus! That Voice didn't sound vengeful, though. The tone was one of forgiveness. Probably Reprobus himself. He sighed inwardly. Reprobus had served with the Third Valerain Cohort of the Marmantae in North Africa. But then he had gone on an odd quest, one that had carried him to many lands where he always found work as a mercenary. Eventually, however, he embraced a new religion, laid down his arms and spent his time carrying people across a river near Antioch. A few years later, however, he was beheaded for his trouble. It was uncertain who killed him—he had a lot of old enemies certainly—but the Cornet of Horse found the whole story troubling. The Vatican eventually embraced his memory, fudged his origins, and called him St. Christopher.

"What are you thinking about?" she asked. Her name was Brana, one of the old names.

"Reprobus."

"I think a cat got him. Goliath too."

"Maybe. But then Reprobus would have just become plain stupid."

"Didn't he?"

"Well, no one has ever claimed he ate someone." The Cornet of Horse shrugged. He was letting his mind wander to avoid mentally rehashing this hunt, something he had already done on the special Janet flight to Rome with a re-fueling stop at Bascombe Down in England. Other than the flight crew, he had been alone on the white jet with the red stripe painted down the middle of the fuselage. Janet, he recalled, was the abbreviation for "Just Another Non-Existent Terminal" but the Cornet of Horse knew Janet flights flew mostly out the secure Gold Coast Terminal in Las Vegas, shuttling workers to Groom Lake—also known as Area 51—and other nearby facilities. But Janet flights also operated internationally from smaller, more discreet airports. The Cornet of Horse had boarded his flight in Farmingdale, New York, a small airport near the midsection of Long Island. The Joyces in Ireland were good at surveillance and had discovered that Derga and presumably the banshee were Rome bound. With Connor as it turned out. He'd been right to request surveillance of Connor in Ireland. He'd been flagged once Connor's name appeared on an airline passenger manifest. And then he'd put a fly watch on Straparola.

Derga and perhaps the banshee were all that remained of a frustrating operation. Most of his Iroquois team was dead. He had missed grabbing the Heer of Dunderberg and had tumbled down the slope of Whiteface Mountain like a skier taking a bad fall. When he finally rolled to a stop and took a minute to recover, it dawned on him that this was a good moment to vanish from the lives of his companions on the mountain lest they wind up dead as well. But that had been wishful thinking. Connor was involved again. And Derga was frankly still a mystery, he had to admit. A victim? A player? An agent for the Other Side? Some kind of interventionist? Human or perhaps not? And was she even within his remit? Was the banshee? Yes, the banshee had consorted with the Heer of Dunderberg but he was unsure of whether she belonged to the Unseelie Court. Well, if there was ever a case of guilt by association, this was it. He'd track her down. Still, there were too many questions. The only positive was that the Heer of Dunderberg had been put out of commission, at least temporarily. But even that thought was tinged with disappointment—the women the Heer of Dunderberg had kidnapped were gone. Overall, he conceded, the mission was mostly a failure. But it wasn't over yet.

The Cornet of Horse struggled to keep his mind in the present. He focused on the pastel colors of the walls lining the narrow Trastevere street. The he turned his attention to his driver.

"What have you got here?"

"It's like you said. What's his name—Straparola—arrived at the airport like you said he would. I tailed him here. A young woman—with the Other Side I don't know—let him in. There is no indication of anyone else in the house and no one has moved since."

"Straparola is of no importance. No sign of the other two?"

"No. But I expect the woman will lead us to them. It will happen soon. You know how they like to move around in the hours before dawn. But if Starparola makes a move, we can follow him as well." She paused. "I love this. They think they have a safe house and it isn't."

"Don't assume too much. It could just be an Internet rental." He paused. "We don't have enough personnel for a proper tail. Straparola won't notice us but if the woman works for the Other Side she will spot us if we follow her." Brana was aware of the Cornet of Horse's general reluctance to increase the roster of operatives knowingly working against the Other Side.

"Agreed. I have it covered." Brana opened the cargo bin between them and retrieved a tablet computer. "There are a lot of rich fathers in this town who are worried about the virtue and safety of their daughters. There is a service that operates drones to keep an eye on them, especially when they are out late with men who drive expensive Italian sports cars. And we all know who owns them," finished Brana, rolling her eyes, before continuing. "I've hacked into this eye-in-the-sky service. We'll commandeer one their drones and have it follow our target—just another young woman under surveillance. The operators are a bit lax in real-time because they are flying multiple drones. Or we can track Straparola if he makes a move. Lots of tiny drones in the sky, all equipped with night vision and infrared cameras. And the new ones are very quiet. I can line up behind him and he won't hear a thing."

He nodded his approval. Brana, like everyone in her family, was an excellent hunter, even if they did tend to roast their captured prey on the spot.

"I'm famished," said Brana and he wondered if she could read his thoughts.

"We wait. And per longstanding operation guidelines, we take no hostile action on the young female until we know which side she plays for."

"I hope she is one of the bad ones," said Brana.

He looked at the six fingers on each of Brana's hands and found himself slowly counting them. Maybe he would have a talk with her later about DNA editing—MEDEA's secret labs, manned by the descendents of the gifted alchemists of the past, were way ahead of known science in this area--but he knew she would be resistant to the idea. There is nothing like six fingers around your throat and a double row of teeth in your face to terrify a target, she would say, and anyone attempting to describe her wouldn't be believed. It was a family trait that she was proud of even if she wouldn't admit it. "I'm a hot babe in Montevun," she once told him. He felt himself fading. There was a pressure on his chest and his legs suddenly felt paralyzed. His mind drifted somewhere between sleep and awake.

The world shifted and he was in another part of Rome, standing in a room with a balding red-headed man dressed in rich robes. He was being introduced to him. He was called The Morholt.

Does a sorcerer stay a sorcerer once he becomes Pope? The Morholt wondered to himself. He had heard the stories, of course, concerning Gerbert of Aurillac, the man now known has Pope Sylvester II and the first Frenchman to head the Papacy. It was said he not only spoke for God but perhaps more importantly—at least in the short term-- Emperor Otto III himself, someone Sylvester II had tutored as a boy. The Emperor was the one who had named Gerbert the new Pope when Gregory V died.

One story had it that Gerbert had stolen a book of spells from a Moorish magician in Spain. The Arab, using his own sorcery, tracked Gerbert as he fled, pursued by soldiers—some said demons—but Gerbert escaped by hanging from the underside of a wooden bridge for, as the practitioners of the black arts know, no man can be found if he is suspended between heaven and earth. The story was enhanced by Gerbert's mysterious origin— no one knew who his parents were and Aurillac was just the name of a monastery he had joined when entering the priesthood. Undoubtedly, the Emperor knew more but he wasn't telling.

Of Gerbert's, now Pope Sylvester II, brilliance The Morholt had no doubt. He had seen and heard for himself the wonderful music played by the hydraulic-powered organ with brass pipes that Gerbert had constructed in Reims. Gerbert had built other devices, all of which were in evidence in the room where The Morholt now stood, one only slightly smaller than the typical Lord's hall. The biggest of these machines was an armillary sphere that could be used to track the stars across the night sky. On a table lay a counting device called an abacus and a square box next to it, a small square box with numbers and arrows called a clock could measure the passage of time. Books lay open on other tables around the room, some in Latin, some in Arabic, some in languages he didn't recognize, with strange symbols and diagrams in the margins. A priest had briefed him on what he would see so he wouldn't waste the Pontiff's time by asking about them.

No one, however, had told him about that brass head sitting on a large table behind which the Pope sat, which made him guess it was not normally on display. The Pope made no effort to rise and he was relieved that he wouldn't have to kiss a ring as a sign of devotion or fealty. The Pope was short on ceremony.

"You are The Morholt, of the race of giants and a fairy hunter?"

This wasn't how The Morholt introduced himself to men even if it was true.

"It is him," said the brass head in a feminine voice. He did his best to conceal his astonishment and peered at the brass head more closely. Its features were finely sculpted and it was well-polished so that sunlight reflected off it, making it difficult to stare at it for any length of time. Truly, Sylvester II remained a sorcerer.

"Don't be alarmed," said the Pope, which did little to quell it. "May I introduce Meridiana. The brass head allows her to speak, hear, and see us from afar and in her view, a safe distance. She thinks if she were actually here you would try to kill her."

"He would," said Meridiana. He looked at the brass head's eyes and noticed a glint of something in the eye sockets but he couldn't name it. She was right but he kept his opinion to himself. The Pope had a demon lover, or so said his detractors. It was worse than that. The Morholt suspected Meridiana was a succubus. A fairy lover of the Unseelie Court, one whose heart was twisted. Eventually, she would kill him, directly or indirectly. If she was here, he would have killed her if only to save the Pope.

The Morholt sensed that the two of them already considered him their subordinate. They expected him to listen and say very little, especially if it was in disagreement. Both were used to getting their own way so in a sense, they were made for each other. The Morholt wondered what unholy bargain had been struck and how it involved him.

"How may I be of service, your Eminence," said The Morholt, observing the forms as far as the Papacy was concerned but implicitly stating that he would not consider himself subservient to Meridiana.

"Clever bastard," said the brass head. The Morholt winced inwardly. Very little escaped a fairy's notice, even when they weren't present, strictly speaking.

The Pope paused as if waiting for hostile thoughts to dissipate like candle smoke.

"The year is 999," began the Pope. Not for the first time did The Morholt wonder why people with power began speaking by stating the obvious. "Next year is The Millenium. An auspicious time and maybe a dangerous time. The Millenium is fraught with symbolism. It is a year that fills many with dread and in that fear, some find opportunity."

The Pope paused, looking at The Morholt as if his meaning was clear. It wasn't. The Morholt knew Brian Boru was destined to become the High King of Ireland and that a clash with the Vikings around Dublin was inevitable. But no Pope had ever said so much as a prayer for Ireland. Or the Vikings, for that matter. The Holy Roman Empire under Otto II was the most powerful state in Europe and that was unlikely to change.

"You're going to have to blunt," said Meridiana with a touch of scorn The Morholt knew was meant for him. "Cat bite your tonque?"

The Morholt ignored the gibe at his biggest vulnerability and the Pope pressed on. "I'm sorry, my love, I know this is a delicate matter for you."

"The perhaps I should continue," said Meridiana, "for time is short and our guest will grasp the situation quickly."

That was almost a compliment, The Morholt realized, and it heightened his guard.

"There is a city on the Baltic Sea called Vineta," said Meridiana. "it must be destroyed. You're the one to do it."

"Why?" asked The Morholt. He had heard about Vineta but he wanted to hear it from her lips, so to speak.

"I hesitate to speak their names for to do so is to attract their attention for they have long ears," said Meridiana. "I call them the Night Orchestra. You know what an orchestra is?"

"As in Greek drama," interjected the Pope.

430

The Morholt nodded. The orchestra was the area in front of the stage reserved for the Chorus. Literally, it meant "the watching place." The Chorus stood apart from the play but sometimes the head chorus member, the coryphaeus, could enter into the story as a character, able to interact with the other actors on the stage.

"Think of Meridiana as a coryphaeus," explained the Pope, "although in this instance, she doesn't speak for the entire Chorus. The Night Orchestra are the ones she doesn't speak for."

"And you know who they are," said Meridiana. This was getting complicated but The Morholt was alarmed that even Meridiana feared to say the name of the Unseelie Court aloud.

"I've killed a few," said The Morholt.

"More than a few by all accounts," said the Pope, "or you wouldn't be here."

The Pope rose and strolled from behind the table, stopping to pick up the abacus, fiddling with the small balls as if tallying an account. "Vineta is in the grips of the Night Orchestra. They're breeding with human women, creating abominations at a rapid pace. This has been going on for some time unbeknownst to us. Their goal is to end the reign of man at the dawn of the new millenium. The number means nothing to them but they know the new millenium has many worried, even expecting the end of the world. They intend to take advantage of that fear and bend it to their own ends. The Night Orchestra wants back in the story and Vineta is where they intend to come onstage."

There was a long silence as if these words had been spoken for the first time and by speaking these words, the danger had now become more imminent.

"I don't understand," said The Morholt after a moment. "I would think this would suit Meridiana just fine."

"Dunce," exclaimed Meridiana. "The Night Orchestra would see the rest of us dead and gone. The balance would end. Those that survive will be slaves."

"There is more," said the Pope. "In return for Merediana's aid, the Church will end its persecution of fairy. The Church will act as if they don't exist. The Church and the world will ignore them."

The Morholt heard more than was said. With fairy ignored, so too would he and his kind.

"No," said The Morholt. "We will destroy Vineta on our own and keep killing her kind until they fear to walk among us."

"You can't," said the Pope. "That's the problem. Vineta is protected by, well, call them spells, that only Merediana can undo."

"Be that as it may, there is more here than meets the eye," said The Merholt. "What is it?"

The Pope's face turned red to match his beard and he turned away, not in anger The Morholt realized but in embarrassment. The Morholt was left staring at the bronze head on the table.

And then it came to him.

"You're pregnant," he said to the bronze head. "That's why you're not here. You're giving birth to the Pope's child."

The Pope turned to face him.

"You don't want the Church going after your own child!"

"And why do you think you are here?" asked the Pope.

"Your sister, the Queen of your kingless kingdom has a lovely little girl named Isolde," said Meridiana. "Odd how no one speaks of her father. And I know you know who her father is."

The Morholt felt his insides shift. It rang true. He suspected but chose not to inquire closely. He had not been present at his sister's wedding—by design it now seemed—and her husband had been accidentally killed soon after the wedding. So he was told. Now The Morholt wondered if he was truly dead at all.

"You're in the same position," said the Pope. "Ultimately, we'd like you to follow the teachings of the Church and end your persecution of fairy." He paused. "Once Vineta no longer exists, of course. Once it has been physically destroyed, I will order Vineta expunged from every map. It will be as if it never existed."

The Morholt paced the room as the Pope spoke. It had been a trap of sorts. Vineta would be triumph but afterwards, it would be like they ceased to exist. All of them. There would be no reason to live.

"No," said The Morholt.

"Isolde won't have very long…" began Merediana.

"Silence," said The Morholt, raising his voice. But his next words were more modulated and reasoned. "The entire Night Orchestra is unlikely to be in Vineta when it is attacked. This will be the case?"

"Most of them will," said Meridiana defensively. "What's your point?"

"I will lead an army that will destroy Vineta," said The Morholt. "But afterwards I will continue to hunt down The Night Orchestra wherever and whenever they appear. As for Merediana and those she does speak for—the Seelie Court to be specific—we will leave them be. Meridiana and her allies will agree to be counted as among them. Call it The Long Truce. Like the Church, we will ignore them as long as they give us no reason not to. But we will still be watching."

"Deal," said the bronze head immediately. The Morholt suspected Merediana knew where they would land all along. Maybe he had been manipulated but some semblance of peace—or at least something less than war-- was something to look forward to.

The idea that perhaps he had been manipulated made him more brazen than he might otherwise be. "What is it between you two?" he blurted.

"She wanted to be loved," said the Pope. "Fortunately, she chose me."

The Morholt nodded and closed his eyes. Perhaps that was the best way to look at it. When a succubus chose a man it was impossible to resist her. But he suspected the Pope knew that already.

Suddenly, he was hit so hard in his shoulder that his head swiveled. Instead of standing, he was sitting with a wide pane of glass in front of him.

"Wake the fuck up," said Brana in his ear. "Straparola is on the move."

Chapter Forty

Connor stared at the two naked white dwarves. It was hard to say exactly how tall they were from a distance but he could see they were powerfully built with broad chests, muscular arms and thick, stout legs. Both wore beards that covered most of their face but what Connor could see he wouldn't have called handsome. Both dwarves stood motionless in the same pose, their backs to an old stone wall, like they were just waiting for Connor to come closer before they made their move. They looked quick. They didn't have any weapons Connor could see but he was sure a punch from one of them would hurt. The Webley holstered under his jacket felt reassuring.

"Who are they?" Connor asked. He was alone with Derga in a dimly lit patch of dirt that passed for a park in the Esquilino district. The park was the principle feature of the Piazza Vittorio Emanuele which was enclosed on four sides by grey six-story buildings from the late 19th century characterized by arcades at ground level that housed a wide variety of shops operated mostly by Asians. This was Rome but Piazza Vittorio wasn't exactly an Italian neighborhood these days even though it had been inhabited since the 7th century BC.

"Egyptians, I think," replied Derga, with a note of distraction in her voice. "Some god called Bes, maybe. They are not important.

Sometimes a statue is just a statue. It's the door we're interested in."

The dwarves flanked what seemed to be a door framed in white stone with some kind of circular emblem above it. The area was lit by an old black streetlight standing a few feet in front of the dwarf to the right of the door. Oddly, while the door frame was set into the stone wall, the stone it framed seemed to be of a different hue that the rest of the wall which appeared to be seven or eight feet in height with a thick tree growing from its top. Connor guessed the wall was about 20 feet wide angled across a corner of the park. Despite its size and mystery, it was easily overlooked by passersby struck by the larger brown ruin in front of it. This was the Nymphaeum of Alexander Severus, a watery folly that had once been on par with the Trevi Fountain that drew tourists by the busload. Both the Magic Door and the Nymphaeum were surrounded by a tall wrought iron fence with tips like pointed spears.

Connor shot Derga glance. She still sported her red eye patch and her red hair was pulled back into a loose knot that draped over her right shoulder. Otherwise, she was a single shade of black in pants and a tight blouse. A black messenger's back was slung over her back. He was dressed in black as well. Night work, she said when she had given him the clothes. Her eyes were focused on what looked like a signature of paper pulled from a larger book and made from what looked like calfskin. Even in the dim light, Connor could see it was strangely illustrated with cartoony looking middle-aged women dancing in the nude and frolicking in baths. The text was in a language Connor didn't recognize.

"What are you reading?"

Derga sighed. "You're a bag of questions." She paused as if debating with herself about how much to reveal. "It's a few pages from a larger work that itself is a copy of a smaller work that was later expanded upon. It is the only book ever written in the language of fairy by someone with human blood, a person who had been raised among them on the other side of that door. It was written, however, on this side of the door and its existence is troubling to them. It cannot be destroyed by them, however, because it is written in vitriol. Do you know what that means?"

"They were pissed off when they wrote it?"

"I'm talking about the ink. Iron gall ink. Vitroil. Look."

Connor bent slightly to look closer at the text. The letters were very tiny and obviously hand-written but the ink on the page seemed to have sunk into the page like a brownish dye.

"Gall nuts, gum arabic, water, sometimes wine but most important, iron sulfate. Vitriol. The iron means they can't touch it. It's how they made books in medieval times. Its why the book themselves are magical. The letters burn them."

"Where's the rest of the book?"

Derga half-chuckled. "In a university library where no one can read it. Mostly it's all about botany and some astronomy as it relates to what's beyond the door. These pages have to do with opening the door. It's a bit complicated and no one has done it in a long time."

"How long?"

"The dwarves weren't here then. So maybe 150 years ago. Thereabouts. The door itself dates back to about 1655 but it's not used very often. Usually there's no need."

Connor felt himself reddening. If he had relinquished the comb, they wouldn't need to use the door. Then again, if he had he felt that he wouldn't be standing here next to her. And next to her was where he wanted to be.

"Where is she?" asked Connor.

"Nearby, I hope. She wants to get back badly."

"Can you take a look?"

Derga shook her head. Connor was asking her to remove her eye patch and use her second sight to confirm the banshee's presence. "I don't want to chance it. It's not likely but if I happen to see someone from the Unseelie Court, they will be all over us. I'll have to trust that she's here."

"When did you see her last?"

"Not since we arrived, actually. I think Rome makes her nervous. And she only half-trusts me."

Connor let his eyes travel around the park. There was no one he could see but he felt like there was someone watching them. His senses were on high alert, thanks in part to the double expresso with a side of anisette that he had with Straparola when they had left Maria Maggiore. Straparola had insisted that he couldn't brief Connor properly on the Magic Door without a proper libation.

"So what's the plan?"

Derga grasped him by the arm. "I need your blood."

"What?" For a moment, Connor half-expected Derga to reveal herself as some kind of vampire. Instead of sharp teeth, however, she showed him a hypodermic needle.

"I told you it was complicated. The door was built by devotees of alchemy so there are numerous symbols on the frame that have to be sequenced in the right order. The last touch is a drop of blood but it has to be a mix of both human and fairy. I already have a vial of the banshee's blood. I just need yours."

Derga paused. "I'm sorry. The human blood for this door has to be male. It's all very medieval. The man who built it didn't want women using it. He had a falling out with an exiled queen named Christina. It's a long story."

"We couldn't do this earlier?"

438

"Yours needs to be fresh. Roll up your sleeve and make a fist, please."

The kids are right, thought Connor. "Please" is a magic word. He rolled up his sleeve and Derga tapped into a vein like a practiced nurse. Connor glanced around. Anyone seeing them would think he was a junkie getting a fix. Still, he saw no one but a flickering light under an arcade spoke of someone in the distance beyond his vision.

"Now what?" said Connor.

"The iron fence keeps our friend from approaching the door. You're going to open the lock and let her through. I'll be watching your back."

"You're expecting trouble?"

"Yes. Let's go."

Derga headed toward the iron fence like she owned it and Connor tried to imitate her sense of purpose but didn't feel like he was doing a convincing job. As they got closer, Connor could see a door in the fence with a massive lock built into it.

"Here's the key," said Derga reaching into her bag and handing it to him. Connor was expecting something the size of his hotel key but instead she handed a ring of skeleton keys. Some were only an inch or two in size but others were almost a half foot in length. It was like something used by jailers in old pirate movies.

Connor took the ring of keys. "Which one?"

"I don't know," said Derga. "It's a universal set. One of them will work."

They reached the fence door and Connor inserted the smallest key into the lock but it wouldn't budge. It was a big lock, Connor realized, so he reversed course and inserted the biggest key into the lock. He could feel it half settle into the lock mechanism but it wouldn't budge. He tried the next biggest, one about five inches long, and felt it settle in comfortably. He turned it to the right and felt the bolt move. The door opened and he pushed it wide. As he did so, the ground in front of him started to move in different directions, bits sliding from one side to another and back again while others seemed to float away from him.

"Cats," said Derga. "The iron fence keeps fairies away from the magic door. The cats, in turn, keep the fairy hunters at bay. It's kind of a de-militarized zone. No one is going to be happy we're here."

"Will she come now? The fence door is wide open."

"Not until the Porto Magico is open. Come on."

They hurried toward the Porto Magico and Connor got his first close look at it. At the top of the door frame was a circular emblem with faded inscriptions.

"What does it say?" asked Connor.

"A dragon guards the entrance of the magic garden of the Hesperides, and without Hercules, Jason would not have tasted the delights of Colchis," recited Derga. "That's along the bottom. Then there is a Hebrew phrase that means 'Spirit of God" above that. At the top it says: "The center is in the triangle of the center.""

Connor eyes traced a path around the door. "There are faint symbols on the door frame and more letters."

"Symbols for the planets," said Derga. "Saturn, Jupiter, Mars, Venus, Mercury and the Sun, plus one for antimony, along with phrases associated with them. My favorite is the one for Saturn. "When in your house black crows will give birth to white doves, then you will be called a sage." On the bottom step is the symbol of the monad. That's kind of like a mile marker for the other side. You kick that last. Just don't sit on the step because then half of you will go through the door and the other half won't. That will kill you."

"What's it all mean?" said Connor. "I'm feeling completely stupid here."

"The antimony is kind of a giveaway. That's an element used for creating alloys. The Sun equals gold. And the planets symbolize iron, tin, copper, lead and mercury."

"And the words? They don't seem to have any meaning."

"It's a code that uses the imagery of alchemy which was all about the transmutation of one material into another. The Porto Magico is about the transmutation from one dimension into another. Basically, the text tells you the activation sequence. The text hints at what's next in the sequence."

"Where do you start the sequence?"

Derga smiled. "That's the secret part. Once I begin, it will become obvious I know the sequence. That's when I expect things will get busy. In the meantime, I want you to turn your back to the door and hold these two vials of blood. Pass them back to me without turning around when I ask for them."

Connor turned his back on the Porto Magico and wondered if he was turning his back on Derga as well. He couldn't see her but he could sense her moving from one side of the door to the other. In front of him, the ground still seemed to be moving with green eyes watching him closely. A flash of orange moved off to his right. A tabby was in the mix.

Suddenly, there was a whisper of air and a pair of green eyes in front of him went dark. A second pair went dark quickly after that. A louder whisper, closer to him, and another pair went dark with a small cat scream. The ground around him moved faster and in multiple directions.

"I think someone is shooting the cats," yelled Connor. "With a silencer."

"Give me the blood now!" shouted Derga.

Connor passed the vials behind him without looking. His eyes were focused across the park. Two large figures were running toward them. He couldn't make out much detail but they looked very tall and one was a bit bulkier than the other. A man and a woman, he guessed. It also looked like they were armed with long guns of some kind. As he looked, one stopped and raised a rifle into a firing position. A second later, he saw a cat fly through the air and crumble to the ground. The first figure kept advancing.

Without thinking, Connor pulled out the Webly revolver and sighted over the rear notch, aiming at the bulkier of the two figures, hoping that was his best chance of actually being on target. He pulled the trigger and it sounded like he had just shot a cannon. The cylinder on the Webly rotated. He couldn't be sure but he thought he saw his target stagger.

Derga appeared beside him. "Aren't you full of surprises," she said as she aimed a short barreled automatic weapon in the direction of the two figures, She opened fire with a long burst that made both targets drop to the ground. Connor thought she had shot them until he saw two more cats drop to the ground. The cats began to move away, slinking close to the ground, looking for cover. One bolted, leaping into the air and was caught mid-flight. Connor fired the Webley again, not aiming so much as firing a warning shot.

"They must have night-vision," said Derga. "Stay behind me. They will want me alive. You, I'm not so sure." Derga shot out the old street light and Connor wondered if that would do any good. He risked a glance behind him at the Porto Magico. The white stone frame seemed to be casting off a glow of its own. Within the frame, what had once been solid stone now seemed to be a shimmering pool of shiny blackness that seemed to be in the midst of changing form. A transmutation, thought Connor.

In the distance, Connor could hear the no-nee sound of a police siren, getting louder as it approached. The carbinieri were responding to reports of shots fired. A second no-nee joined in with the first but the sound came from another direction. Derga fired another burst.

"Now!" she yelled. Connor assumed she yelling for the banshee to make her move and Connor expected her to materialize on the run and dive through the Porto Magico like it was some kind of swimming pool set on its side. Once she was gone, Connor figured he and Derga would run, evading police and other pursuers somehow. But at least they would be together.

Connor knew that vision of the future wouldn't occur when the banshee materialized directly in front of him and he recoiled at the sight. Her head was thatched with grey dreadlocks inextricably tangled above an ulcerated forehead that seemed to be the source of a foul odor. Her eyebrows looked like fish hooks and below them were red and bleary eyes that gazed with malignant fire. Her nose was blueish, flattened and wide, dripping of some brackish fluid. Her lips were livid and pushed outwards like the beginnings of a snout.

The banshee's eyes flared and she tossed her head skyward. Something was happening to her throat: it stretched in places and bulged in others. Her cheeks filled and expanded. Her mouth opened and a sound began to fill the air. In the beginning it sounded like a horde of crickets. Then it shifted higher. The sound became more piercing. It was everywhere. Connor instinctively clasped his hands over his ears to protect them. But he was unprepared.

The sound didn't hurt his ears. It crippled his heart. He was gripped first by melancholy and then by an incredible sadness that buckled his knees. He fell over. Tears clouded his vision. Grief overcame him for the uncle who had died in Ireland. Sorrow and regret for the pain suffered by his cousin—something he had put in the back of his mind and never addressed. He felt a sense of impending loss as well, unclear and ill-defined, at some distant future point. Waiting. The banshee as the harbinger of death. Sobs tour themselves from his body and he crumpled to the ground. His chest hurt—the sobbing was about to break his ribs. He sucked in huge breaths of air but he felt like he was suffocating. All he wanted to do was to dissolve into the dirt and let the earth embrace him and give him comfort. Somewhere he heard a scream of agony and he drew solace from it, knowing he was not alone his sorrow. Then he realized it was him. The no-nee died away. And he heard more crying. People were coming out of the surrounding buildings sobbing. Above it all then, a wail that vibrated to a higher and higher pitch until it vanished to a place beyond his ability to hear. Windows shattered all at once like an explosion of glass, crashing and tinkling as it hit the street to become even smaller pieces.

Connor couldn't move. The sound had stopped and his heart felt like a heavy boot had been lifted from it. Still, he didn't move, giving the earth once last chance to claim him. It didn't and then thoughts of Derga entered his mind and he sat bolt upright like he had been jolted with electricity.

Derga was nowhere to be seen. Neither was the banshee. The Porto Magico was rock solid stone. The two white stone dwarves stared him down. It was like they were watching him and ignoring him at same time. The no-nee sound of sirens had resumed. There were more than before.

"Walk away," said the dwarves. "Now."

"Fuck you," said Connor.

But it wasn't the dwarves talking. It was Straparola.

"Connor, listen. It's me. We have to walk away. Now!" said Straparola. "They're going to call this a terrorist attack. Every window in the piazza is busted. People have cuts from the glass. There are a lot of dead cats all over the place. Shots were fired. I don't think anyone is dead but it would be best for us to disappear."

"Like Derga."

"Where is she, Connor?"

"Call me Aenghus. She's gone. Through the Porto Magico."

"Well, I'm sure she is safe," said Straparola without sounding sure at all. Straparola helped Connor to feet. "And enough with the Yeats already."

"My heart is broken," said Connor.

"Mine too," said Straparola. "I think everyone's heart is broken. Everyone has tears on their face. This is now the Piazza di Cuori Spezzati."

Connor stared at him.

"The Piazza of Broken Hearts,' said Straparola. "And we're leaving."

Chapter Forty-One

The Cornet of Horse lay face up on the pavement. A figure hovered over him, shaking his shoulders. He wasn't gentle. The Cornet of Horse opened his eyes. He was in Rome, he knew. In a park. The last thing he remembered was a world of broken glass. Then he remembered the moment before that. He had been shot. Just below the rib cage. There was pain but he mentally shut it down. Not completely but enough so that the pain didn't own him. He focused on the figure that had now stopped shaking him. In another minute, he would have broken his arms.

The man looked middle-aged with a slender figure which puzzled him a bit at first due to the strength with which the man had shaken him. His hair was jet black as was the beard. Brown eyes gazed at him with a peculiar intensity and beauty. The man wore a black scarf and the Cornet of Horse noticed the diamonds embedded in the cloth. He should have been surprised but he wasn't, even though he hadn't seen the man in a few centuries.

"Hello, Count. Where have you been?"

"Oh, you know. Keeping an eye on things. Making sure things don't get out of hand. Mostly on the Silk Road of late. I go by a different name these days. And I keep a very low profile. Getting harder to do, though. Cameras are my worst enemy. I'm sure you understand. You have had a few names yourself."

"You'll always be the Count to me. Still a ladies man, I bet."

The Count St. Germain smiled. "We'll always have Pollepel Island and the Heer of Dunderberg. Sorry I missed your return engagement with him. But this isn't Casablanca and you're not Ingrid Bergman."

"Classic film fan these days, eh?"

"A recent interest. You'll be okay?"

"My ears hurt. And there is a bullet in my gut. Other than that, I'm fine." said the Cornet of Horse, sitting up with a grimace. He hadn't expected Connor to have a pistol. *He was nearly your Jack. You would have died like Cormoran.* The Voices wouldn't let him forget this.

"Fuck off." Connor had shot him but he was a long way from being a giant-killer like Jack.

The Count raised his eyebrows.

"Not you." Funny how you could still like someone after they'd had shot you. Sounded like an old Webley. Where did Connor get that relic? If he was smart, Connor would have chucked it into the Tiber River by now.

"Still hearing things, I see," said the Count.

The Cornet of Horse ignored the comment. "There was a woman with me. She didn't look like Ingrid Bergman either."

"No, definitely not. Shaken but unharmed, I think. A little deaf perhaps. Hopefully, only temporarily. I have already sent Brana on her way. She cleaned things up a bit before she left. She's very quick and efficient. She even stopped your bleeding and put a bandage on you. I told her you would be fine. You're hard to kill."

The Cornet of Horse realized he was without weapons. He was shot and felt naked.

"She'll be back in Istria within hours. It will be easier if you are no longer a pair. That's who the police will be looking for. You should leave here before the authorities arrive in force," said the Count, straightening. The sirens were getting louder. "You're not the sort that should be interrogated."

"I will.

"I assume you have a place where that wound can be attended to."

"Yes." MEDEA had a local doctor on the payroll.

"Good." The Count paused. "The Learmont woman is interesting. Think she will turn into a vampire?"

The ancient Greeks believed redheads turned into vampires when they died. The Cornet of Horse assumed the Count was joking but the old belief spoke to how redheads were often persecuted in days gone by. The ancient Greeks were very good at giving those they didn't like a bad name. He shared that much with redheads certainly.

"The old Greeks didn't know everything but you're very well informed."

"And that surprises you?" The Count started to walk away. "I'll distract the police a little. Mind the cats. I wouldn't want you to get bitten."

The Cornet of Horse watched the Count disappear into the darkness.

Cavalier bastard. The Voices wanted the last word.

Chapter Forty-Two

The tiny winged creature swooped toward the smiling little blond girl outfitted in a red dress that came to her knees and wiped the smile from her face with a cut across the front of her nose. Up close it looked like a little skeleton with wings the color of dead leaves. The little girl had a British accent and she had wandered into an English wood that would have sent any kid who had ever heard of Little Red Riding Hood running toward the nearest village. More evil little bastards arrived and soon the girl's face was red lined and the fear in her eyes was plain to see. They swarmed around her like a swarm of angry mosquitoes and she raised her arms to protect herself. To no avail.

Thank goodness the film was only three minutes long. Connor clicked on the stop button and sighed. He wondered if the director of this film required psychiatric help or was perhaps ahead of his time, God forbid. After all, one of the most successful blockbuster films of recent years revolved around teenagers killing each other for the amusement of an audience. Maybe pre-teens dying on screen was next. Well, not on his watch.

The good news was that the number of short films entering the festival had exceeded his expectations and the entry fees were keeping him fed, albeit modestly. The bad news was that he had to watch a lot of films like the one he had just seen and they all contributed to a despondency he'd felt since leaving Rome. True, it had only been a few days and perhaps time would make things better, just like the cliché promised. Connor wasn't so sure. He felt like he was wearing a necktie made of lead: grey, dull and heavy. A rueful smile crossed his lips. The one tie he owned would be described as vintage by a kind fashion critic. He wondered where it was.

Connor tried to shift his mood by burying himself in his work. He liked staying in his office these days. Every time Connor went for a walk he couldn't help but notice all the different sizes and shapes of the people he saw on the street. Tall ones, short ones, round ones, skinny ones. There was a time when his eyes would have glanced over them, almost ignoring them all unless he had to engage with someone specifically. Now he wondered if they were all human.

Once again, Connor reviewed the specifications for the digital cinema package (DCP) he shipped to theater owners. Due to differences in respective power grids, European films used a 25p video frame rate that needed to be converted to the 24p standard for use in the USA; otherwise, motions sequences on the European films would look choppy on screen.

Connor's phone chirped with a notification of an incoming message. "Someone has put a spell on you. Snap out of it!" It was from Urs. The hotel owner was not above revoking his artist-in-residence status if he didn't see results. He hadn't booked the roof terrace for any film-related events since his return from Rome. He hadn't been invited to this week's card game and that was a bad sign. Connor could sense that Urs held him somehow responsible for the melee during the *Bada Bing* premiere. Connor was sure the mobbed-up guests blamed Urs. They were experts in the blame game. The repercussions remained to be seen but if Connor focused on his job, he'd likely weather the storm.

The first thing to do was to get Derga out of his mind. Connor shifted his attention by opening a file on his computer that revealed the poster that would be sent to theaters for lobby display. He bought them in packets of 36 from the printer. The artwork featured a globe wrapped by three film strips filled with still photos from each of the short films in the program. No one used film anymore. It was a digital world. Yet the image of a film strip was still instantly recognizable even by a generation that had never actually seen one. He'd use the same image on the program that would be given to each ticket holder. The program, though, had been modified from its initial magazine size down to a digest form thanks to the elimination of the director's interviews. These were moved to the festival's website. The program now contained just a quote from the director, a synopsis of each film and notes on the cast and country of origin. Producing a program wasn't strictly necessary but Connor felt the addition of something tangible that could be put in viewers' hands made the festival feel like a special event. The only thing that wasn't special was the day he would have to spend filling mailing tubes with rolled up posters and the inevitable waiting on line at the post office that followed.

The phone on his desk rang. A vintage moment. The old landline phones had been converted for internal use at the Gershwin Hotel.

"Yes?"

"Front desk. There is a man here with a package for you." A strange woman's voice. Lisa had come and gone and Connor had yet to learn the new front desk clerk's name.

"Can't you just sign for it?"

"He says it must be delivered into your hands personally."

That gave Connor pause. "He's not a really big guy is he?"

"Not especially."

"He's not wearing a dark pin-striped suit?"

"No."

"Well, what does he look like?"

451

A few beats of silence. "A musician maybe. Or a poet?"

Killer guitar players were just part of a critic's vocabulary, he hoped. "OK. I'll be right down."

Connor soon found himself looking across the counter at a young man with longish black hair that swept around the sides of long thin face. He wore a tweedy suit that was either hopelessly out of fashion or completely hip in a steampunk sort of way.

"You have a package for me?" asked Connor. The young man nodded in a way that pegged him as Irish in Connor's mind and handed Connor a small yellow manila envelope. His name was on the front, written in a brownish ink.

"Whereabouts in Ireland are you from?" asked Connor as he considered the envelope. Something nagged at him but he couldn't pin it.

"My father would be well-known in Sligo although few would know myself."

"I have family in Sligo and I spend a lot of time there," replied Connor.

"Aye. I know." The man paused and then ventured. "I'm told you are an admirer of my father's work."

There was a mischievous tone in the young man's voice that made Connor take his eyes off the envelope and give the man his full attention. "And who is your father?"

"A local poet. I'd be his son, like." Connor worked his memory and something began to tingle at the edges of his mind.

"And your mother?"

"A glimmering girl with apple blossom in her hair." Connor recognized the phrase as a line from The Song of the Wandering Aenghus, a poem by W.B. Yeats.

"What did you say your name was?" Yeats died on the eve of World War II. The man standing before him was too young to be his son.

"Aye. That will be enough for now," he said as he headed for the front door.

"Wait!" The man turned and nodded at the package in Connor hands. Then he walked out the door and disappeared into the streets of New York City.

Connor stared after the man for what seemed like a long moment. "I'm hoping that was just some mad bastard."

The desk clerk gave him an odd look and Connor shifted his gaze down at the yellow manila envelope. He grabbed a letter opener from a draw beneath the counter and sliced opened the envelope, turning it upside down so that the contents spilled on the counter surface. It was a palm sized piece of calfskin cut into the shape of a heart. Connor picked it up. The words were written in a brownish dye.

Vitriol. There was iron in these words.

"I'll see you sooner than you think but not as soon as you would like."

It was unsigned.

Connor inhaled sharply and his heart missed a beat.

The End.

Frank Vizard's journalistic career includes stints as an editor with *Popular Science* magazine and as the motoring correspondent for *Departures* magazine. His byline has appeared in numerous publications, ranging from *Business Week to USA Today*. He is the author of *Why A Curveball Curves* and co-author of *The 21ˢᵗ Century Soldier*. His Norman-Irish family has moved between Ireland and the United States for generations. *Screamer* is his first novel. A short story with his byline appeared in *An Gael* magazine.

Made in the USA
Middletown, DE
06 November 2018